KEVIN Keller™

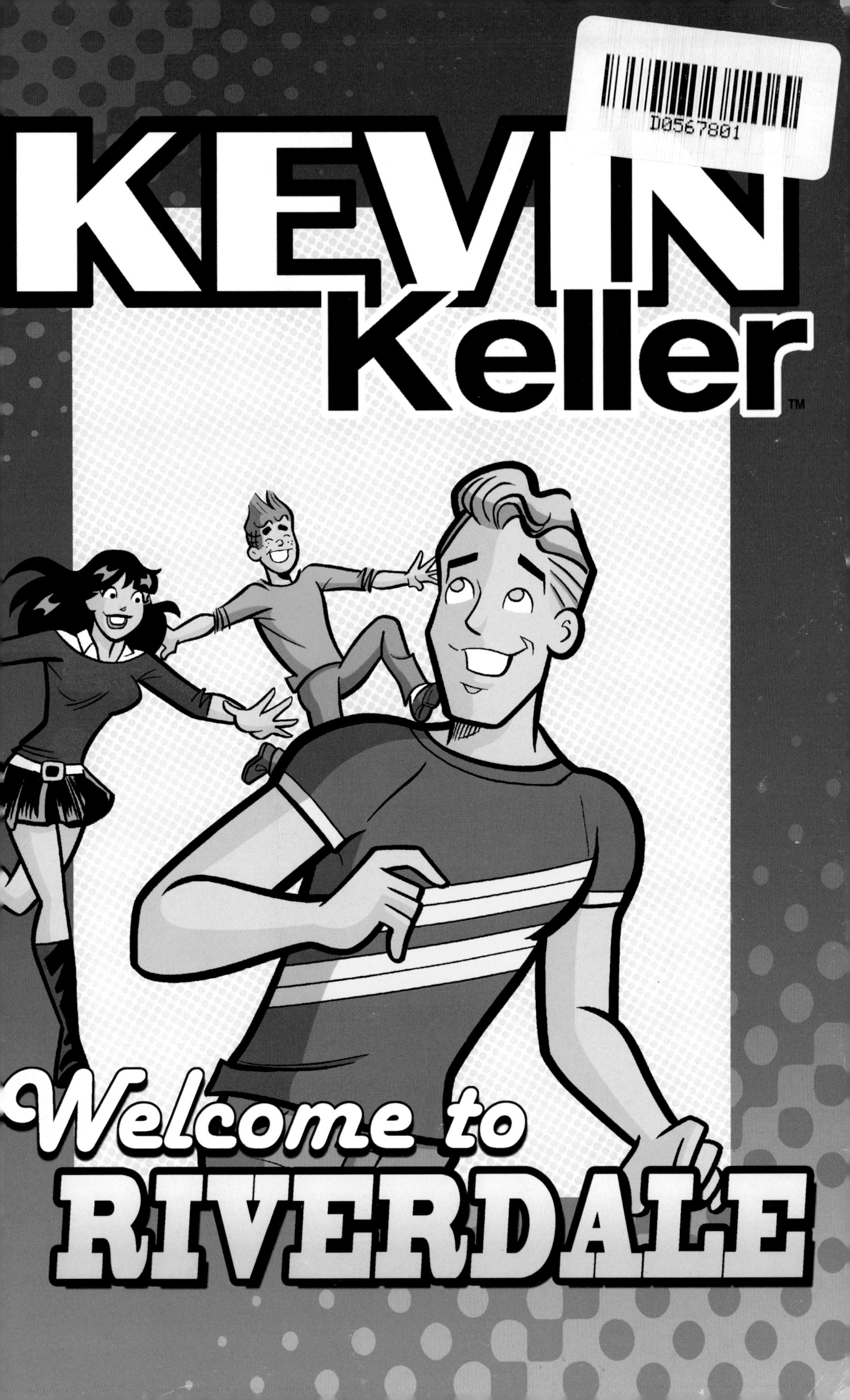

Welcome to RIVERDALE

Kevin Keller: Welcome to Riverdale
Published by Archie Comic Publications, Inc.
325 Fayette Avenue, Mamaroneck, NY 10543-2318.

FIRST PRINTING.

ISBN: 978-1-936975-23-5

Printed in USA.

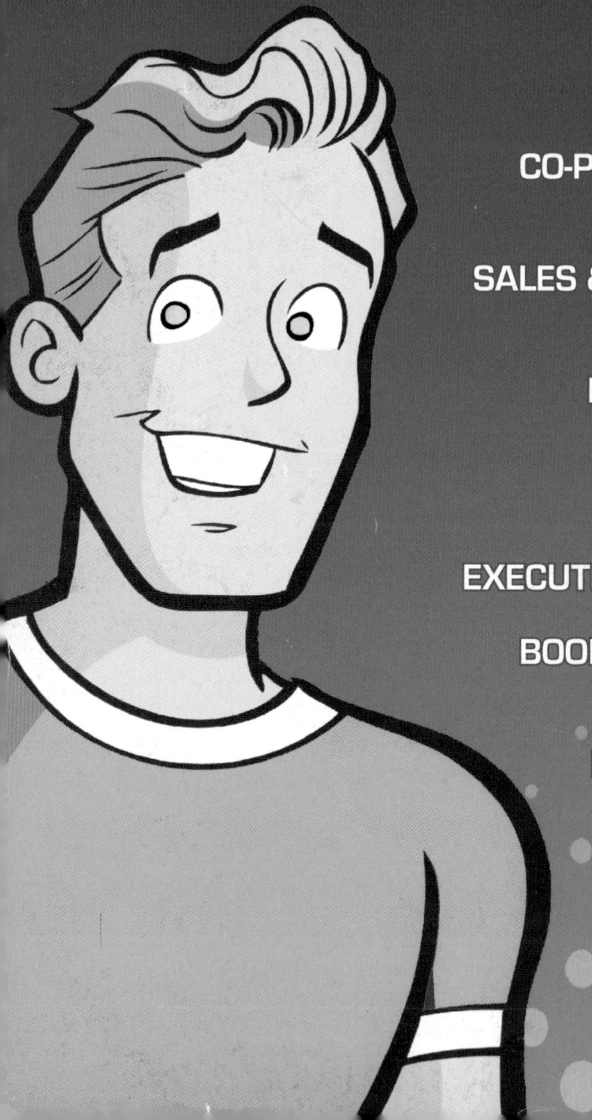

PUBLISHER/CO-CEO: Jonathan Goldwater
CO-CEO: Nancy Silberkleit
PRESIDENT: Mike Pellerito
CO-PRESIDENT/EDITOR-IN-CHIEF: Victor Gorelick
SENIOR VICE PRESIDENT, SALES & BUSINESS DEVELOPMENT: Jim Sokolowski
SENIOR VICE PRESIDENT, PUBLISHING & OPERATIONS: Harold Buchholz
DIRECTOR OF PUBLICITY & MARKETING: Adam Tracey
EXECUTIVE DIRECTOR OF EDITORIAL: Paul Kaminski
BOOK DESIGN: Duncan McLachlan
PRODUCTION MANAGER: Stephen Oswald
PRODUCTION: Kari Silbergleit, Suzannah Rowntree
EDITORIAL ASSISTANT/ PROOFREADER: Jamie Lee Rotante

SCRIPT & PENCILS: Dan Parent

INKS: Rich Koslowski

LETTERS: Jack Morelli

COLORS: Digikore Studios

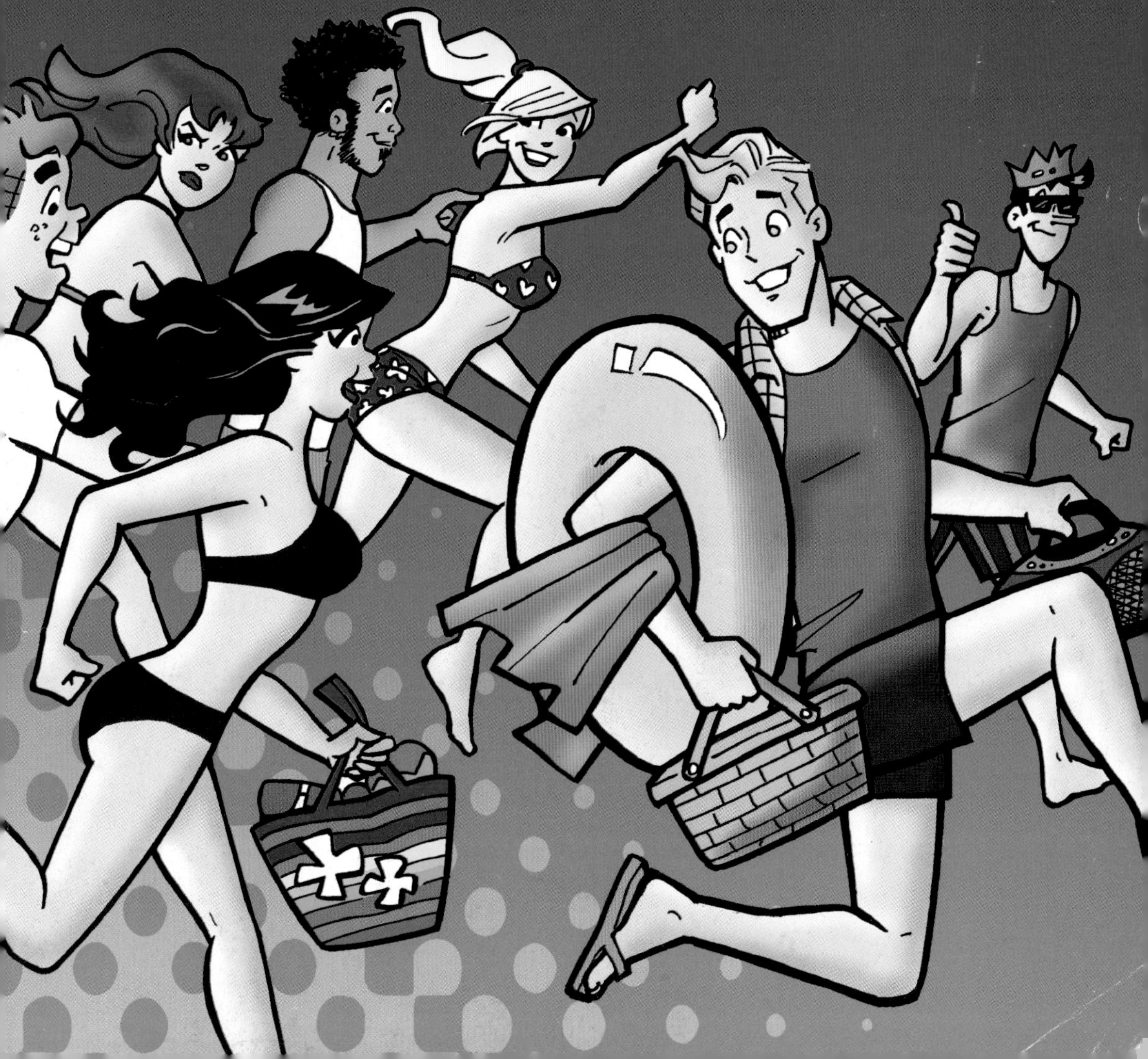

KEVIN Keller™

CATCH UP WITH THE CHARACTERS

Kevin's the nicest "brat" you'll ever meet—army brat, that is! Born in England to parents KATHY and COLONEL THOMAS KELLER, Kevin's seen more of the world in his seventeen years than most people do their entire lives! From a very young age, Kevin had to get used to not seeing his father for long periods of time. However, it was always the highlight of his life when he would hear the honk of his father's army jeep to indicate his return.

After living in England for a bit, the Keller family moved to France and welcomed in a new member of their family: Kevin's little sister DENISE. With his dad still in the army, Kevin became the man of the house, and though he wasn't even in middle school yet, he watched closely over and cared after both his mother and sister—just like his father would. It was during this time that Kevin developed a passion for writing, often creating fantastical stories of himself as a super hero battling dragons, dinosaurs and evil wizards!

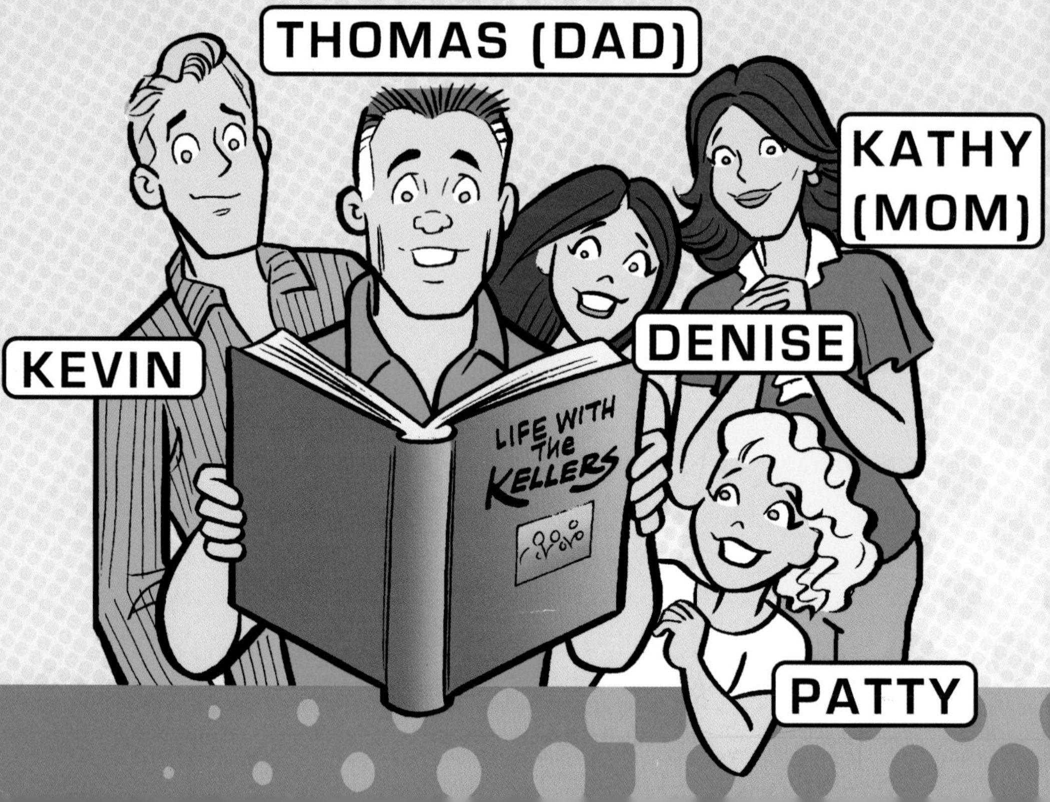

THOMAS (DAD)
KATHY (MOM)
KEVIN
DENISE
LIFE WITH The KELLERS
PATTY

The Kellers then relocated to the United States where they welcomed their last addition: PATTY. Now the older brother to two sisters, Kevin felt more responsible and in charge than ever before! Unfortunately, school was a whole different world than at home and he couldn't help but feel vulnerable. Now living in Bricktown, Kevin had to face the challenges of adolescence in a brand new school all on his own. Fortunately, it was here that he met WENDY and WILLIAM. With their friendship, Kevin's creative intuition, and his growing strength and confidence, Kevin had the tools necessary to survive this awkward and uncomfortable time. He then moved to Honesdale, where he not only rose above the adversity he faced because he was gay, but also helped fellow schoolmates fight against any sort of bullying or injustices.

Now the Kellers are in Riverdale to stay and Kevin couldn't be happier! With plenty of friends both old and new, a growing interest in journalism, his involvement in the Army ROTC, Chess Club, Debate Team and Yearbook Committee as well as being the new class president at Riverdale High, Kevin certainly has a bright future ahead of him!

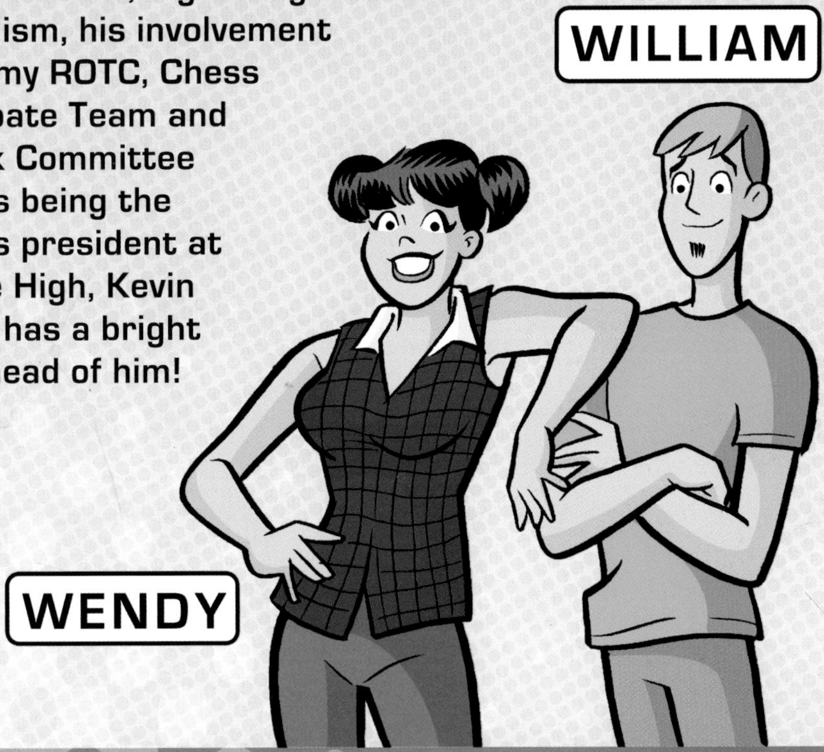
WILLIAM
WENDY

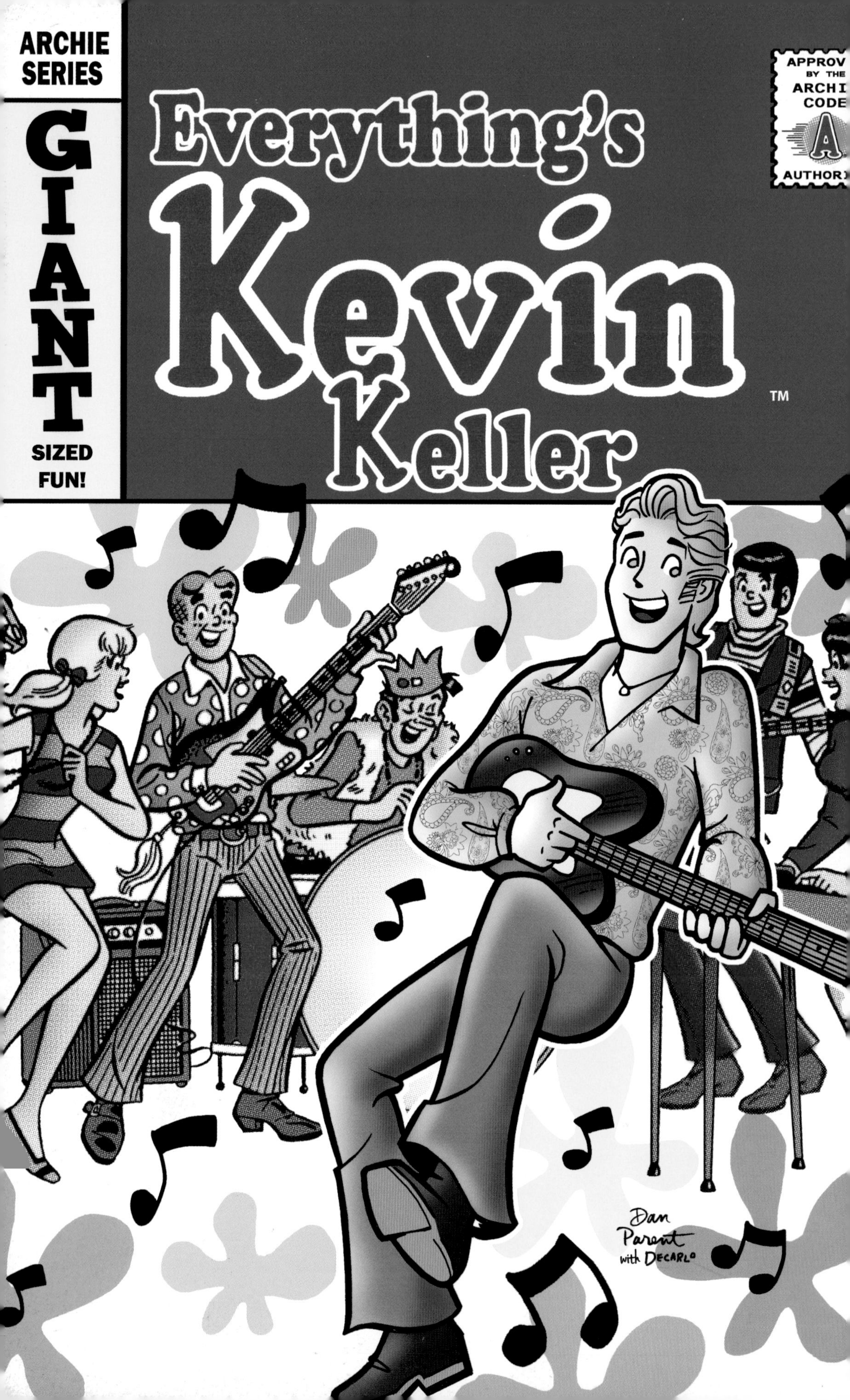
ARCHIE SERIES
GIANT
SIZED FUN!
Everything's Kevin Keller™
APPROV
BY THE
ARCHI
CODE
AUTHORI
Dan Parent with DeCarlo

Chapter 1

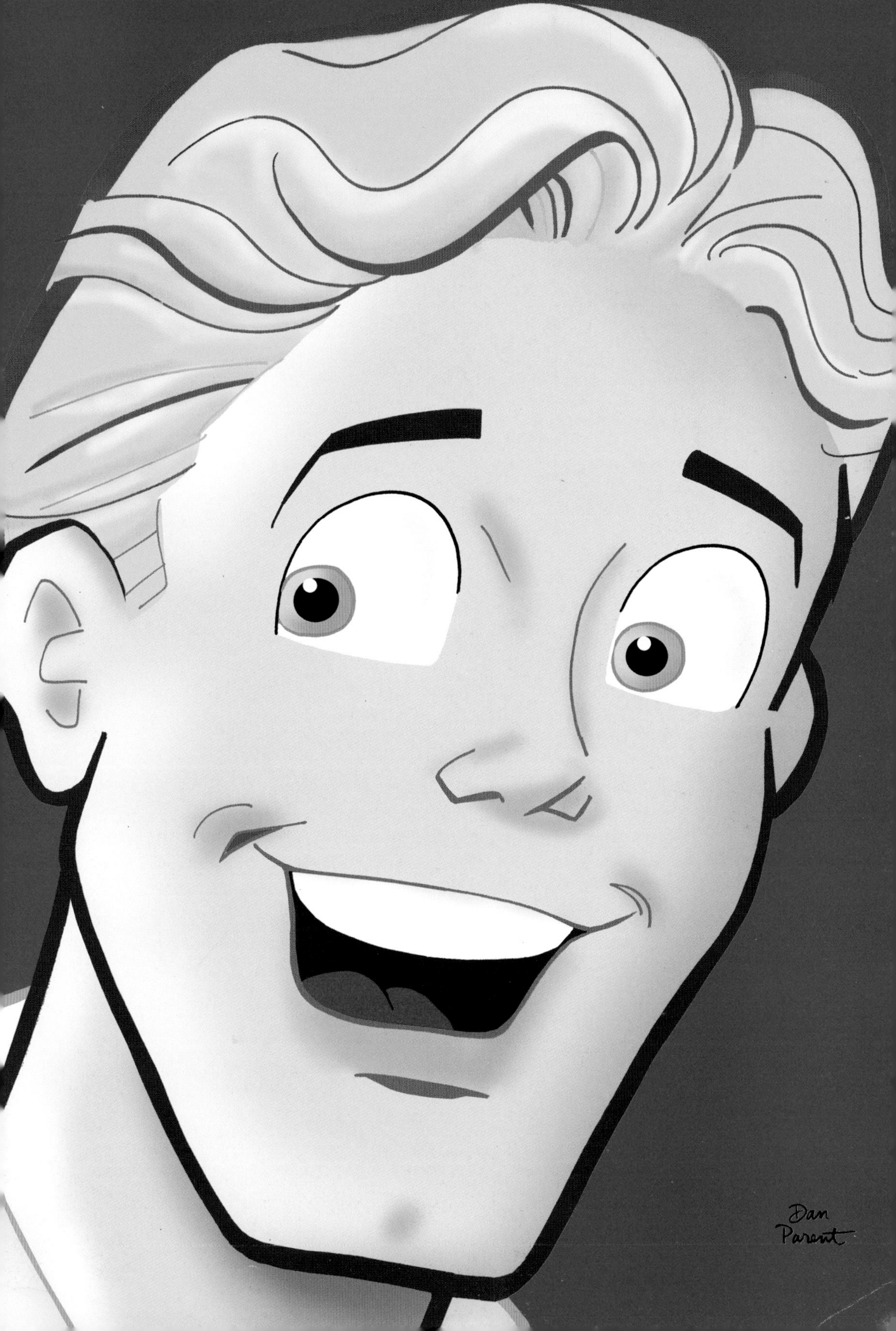
Dan Parent

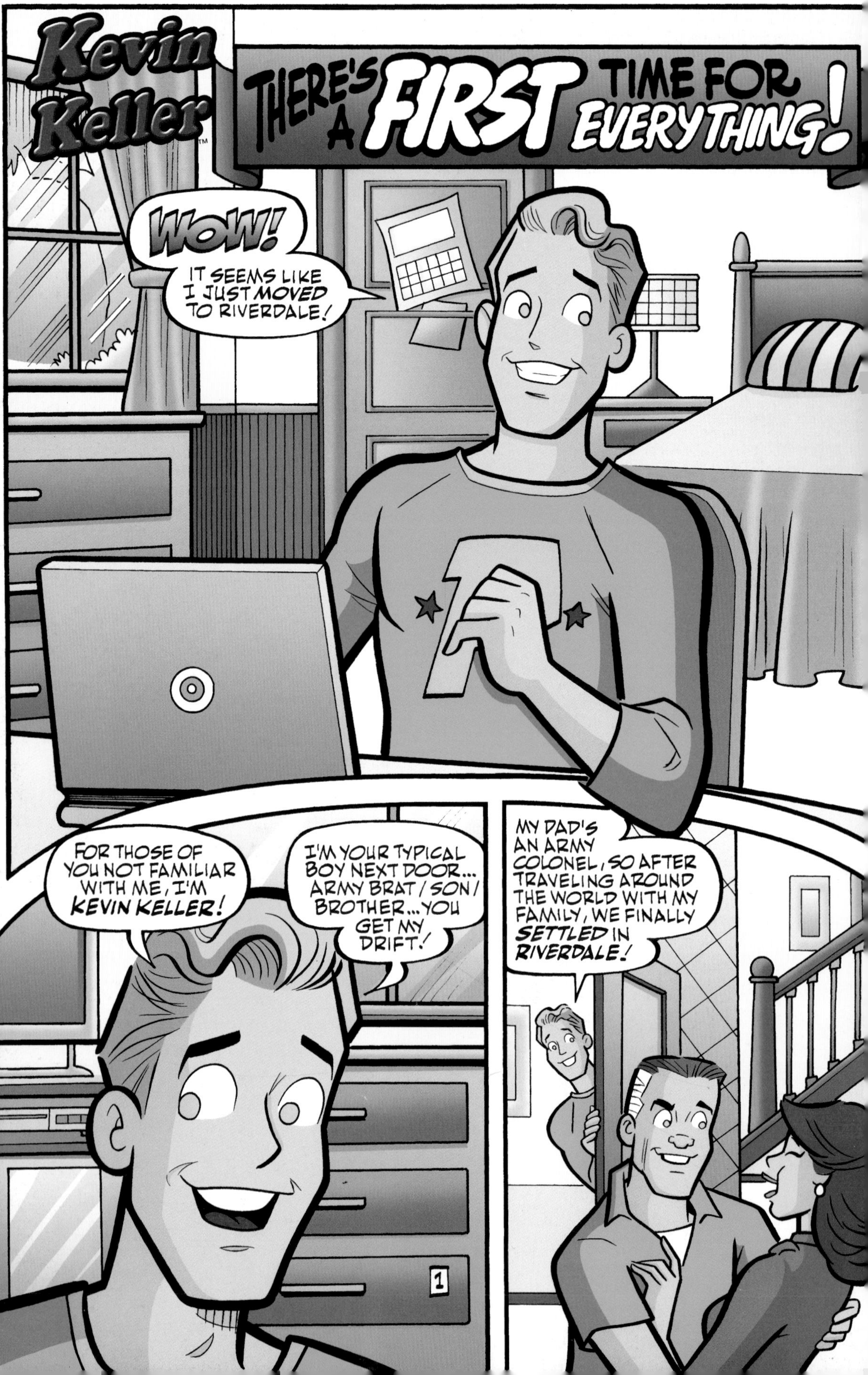
Kevin Keller™
THERE'S A FIRST TIME FOR EVERYTHING!
WOW! IT SEEMS LIKE I JUST MOVED TO RIVERDALE!
FOR THOSE OF YOU NOT FAMILIAR WITH ME, I'M KEVIN KELLER!
I'M YOUR TYPICAL BOY NEXT DOOR... ARMY BRAT / SON / BROTHER... YOU GET MY DRIFT!
MY DAD'S AN ARMY COLONEL, SO AFTER TRAVELING AROUND THE WORLD WITH MY FAMILY, WE FINALLY SETTLED IN RIVERDALE!
1

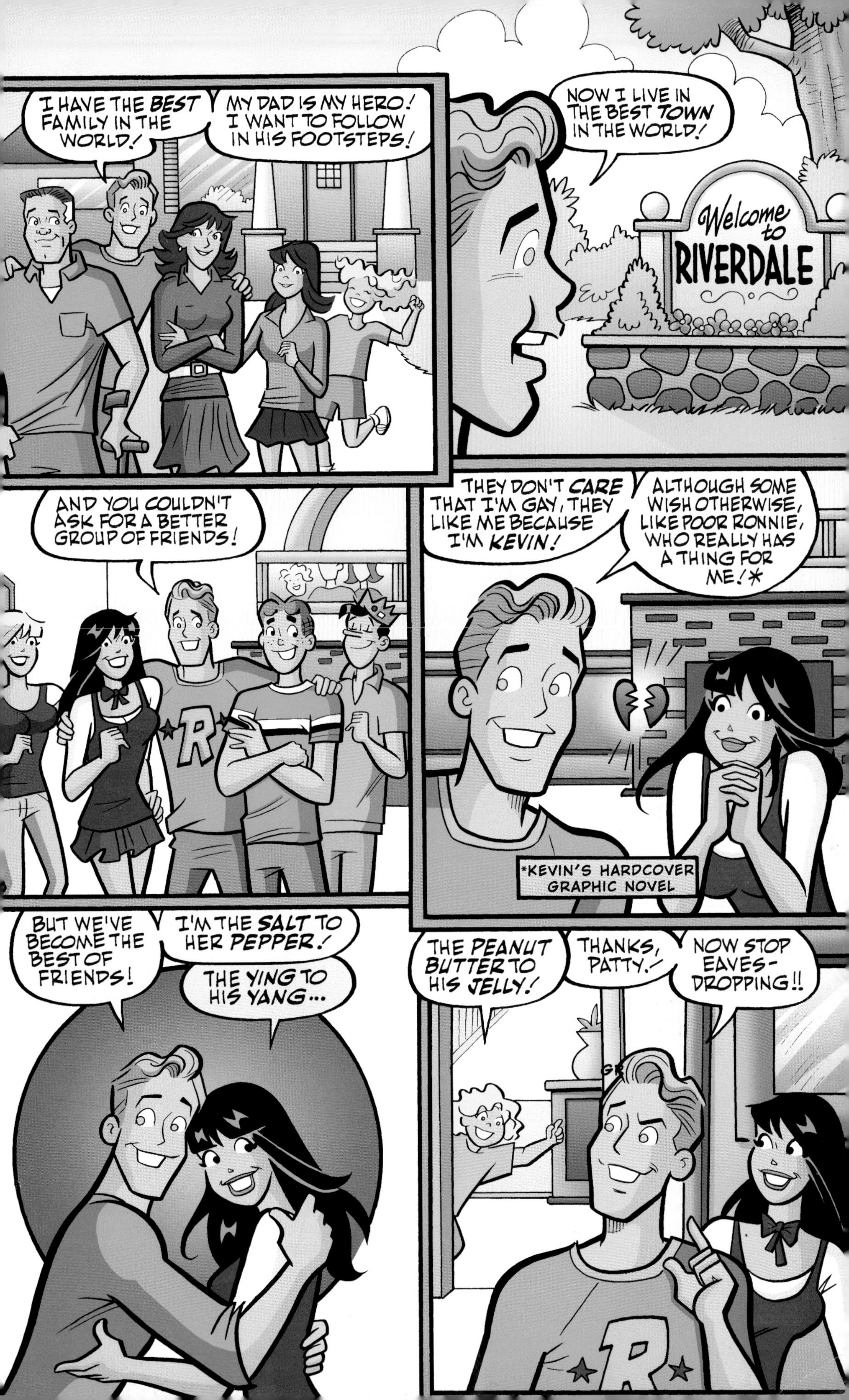
I HAVE THE BEST FAMILY IN THE WORLD!
MY DAD IS MY HERO! I WANT TO FOLLOW IN HIS FOOTSTEPS!
NOW I LIVE IN THE BEST TOWN IN THE WORLD!
Welcome to RIVERDALE
AND YOU COULDN'T ASK FOR A BETTER GROUP OF FRIENDS!
THEY DON'T CARE THAT I'M GAY, THEY LIKE ME BECAUSE I'M KEVIN!
ALTHOUGH SOME WISH OTHERWISE, LIKE POOR RONNIE, WHO REALLY HAS A THING FOR ME!*
*KEVIN'S HARDCOVER GRAPHIC NOVEL
BUT WE'VE BECOME THE BEST OF FRIENDS!
I'M THE SALT TO HER PEPPER!
THE YING TO HIS YANG...
THE PEANUT BUTTER TO HIS JELLY!
THANKS, PATTY.!
NOW STOP EAVES-DROPPING!!

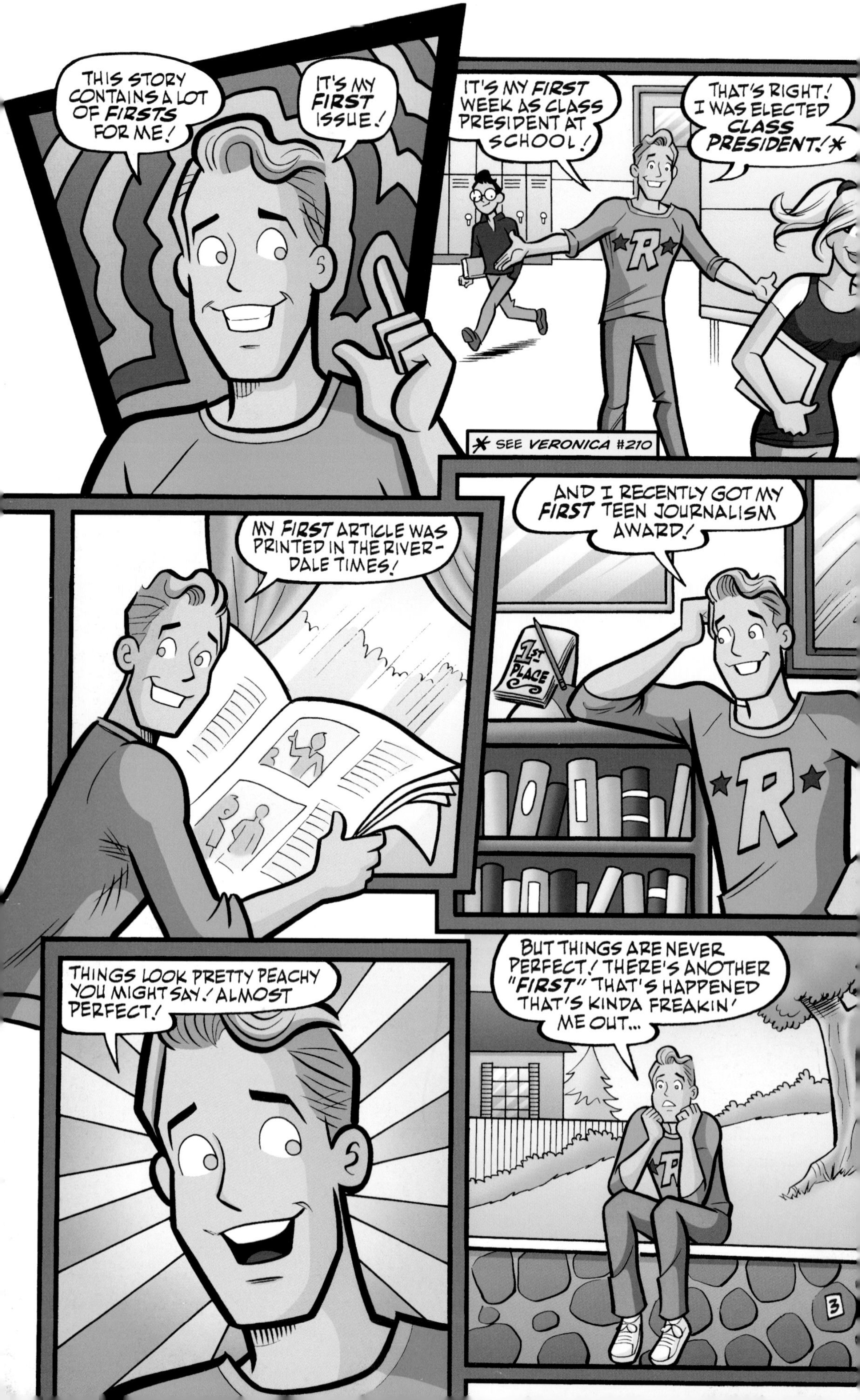
THIS STORY CONTAINS A LOT OF FIRSTS FOR ME!
IT'S MY FIRST ISSUE!
IT'S MY FIRST WEEK AS CLASS PRESIDENT AT SCHOOL!
THAT'S RIGHT! I WAS ELECTED CLASS PRESIDENT!*
* SEE VERONICA #210
MY FIRST ARTICLE WAS PRINTED IN THE RIVER-DALE TIMES!
AND I RECENTLY GOT MY FIRST TEEN JOURNALISM AWARD!
1ST PLACE
THINGS LOOK PRETTY PEACHY YOU MIGHT SAY! ALMOST PERFECT!
BUT THINGS ARE NEVER PERFECT! THERE'S ANOTHER "FIRST" THAT'S HAPPENED THAT'S KINDA FREAKIN' ME OUT...
3

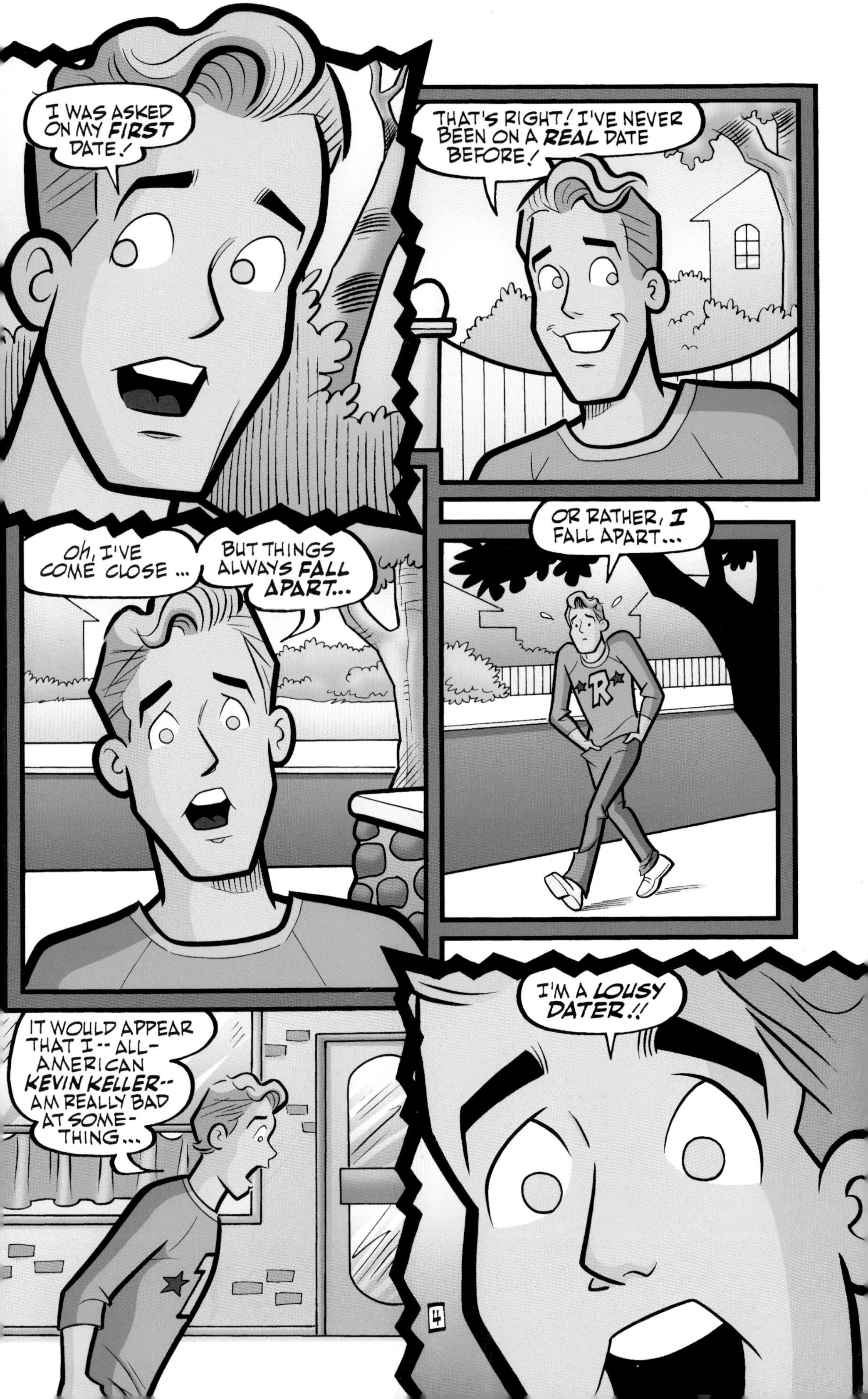
I WAS ASKED ON MY FIRST DATE!
THAT'S RIGHT! I'VE NEVER BEEN ON A REAL DATE BEFORE!
OH, I'VE COME CLOSE ...
BUT THINGS ALWAYS FALL APART...
OR RATHER, I FALL APART...
IT WOULD APPEAR THAT I -- ALL-AMERICAN KEVIN KELLER -- AM REALLY BAD AT SOME-THING...
I'M A LOUSY DATER!!
R
4

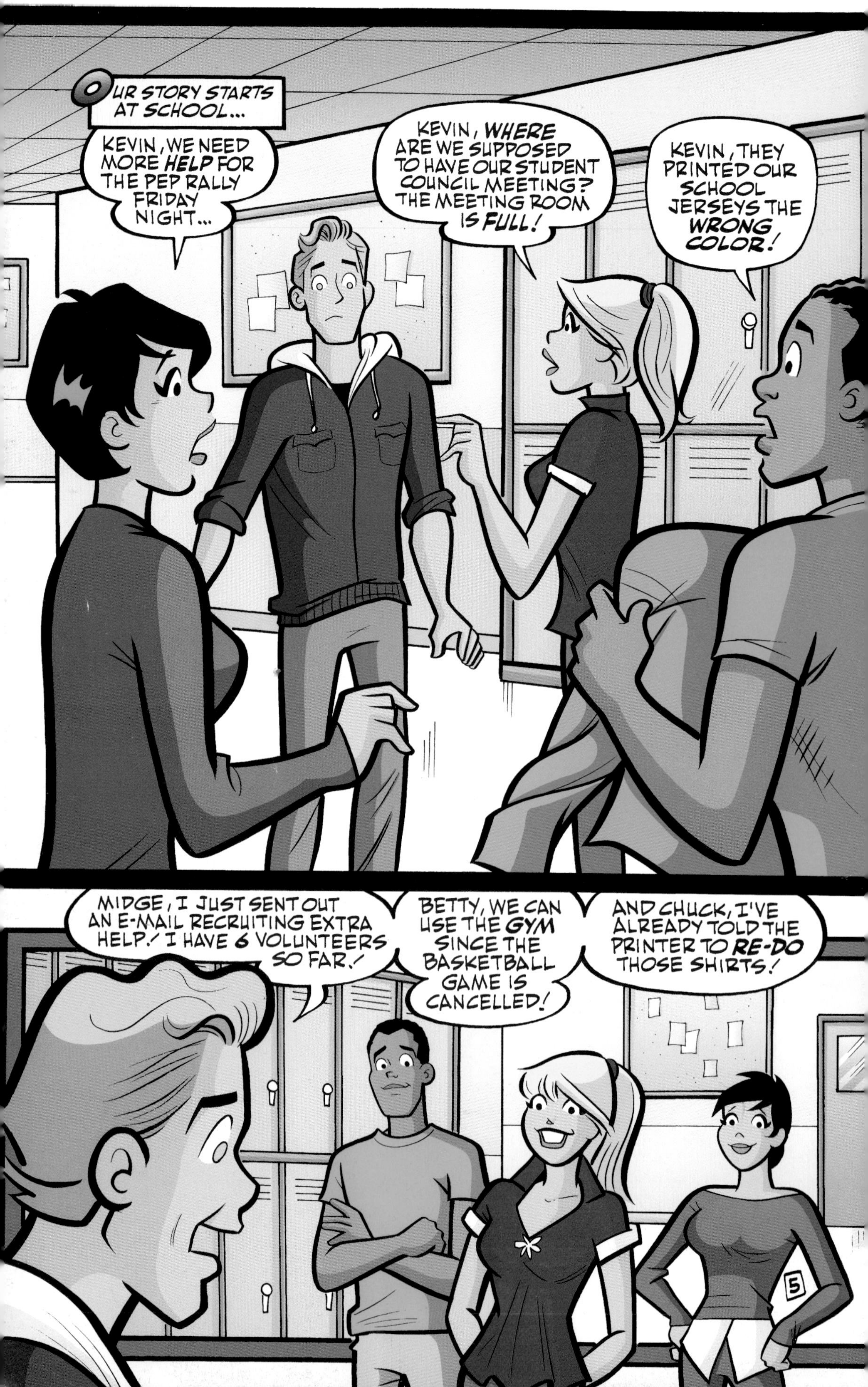
OUR STORY STARTS AT SCHOOL...
KEVIN, WE NEED MORE HELP FOR THE PEP RALLY FRIDAY NIGHT...
KEVIN, WHERE ARE WE SUPPOSED TO HAVE OUR STUDENT COUNCIL MEETING? THE MEETING ROOM IS FULL!
KEVIN, THEY PRINTED OUR SCHOOL JERSEYS THE WRONG COLOR!
MIDGE, I JUST SENT OUT AN E-MAIL RECRUITING EXTRA HELP! I HAVE 6 VOLUNTEERS SO FAR!
BETTY, WE CAN USE THE GYM SINCE THE BASKETBALL GAME IS CANCELLED!
AND CHUCK, I'VE ALREADY TOLD THE PRINTER TO RE-DO THOSE SHIRTS!
5

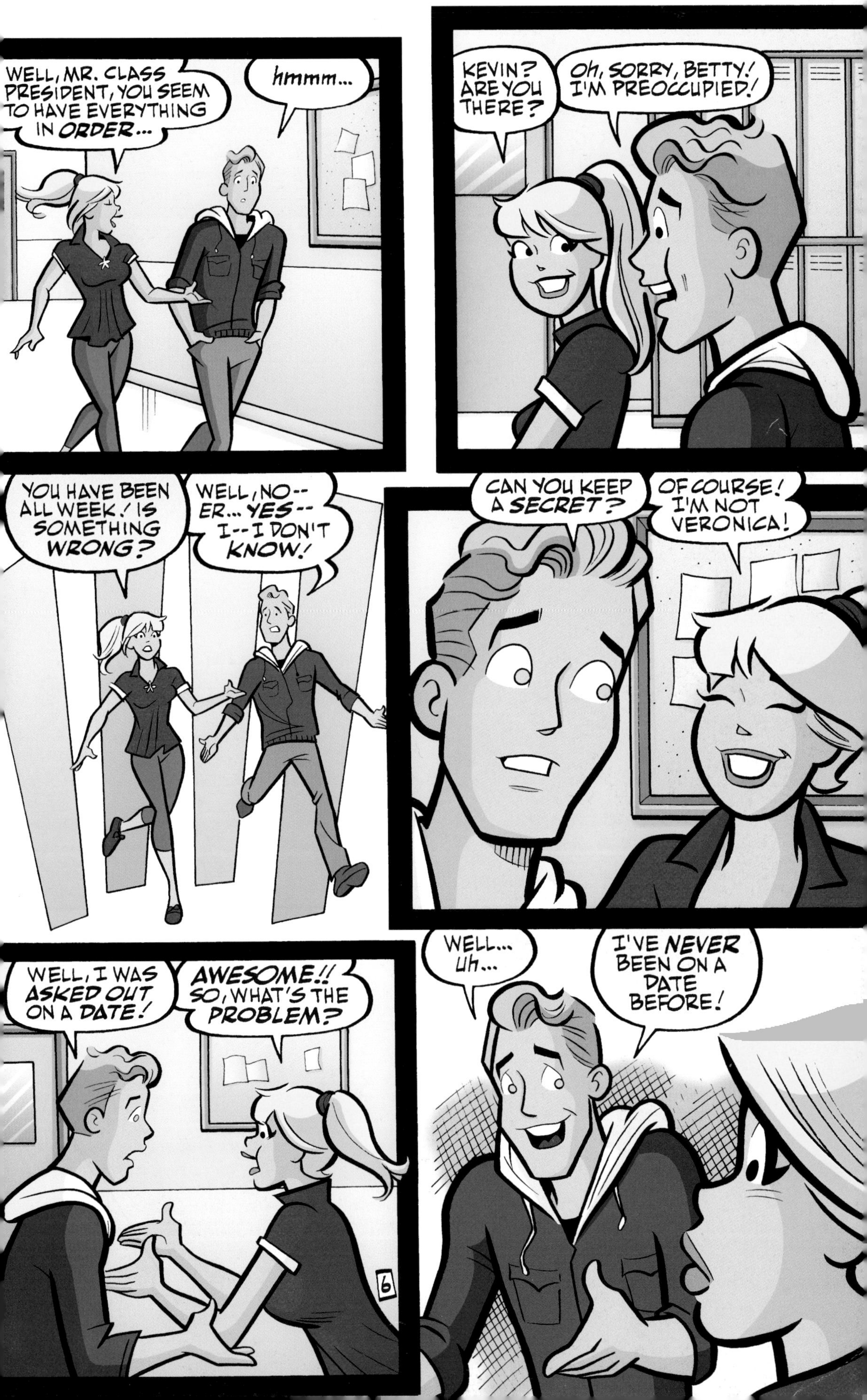
WELL, MR. CLASS PRESIDENT, YOU SEEM TO HAVE EVERYTHING IN ORDER...
hmmm...
KEVIN? ARE YOU THERE?
Oh, SORRY, BETTY! I'M PREOCCUPIED!
YOU HAVE BEEN ALL WEEK! IS SOMETHING WRONG?
WELL, NO-- ER... YES-- I--I DON'T KNOW!
CAN YOU KEEP A SECRET?
OF COURSE! I'M NOT VERONICA!
WELL, I WAS ASKED OUT ON A DATE!
AWESOME!! SO, WHAT'S THE PROBLEM?
6
WELL... uh...
I'VE NEVER BEEN ON A DATE BEFORE!

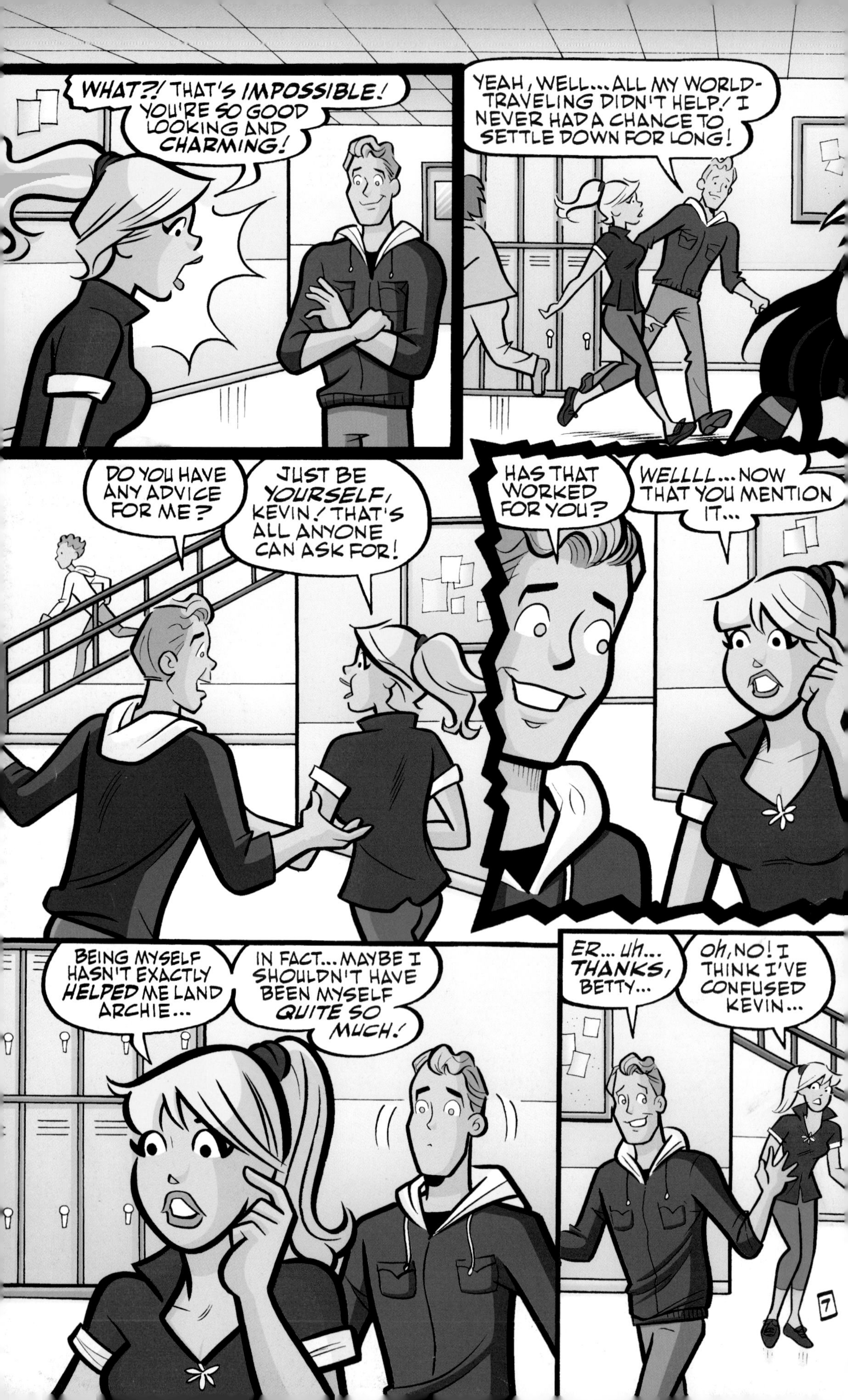
WHAT?! THAT'S IMPOSSIBLE! YOU'RE SO GOOD LOOKING AND CHARMING!
YEAH, WELL... ALL MY WORLD-TRAVELING DIDN'T HELP! I NEVER HAD A CHANCE TO SETTLE DOWN FOR LONG!
DO YOU HAVE ANY ADVICE FOR ME?
JUST BE YOURSELF, KEVIN! THAT'S ALL ANYONE CAN ASK FOR!
HAS THAT WORKED FOR YOU?
WELLLL... NOW THAT YOU MENTION IT...
BEING MYSELF HASN'T EXACTLY HELPED ME LAND ARCHIE...
IN FACT... MAYBE I SHOULDN'T HAVE BEEN MYSELF QUITE SO MUCH!
ER... uh... THANKS, BETTY...
oh, NO! I THINK I'VE CONFUSED KEVIN...
7

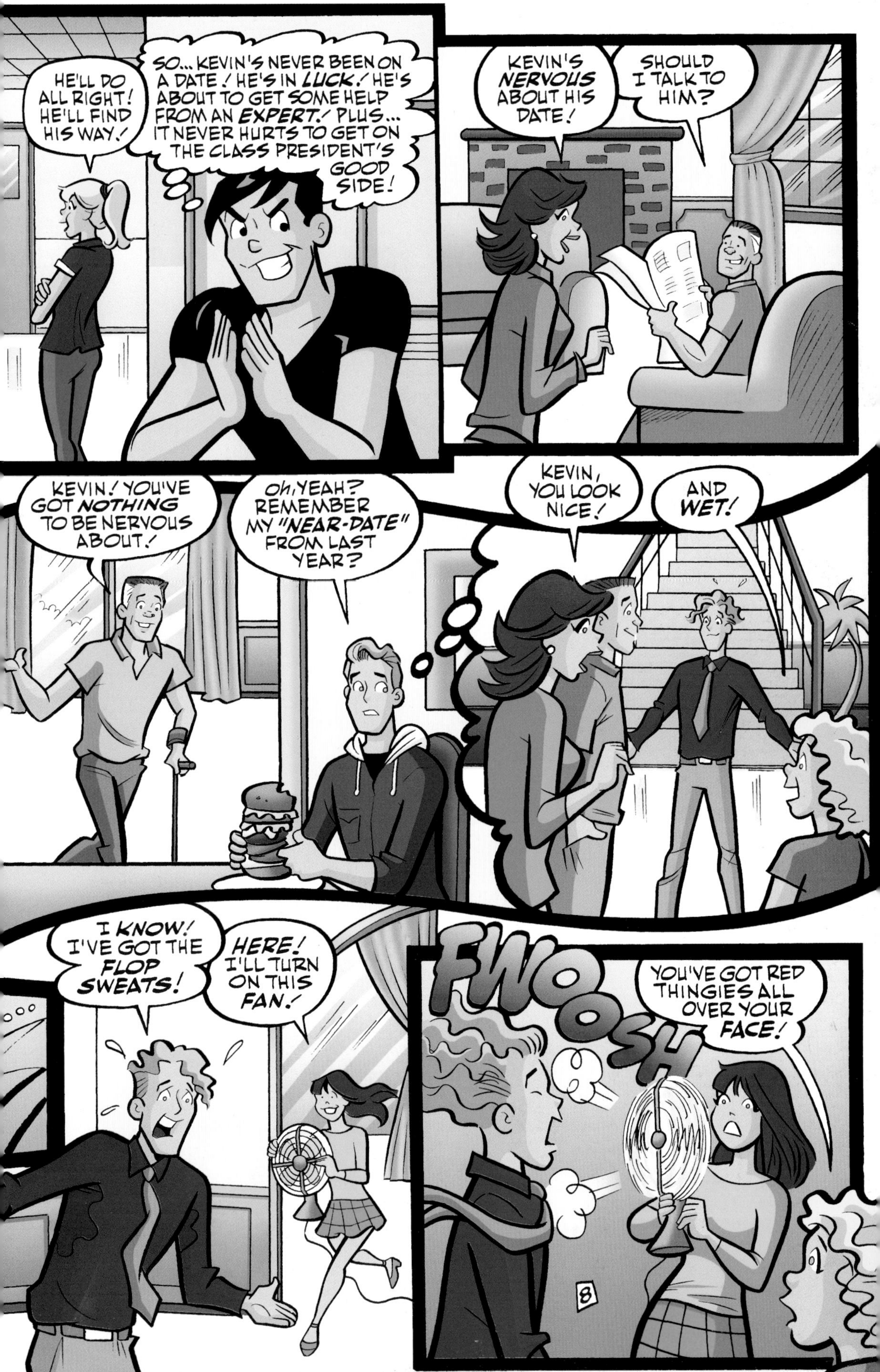
HE'LL DO ALL RIGHT! HE'LL FIND HIS WAY!
SO... KEVIN'S NEVER BEEN ON A DATE! HE'S IN LUCK! HE'S ABOUT TO GET SOME HELP FROM AN EXPERT! PLUS... IT NEVER HURTS TO GET ON THE CLASS PRESIDENT'S GOOD SIDE!
KEVIN'S NERVOUS ABOUT HIS DATE!
SHOULD I TALK TO HIM?
KEVIN! YOU'VE GOT NOTHING TO BE NERVOUS ABOUT!
OH, YEAH? REMEMBER MY "NEAR-DATE" FROM LAST YEAR?
KEVIN, YOU LOOK NICE!
AND WET!
I KNOW! I'VE GOT THE FLOP SWEATS!
HERE! I'LL TURN ON THIS FAN!
FWOOSH
YOU'VE GOT RED THINGIES ALL OVER YOUR FACE!
8

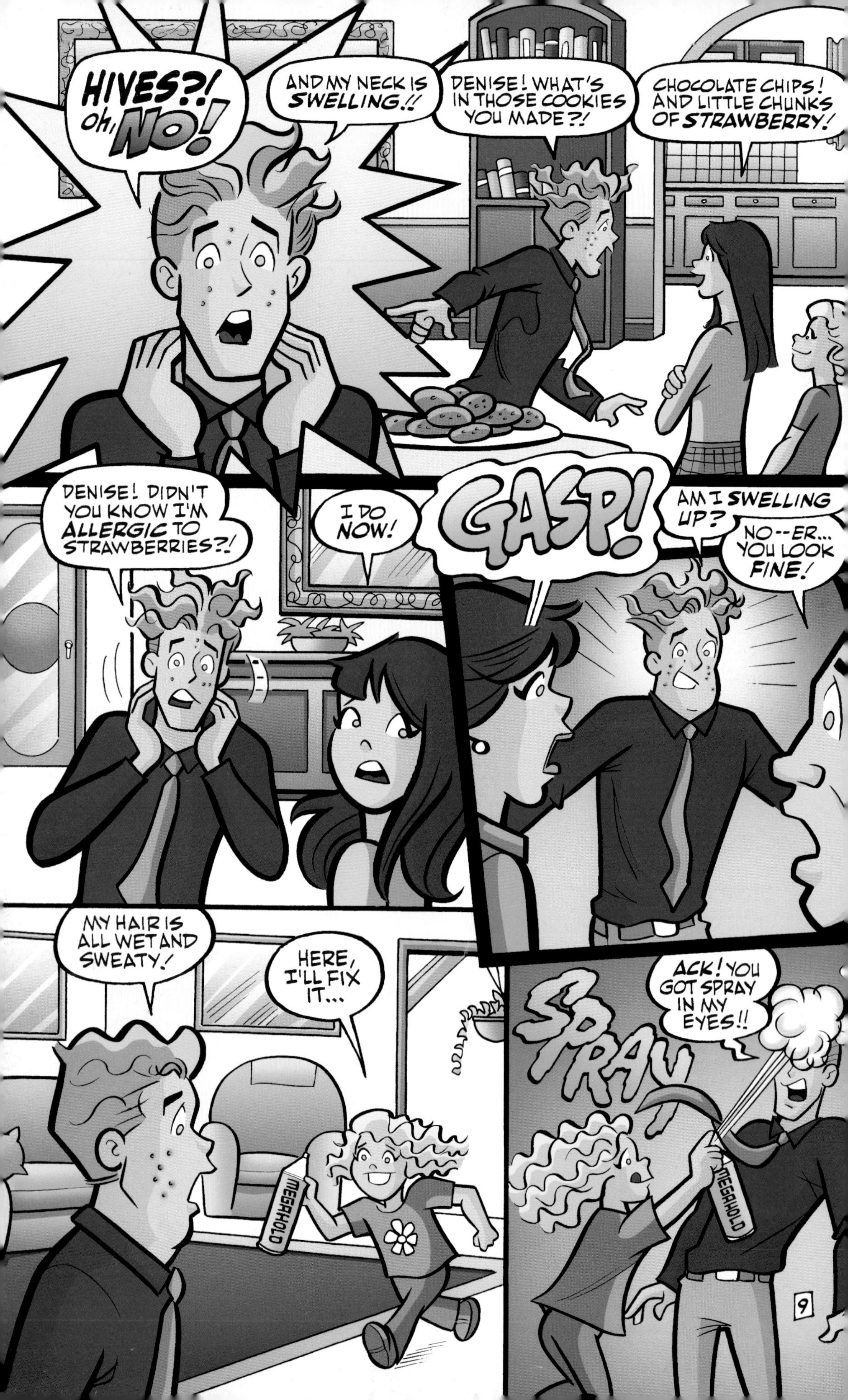
HIVES?! oh, NO!
AND MY NECK IS SWELLING.!!
DENISE! WHAT'S IN THOSE COOKIES YOU MADE?!
CHOCOLATE CHIPS! AND LITTLE CHUNKS OF STRAWBERRY!
DENISE! DIDN'T YOU KNOW I'M ALLERGIC TO STRAWBERRIES?!
I DO NOW!
GASP!
AM I SWELLING UP?
NO--ER... YOU LOOK FINE!
MY HAIR IS ALL WET AND SWEATY!
HERE, I'LL FIX IT...
MEGAHOLD
SPRAY
ACK! YOU GOT SPRAY IN MY EYES!!
MEGAHOLD

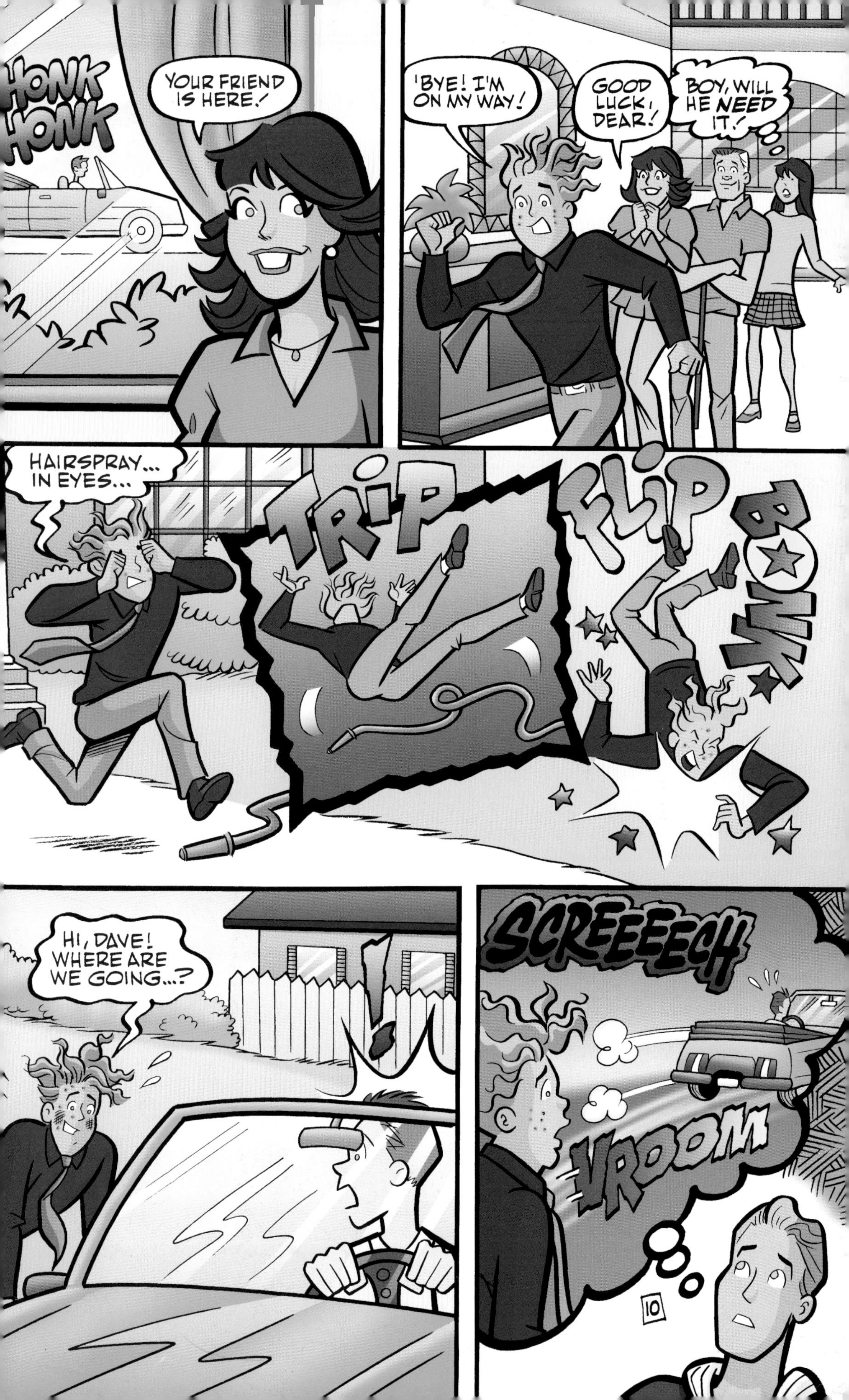
HONK HONK
YOUR FRIEND IS HERE!
'BYE! I'M ON MY WAY!
GOOD LUCK, DEAR!
BOY, WILL HE NEED IT!
HAIRSPRAY... IN EYES...
TRIP
FLIP
BONK
HI, DAVE! WHERE ARE WE GOING...?
!
SCREEEECH
VROOM
10

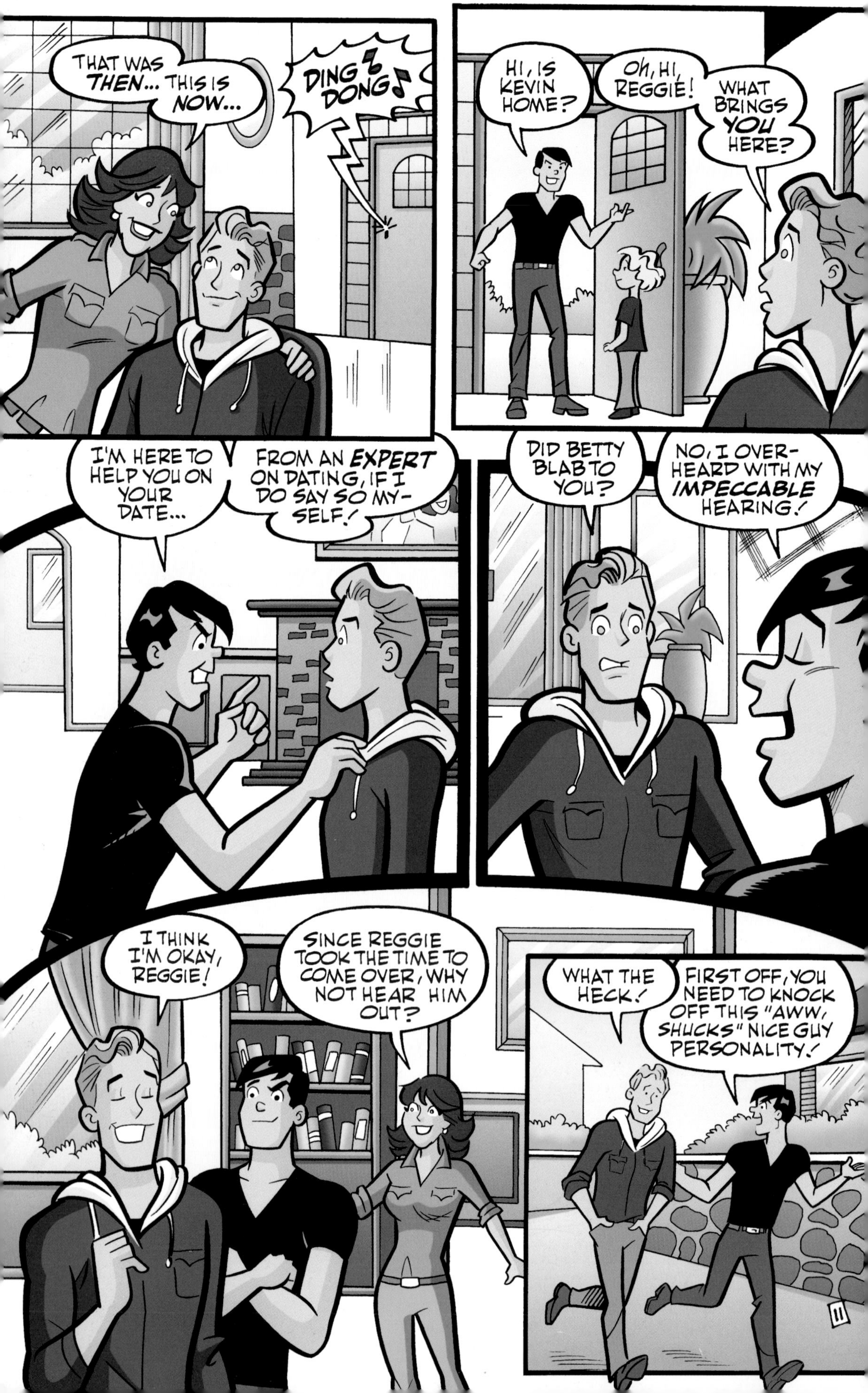

THAT WAS THEN... THIS IS NOW...
DING DONG
HI, IS KEVIN HOME?
OH, HI, REGGIE!
WHAT BRINGS YOU HERE?
I'M HERE TO HELP YOU ON YOUR DATE...
FROM AN EXPERT ON DATING, IF I DO SAY SO MYSELF!
DID BETTY BLAB TO YOU?
NO, I OVERHEARD WITH MY IMPECCABLE HEARING!
I THINK I'M OKAY, REGGIE!
SINCE REGGIE TOOK THE TIME TO COME OVER, WHY NOT HEAR HIM OUT?
WHAT THE HECK!
FIRST OFF, YOU NEED TO KNOCK OFF THIS "AWW, SHUCKS" NICE GUY PERSONALITY!
11

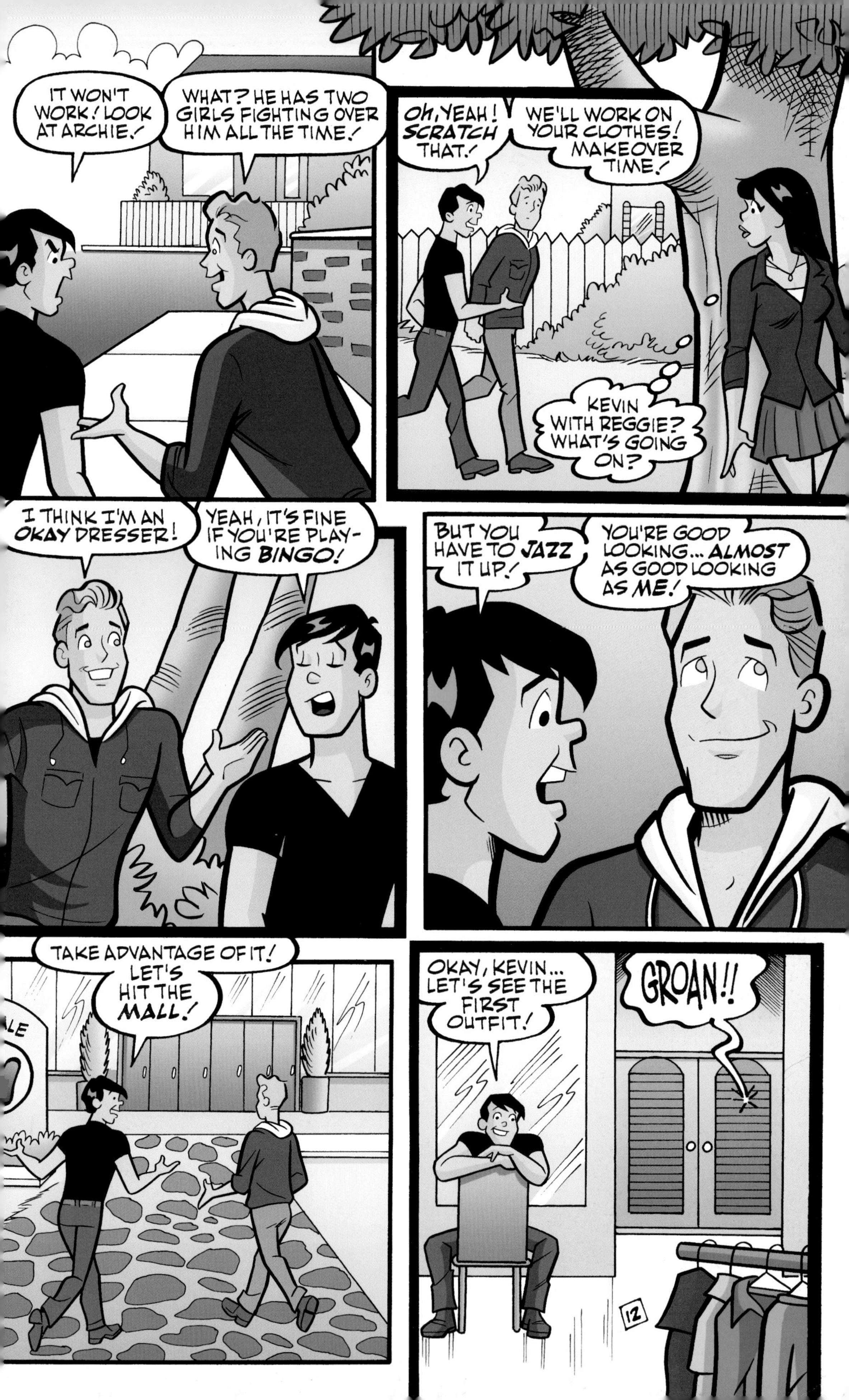
IT WON'T WORK! LOOK AT ARCHIE!
WHAT? HE HAS TWO GIRLS FIGHTING OVER HIM ALL THE TIME!
OH, YEAH! SCRATCH THAT!
WE'LL WORK ON YOUR CLOTHES! MAKEOVER TIME!
KEVIN WITH REGGIE? WHAT'S GOING ON?
I THINK I'M AN OKAY DRESSER!
YEAH, IT'S FINE IF YOU'RE PLAYING BINGO!
BUT YOU HAVE TO JAZZ IT UP!
YOU'RE GOOD LOOKING... ALMOST AS GOOD LOOKING AS ME!
TAKE ADVANTAGE OF IT! LET'S HIT THE MALL!
OKAY, KEVIN... LET'S SEE THE FIRST OUTFIT!
GROAN!!
12

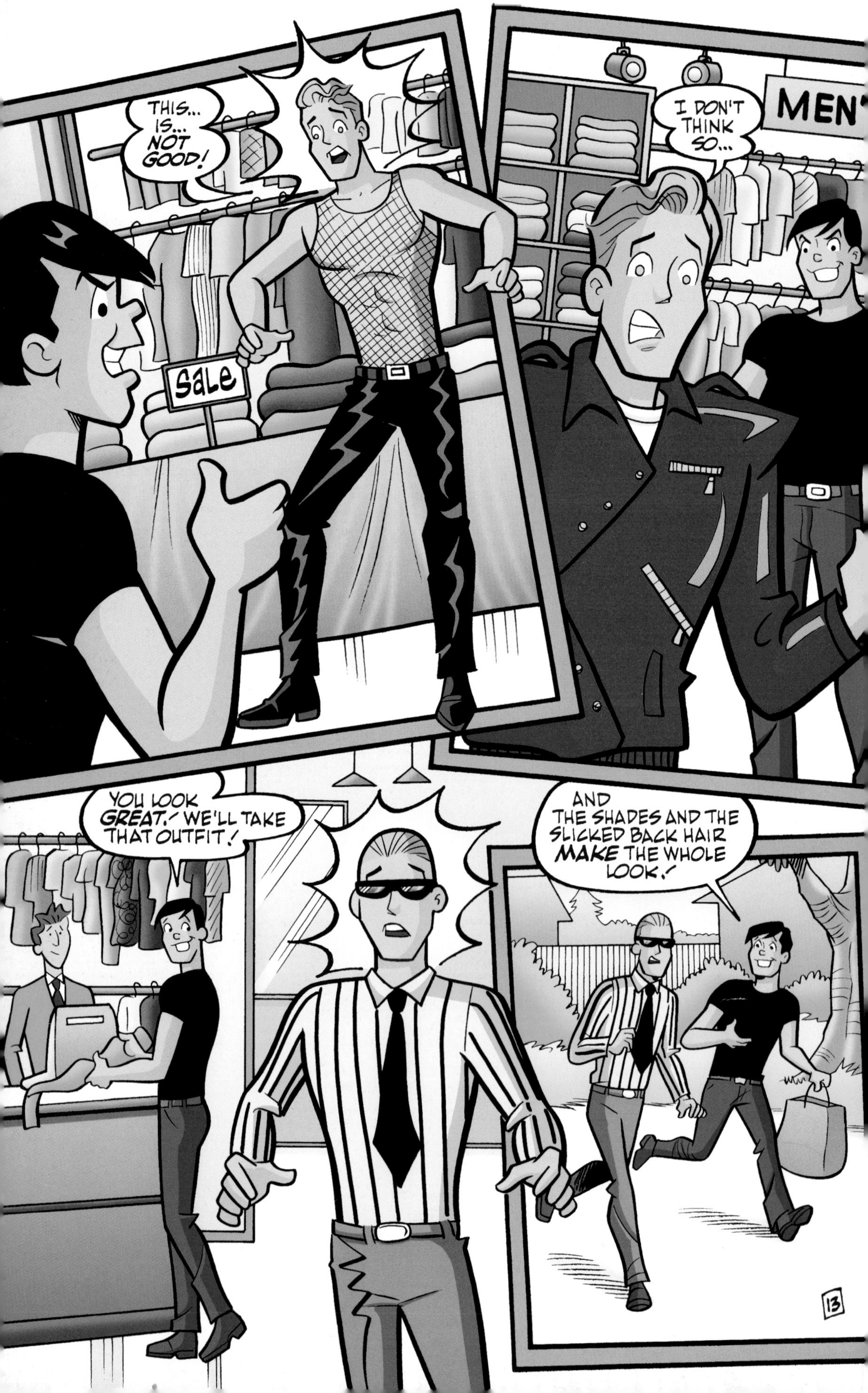
THIS... IS... NOT GOOD!
SALE
I DON'T THINK SO...
MEN'
YOU LOOK GREAT! WE'LL TAKE THAT OUTFIT!
AND THE SHADES AND THE SLICKED BACK HAIR MAKE THE WHOLE LOOK!

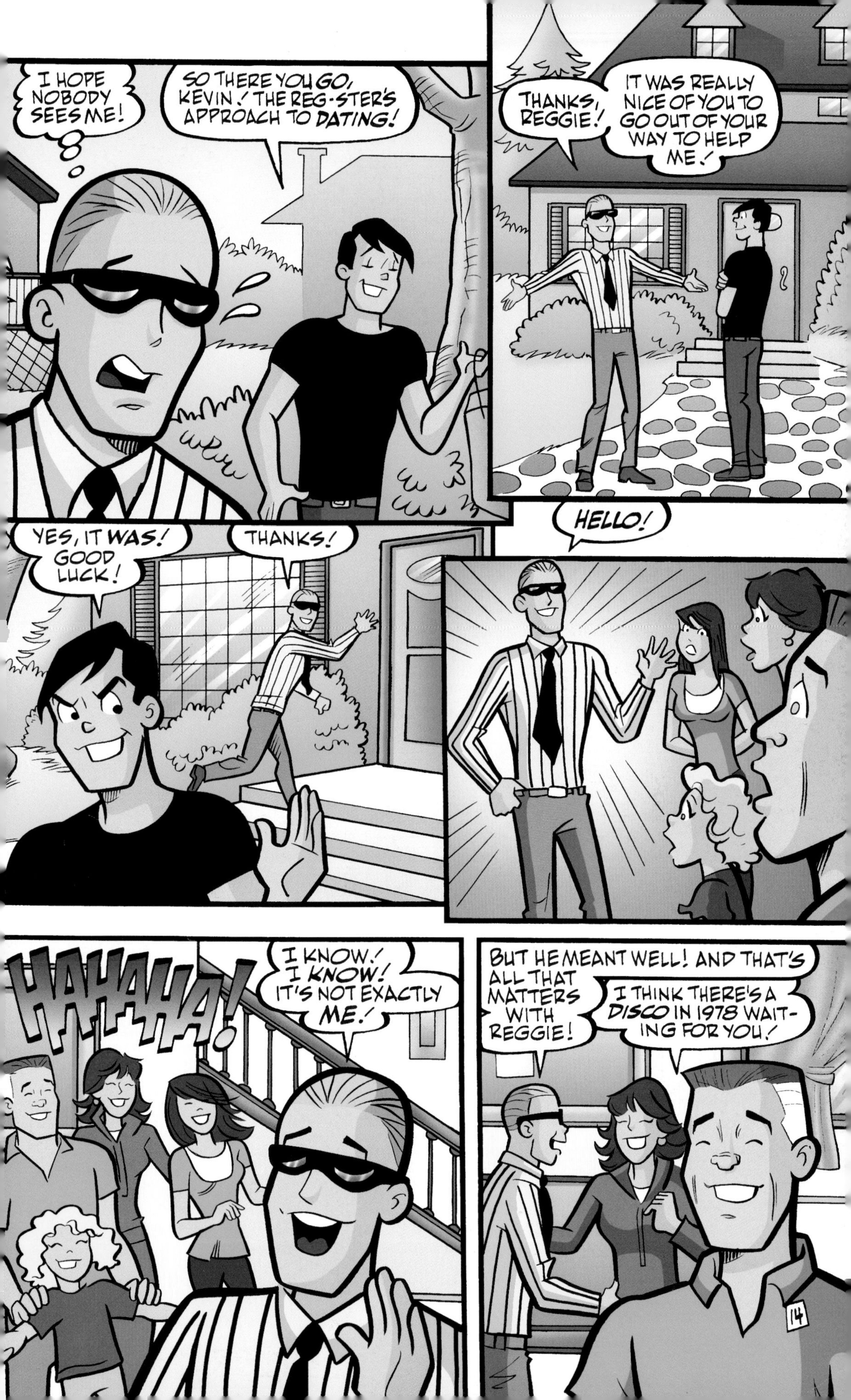
I HOPE NOBODY SEES ME!
SO THERE YOU GO, KEVIN! THE REG-STER'S APPROACH TO DATING!
THANKS, REGGIE!
IT WAS REALLY NICE OF YOU TO GO OUT OF YOUR WAY TO HELP ME!
YES, IT WAS! GOOD LUCK!
THANKS!
HELLO!
HAHAHA!
I KNOW! I KNOW! IT'S NOT EXACTLY ME!
BUT HE MEANT WELL! AND THAT'S ALL THAT MATTERS WITH REGGIE!
I THINK THERE'S A DISCO IN 1978 WAITING FOR YOU!
14

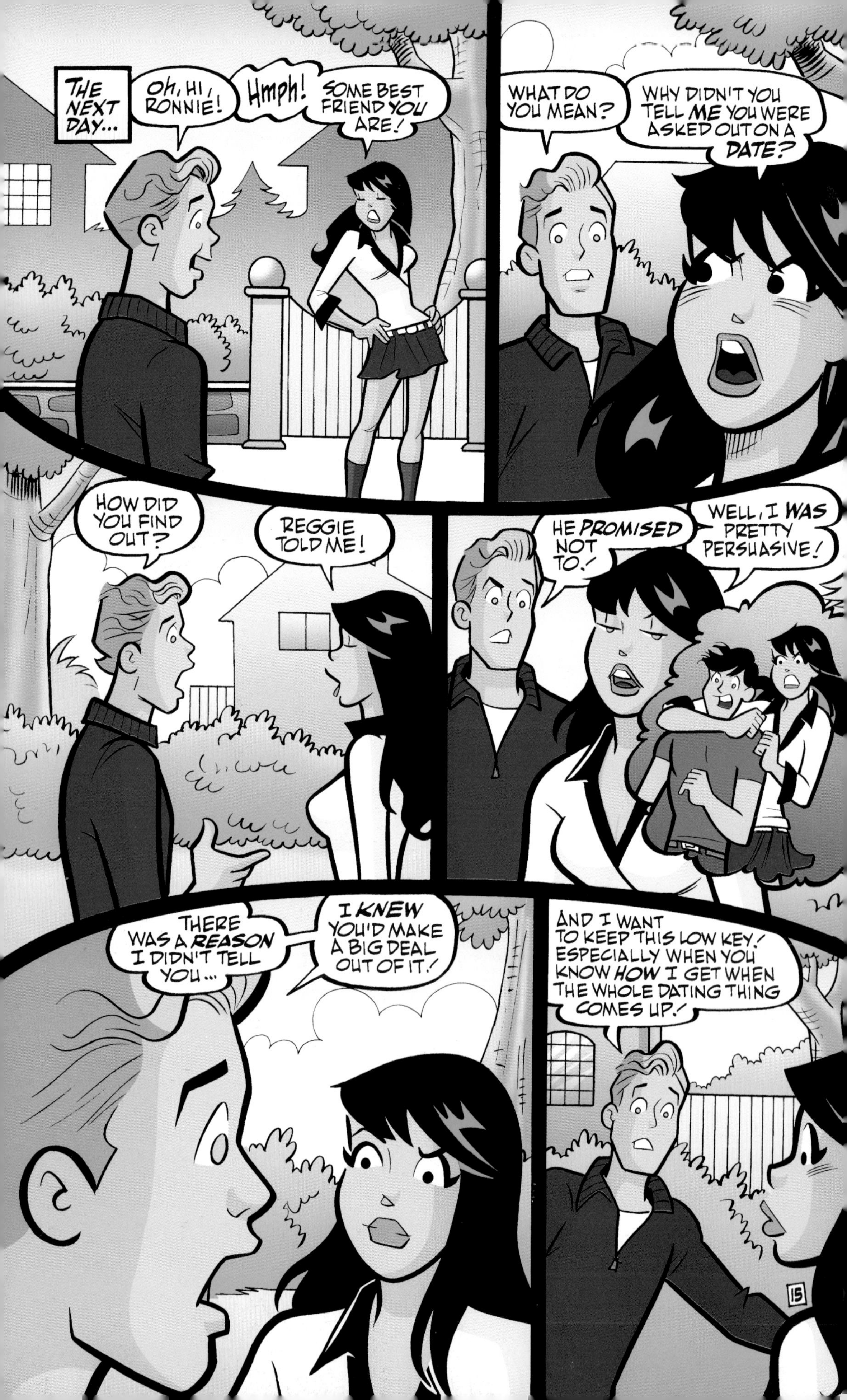
THE NEXT DAY...
OH, HI, RONNIE!
Hmph!
SOME BEST FRIEND YOU ARE!
WHAT DO YOU MEAN?
WHY DIDN'T YOU TELL ME YOU WERE ASKED OUT ON A DATE?
HOW DID YOU FIND OUT?
REGGIE TOLD ME!
HE PROMISED NOT TO!
WELL, I WAS PRETTY PERSUASIVE!
THERE WAS A REASON I DIDN'T TELL YOU...
I KNEW YOU'D MAKE A BIG DEAL OUT OF IT!
AND I WANT TO KEEP THIS LOW KEY! ESPECIALLY WHEN YOU KNOW HOW I GET WHEN THE WHOLE DATING THING COMES UP!
15

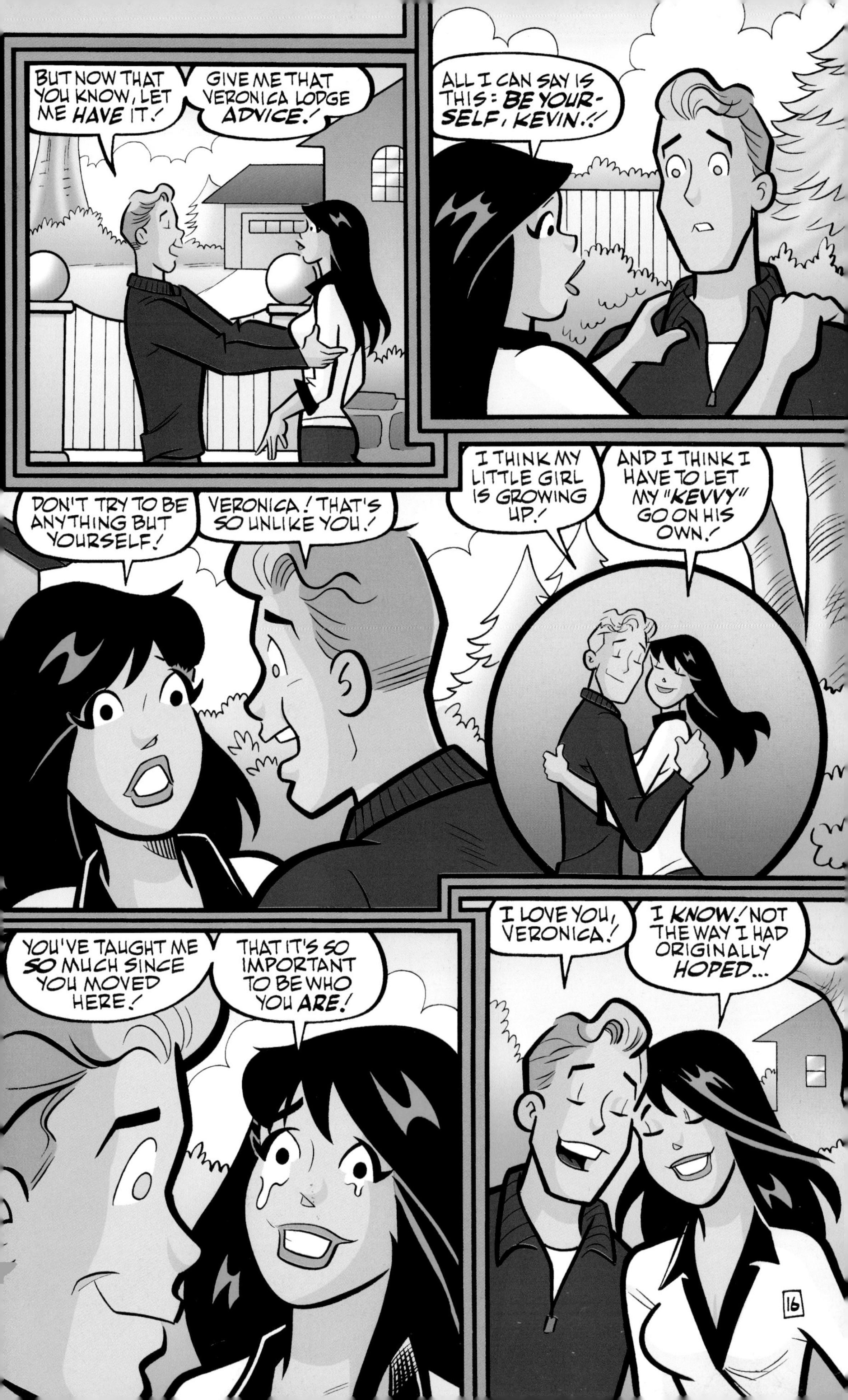
BUT NOW THAT YOU KNOW, LET ME HAVE IT!
GIVE ME THAT VERONICA LODGE ADVICE!
ALL I CAN SAY IS THIS: BE YOURSELF, KEVIN!!
DON'T TRY TO BE ANYTHING BUT YOURSELF!
VERONICA! THAT'S SO UNLIKE YOU!
I THINK MY LITTLE GIRL IS GROWING UP!
AND I THINK I HAVE TO LET MY "KEVVY" GO ON HIS OWN!
YOU'VE TAUGHT ME SO MUCH SINCE YOU MOVED HERE!
THAT IT'S SO IMPORTANT TO BE WHO YOU ARE!
I LOVE YOU, VERONICA!
I KNOW! NOT THE WAY I HAD ORIGINALLY HOPED...
16

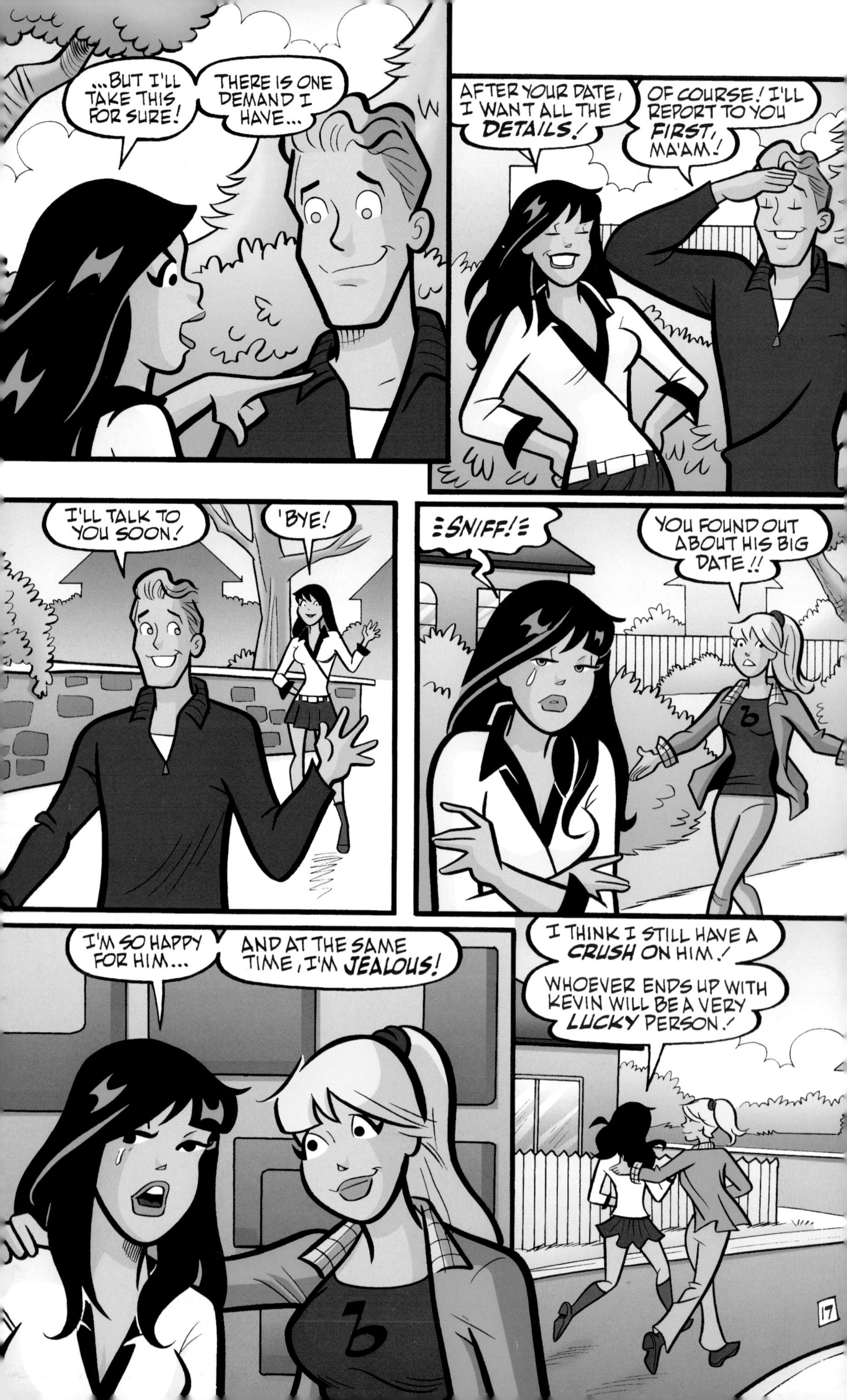
...BUT I'LL TAKE THIS FOR SURE!
THERE IS ONE DEMAND I HAVE...
AFTER YOUR DATE, I WANT ALL THE DETAILS!
OF COURSE! I'LL REPORT TO YOU FIRST, MA'AM!
I'LL TALK TO YOU SOON!
'BYE!
SNIFF!
YOU FOUND OUT ABOUT HIS BIG DATE!!
I'M SO HAPPY FOR HIM...
AND AT THE SAME TIME, I'M JEALOUS!
I THINK I STILL HAVE A CRUSH ON HIM!
WHOEVER ENDS UP WITH KEVIN WILL BE A VERY LUCKY PERSON!
17

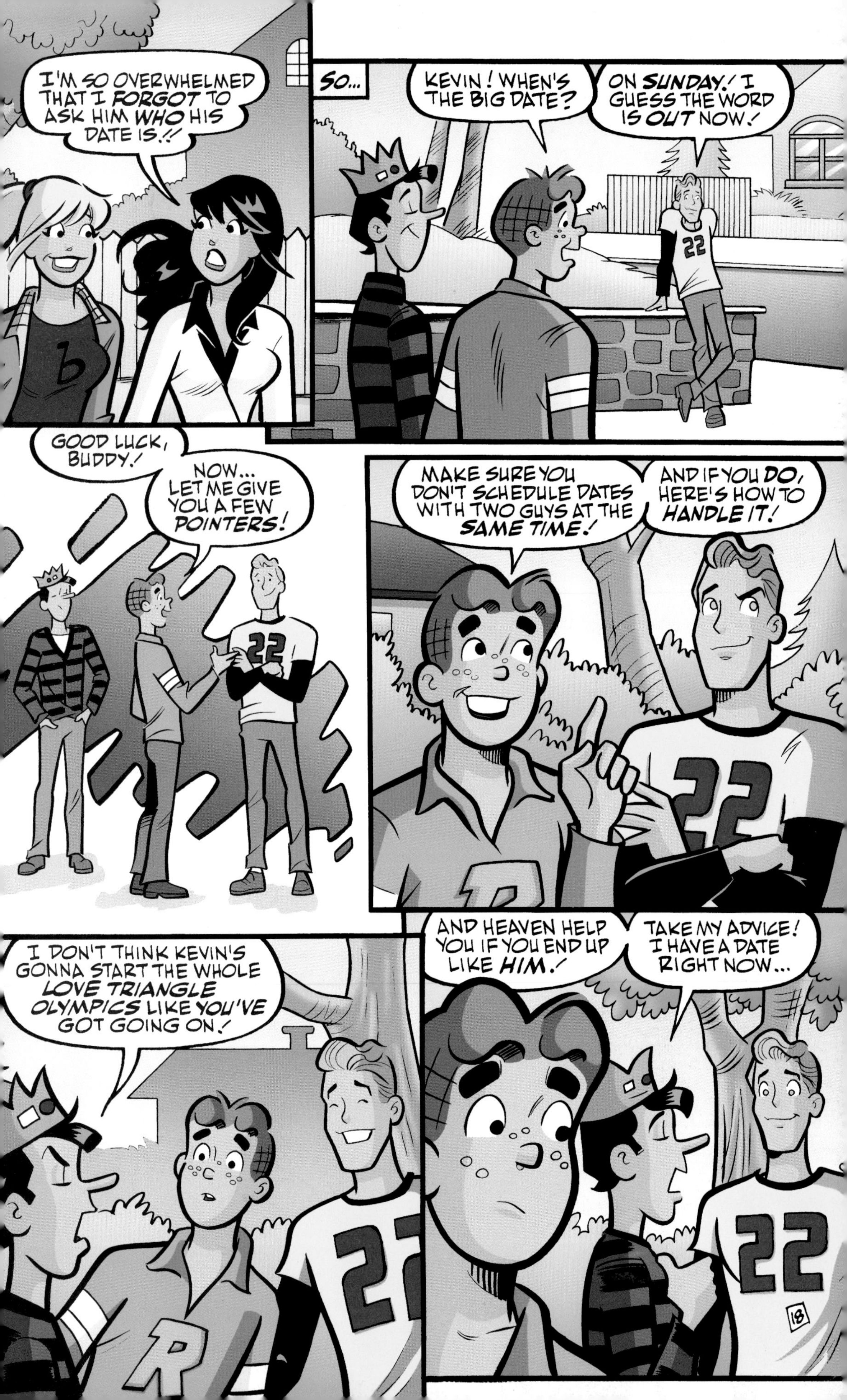

I'M SO OVERWHELMED THAT I FORGOT TO ASK HIM WHO HIS DATE IS!!
SO...
KEVIN! WHEN'S THE BIG DATE?
ON SUNDAY! I GUESS THE WORD IS OUT NOW!
GOOD LUCK, BUDDY!
NOW... LET ME GIVE YOU A FEW POINTERS!
MAKE SURE YOU DON'T SCHEDULE DATES WITH TWO GUYS AT THE SAME TIME!
AND IF YOU DO, HERE'S HOW TO HANDLE IT!
I DON'T THINK KEVIN'S GONNA START THE WHOLE LOVE TRIANGLE OLYMPICS LIKE YOU'VE GOT GOING ON!
AND HEAVEN HELP YOU IF YOU END UP LIKE HIM!
TAKE MY ADVICE! I HAVE A DATE RIGHT NOW...
18

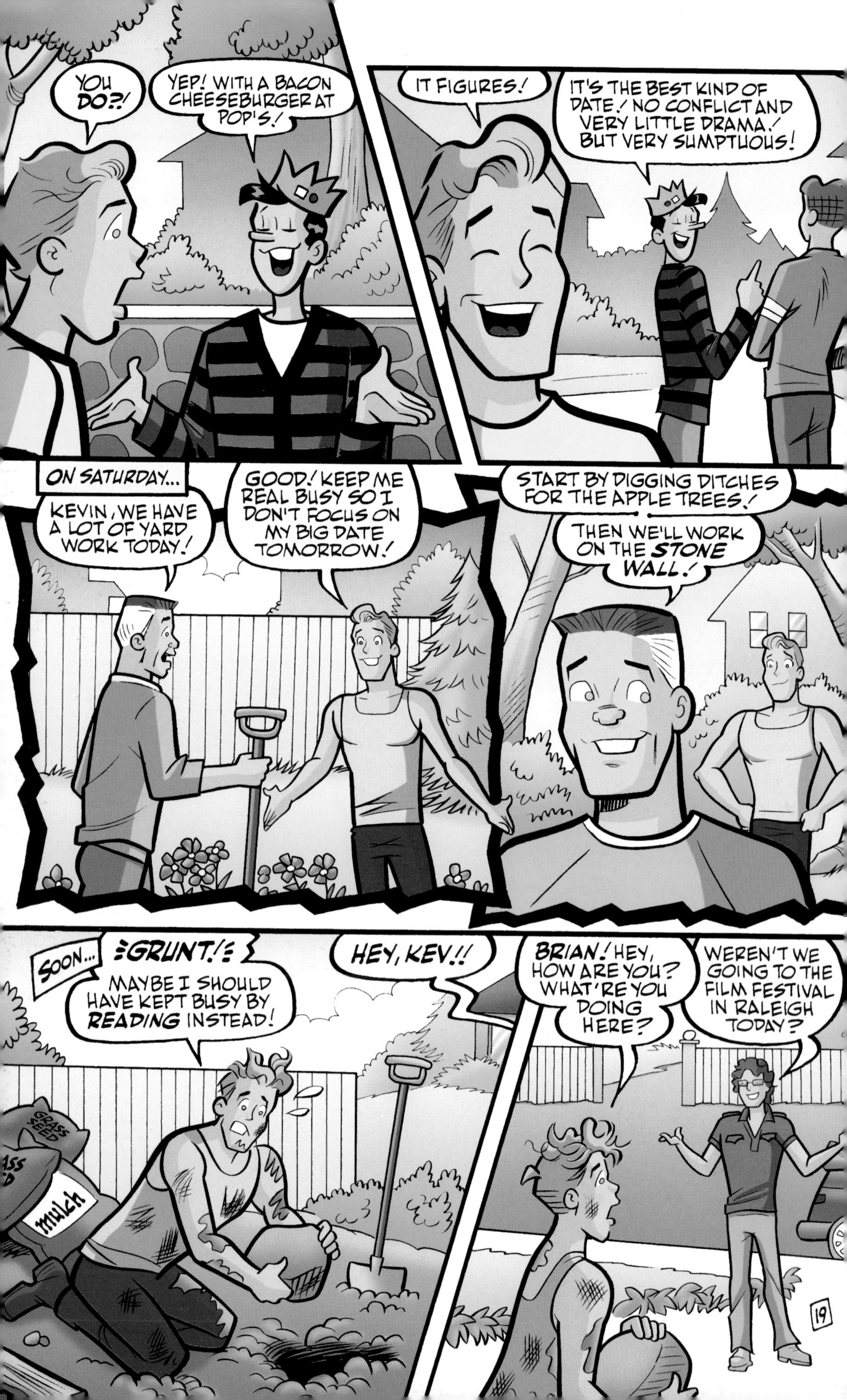

YOU DO?!
YEP! WITH A BACON CHEESEBURGER AT POP'S!
IT FIGURES!
IT'S THE BEST KIND OF DATE! NO CONFLICT AND VERY LITTLE DRAMA! BUT VERY SUMPTUOUS!
ON SATURDAY...
KEVIN, WE HAVE A LOT OF YARD WORK TODAY!
GOOD! KEEP ME REAL BUSY SO I DON'T FOCUS ON MY BIG DATE TOMORROW!
START BY DIGGING DITCHES FOR THE APPLE TREES!
THEN WE'LL WORK ON THE STONE WALL!
SOON...
GRUNT!
MAYBE I SHOULD HAVE KEPT BUSY BY READING INSTEAD!
GRASS SEED
mulch
HEY, KEV!!
BRIAN! HEY, HOW ARE YOU? WHAT'RE YOU DOING HERE?
WEREN'T WE GOING TO THE FILM FESTIVAL IN RALEIGH TODAY?

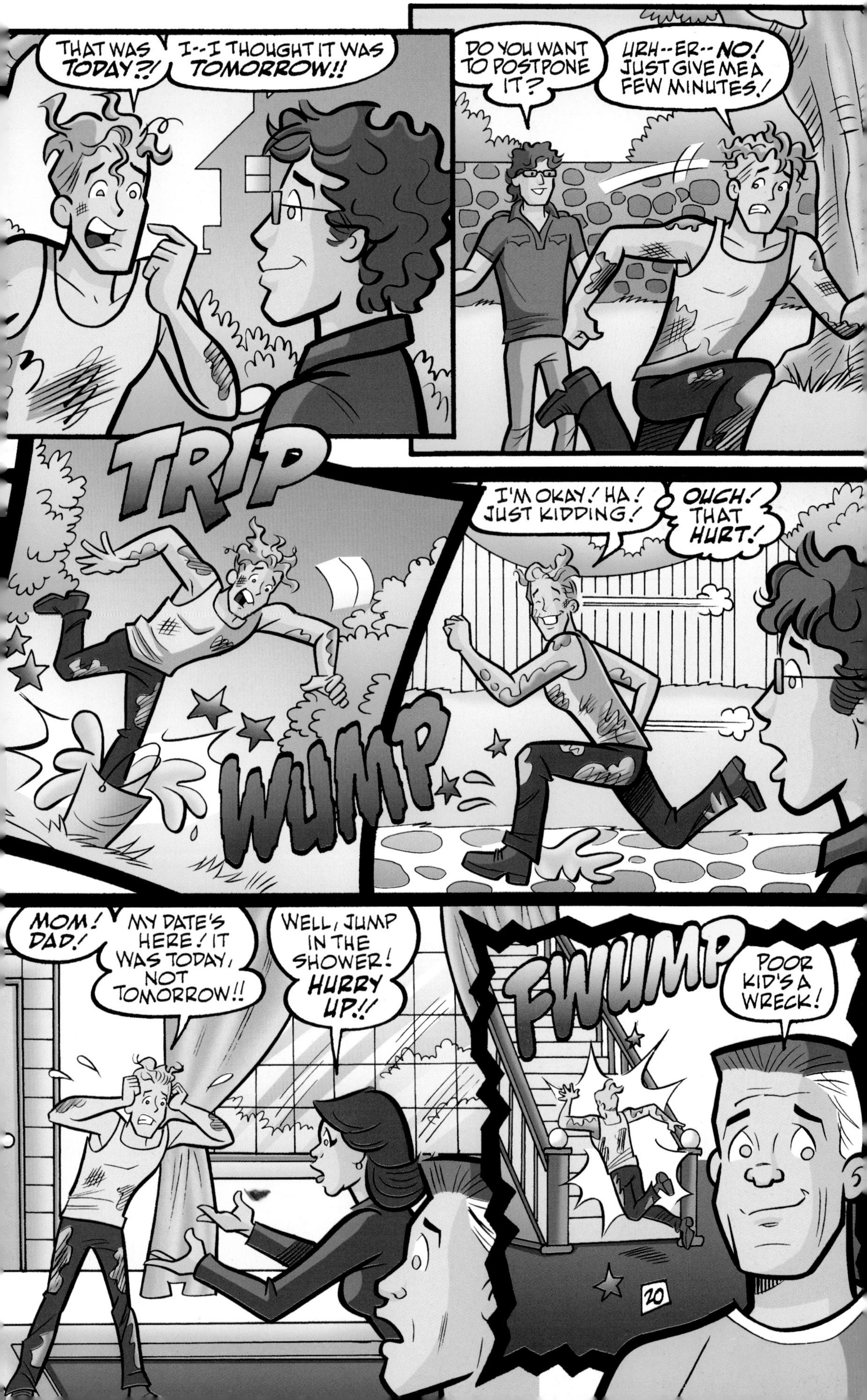
THAT WAS TODAY?!
I--I THOUGHT IT WAS TOMORROW!!
DO YOU WANT TO POSTPONE IT?
URH--ER--NO! JUST GIVE ME A FEW MINUTES!
TRIP
WUMP
I'M OKAY! HA! JUST KIDDING!
OUCH! THAT HURT!
MOM! DAD!
MY DATE'S HERE! IT WAS TODAY, NOT TOMORROW!!
WELL, JUMP IN THE SHOWER! HURRY UP!!
FWUMP
POOR KID'S A WRECK!
20

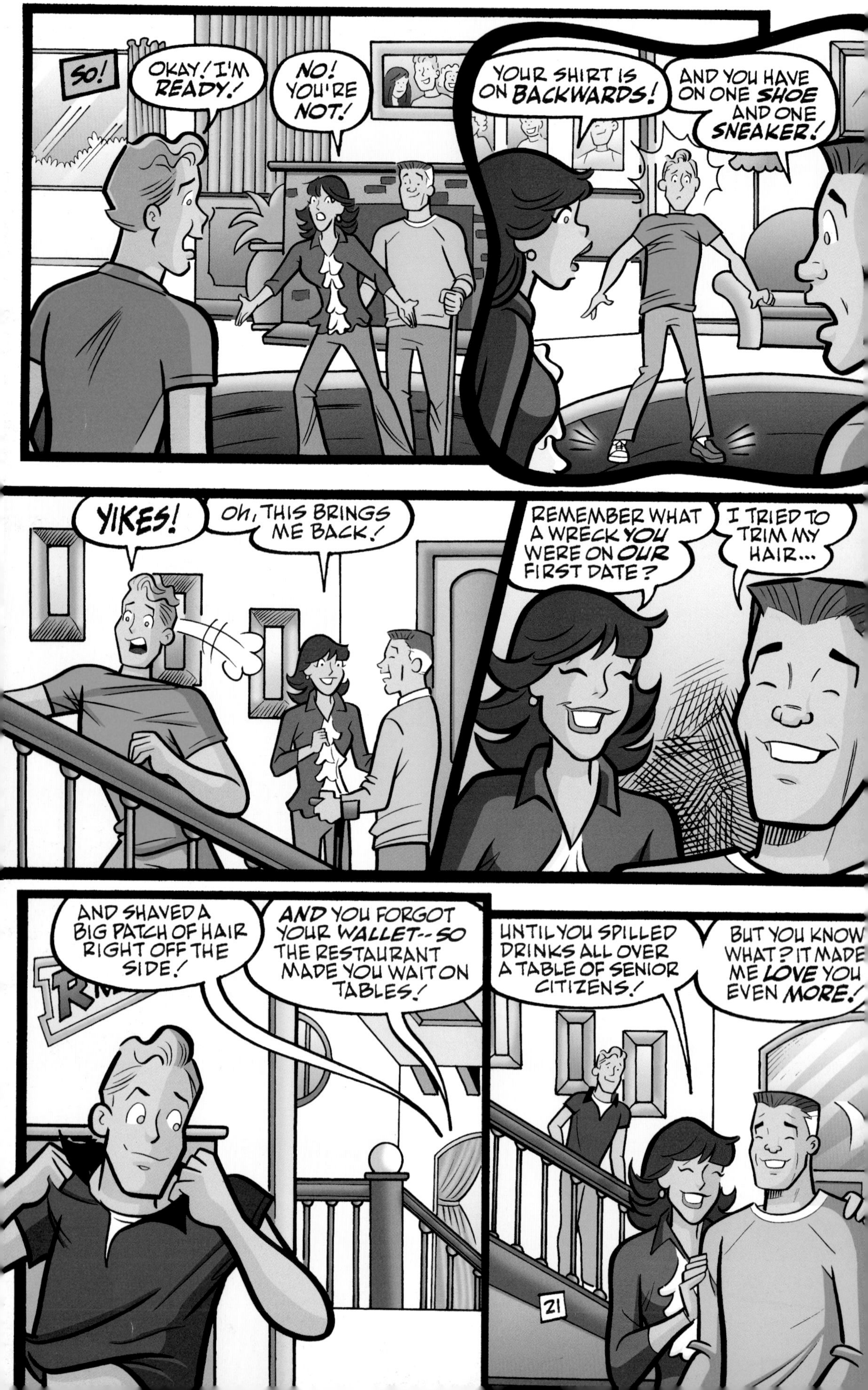
SO!
OKAY! I'M READY!
NO! YOU'RE NOT!
YOUR SHIRT IS ON BACKWARDS!
AND YOU HAVE ON ONE SHOE AND ONE SNEAKER!
YIKES!
Oh, THIS BRINGS ME BACK!
REMEMBER WHAT A WRECK YOU WERE ON OUR FIRST DATE?
I TRIED TO TRIM MY HAIR...
AND SHAVED A BIG PATCH OF HAIR RIGHT OFF THE SIDE!
AND YOU FORGOT YOUR WALLET-- SO THE RESTAURANT MADE YOU WAIT ON TABLES!
UNTIL YOU SPILLED DRINKS ALL OVER A TABLE OF SENIOR CITIZENS!
BUT YOU KNOW WHAT? IT MADE ME LOVE YOU EVEN MORE!
21

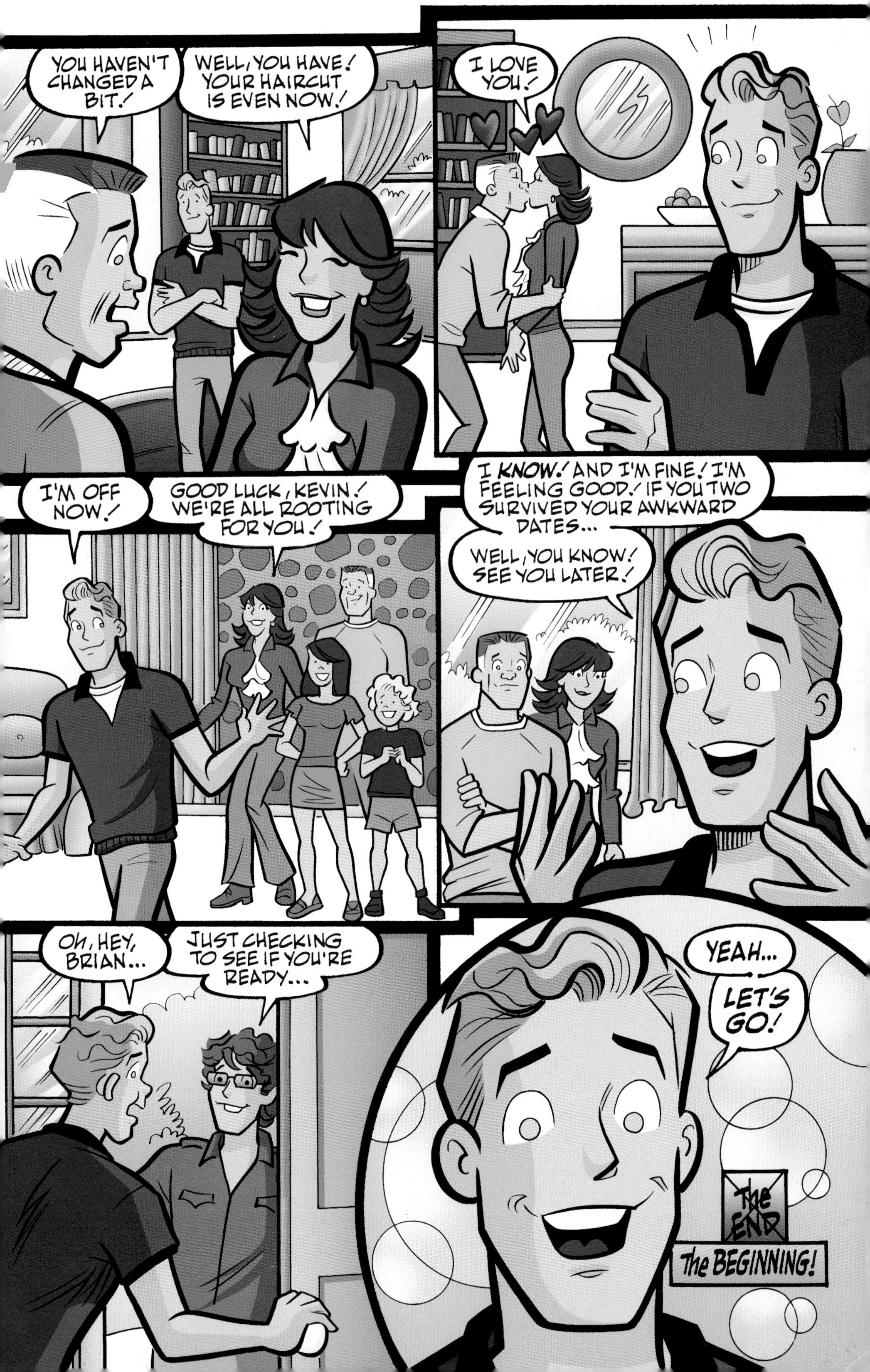
YOU HAVEN'T CHANGED A BIT!
WELL, YOU HAVE! YOUR HAIRCUT IS EVEN NOW!
I LOVE YOU!
I'M OFF NOW!
GOOD LUCK, KEVIN! WE'RE ALL ROOTING FOR YOU!
I KNOW! AND I'M FINE! I'M FEELING GOOD! IF YOU TWO SURVIVED YOUR AWKWARD DATES...
WELL, YOU KNOW! SEE YOU LATER!
OH, HEY, BRIAN...
JUST CHECKING TO SEE IF YOU'RE READY...
YEAH...
LET'S GO!
The END
The BEGINNING!

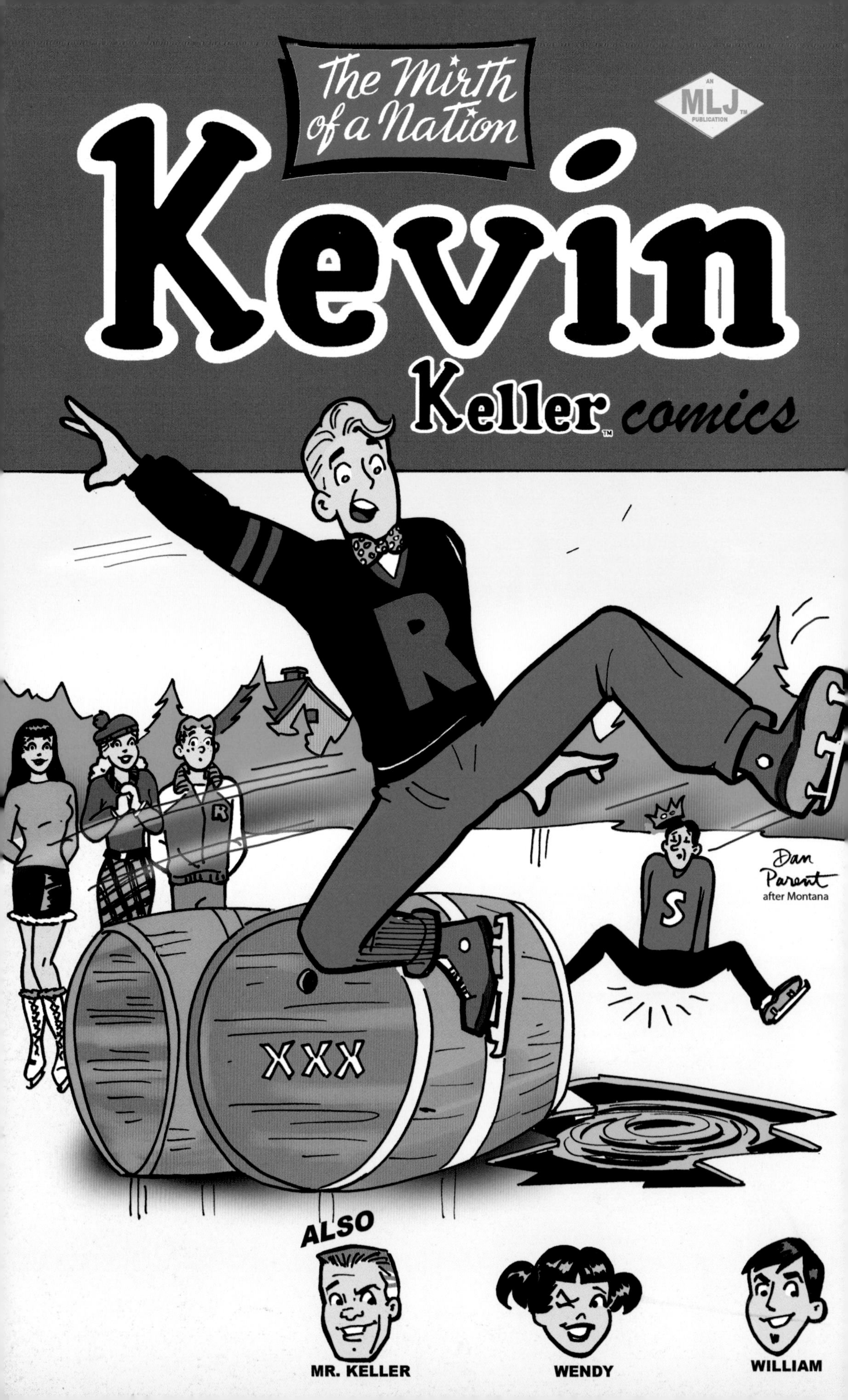

The Mirth of a Nation
AN MLJ PUBLICATION
Kevin Keller comics
XXX
Dan Parent after Montana
ALSO
MR. KELLER
WENDY
WILLIAM

Chapter 2

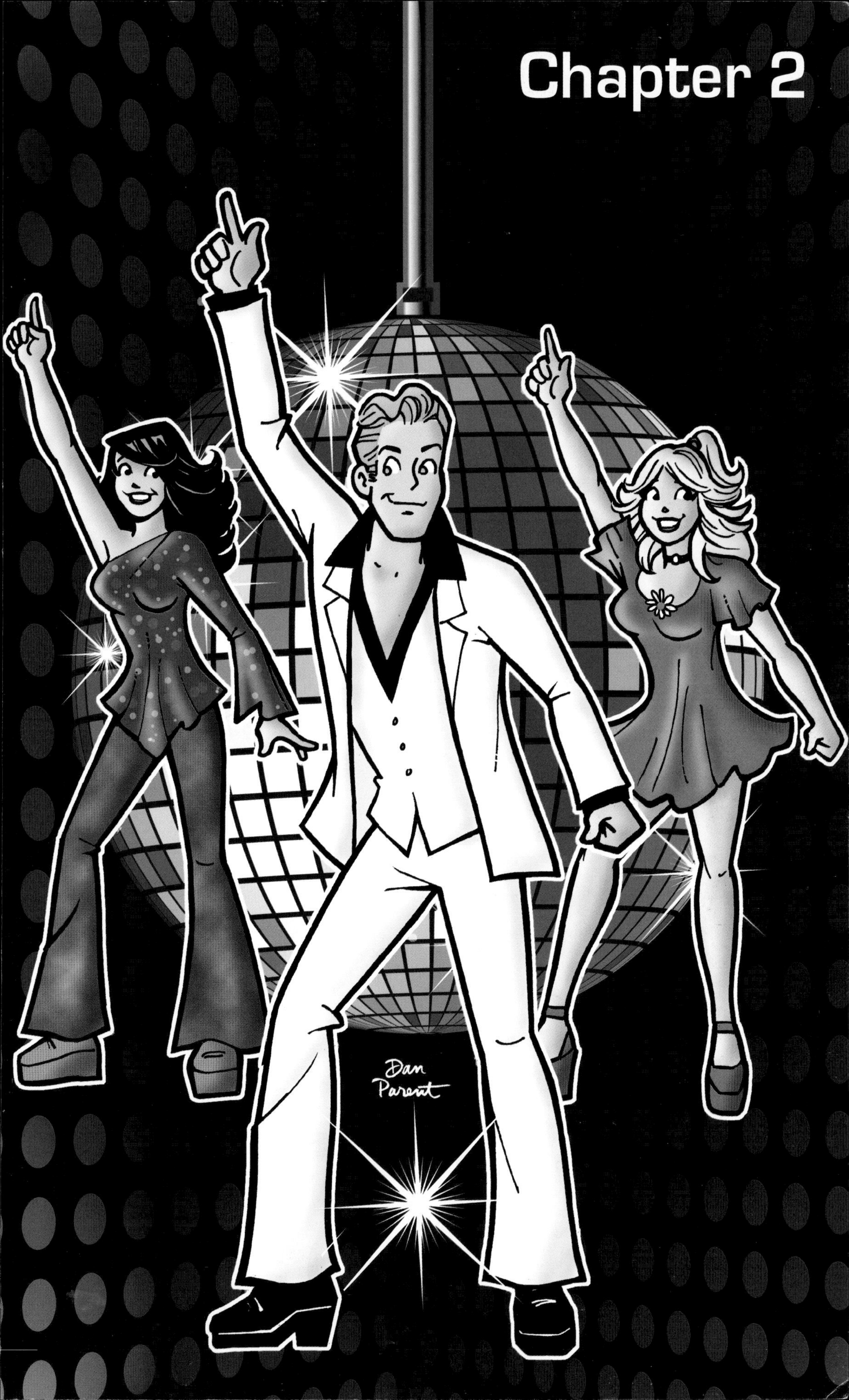
Dan Parent

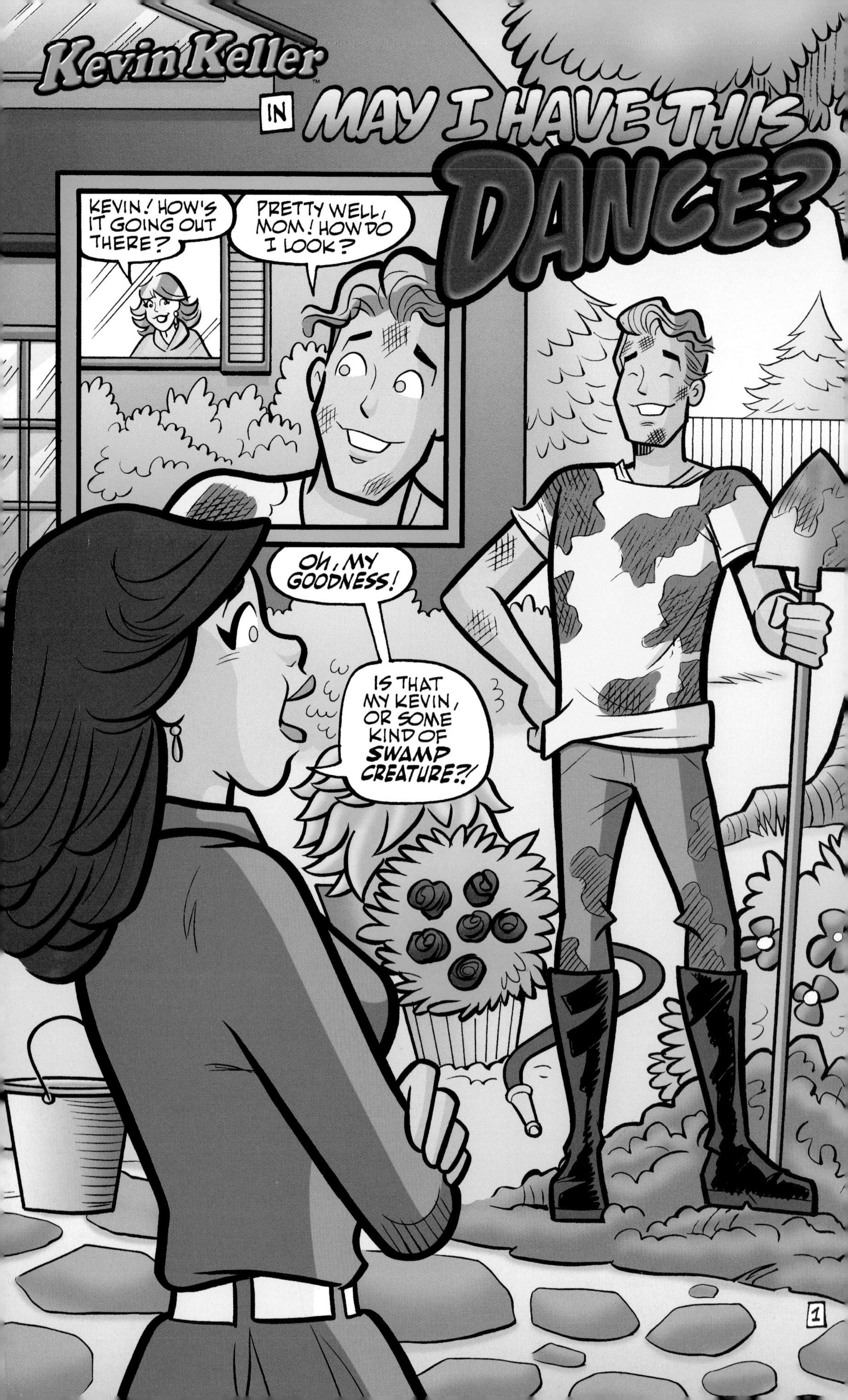

Kevin Keller™
IN MAY I HAVE THIS DANCE?
KEVIN! HOW'S IT GOING OUT THERE?
PRETTY WELL, MOM! HOW DO I LOOK?
Oh, MY GOODNESS!
IS THAT MY KEVIN, OR SOME KIND OF SWAMP CREATURE?!
1

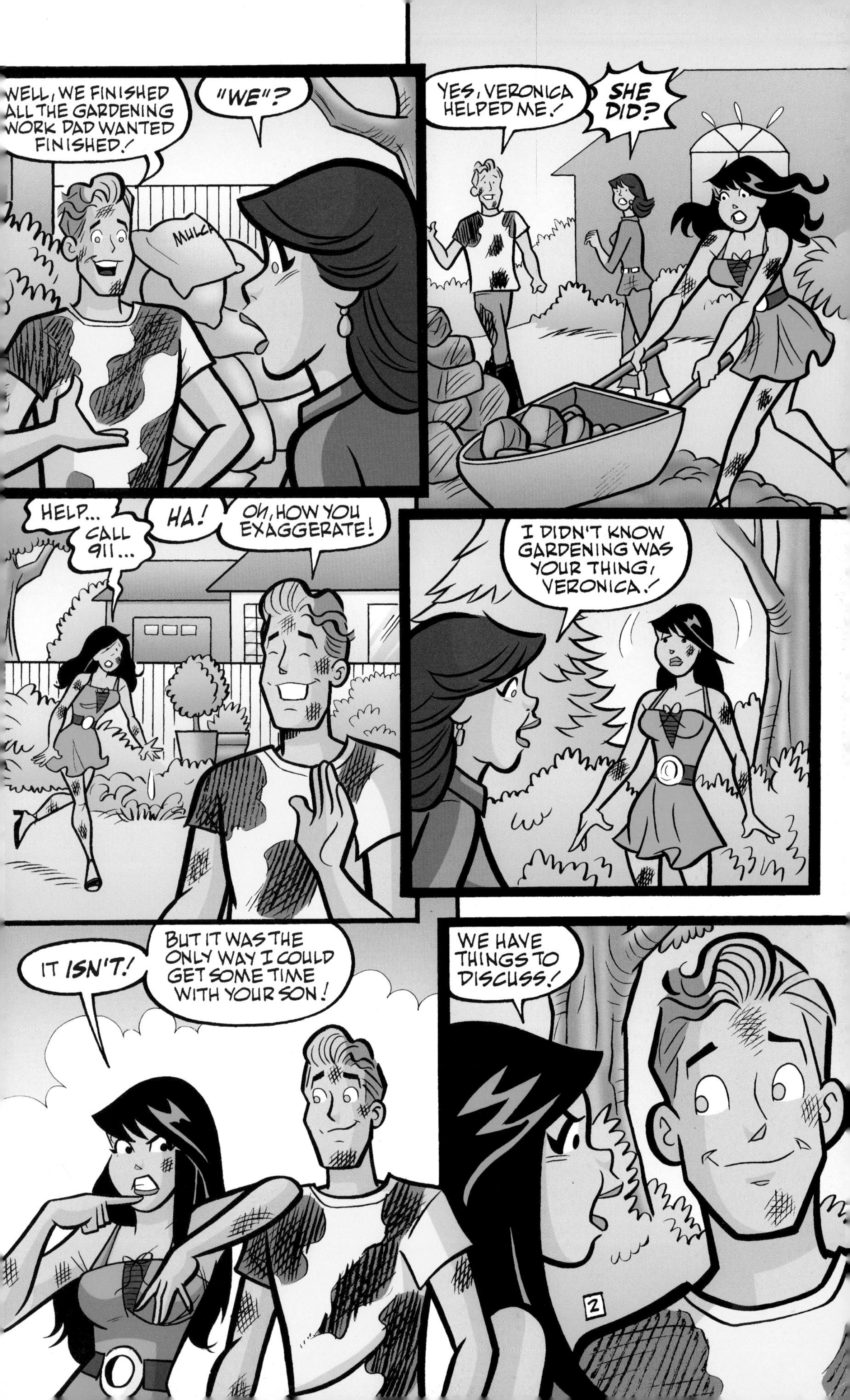
WELL, WE FINISHED ALL THE GARDENING WORK DAD WANTED FINISHED!
"WE"?
MULCH
YES, VERONICA HELPED ME!
SHE DID?
HELP... CALL 911...
HA!
OH, HOW YOU EXAGGERATE!
I DIDN'T KNOW GARDENING WAS YOUR THING, VERONICA!
IT ISN'T!
BUT IT WAS THE ONLY WAY I COULD GET SOME TIME WITH YOUR SON!
WE HAVE THINGS TO DISCUSS!
2

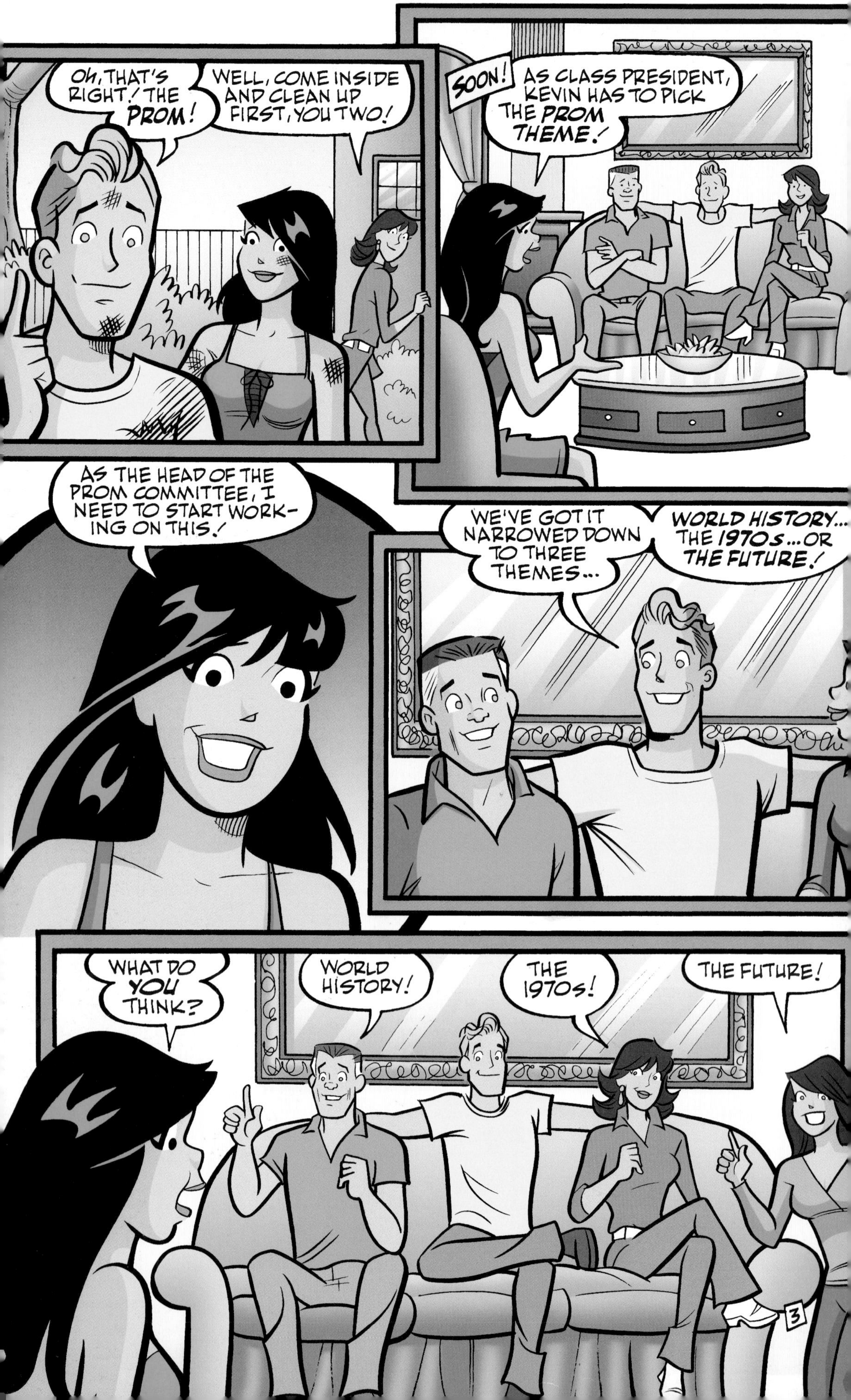

OH, THAT'S RIGHT! THE PROM!
WELL, COME INSIDE AND CLEAN UP FIRST, YOU TWO!
SOON!
AS CLASS PRESIDENT, KEVIN HAS TO PICK THE PROM THEME!
AS THE HEAD OF THE PROM COMMITTEE, I NEED TO START WORKING ON THIS!
WE'VE GOT IT NARROWED DOWN TO THREE THEMES...
WORLD HISTORY... THE 1970s...OR THE FUTURE!
WHAT DO YOU THINK?
WORLD HISTORY!
THE 1970s!
THE FUTURE!
3

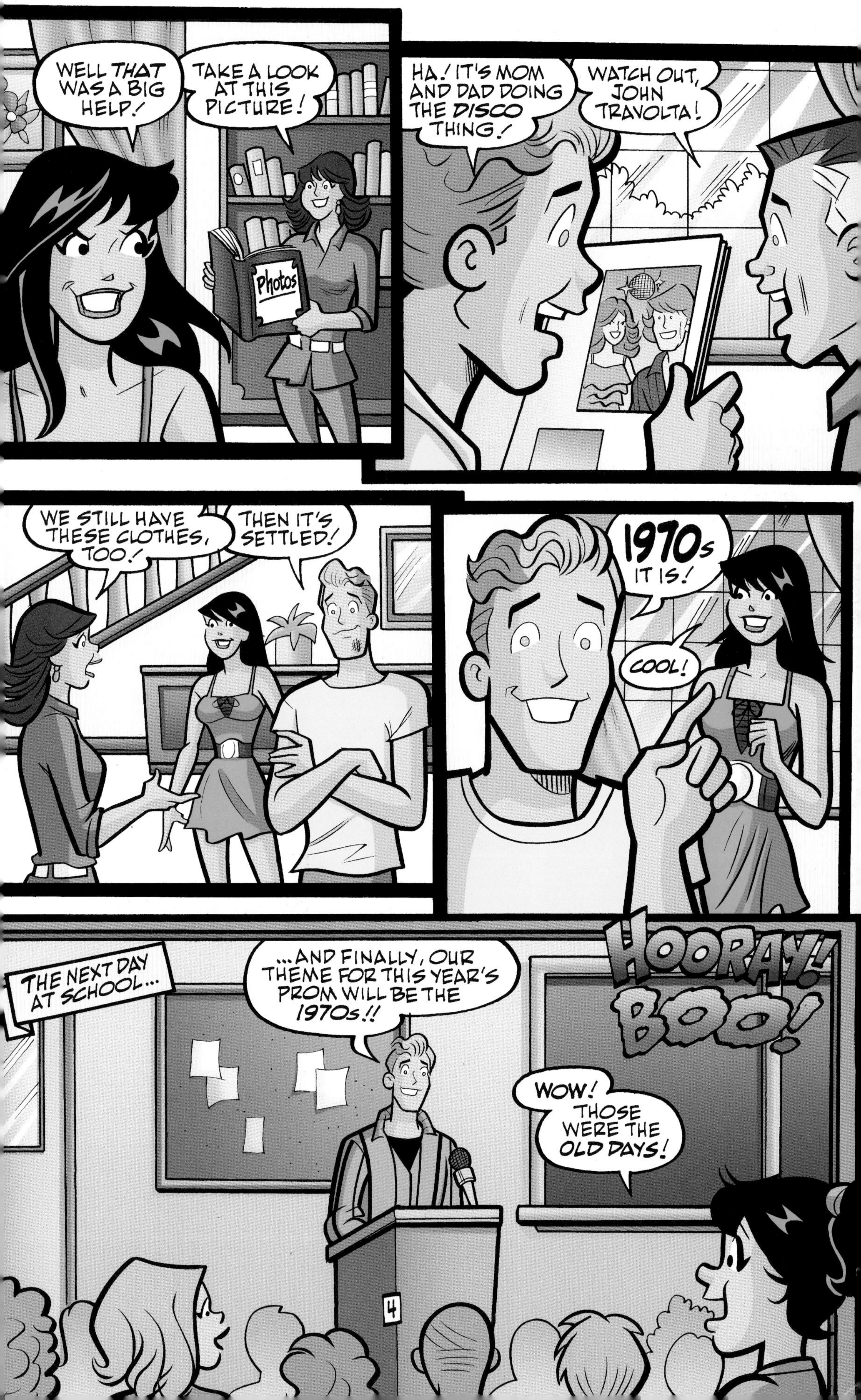
WELL THAT WAS A BIG HELP!
TAKE A LOOK AT THIS PICTURE!
Photos
HA! IT'S MOM AND DAD DOING THE DISCO THING!
WATCH OUT, JOHN TRAVOLTA!
WE STILL HAVE THESE CLOTHES, TOO!
THEN IT'S SETTLED!
1970s IT IS!
COOL!
THE NEXT DAY AT SCHOOL...
...AND FINALLY, OUR THEME FOR THIS YEAR'S PROM WILL BE THE 1970s!!
HOORAY! BOO!
WOW! THOSE WERE THE OLD DAYS!
4

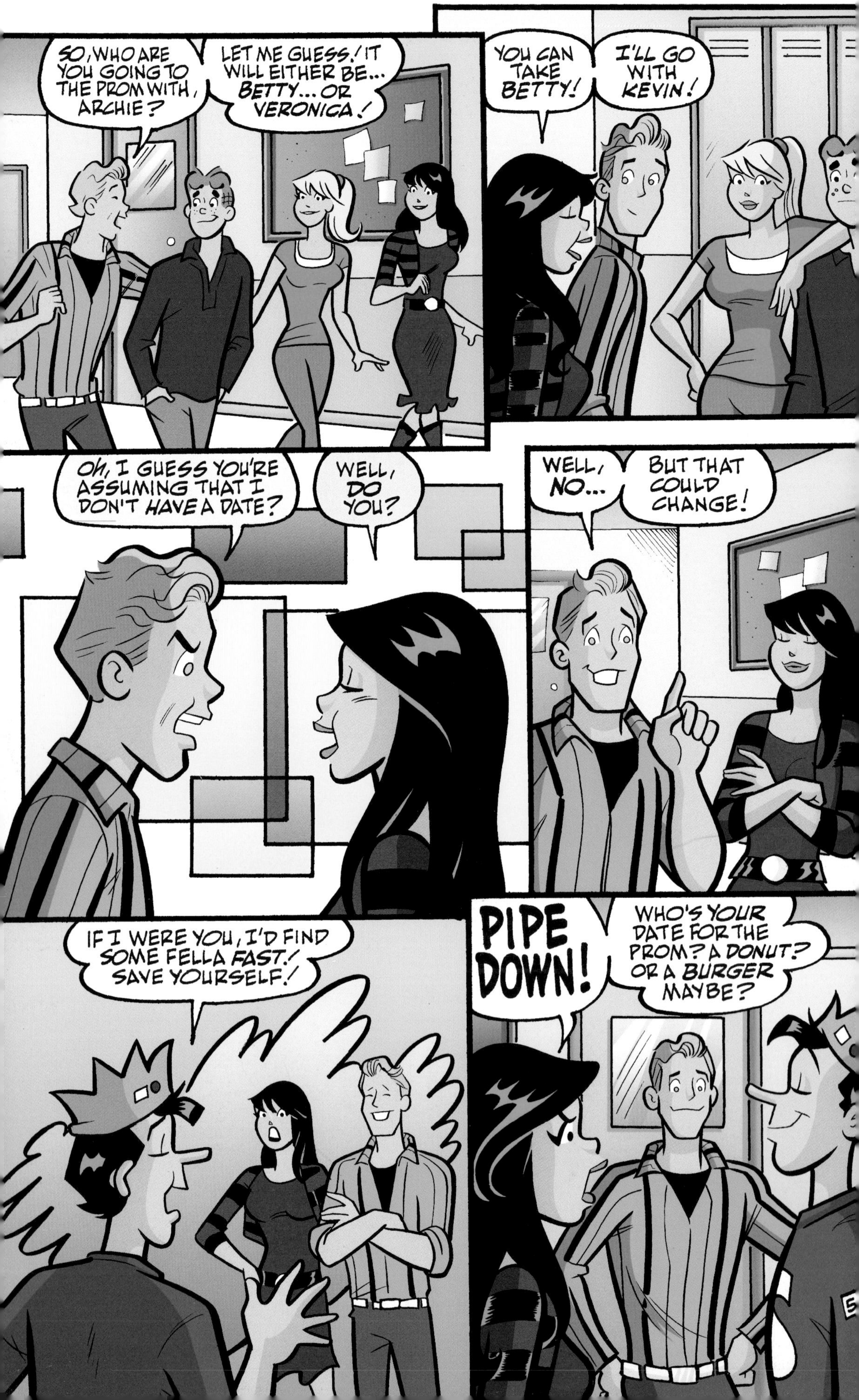
SO, WHO ARE YOU GOING TO THE PROM WITH, ARCHIE?
LET ME GUESS! IT WILL EITHER BE... BETTY... OR VERONICA!
YOU CAN TAKE BETTY!
I'LL GO WITH KEVIN!
OH, I GUESS YOU'RE ASSUMING THAT I DON'T HAVE A DATE?
WELL, DO YOU?
WELL, NO...
BUT THAT COULD CHANGE!
IF I WERE YOU, I'D FIND SOME FELLA FAST! SAVE YOURSELF!
PIPE DOWN!
WHO'S YOUR DATE FOR THE PROM? A DONUT? OR A BURGER MAYBE?

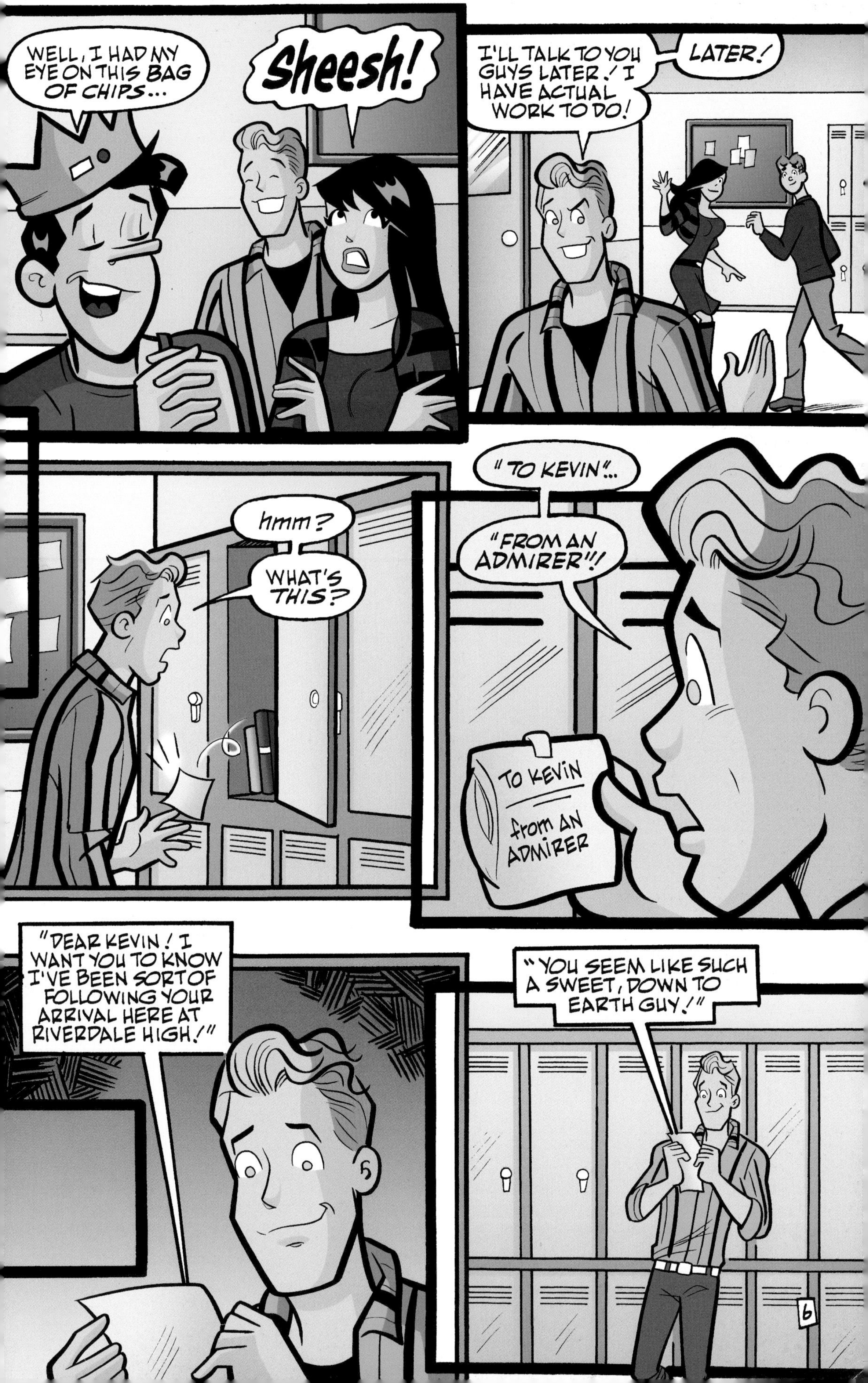
WELL, I HAD MY EYE ON THIS BAG OF CHIPS...
Sheesh!
I'LL TALK TO YOU GUYS LATER! I HAVE ACTUAL WORK TO DO!
LATER!
hmm?
WHAT'S THIS?
"TO KEVIN"...
"FROM AN ADMIRER"!
TO KEVIN
from AN ADMIRER
"DEAR KEVIN! I WANT YOU TO KNOW I'VE BEEN SORT OF FOLLOWING YOUR ARRIVAL HERE AT RIVERDALE HIGH!"
"YOU SEEM LIKE SUCH A SWEET, DOWN TO EARTH GUY!"
6

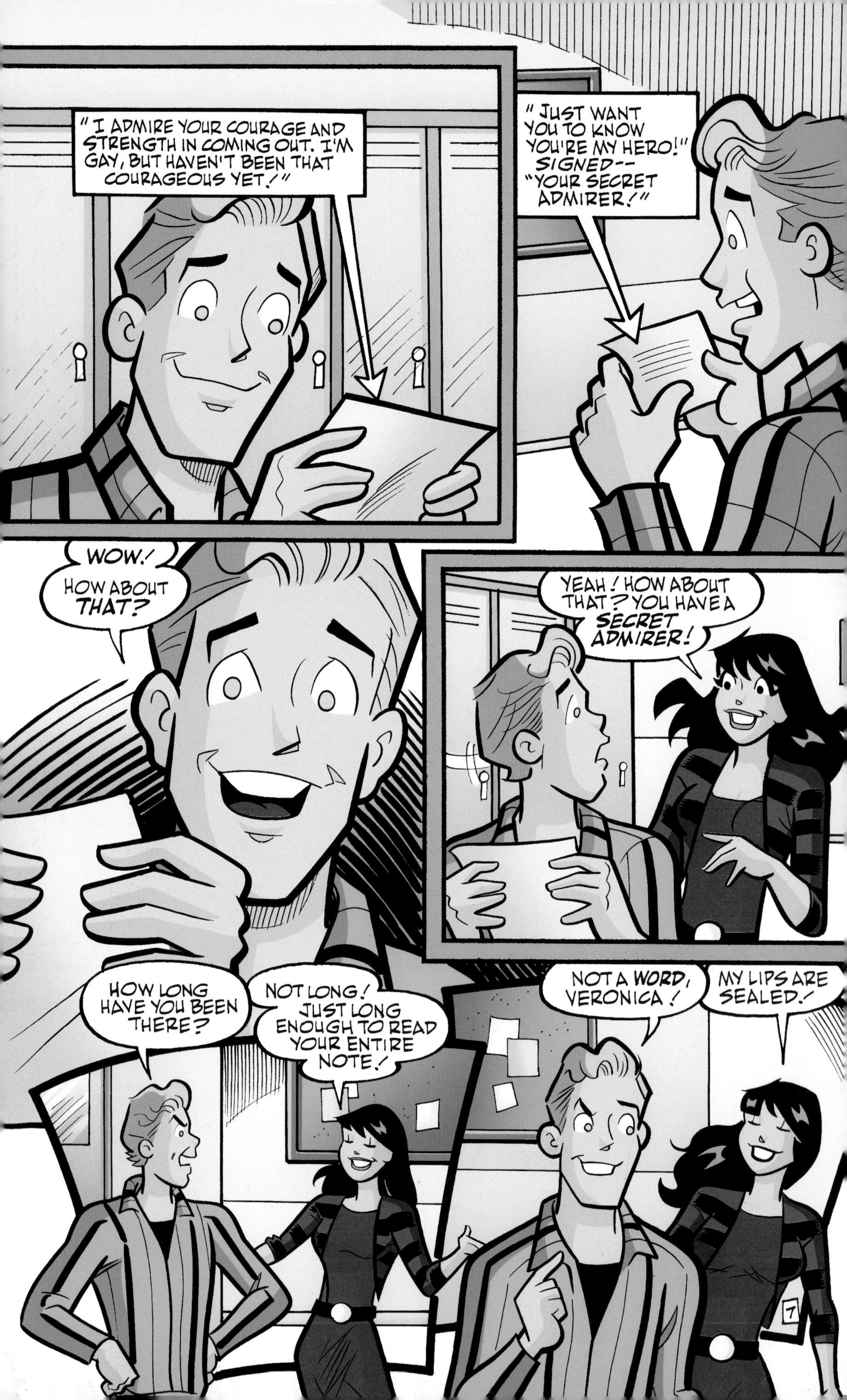
"I ADMIRE YOUR COURAGE AND STRENGTH IN COMING OUT. I'M GAY, BUT HAVEN'T BEEN THAT COURAGEOUS YET!"
"JUST WANT YOU TO KNOW YOU'RE MY HERO!" SIGNED-- "YOUR SECRET ADMIRER!"
WOW! HOW ABOUT THAT?
YEAH! HOW ABOUT THAT? YOU HAVE A SECRET ADMIRER!
HOW LONG HAVE YOU BEEN THERE?
NOT LONG! JUST LONG ENOUGH TO READ YOUR ENTIRE NOTE!
NOT A WORD, VERONICA!
MY LIPS ARE SEALED!
7

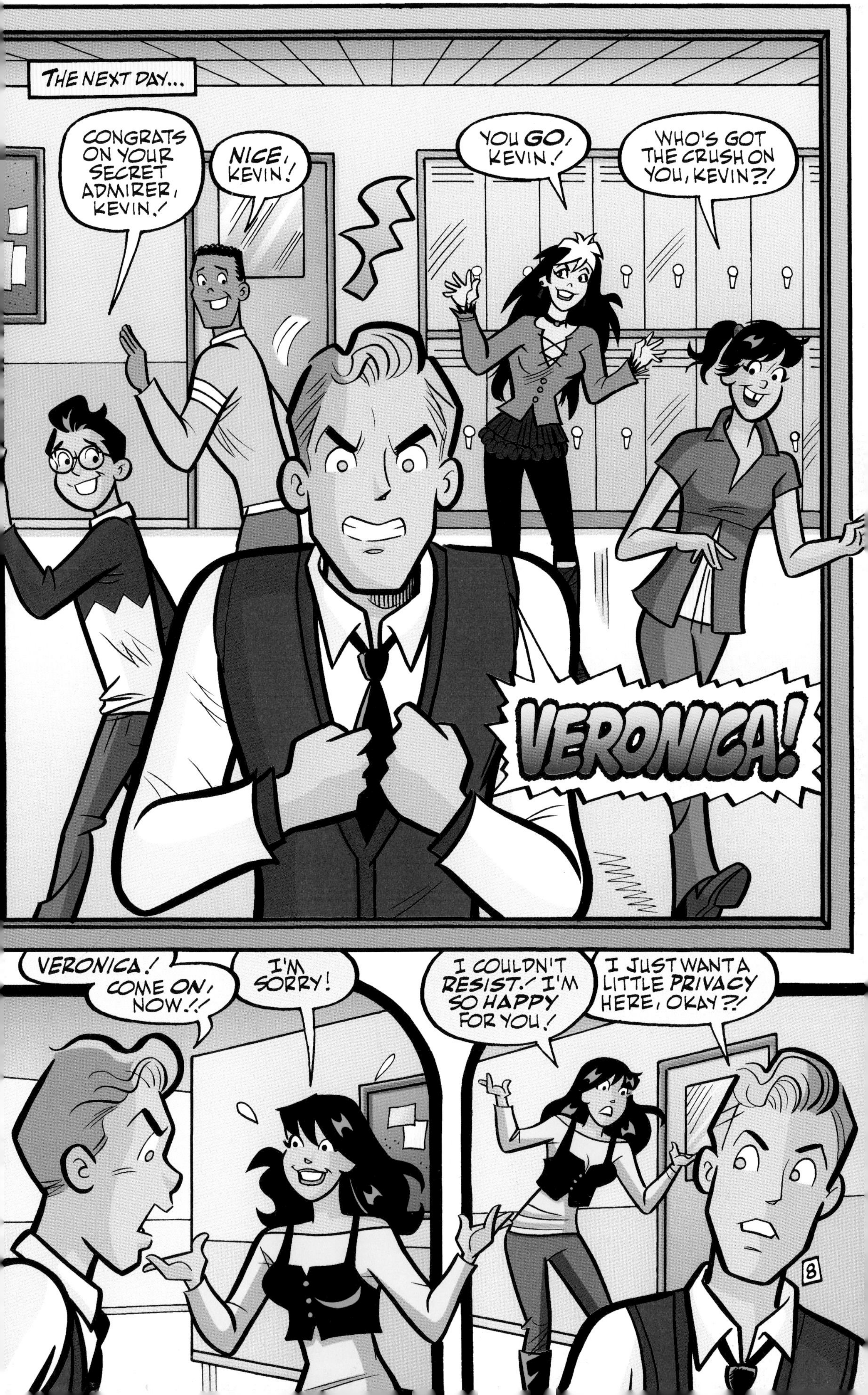
THE NEXT DAY...
CONGRATS ON YOUR SECRET ADMIRER, KEVIN!
NICE, KEVIN!
YOU GO, KEVIN!
WHO'S GOT THE CRUSH ON YOU, KEVIN?!
VERONICA!
VERONICA! COME ON, NOW!!
I'M SORRY!
I COULDN'T RESIST! I'M SO HAPPY FOR YOU!
I JUST WANT A LITTLE PRIVACY HERE, OKAY?!
8

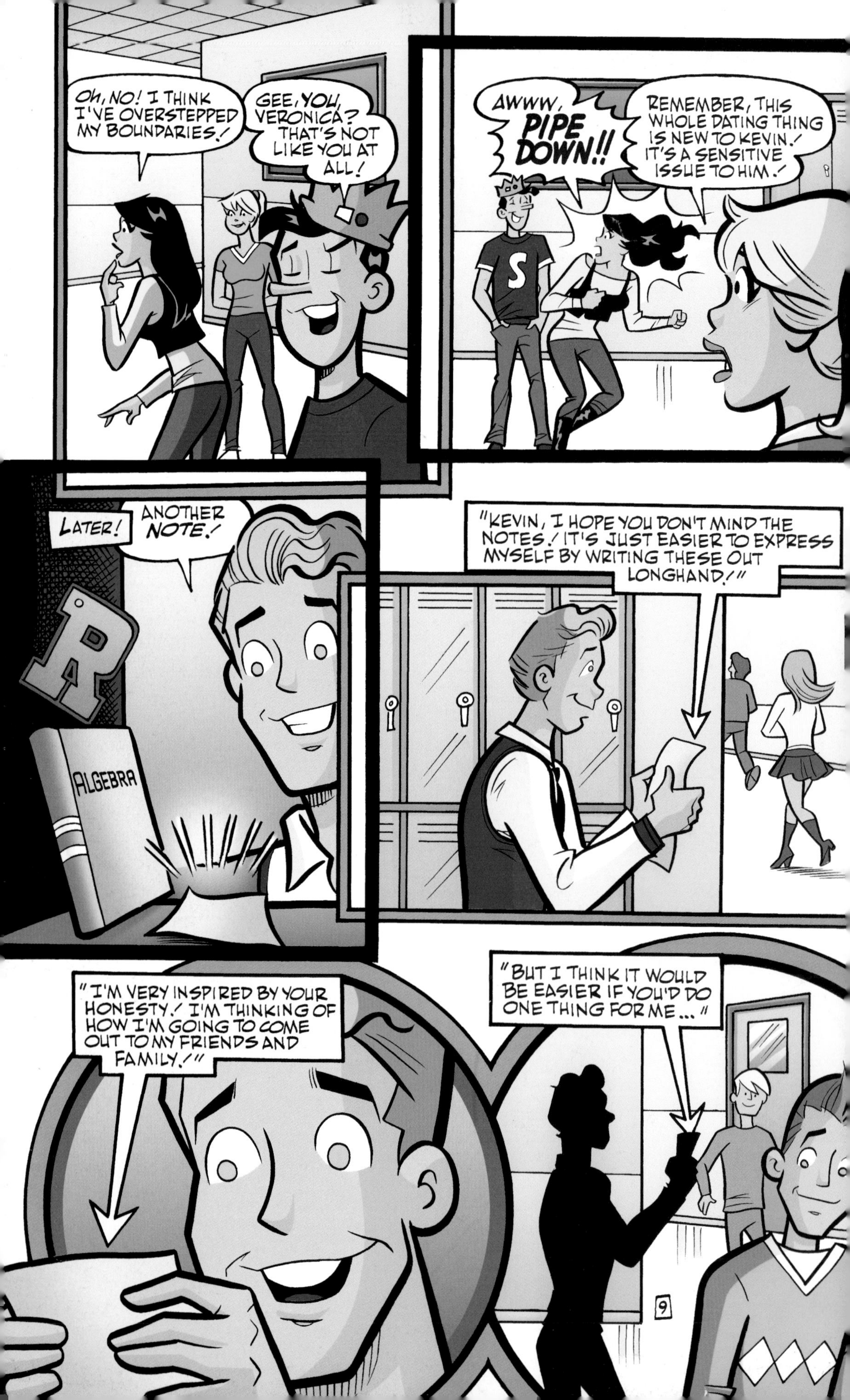

OH, NO! I THINK I'VE OVERSTEPPED MY BOUNDARIES!
GEE, YOU, VERONICA? THAT'S NOT LIKE YOU AT ALL!
AWWW, PIPE DOWN!!
REMEMBER, THIS WHOLE DATING THING IS NEW TO KEVIN! IT'S A SENSITIVE ISSUE TO HIM!
LATER!
ANOTHER NOTE!
R
ALGEBRA
"KEVIN, I HOPE YOU DON'T MIND THE NOTES! IT'S JUST EASIER TO EXPRESS MYSELF BY WRITING THESE OUT LONGHAND!"
"I'M VERY INSPIRED BY YOUR HONESTY! I'M THINKING OF HOW I'M GOING TO COME OUT TO MY FRIENDS AND FAMILY!"
"BUT I THINK IT WOULD BE EASIER IF YOU'D DO ONE THING FOR ME..."
S
9

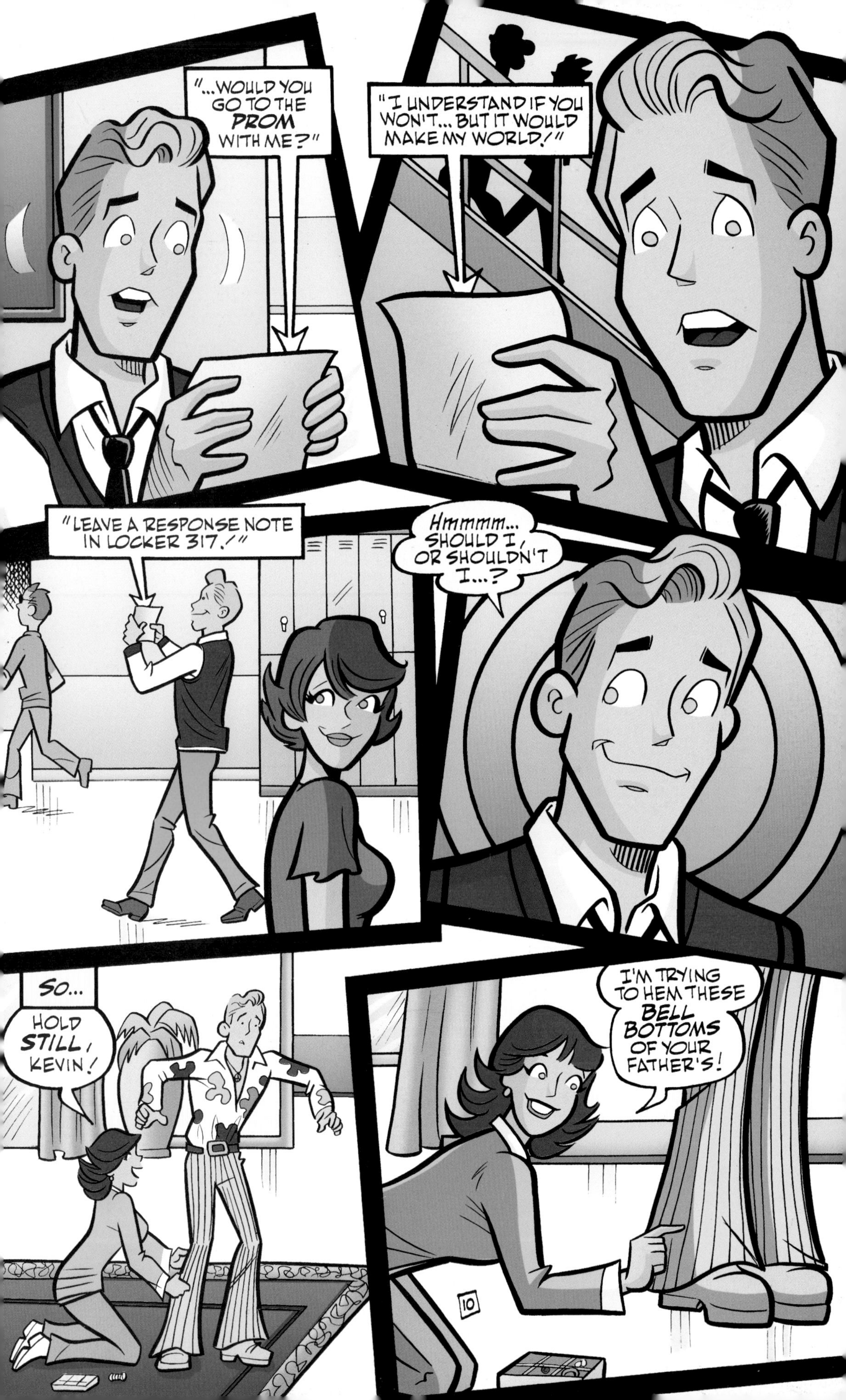
"...WOULD YOU GO TO THE PROM WITH ME?"
"I UNDERSTAND IF YOU WON'T... BUT IT WOULD MAKE MY WORLD!"
"LEAVE A RESPONSE NOTE IN LOCKER 317!"
Hmmmm... SHOULD I, OR SHOULDN'T I...?
SO...
HOLD STILL, KEVIN!
I'M TRYING TO HEM THESE BELL BOTTOMS OF YOUR FATHER'S!
10

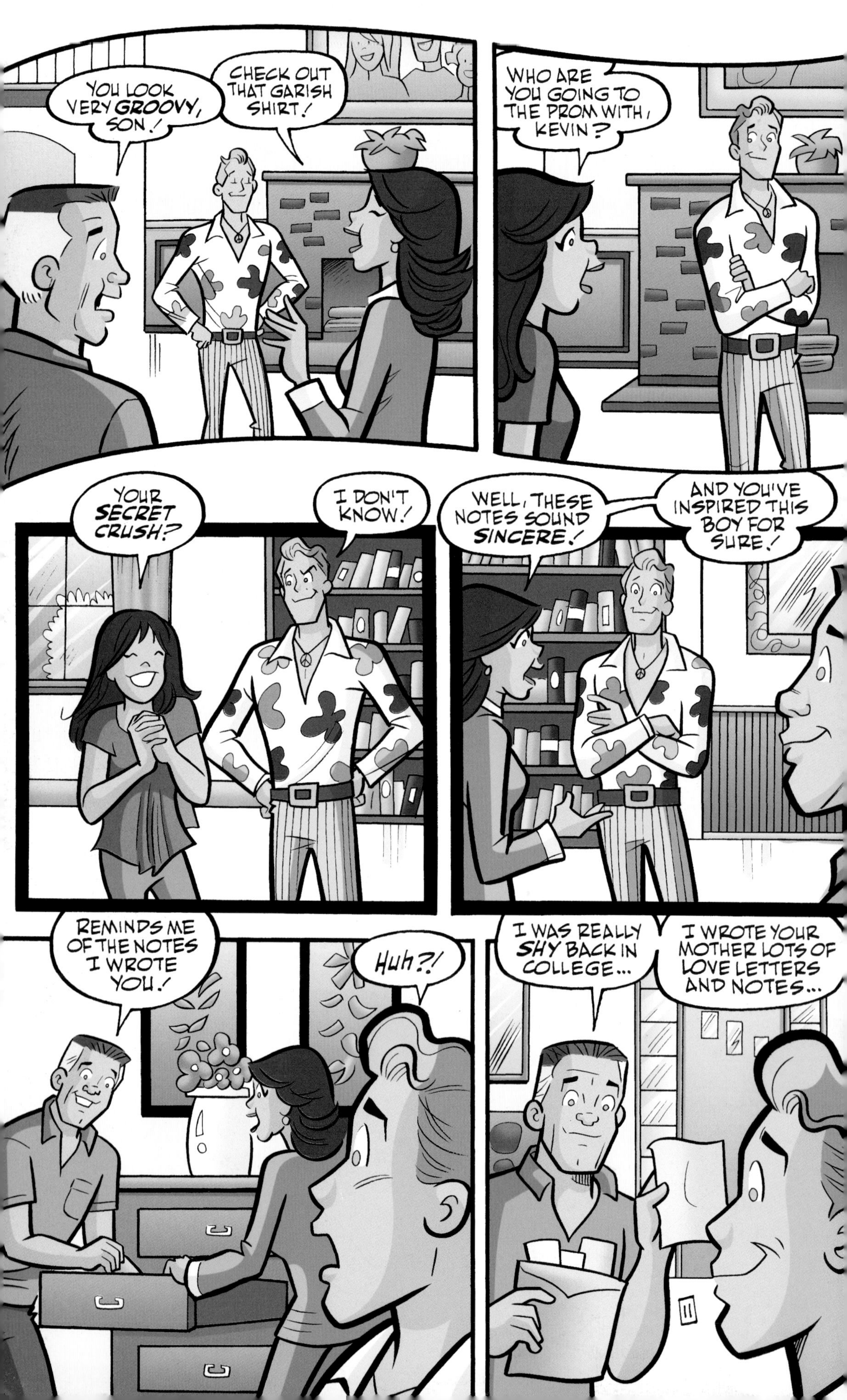
YOU LOOK VERY GROOVY, SON!
CHECK OUT THAT GARISH SHIRT!
WHO ARE YOU GOING TO THE PROM WITH, KEVIN?
YOUR SECRET CRUSH?
I DON'T KNOW!
WELL, THESE NOTES SOUND SINCERE!
AND YOU'VE INSPIRED THIS BOY FOR SURE!
REMINDS ME OF THE NOTES I WROTE YOU!
Huh?!
I WAS REALLY SHY BACK IN COLLEGE...
I WROTE YOUR MOTHER LOTS OF LOVE LETTERS AND NOTES...
11

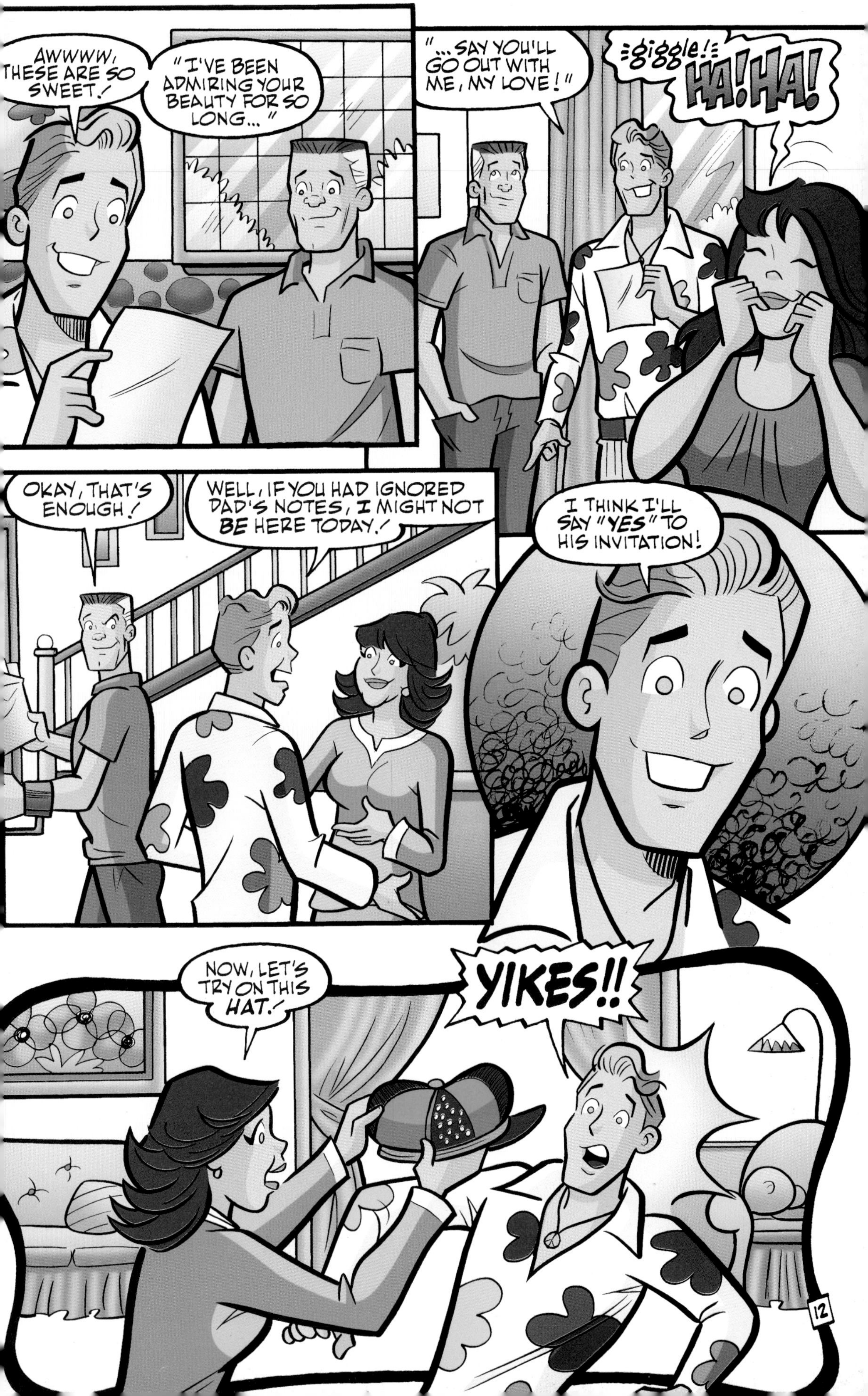
AWWWW, THESE ARE SO SWEET.!
"I'VE BEEN ADMIRING YOUR BEAUTY FOR SO LONG..."
"...SAY YOU'LL GO OUT WITH ME, MY LOVE!"
giggle!
HA! HA!
OKAY, THAT'S ENOUGH!
WELL, IF YOU HAD IGNORED DAD'S NOTES, I MIGHT NOT BE HERE TODAY.!
I THINK I'LL SAY "YES" TO HIS INVITATION!
NOW, LET'S TRY ON THIS HAT.!
YIKES!!
12

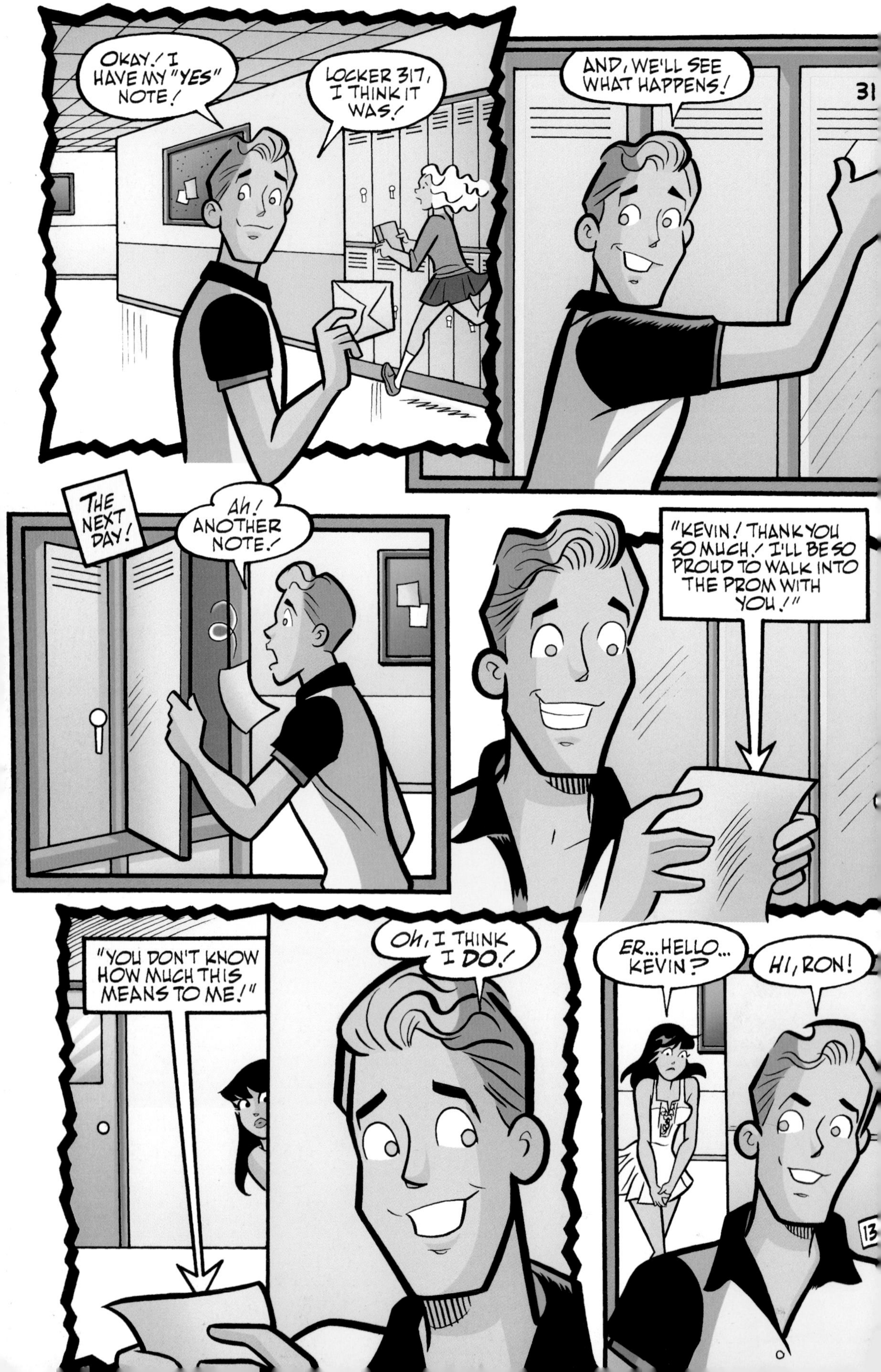
OKAY! I HAVE MY "YES" NOTE!
LOCKER 317, I THINK IT WAS!
AND, WE'LL SEE WHAT HAPPENS!
31
THE NEXT DAY!
Ah! ANOTHER NOTE!
"KEVIN! THANK YOU SO MUCH! I'LL BE SO PROUD TO WALK INTO THE PROM WITH YOU!"
"YOU DON'T KNOW HOW MUCH THIS MEANS TO ME!"
Oh, I THINK I DO!
ER... HELLO... KEVIN?
HI, RON!
13

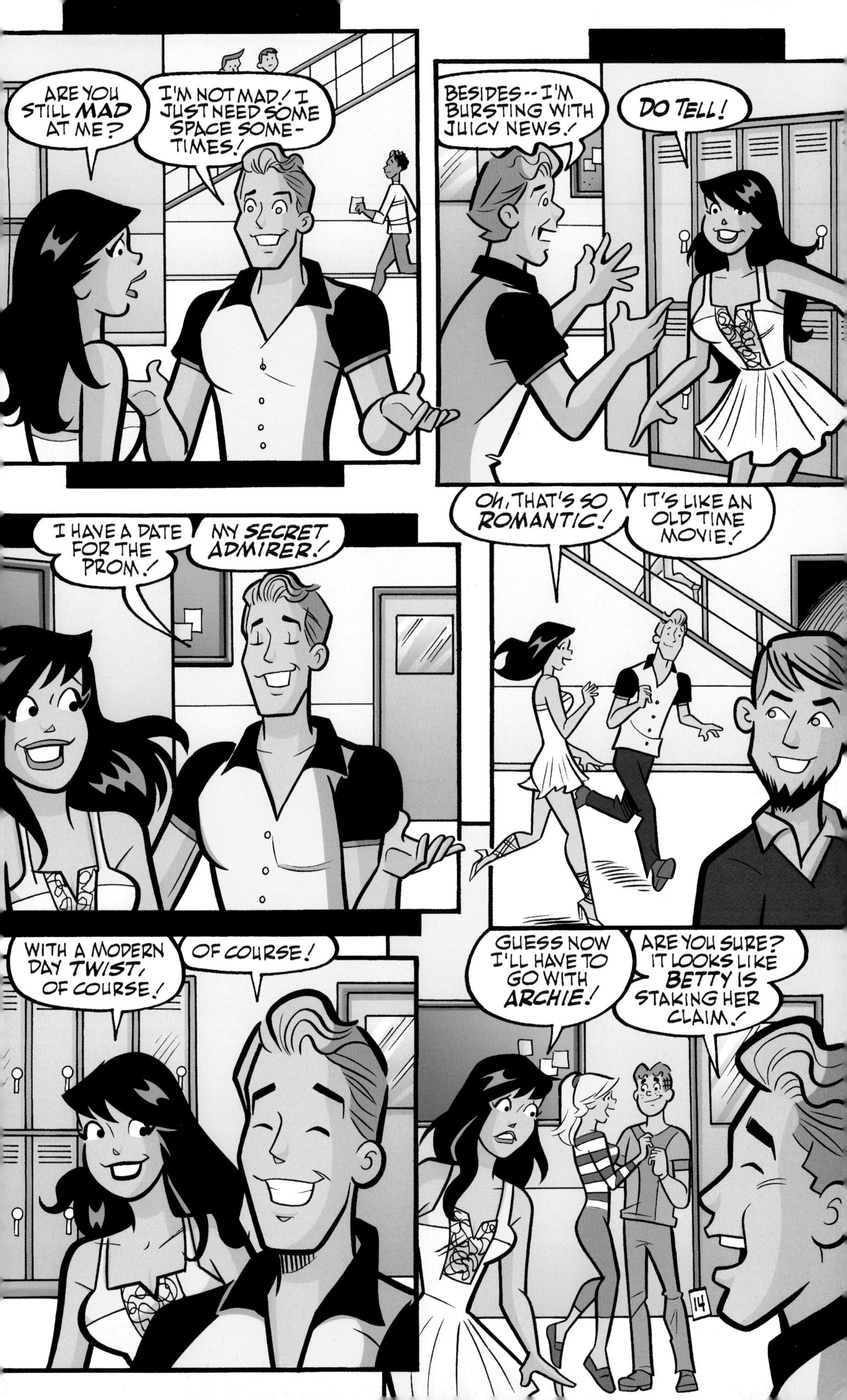
ARE YOU STILL MAD AT ME?
I'M NOT MAD! I JUST NEED SOME SPACE SOME-TIMES!
BESIDES-- I'M BURSTING WITH JUICY NEWS!
DO TELL!
I HAVE A DATE FOR THE PROM!
MY SECRET ADMIRER!
Oh, THAT'S SO ROMANTIC!
IT'S LIKE AN OLD TIME MOVIE!
WITH A MODERN DAY TWIST, OF COURSE!
OF COURSE!
GUESS NOW I'LL HAVE TO GO WITH ARCHIE!
ARE YOU SURE? IT LOOKS LIKE BETTY IS STAKING HER CLAIM!
14

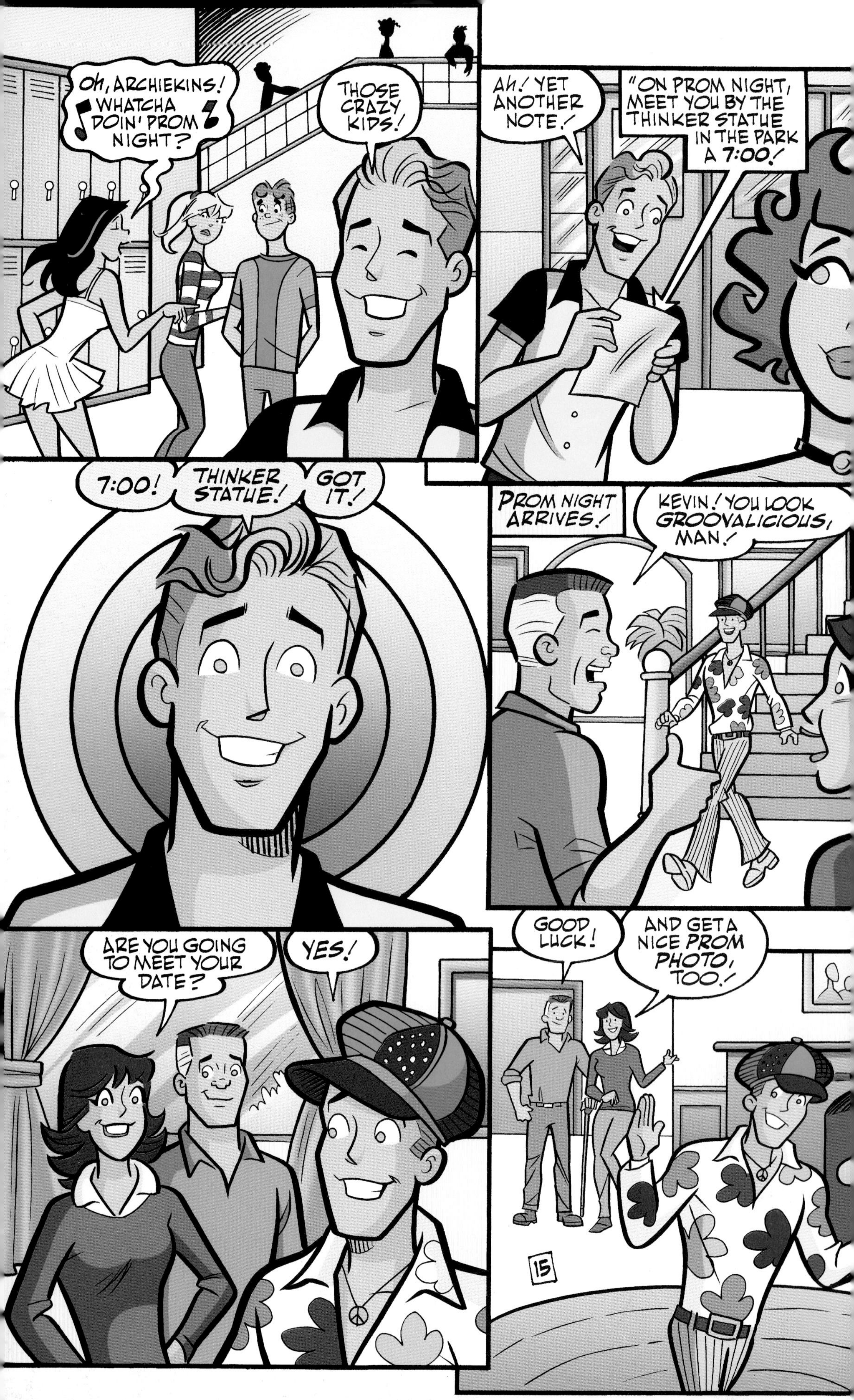
OH, ARCHIEKINS! WHATCHA DOIN' PROM NIGHT?
THOSE CRAZY KIDS!
AH! YET ANOTHER NOTE!
"ON PROM NIGHT, MEET YOU BY THE THINKER STATUE IN THE PARK A 7:00!
7:00!
THINKER STATUE!
GOT IT!
PROM NIGHT ARRIVES!
KEVIN! YOU LOOK GROOVALICIOUS, MAN!
ARE YOU GOING TO MEET YOUR DATE?
YES!
GOOD LUCK!
AND GET A NICE PROM PHOTO, TOO!
15

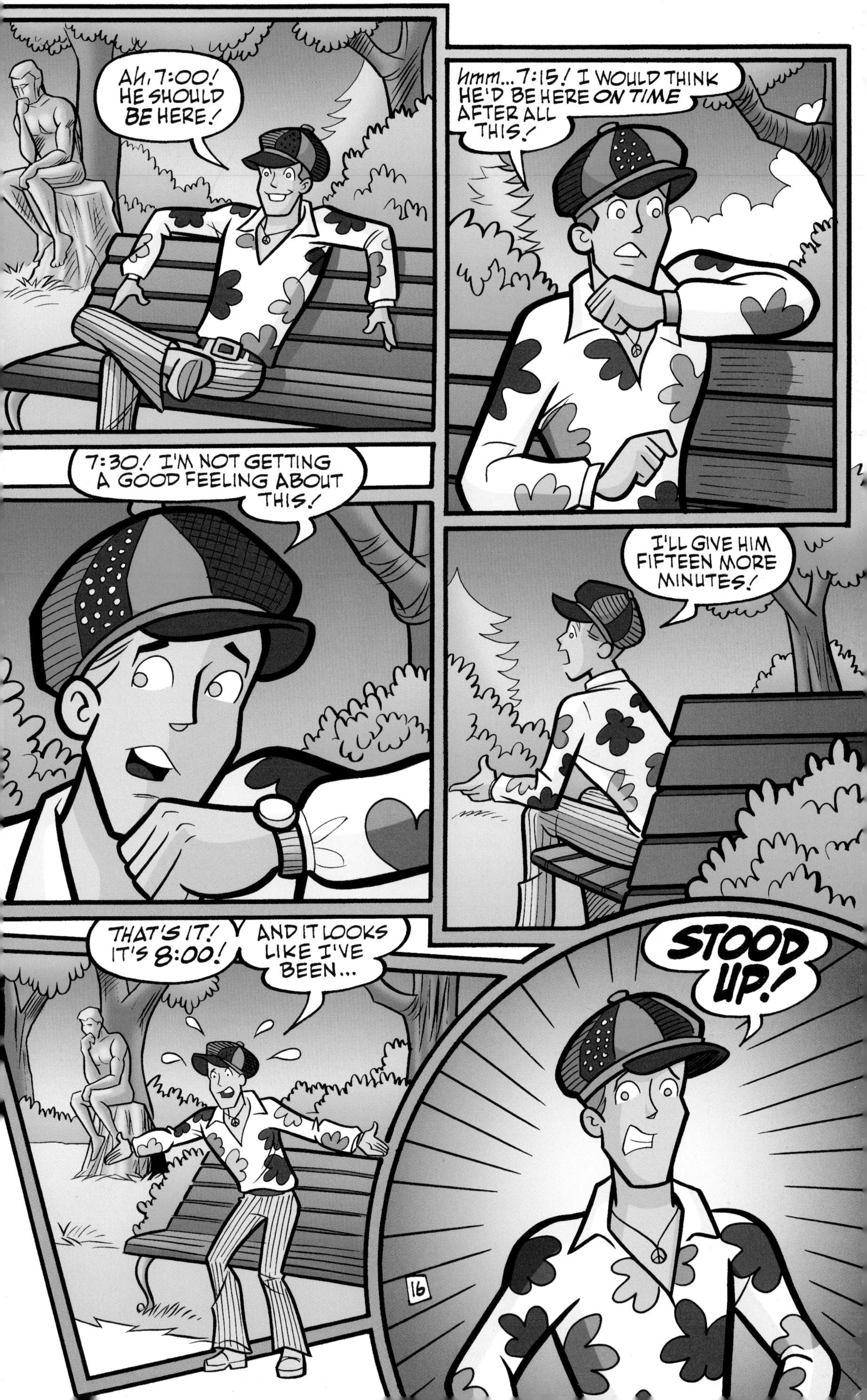
AH, 7:00! HE SHOULD BE HERE!
hmm... 7:15! I WOULD THINK HE'D BE HERE ON TIME AFTER ALL THIS!
7:30! I'M NOT GETTING A GOOD FEELING ABOUT THIS!
I'LL GIVE HIM FIFTEEN MORE MINUTES!
THAT'S IT! IT'S 8:00!
AND IT LOOKS LIKE I'VE BEEN...
STOOD UP!
16

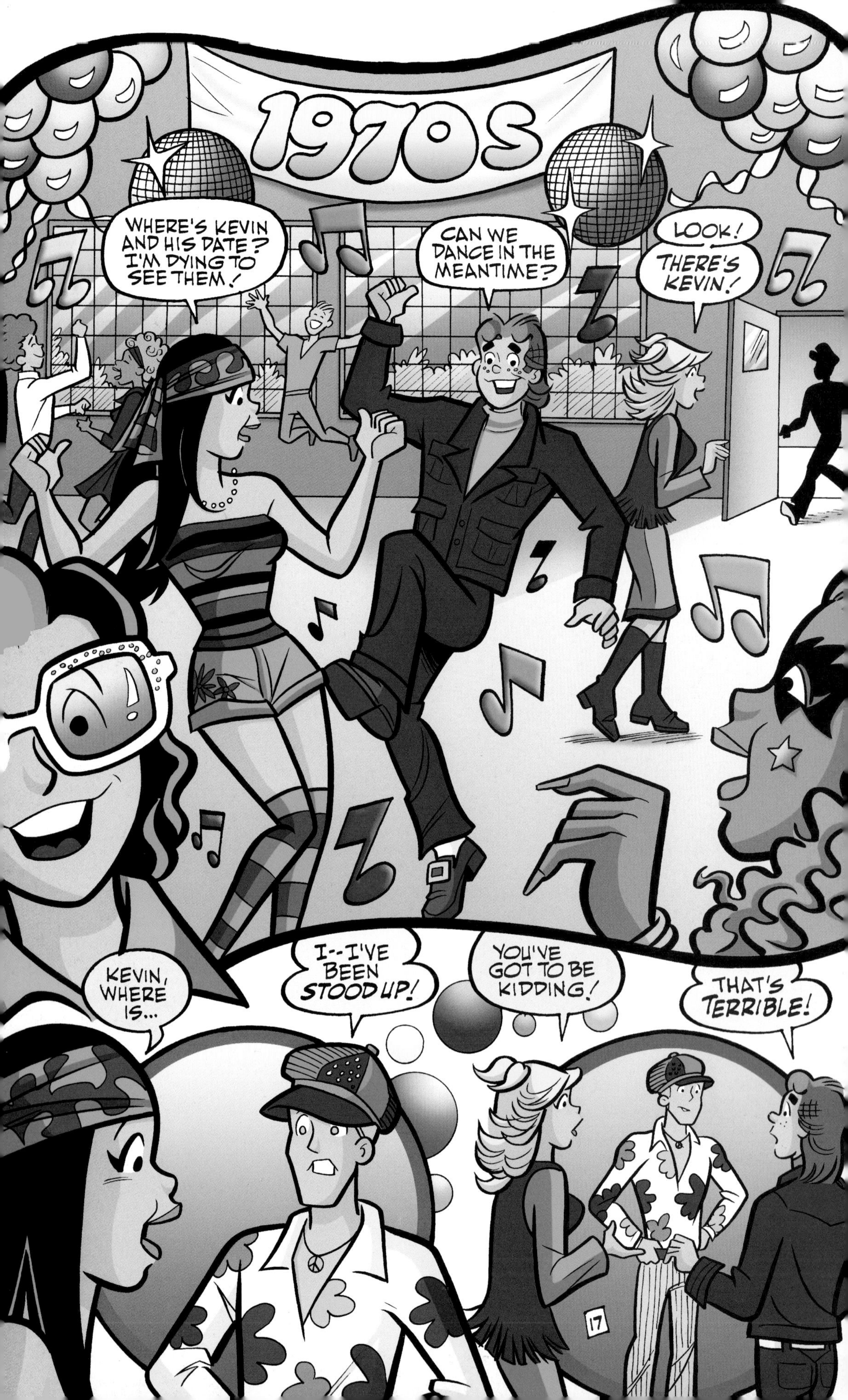
1970S
WHERE'S KEVIN AND HIS DATE? I'M DYING TO SEE THEM!
CAN WE DANCE IN THE MEANTIME?
LOOK! THERE'S KEVIN!
KEVIN, WHERE IS...
I--I'VE BEEN STOOD UP!
YOU'VE GOT TO BE KIDDING!
THAT'S TERRIBLE!

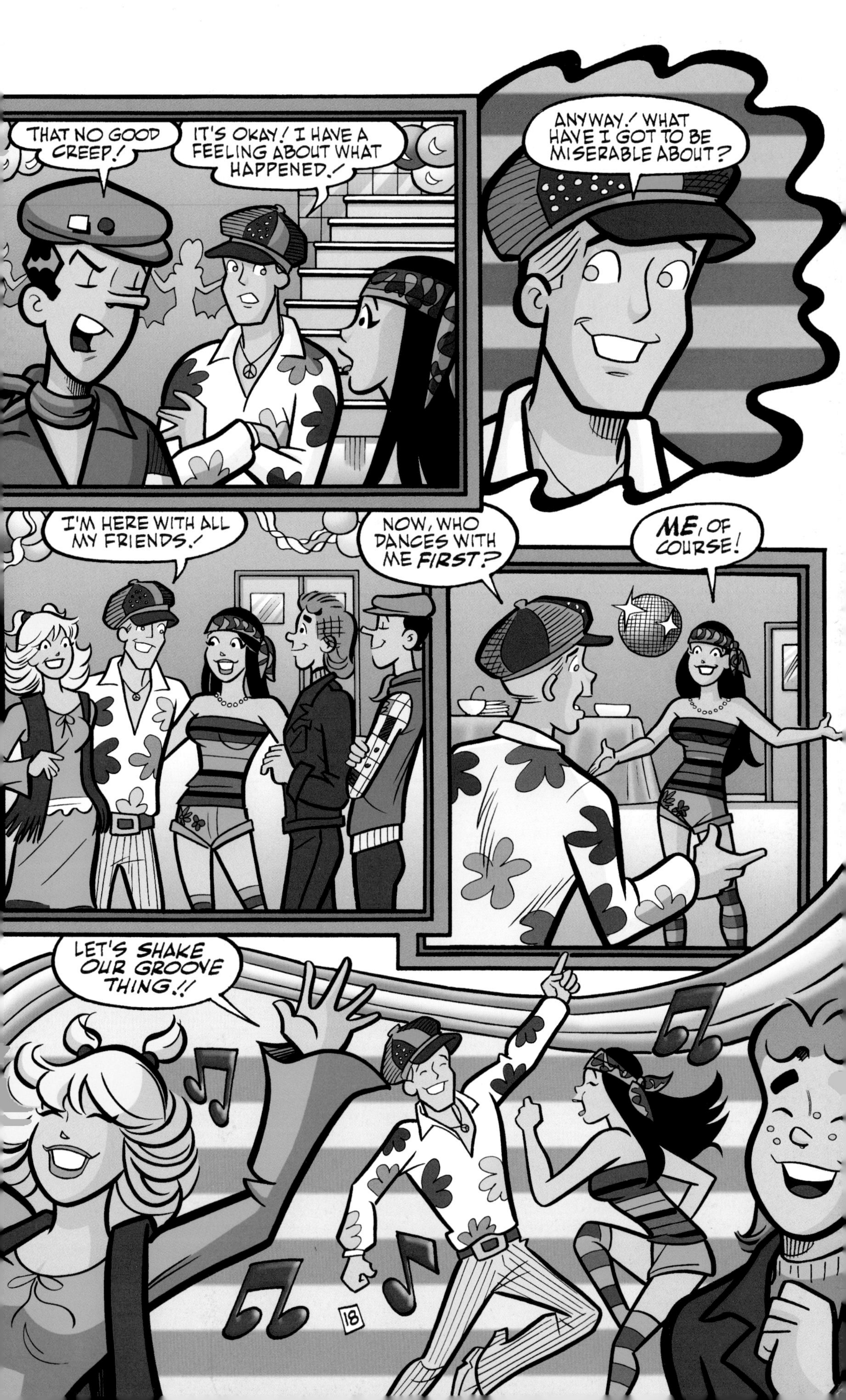
THAT NO GOOD CREEP!
IT'S OKAY! I HAVE A FEELING ABOUT WHAT HAPPENED!
ANYWAY! WHAT HAVE I GOT TO BE MISERABLE ABOUT?
I'M HERE WITH ALL MY FRIENDS!
NOW, WHO DANCES WITH ME FIRST?
ME, OF COURSE!
LET'S SHAKE OUR GROOVE THING!!
18

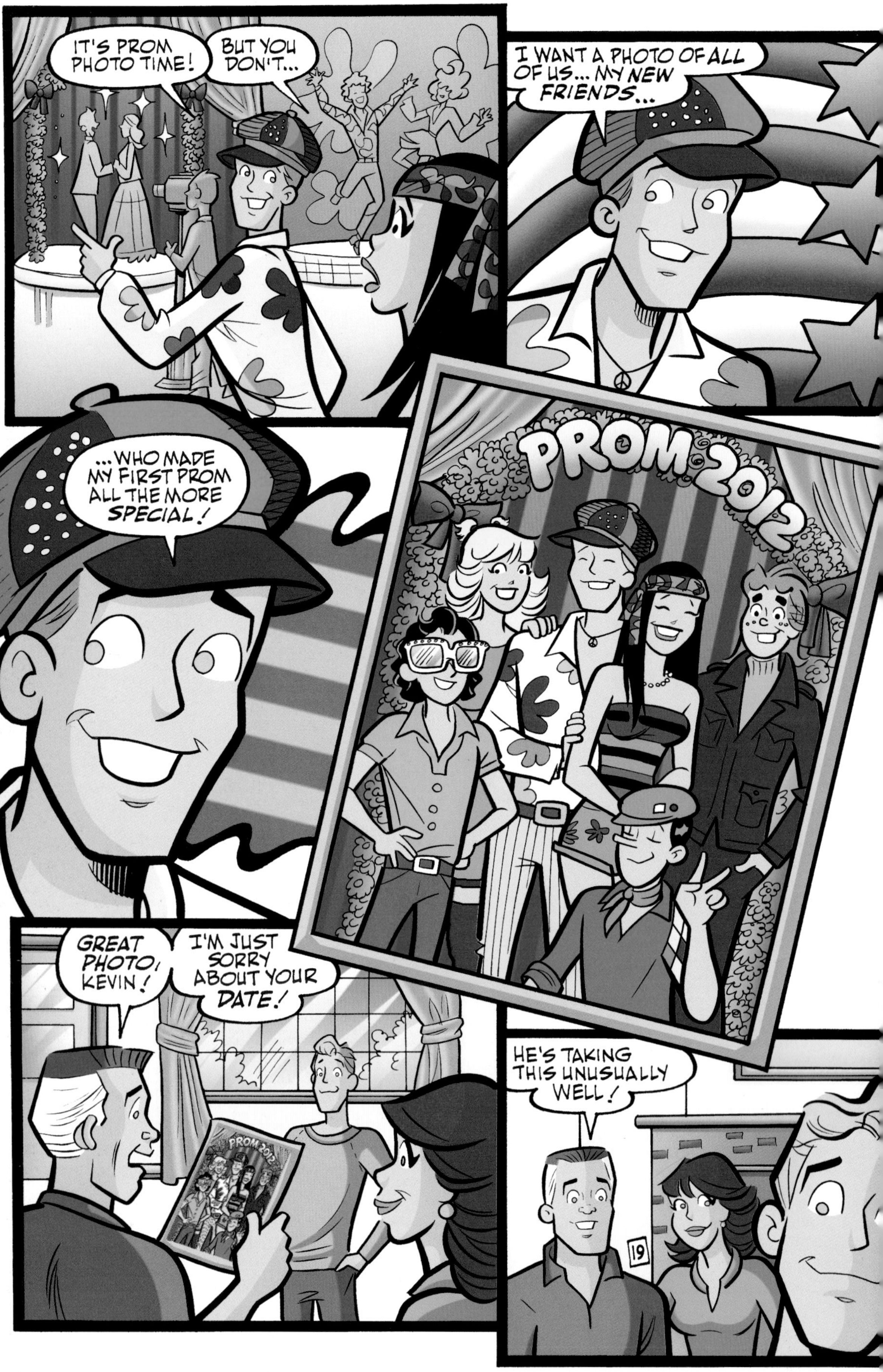
IT'S PROM PHOTO TIME!
BUT YOU DON'T...
I WANT A PHOTO OF ALL OF US... MY NEW FRIENDS...
...WHO MADE MY FIRST PROM ALL THE MORE SPECIAL!
PROM 2012
GREAT PHOTO, KEVIN!
I'M JUST SORRY ABOUT YOUR DATE!
HE'S TAKING THIS UNUSUALLY WELL!
19

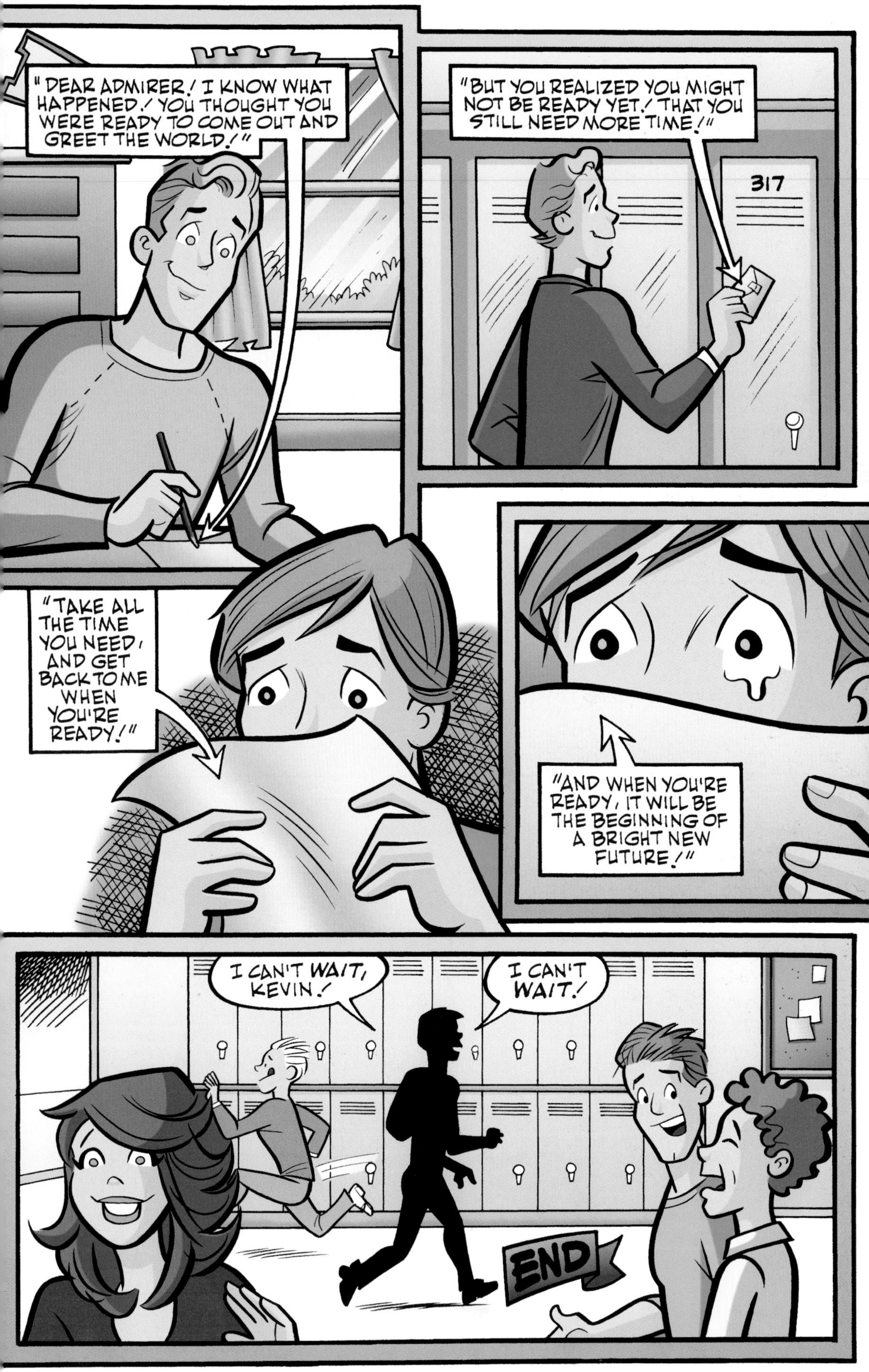
"DEAR ADMIRER! I KNOW WHAT HAPPENED! YOU THOUGHT YOU WERE READY TO COME OUT AND GREET THE WORLD!"
"BUT YOU REALIZED YOU MIGHT NOT BE READY YET! THAT YOU STILL NEED MORE TIME!"
317
"TAKE ALL THE TIME YOU NEED, AND GET BACK TO ME WHEN YOU'RE READY!"
"AND WHEN YOU'RE READY, IT WILL BE THE BEGINNING OF A BRIGHT NEW FUTURE!"
I CAN'T WAIT, KEVIN!
I CAN'T WAIT!
END

ARCHIE SERIES

GIANT

FUN SIZED!

Kevin's™ SUMMER FUN

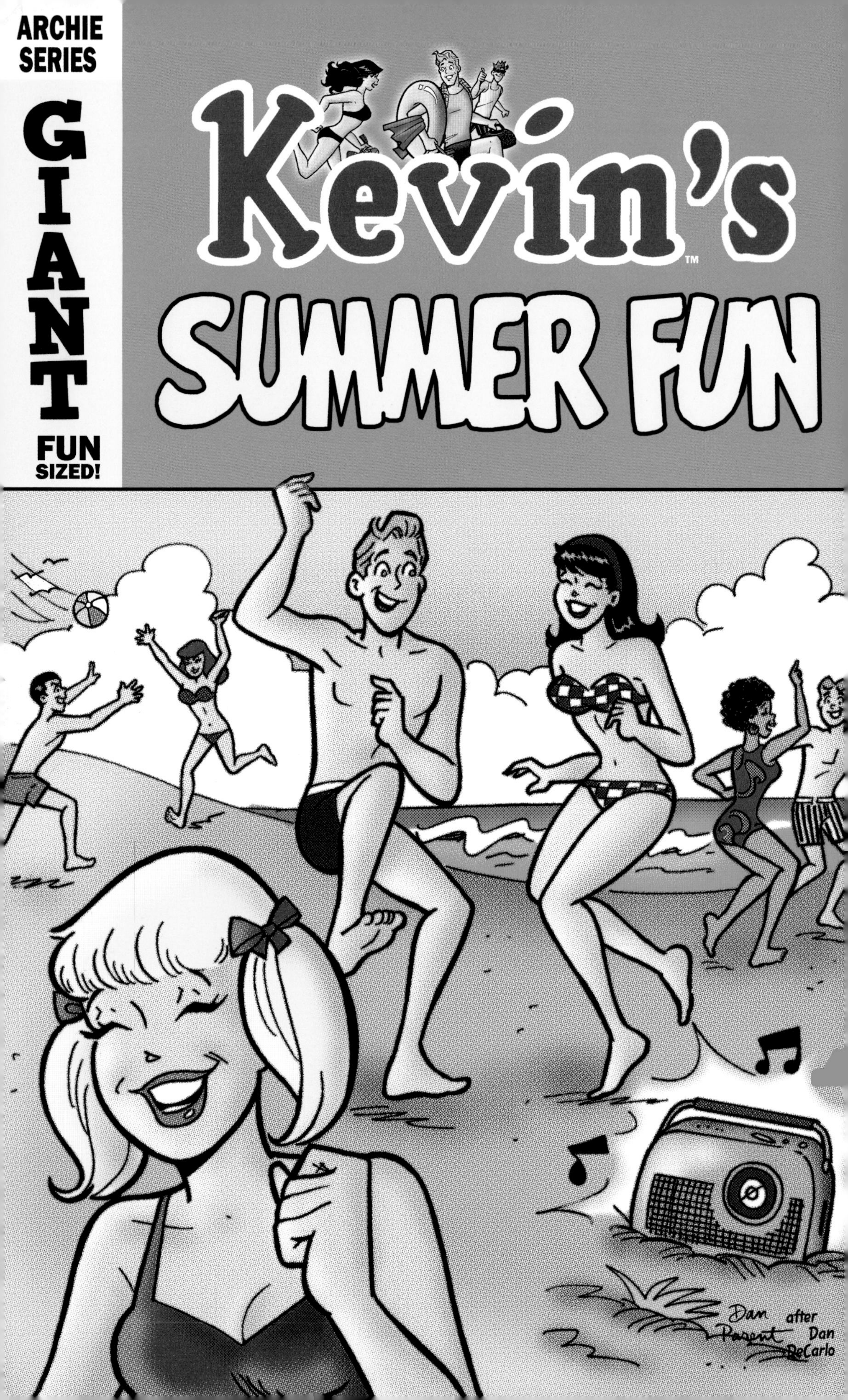

Dan Parent after Dan DeCarlo

Chapter 3

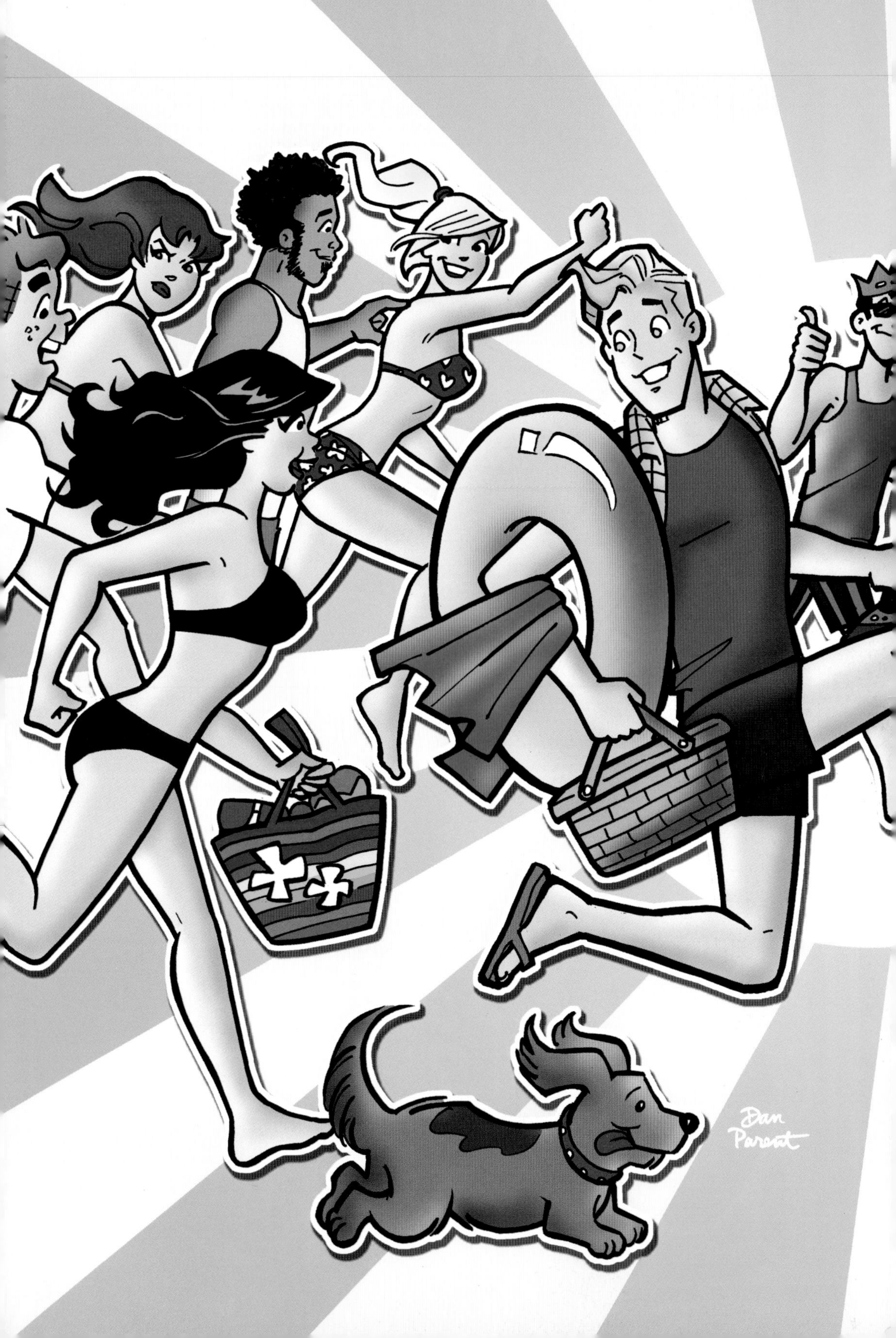
Dan Parent

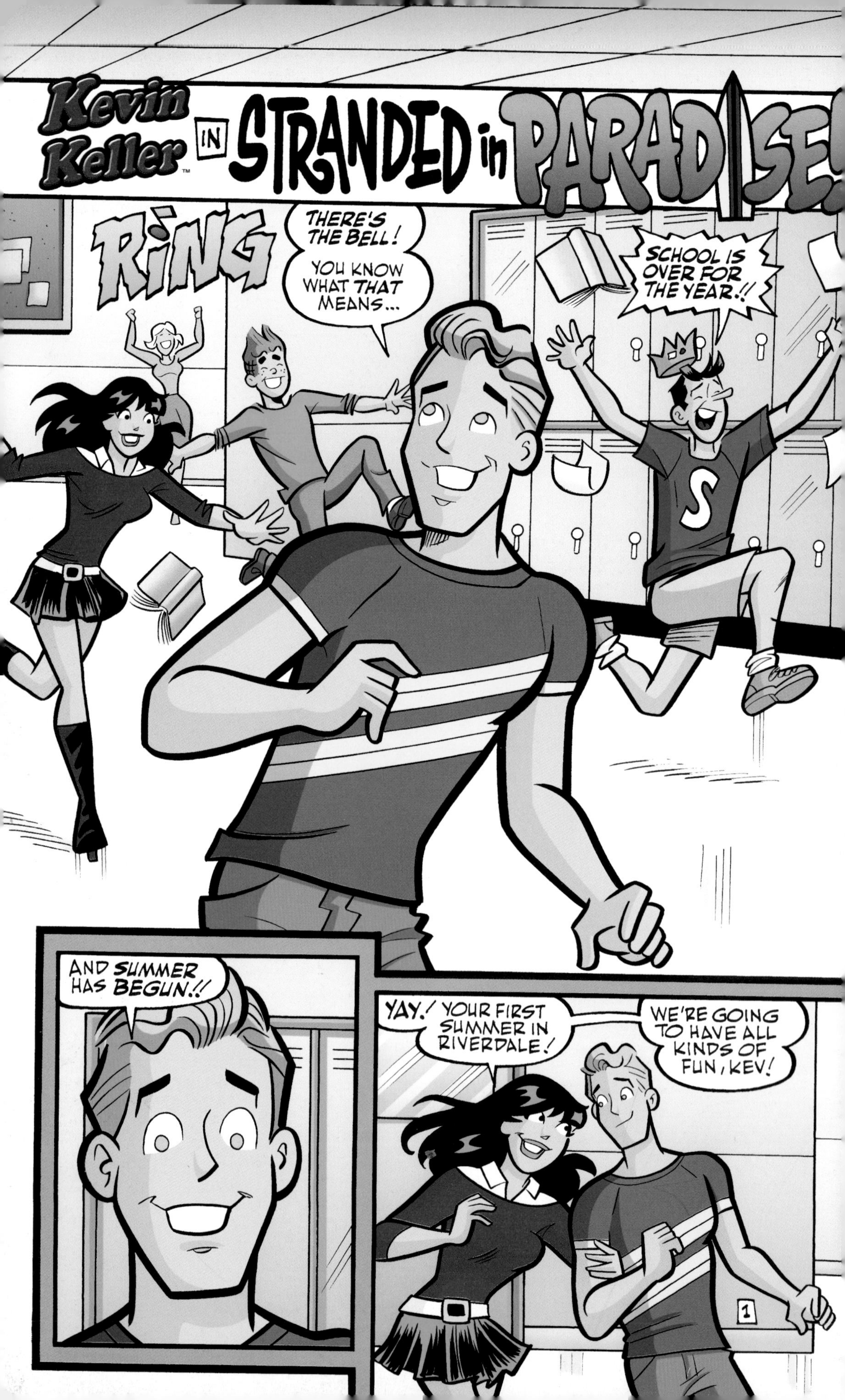
Kevin Keller™ IN STRANDED in PARADISE!
RING
THERE'S THE BELL!
YOU KNOW WHAT THAT MEANS...
SCHOOL IS OVER FOR THE YEAR.!!
S
AND SUMMER HAS BEGUN.!!
YAY.! YOUR FIRST SUMMER IN RIVERDALE!
WE'RE GOING TO HAVE ALL KINDS OF FUN, KEV!
1

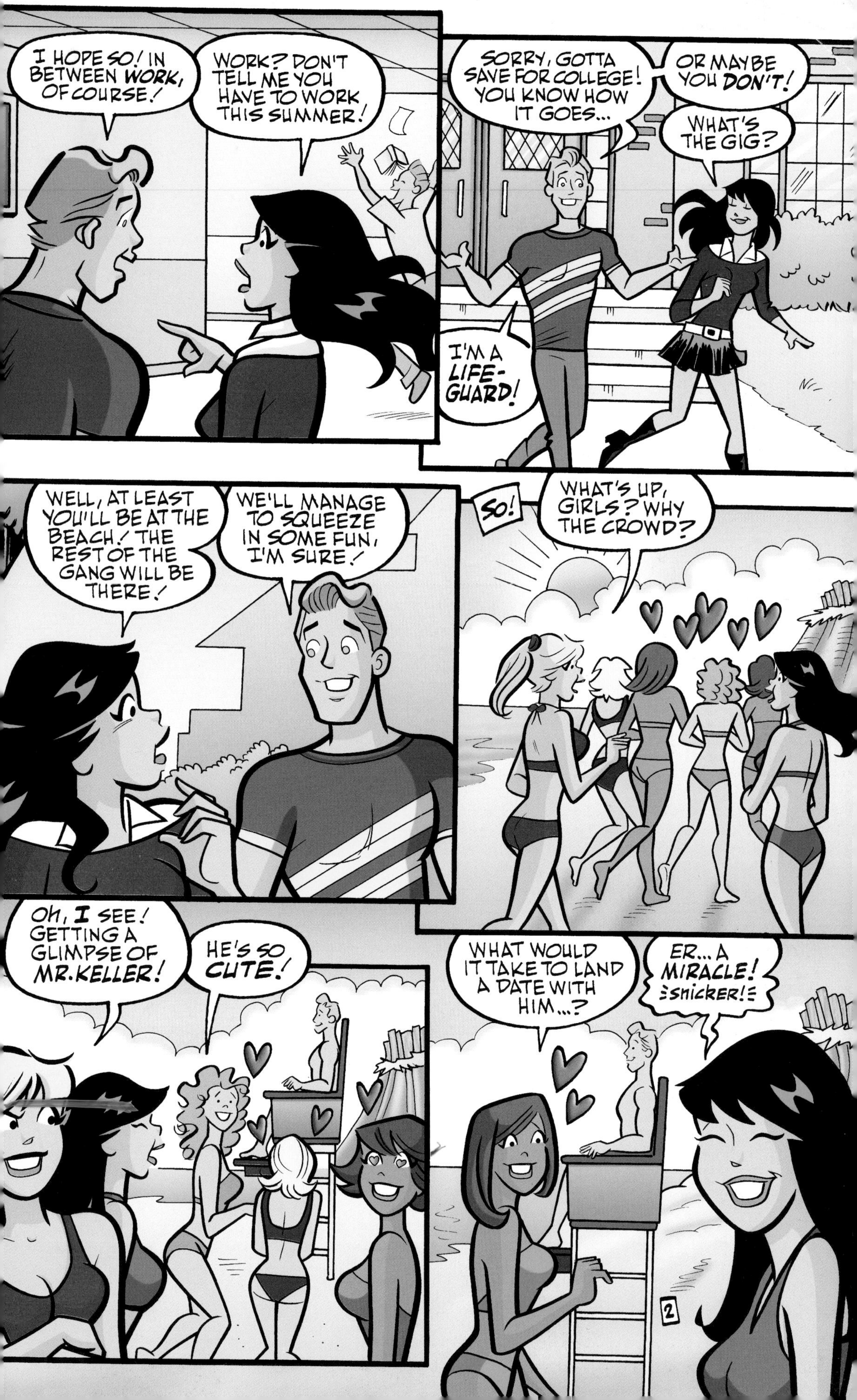
I HOPE SO! IN BETWEEN WORK, OF COURSE!
WORK? DON'T TELL ME YOU HAVE TO WORK THIS SUMMER!
SORRY, GOTTA SAVE FOR COLLEGE! YOU KNOW HOW IT GOES...
OR MAYBE YOU DON'T!
WHAT'S THE GIG?
I'M A LIFE-GUARD!
WELL, AT LEAST YOU'LL BE AT THE BEACH! THE REST OF THE GANG WILL BE THERE!
WE'LL MANAGE TO SQUEEZE IN SOME FUN, I'M SURE!
SO!
WHAT'S UP, GIRLS? WHY THE CROWD?
OH, I SEE! GETTING A GLIMPSE OF MR. KELLER!
HE'S SO CUTE!
WHAT WOULD IT TAKE TO LAND A DATE WITH HIM...?
ER... A MIRACLE!
snicker!
2

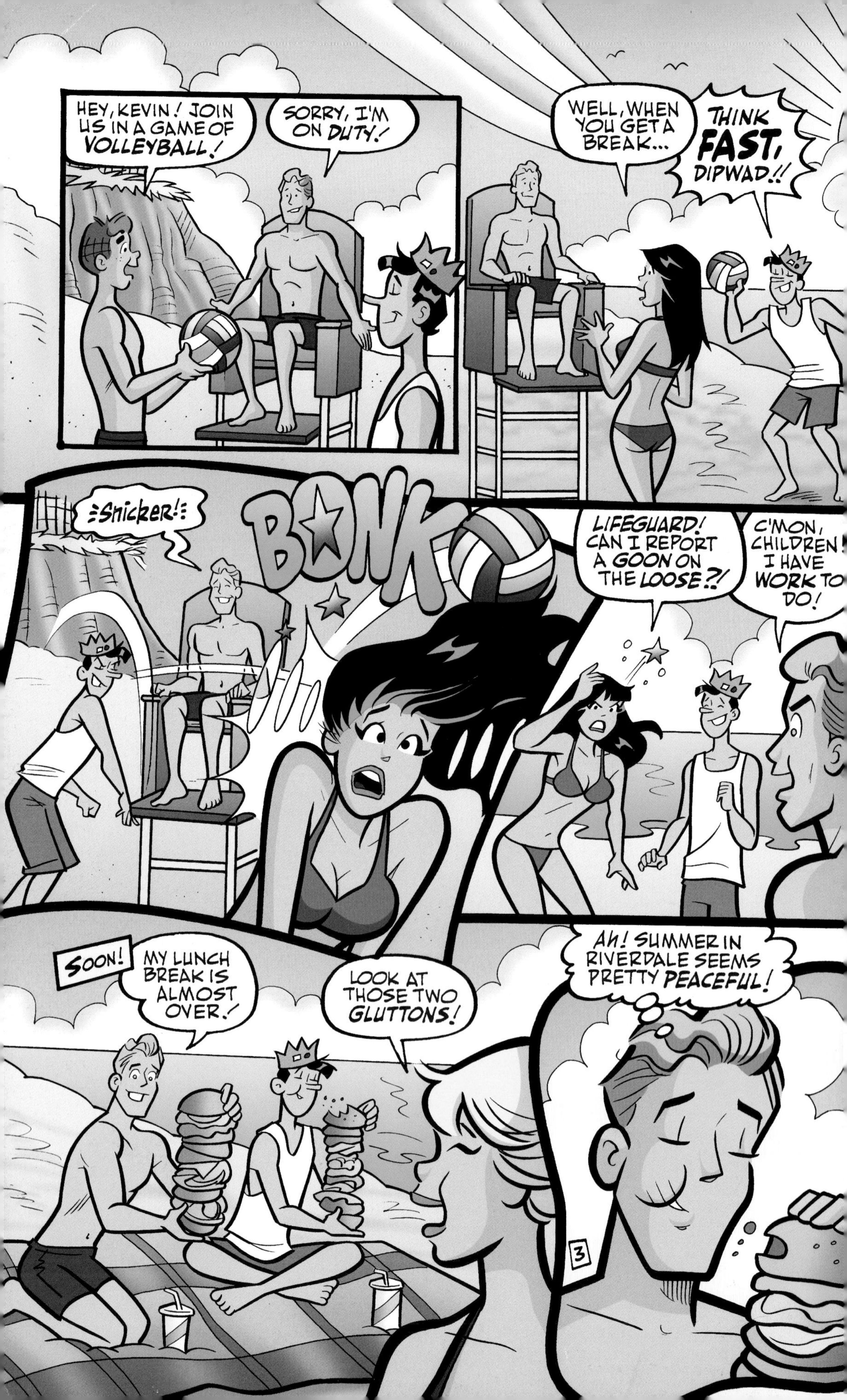
HEY, KEVIN! JOIN US IN A GAME OF VOLLEYBALL!
SORRY, I'M ON DUTY!
WELL, WHEN YOU GET A BREAK...
THINK FAST, DIPWAD!!
:Snicker!:
BONK
LIFEGUARD! CAN I REPORT A GOON ON THE LOOSE?!
C'MON, CHILDREN! I HAVE WORK TO DO!
SOON!
MY LUNCH BREAK IS ALMOST OVER!
LOOK AT THOSE TWO GLUTTONS!
AH! SUMMER IN RIVERDALE SEEMS PRETTY PEACEFUL!
3

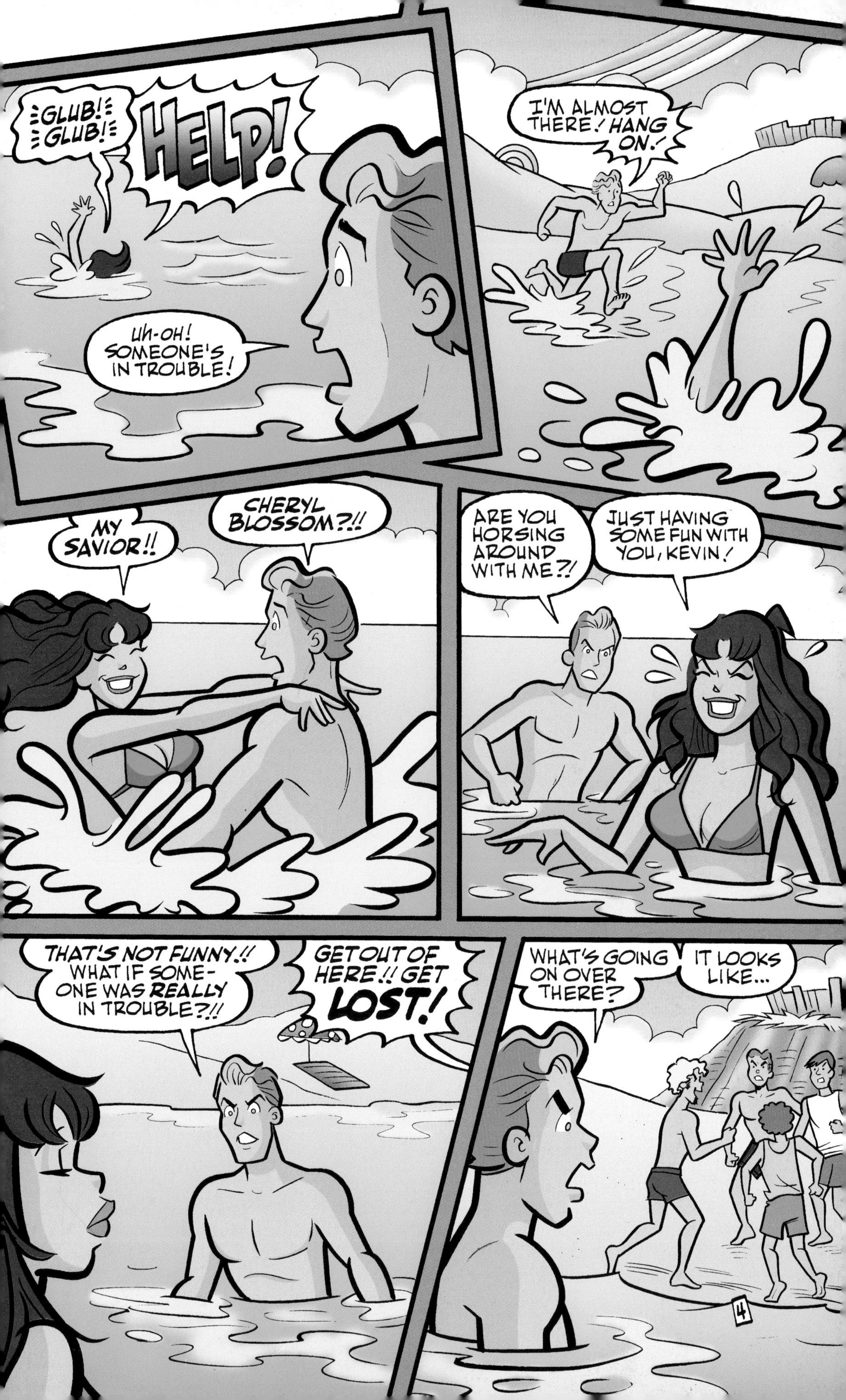
GLUB! GLUB!
HELP!
UH-OH! SOMEONE'S IN TROUBLE!
I'M ALMOST THERE! HANG ON!
MY SAVIOR!!
CHERYL BLOSSOM?!!
ARE YOU HORSING AROUND WITH ME?!
JUST HAVING SOME FUN WITH YOU, KEVIN!
THAT'S NOT FUNNY!! WHAT IF SOME-ONE WAS REALLY IN TROUBLE?!!
GET OUT OF HERE!! GET LOST!
WHAT'S GOING ON OVER THERE?
IT LOOKS LIKE...
4

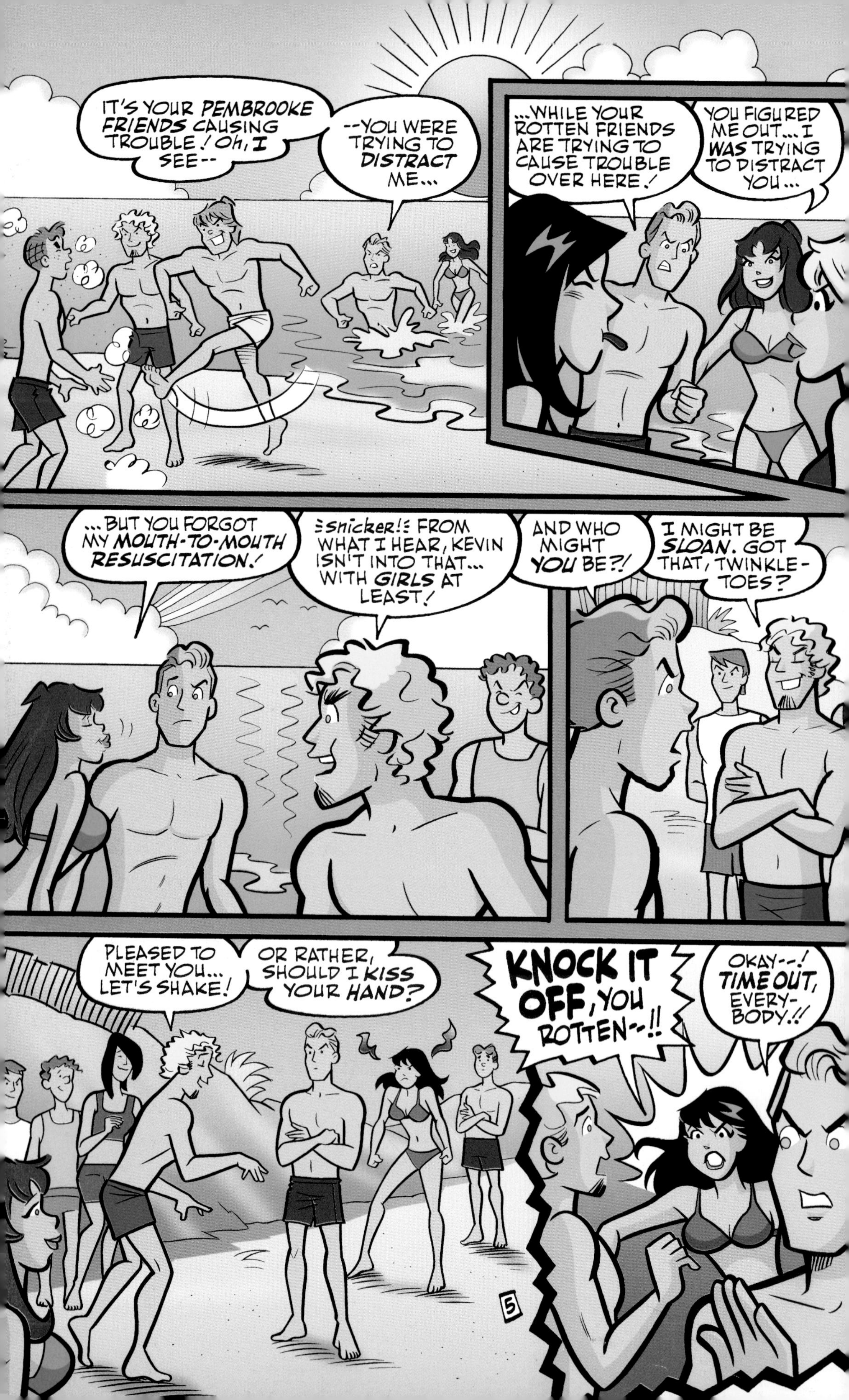
IT'S YOUR PEMBROOKE FRIENDS CAUSING TROUBLE! Oh, I SEE--
--YOU WERE TRYING TO DISTRACT ME...
...WHILE YOUR ROTTEN FRIENDS ARE TRYING TO CAUSE TROUBLE OVER HERE!
YOU FIGURED ME OUT... I WAS TRYING TO DISTRACT YOU...
...BUT YOU FORGOT MY MOUTH-TO-MOUTH RESUSCITATION!
=snicker!= FROM WHAT I HEAR, KEVIN ISN'T INTO THAT... WITH GIRLS AT LEAST!
AND WHO MIGHT YOU BE?!
I MIGHT BE SLOAN. GOT THAT, TWINKLE-TOES?
PLEASED TO MEET YOU... LET'S SHAKE!
OR RATHER, SHOULD I KISS YOUR HAND?
KNOCK IT OFF, YOU ROTTEN--!!
OKAY--! TIME OUT, EVERY-BODY!!
5

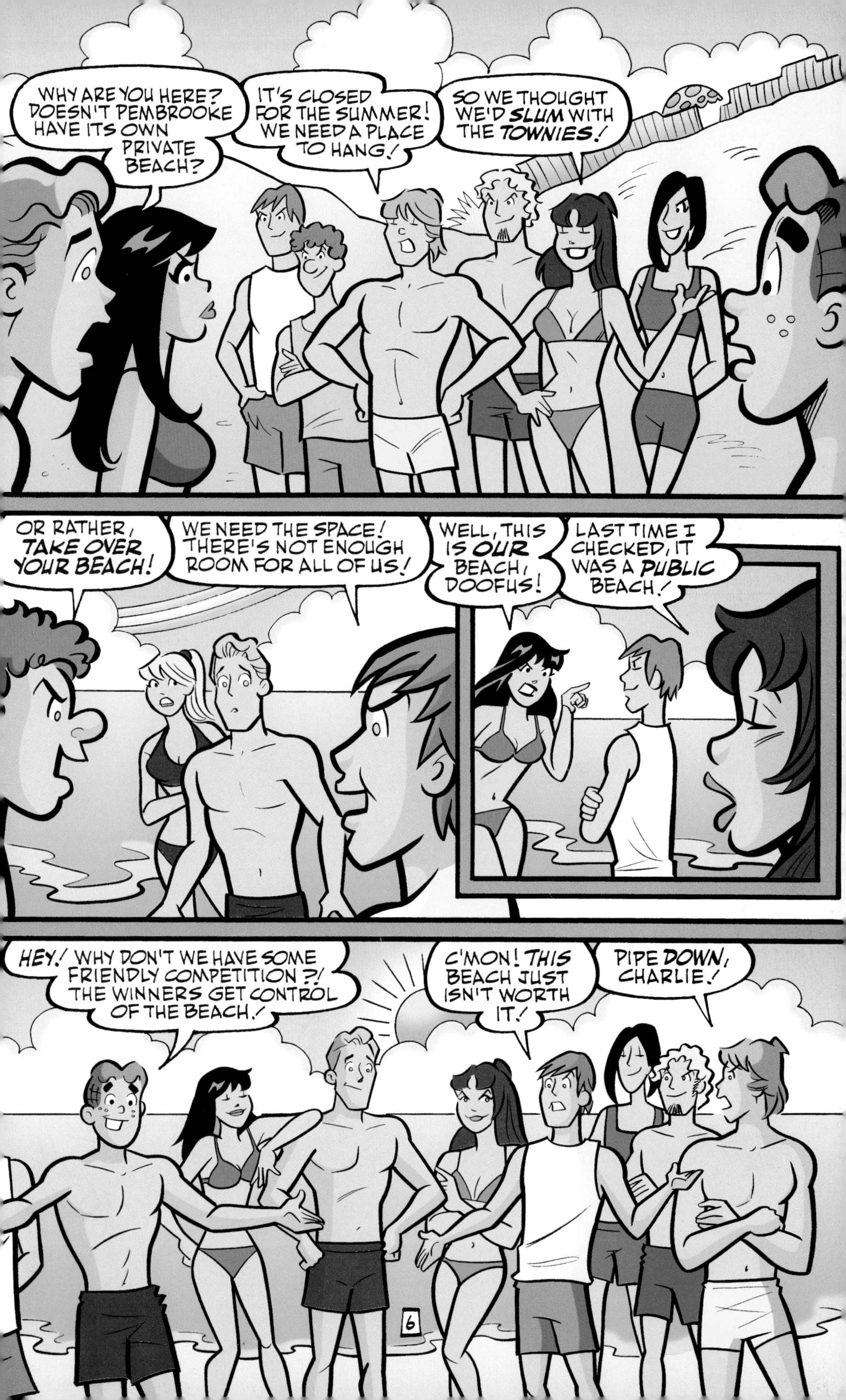
WHY ARE YOU HERE? DOESN'T PEMBROOKE HAVE ITS OWN PRIVATE BEACH?
IT'S CLOSED FOR THE SUMMER! WE NEED A PLACE TO HANG!
SO WE THOUGHT WE'D SLUM WITH THE TOWNIES!
OR RATHER, TAKE OVER YOUR BEACH!
WE NEED THE SPACE! THERE'S NOT ENOUGH ROOM FOR ALL OF US!
WELL, THIS IS OUR BEACH, DOOFUS!
LAST TIME I CHECKED, IT WAS A PUBLIC BEACH!
HEY! WHY DON'T WE HAVE SOME FRIENDLY COMPETITION ?! THE WINNERS GET CONTROL OF THE BEACH!
C'MON! THIS BEACH JUST ISN'T WORTH IT!
PIPE DOWN, CHARLIE!
6

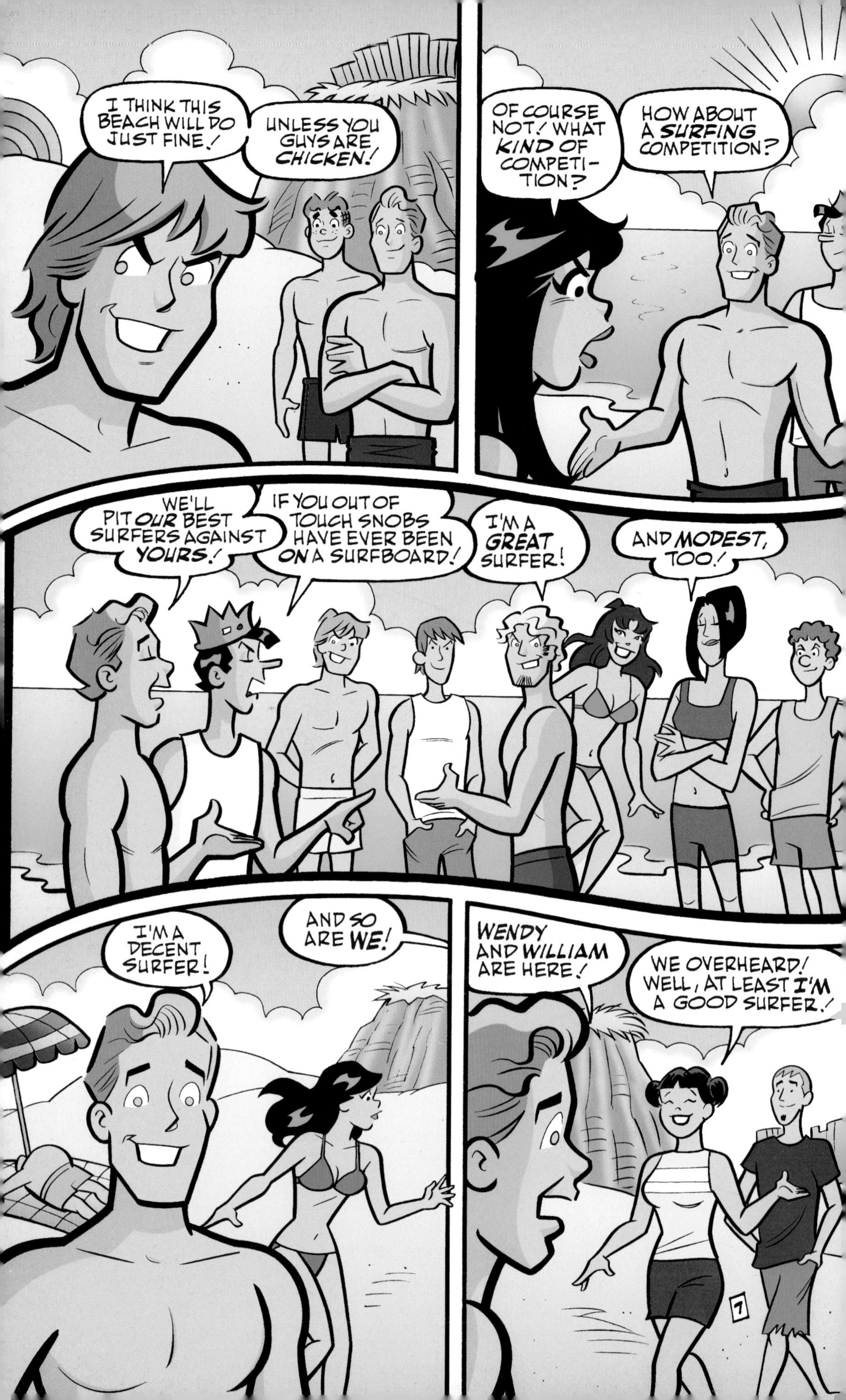
I THINK THIS BEACH WILL DO JUST FINE!
UNLESS YOU GUYS ARE CHICKEN!
OF COURSE NOT! WHAT KIND OF COMPETITION?
HOW ABOUT A SURFING COMPETITION?
WE'LL PIT OUR BEST SURFERS AGAINST YOURS!
IF YOU OUT OF TOUCH SNOBS HAVE EVER BEEN ON A SURFBOARD!
I'M A GREAT SURFER!
AND MODEST, TOO!
I'M A DECENT SURFER!
AND SO ARE WE!
WENDY AND WILLIAM ARE HERE!
WE OVERHEARD! WELL, AT LEAST I'M A GOOD SURFER!
7

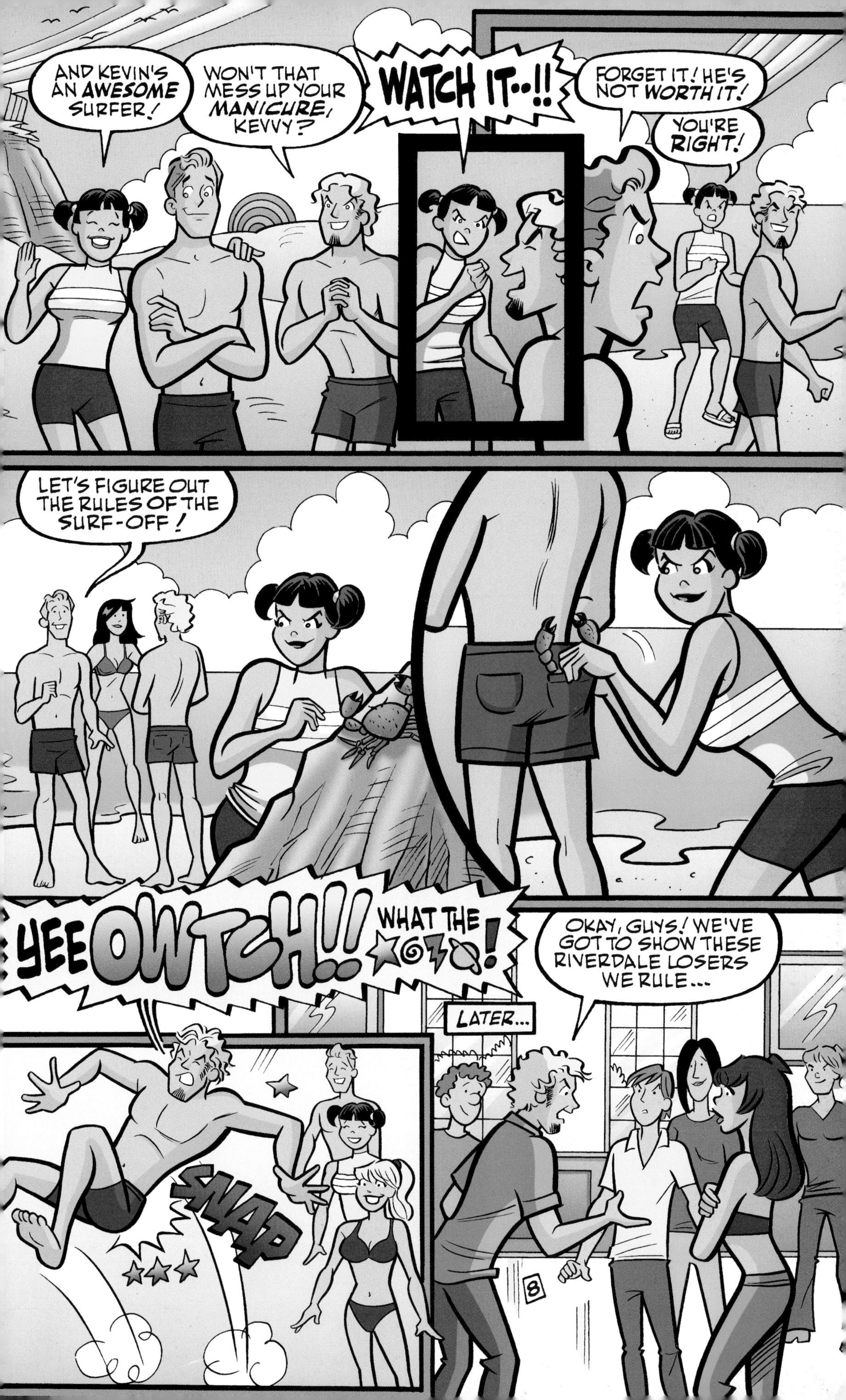

AND KEVIN'S AN AWESOME SURFER!
WON'T THAT MESS UP YOUR MANICURE, KEVVY?
WATCH IT..!!
FORGET IT! HE'S NOT WORTH IT!
YOU'RE RIGHT!
LET'S FIGURE OUT THE RULES OF THE SURF-OFF!
YEEOWTCH!!
WHAT THE !
SNAP
LATER...
OKAY, GUYS! WE'VE GOT TO SHOW THESE RIVERDALE LOSERS WE RULE...
8

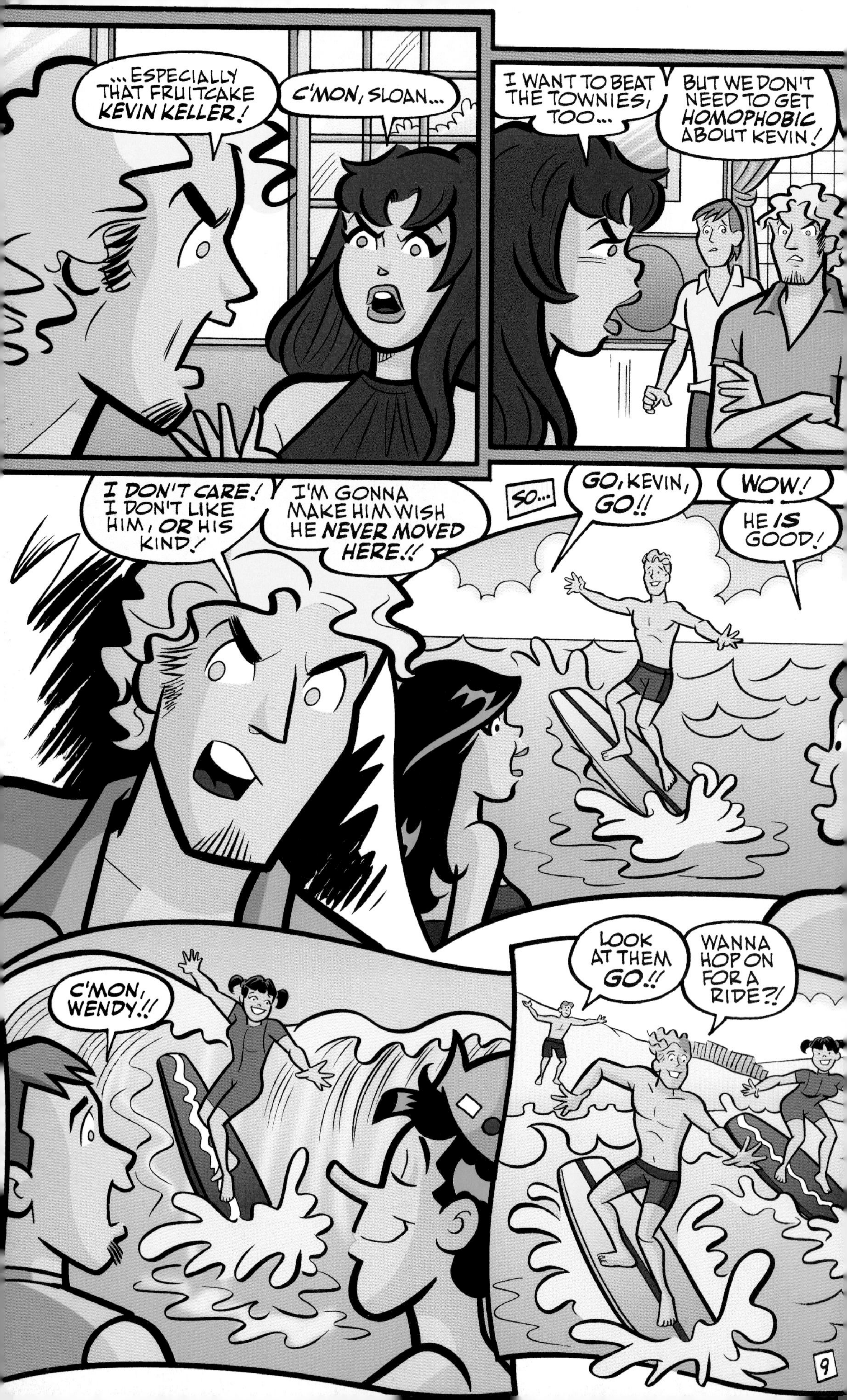
...ESPECIALLY THAT FRUITCAKE KEVIN KELLER!
C'MON, SLOAN...
I WANT TO BEAT THE TOWNIES, TOO...
BUT WE DON'T NEED TO GET HOMOPHOBIC ABOUT KEVIN!
I DON'T CARE! I DON'T LIKE HIM, OR HIS KIND!
I'M GONNA MAKE HIM WISH HE NEVER MOVED HERE!!
SO...
GO, KEVIN, GO!!
WOW!
HE IS GOOD!
C'MON, WENDY!!
LOOK AT THEM GO!!
WANNA HOP ON FOR A RIDE?!
9

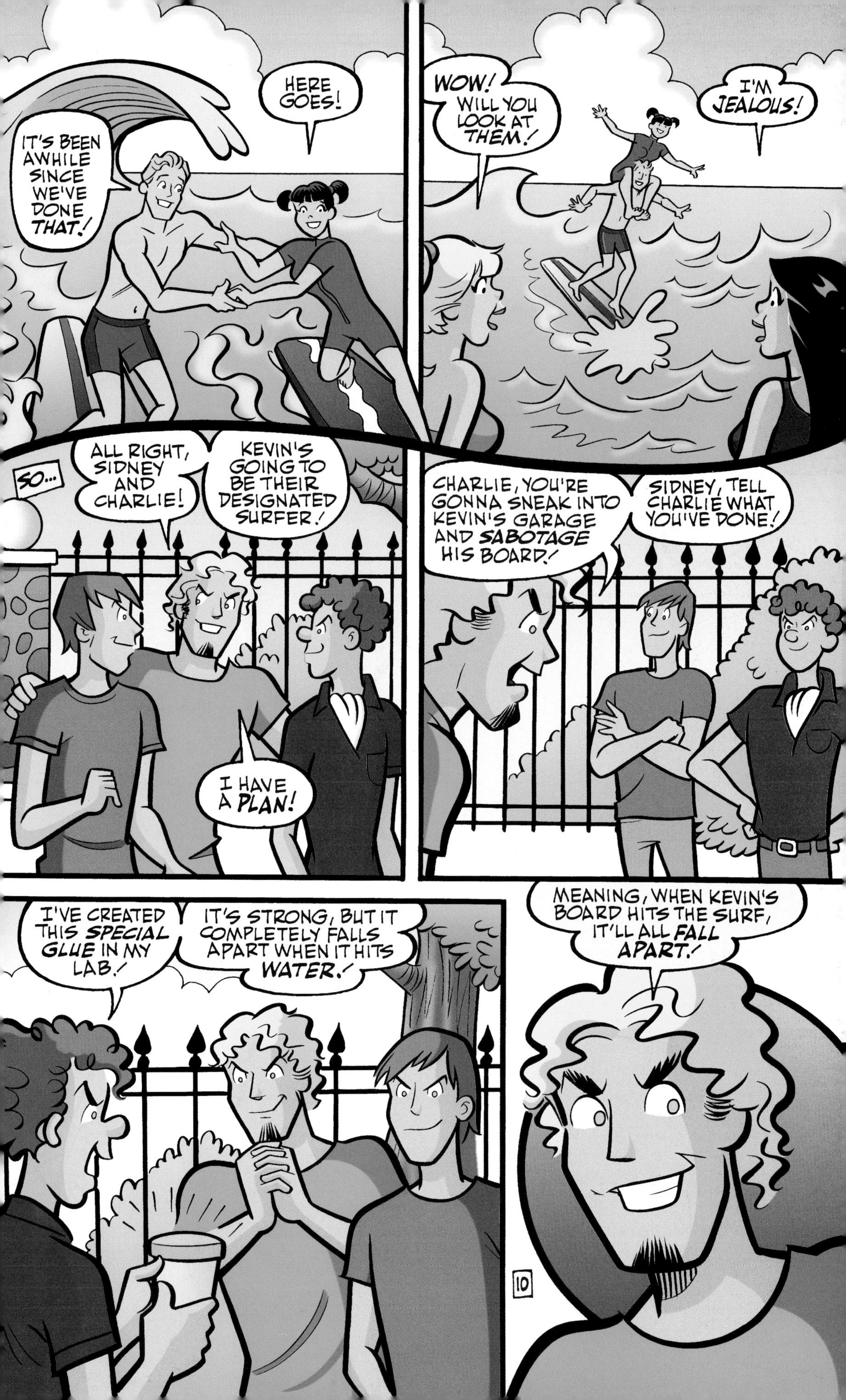

HERE GOES!
IT'S BEEN AWHILE SINCE WE'VE DONE THAT!
WOW! WILL YOU LOOK AT THEM!
I'M JEALOUS!
SO...
ALL RIGHT, SIDNEY AND CHARLIE!
KEVIN'S GOING TO BE THEIR DESIGNATED SURFER!
I HAVE A PLAN!
CHARLIE, YOU'RE GONNA SNEAK INTO KEVIN'S GARAGE AND SABOTAGE HIS BOARD!
SIDNEY, TELL CHARLIE WHAT YOU'VE DONE!
I'VE CREATED THIS SPECIAL GLUE IN MY LAB!
IT'S STRONG, BUT IT COMPLETELY FALLS APART WHEN IT HITS WATER!
MEANING, WHEN KEVIN'S BOARD HITS THE SURF, IT'LL ALL FALL APART!
10

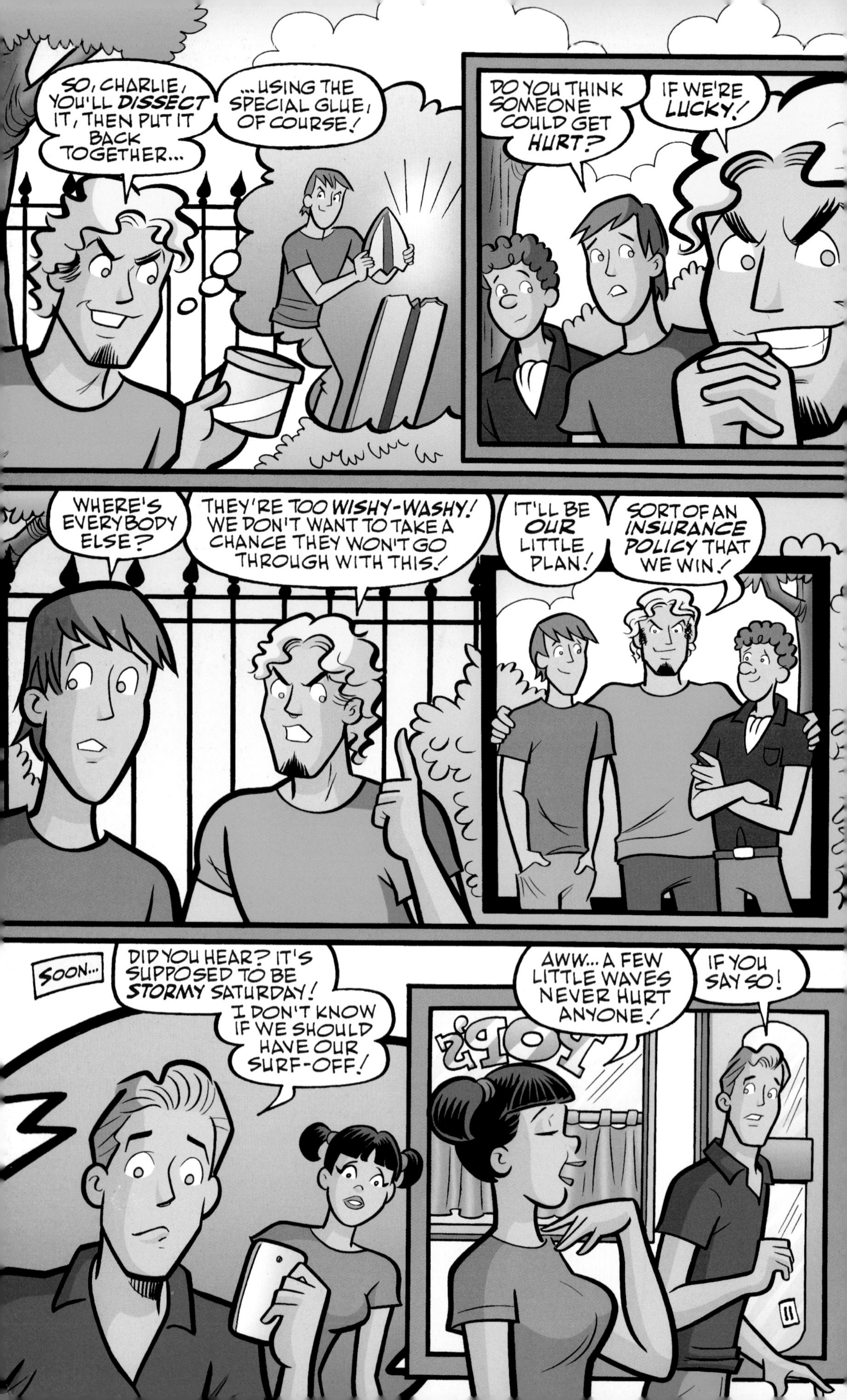
SO, CHARLIE, YOU'LL DISSECT IT, THEN PUT IT BACK TOGETHER...
...USING THE SPECIAL GLUE, OF COURSE!
DO YOU THINK SOMEONE COULD GET HURT?
IF WE'RE LUCKY!
WHERE'S EVERYBODY ELSE?
THEY'RE TOO WISHY-WASHY! WE DON'T WANT TO TAKE A CHANCE THEY WON'T GO THROUGH WITH THIS!
IT'LL BE OUR LITTLE PLAN!
SORT OF AN INSURANCE POLICY THAT WE WIN!
SOON...
DID YOU HEAR? IT'S SUPPOSED TO BE STORMY SATURDAY!
I DON'T KNOW IF WE SHOULD HAVE OUR SURF-OFF!
AWW... A FEW LITTLE WAVES NEVER HURT ANYONE!
IF YOU SAY SO!

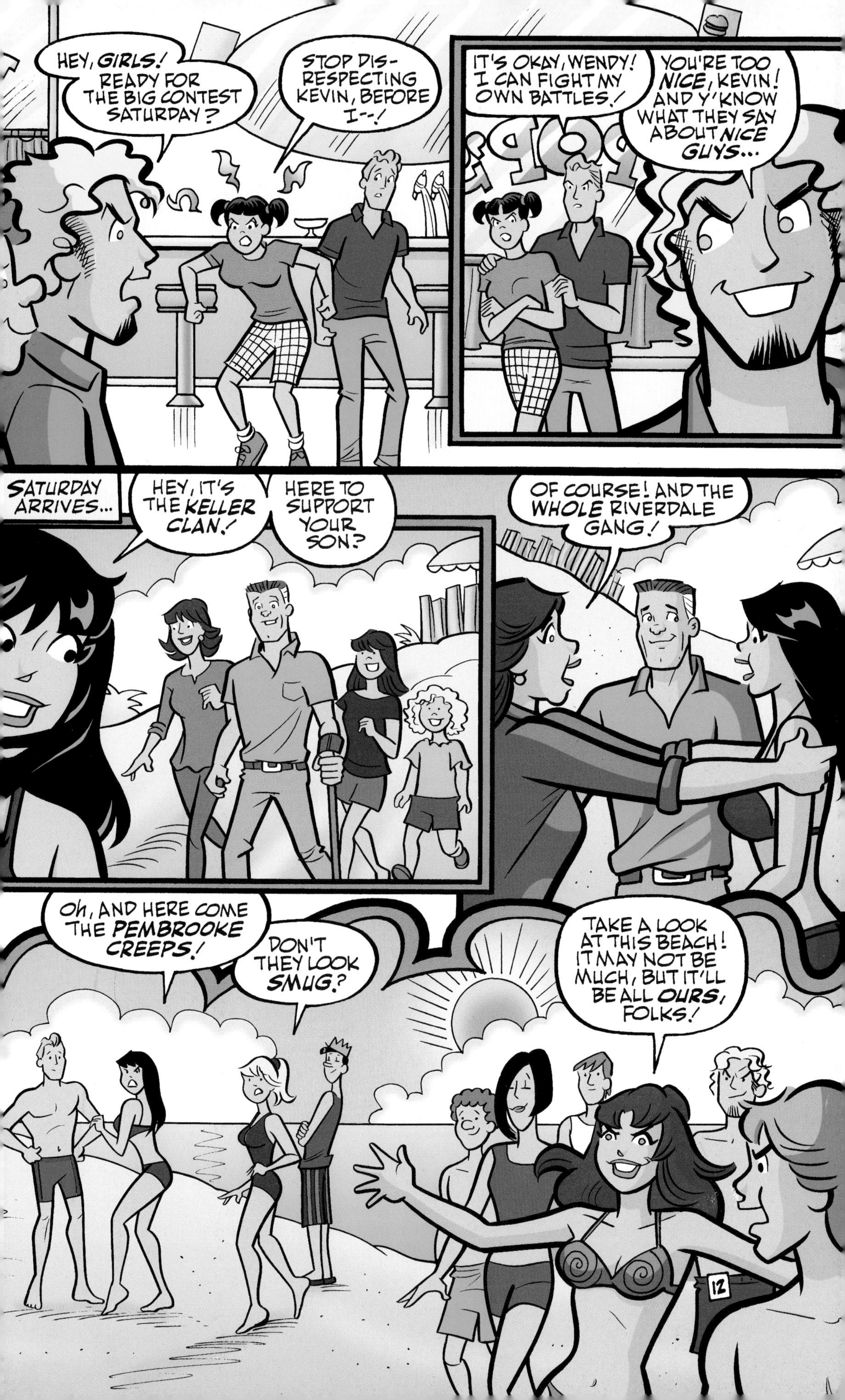

HEY, GIRLS! READY FOR THE BIG CONTEST SATURDAY?
STOP DIS-RESPECTING KEVIN, BEFORE I--!
IT'S OKAY, WENDY! I CAN FIGHT MY OWN BATTLES!
YOU'RE TOO NICE, KEVIN! AND Y'KNOW WHAT THEY SAY ABOUT NICE GUYS...
SATURDAY ARRIVES...
HEY, IT'S THE KELLER CLAN!
HERE TO SUPPORT YOUR SON?
OF COURSE! AND THE WHOLE RIVERDALE GANG!
Oh, AND HERE COME THE PEMBROOKE CREEPS!
DON'T THEY LOOK SMUG?
TAKE A LOOK AT THIS BEACH! IT MAY NOT BE MUCH, BUT IT'LL BE ALL OURS, FOLKS!
12

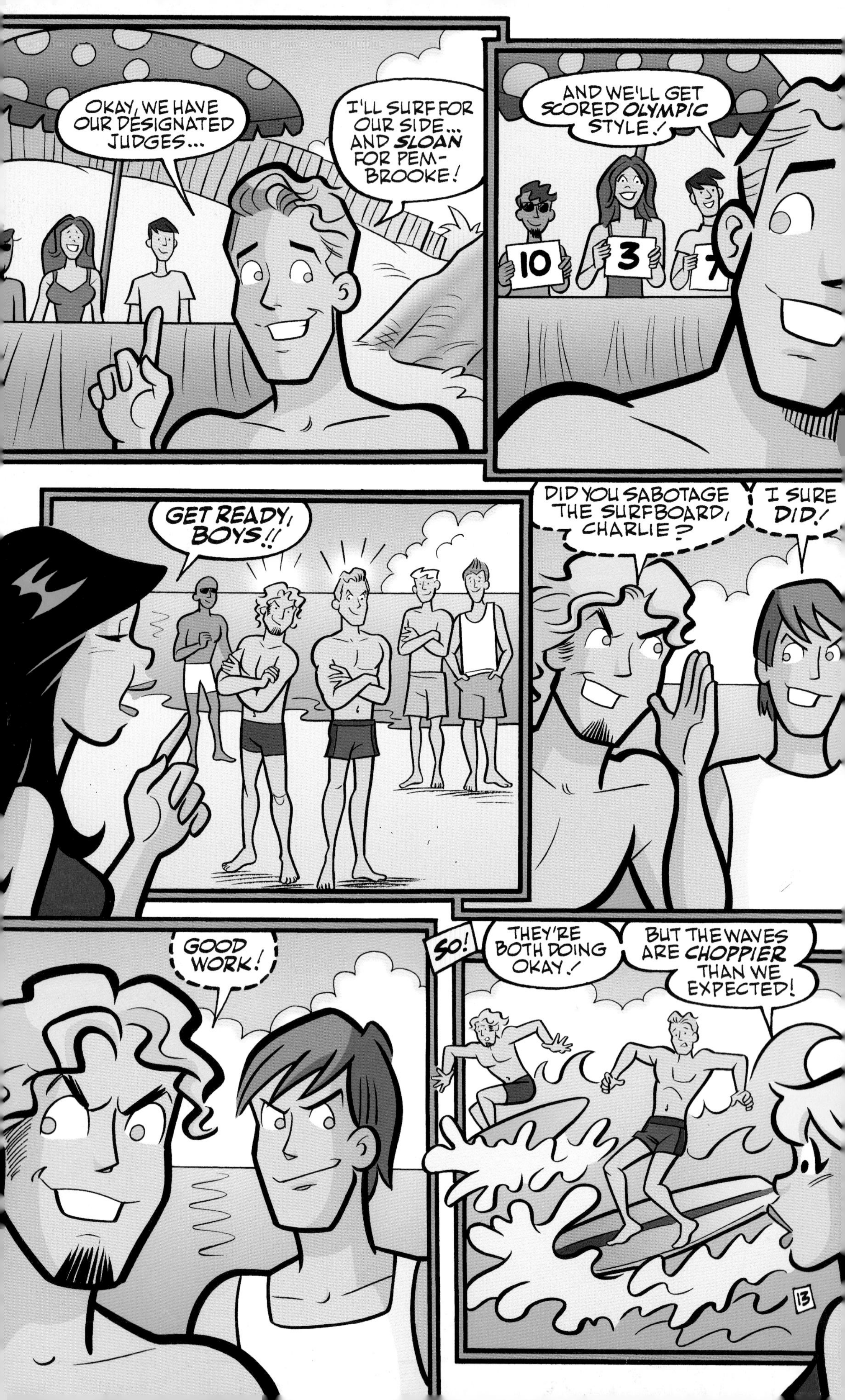
OKAY, WE HAVE OUR DESIGNATED JUDGES...
I'LL SURF FOR OUR SIDE... AND SLOAN FOR PEM-BROOKE!
AND WE'LL GET SCORED OLYMPIC STYLE!
10
3
GET READY, BOYS!!
DID YOU SABOTAGE THE SURFBOARD, CHARLIE?
I SURE DID!
GOOD WORK!
SO!
THEY'RE BOTH DOING OKAY!
BUT THE WAVES ARE CHOPPIER THAN WE EXPECTED!
13

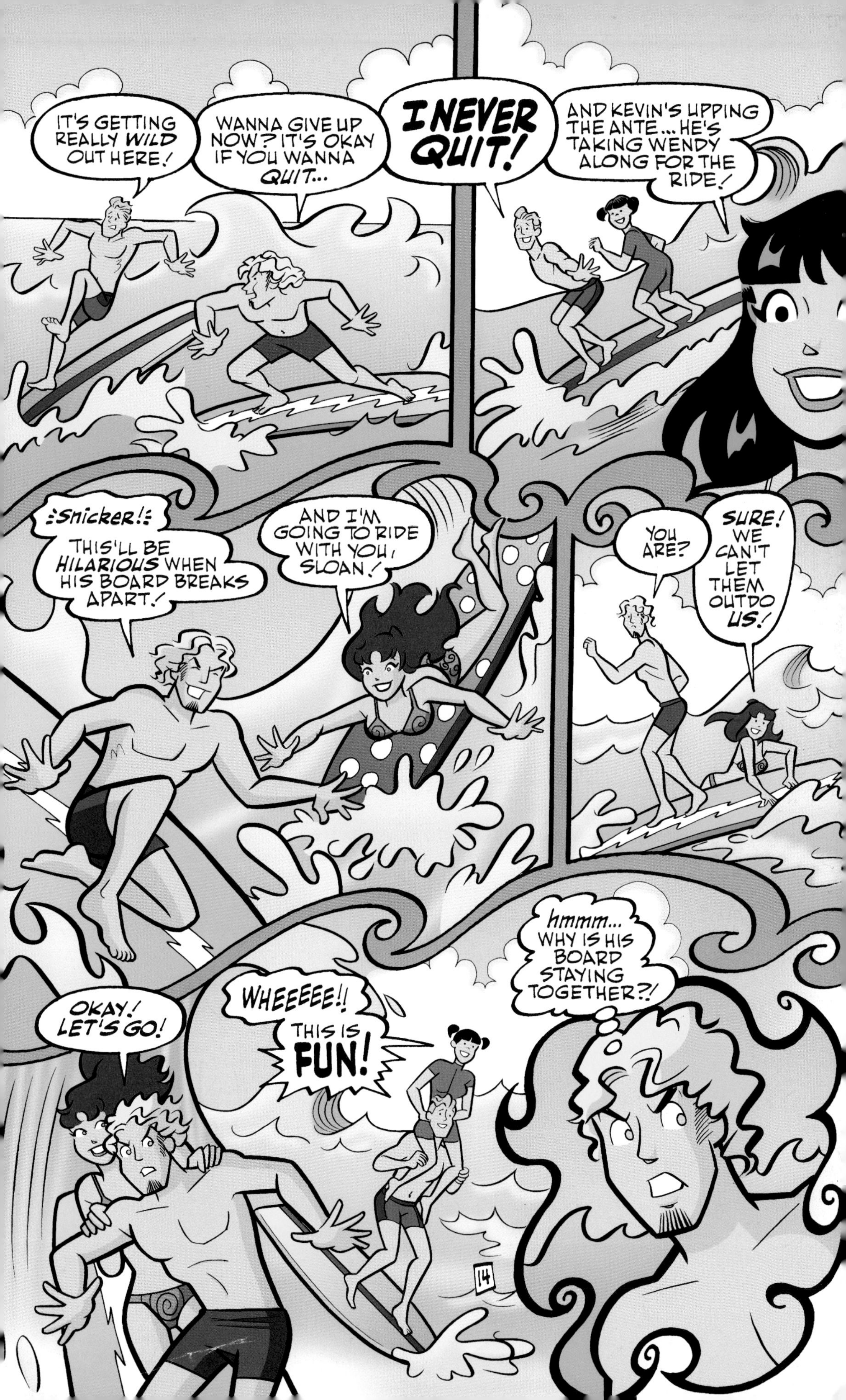
IT'S GETTING REALLY WILD OUT HERE!
WANNA GIVE UP NOW? IT'S OKAY IF YOU WANNA QUIT...
I NEVER QUIT!
AND KEVIN'S UPPING THE ANTE... HE'S TAKING WENDY ALONG FOR THE RIDE!
:Snicker!: THIS'LL BE HILARIOUS WHEN HIS BOARD BREAKS APART!
AND I'M GOING TO RIDE WITH YOU, SLOAN!
YOU ARE?
SURE! WE CAN'T LET THEM OUTDO US!
OKAY! LET'S GO!
WHEEEEE!! THIS IS FUN!
hmmm... WHY IS HIS BOARD STAYING TOGETHER?!
14

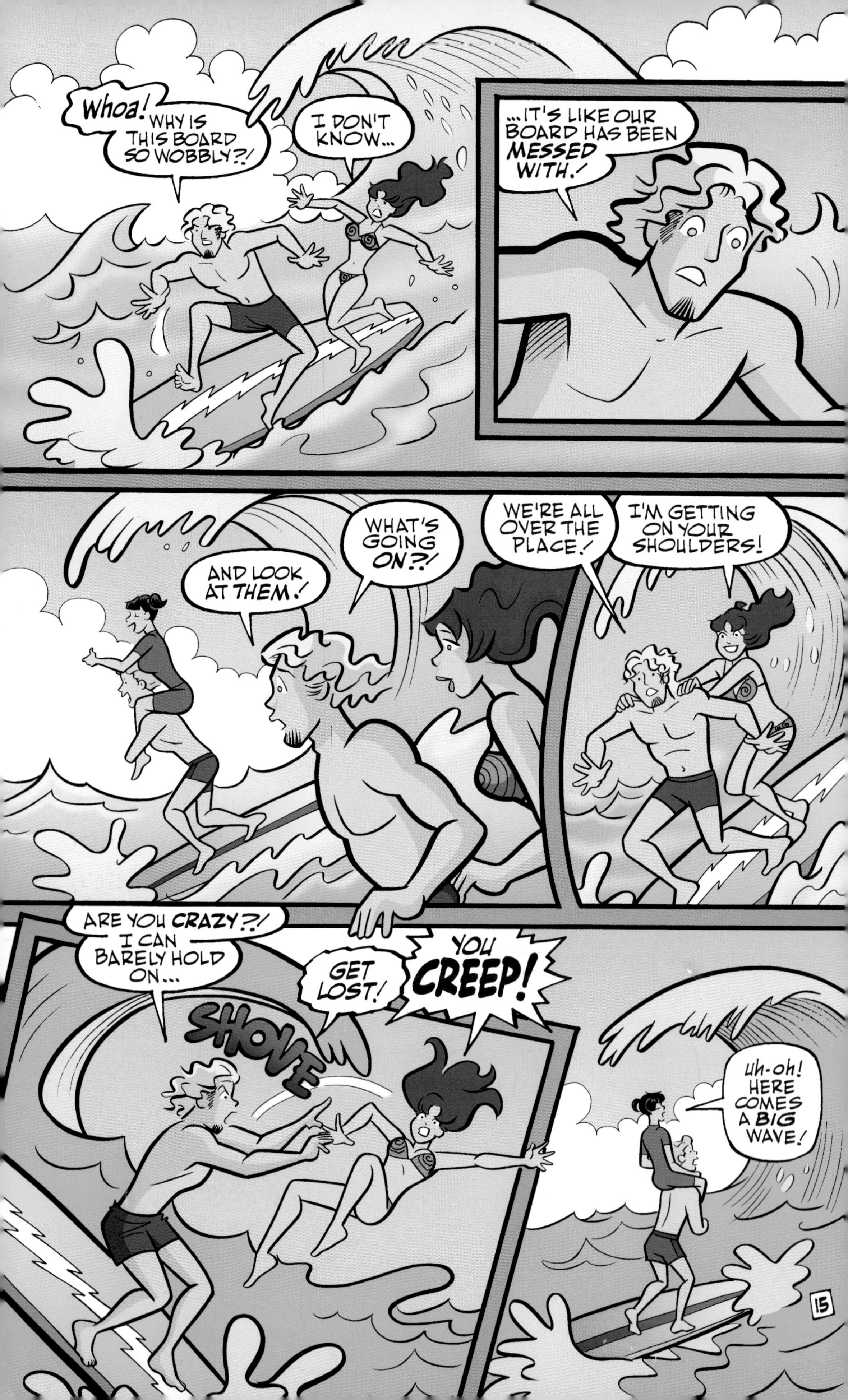
Whoa! WHY IS THIS BOARD SO WOBBLY?!
I DON'T KNOW...
...IT'S LIKE OUR BOARD HAS BEEN MESSED WITH!
AND LOOK AT THEM!
WHAT'S GOING ON?!
WE'RE ALL OVER THE PLACE!
I'M GETTING ON YOUR SHOULDERS!
ARE YOU CRAZY?! I CAN BARELY HOLD ON...
SHOVE
GET LOST!
YOU CREEP!
Uh-oh! HERE COMES A BIG WAVE!

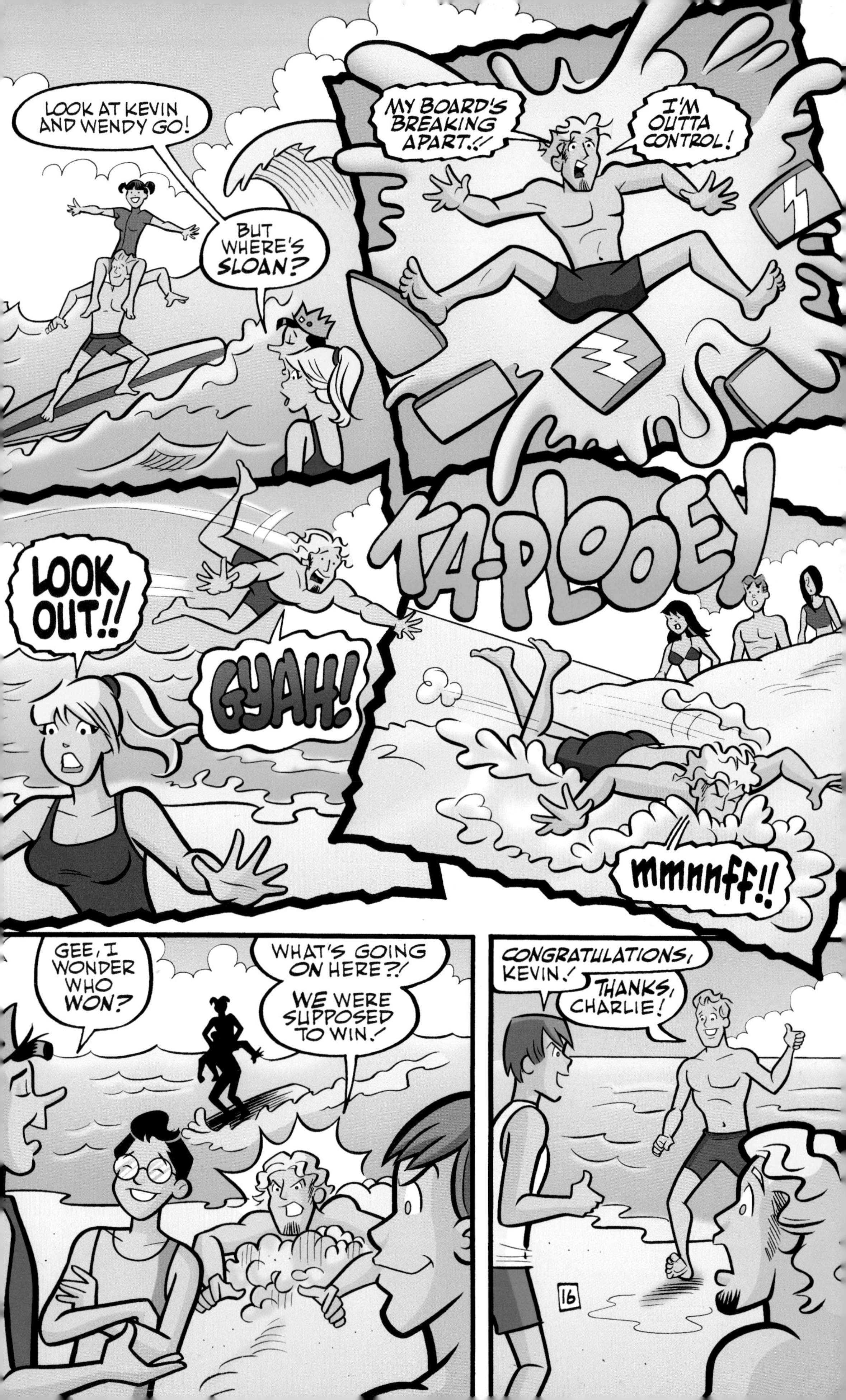

LOOK AT KEVIN AND WENDY GO!
BUT WHERE'S SLOAN?
MY BOARD'S BREAKING APART.!!
I'M OUTTA CONTROL!
KA-PLOOEY
LOOK OUT!!
GYAH!
mmnnff!!
GEE, I WONDER WHO WON?
WHAT'S GOING ON HERE?!
WE WERE SUPPOSED TO WIN.!
CONGRATULATIONS, KEVIN!
THANKS, CHARLIE!
16

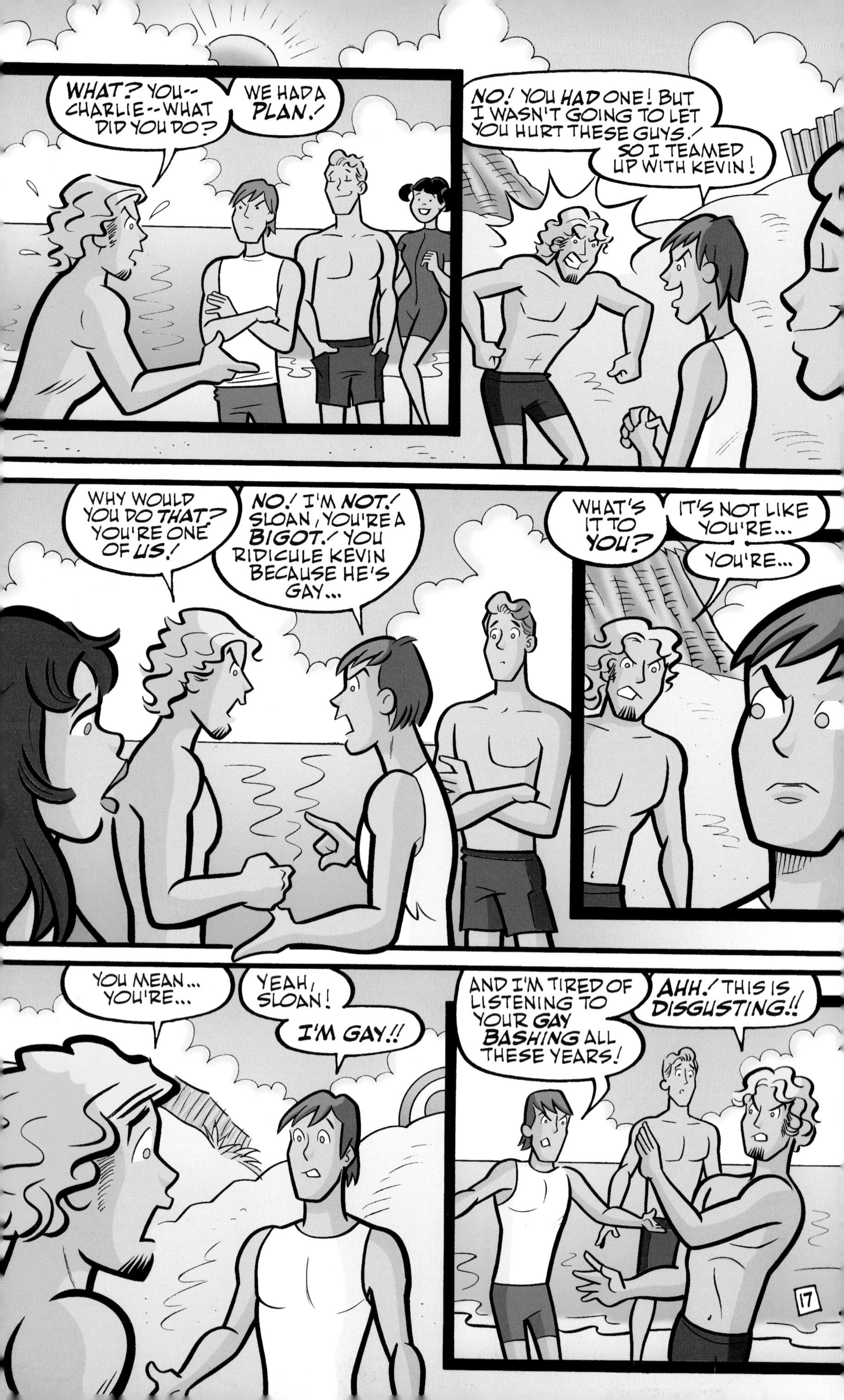
WHAT? YOU-- CHARLIE--WHAT DID YOU DO?
WE HAD A PLAN!
NO! YOU HAD ONE! BUT I WASN'T GOING TO LET YOU HURT THESE GUYS!
SO I TEAMED UP WITH KEVIN!
WHY WOULD YOU DO THAT? YOU'RE ONE OF US!
NO! I'M NOT! SLOAN, YOU'RE A BIGOT! YOU RIDICULE KEVIN BECAUSE HE'S GAY...
WHAT'S IT TO YOU?
IT'S NOT LIKE YOU'RE...
YOU'RE...
YOU MEAN... YOU'RE...
YEAH, SLOAN!
I'M GAY!!
AND I'M TIRED OF LISTENING TO YOUR GAY BASHING ALL THESE YEARS!
AHH! THIS IS DISGUSTING!!
17

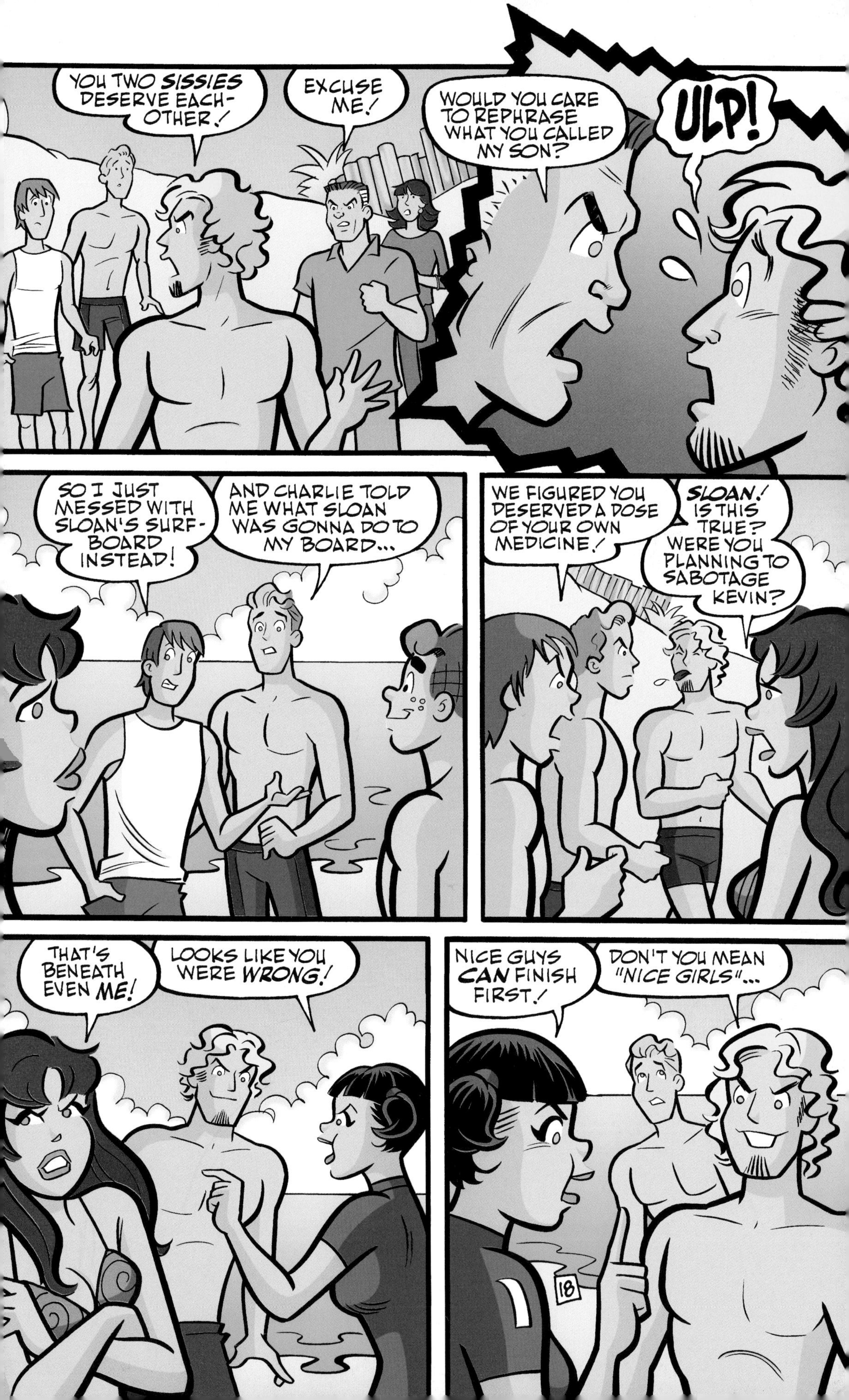
YOU TWO SISSIES DESERVE EACH-OTHER!
EXCUSE ME!
WOULD YOU CARE TO REPHRASE WHAT YOU CALLED MY SON?
ULP!
SO I JUST MESSED WITH SLOAN'S SURF-BOARD INSTEAD!
AND CHARLIE TOLD ME WHAT SLOAN WAS GONNA DO TO MY BOARD...
WE FIGURED YOU DESERVED A DOSE OF YOUR OWN MEDICINE!
SLOAN! IS THIS TRUE? WERE YOU PLANNING TO SABOTAGE KEVIN?
THAT'S BENEATH EVEN ME!
LOOKS LIKE YOU WERE WRONG!
NICE GUYS CAN FINISH FIRST!
DON'T YOU MEAN "NICE GIRLS"...
18

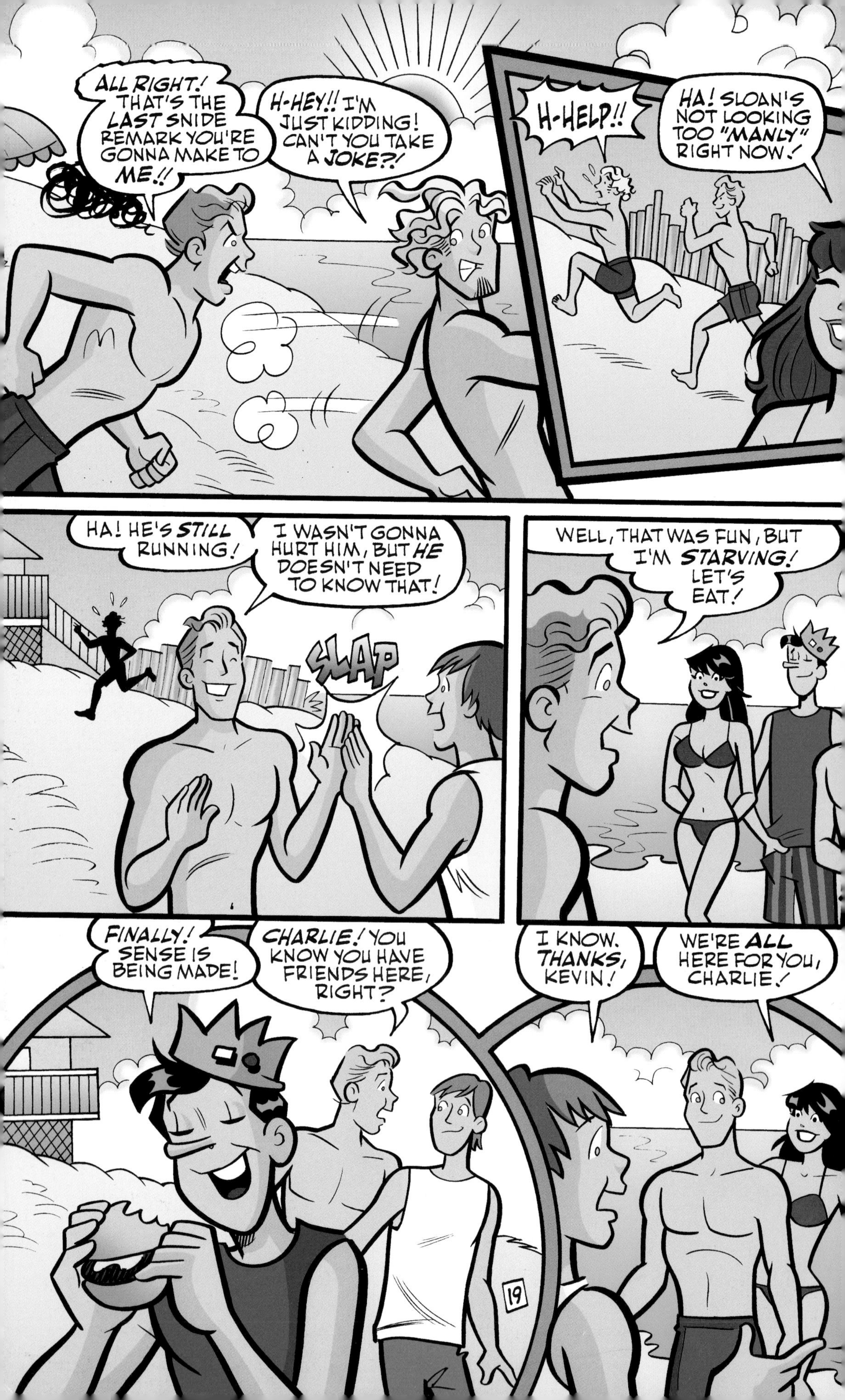
ALL RIGHT! THAT'S THE LAST SNIDE REMARK YOU'RE GONNA MAKE TO ME!!
H-HEY!! I'M JUST KIDDING! CAN'T YOU TAKE A JOKE?!
H-HELP!!
HA! SLOAN'S NOT LOOKING TOO "MANLY" RIGHT NOW!
HA! HE'S STILL RUNNING!
I WASN'T GONNA HURT HIM, BUT HE DOESN'T NEED TO KNOW THAT!
SLAP
WELL, THAT WAS FUN, BUT I'M STARVING! LET'S EAT!
FINALLY! SENSE IS BEING MADE!
CHARLIE! YOU KNOW YOU HAVE FRIENDS HERE, RIGHT?
I KNOW. THANKS, KEVIN!
WE'RE ALL HERE FOR YOU, CHARLIE!
19

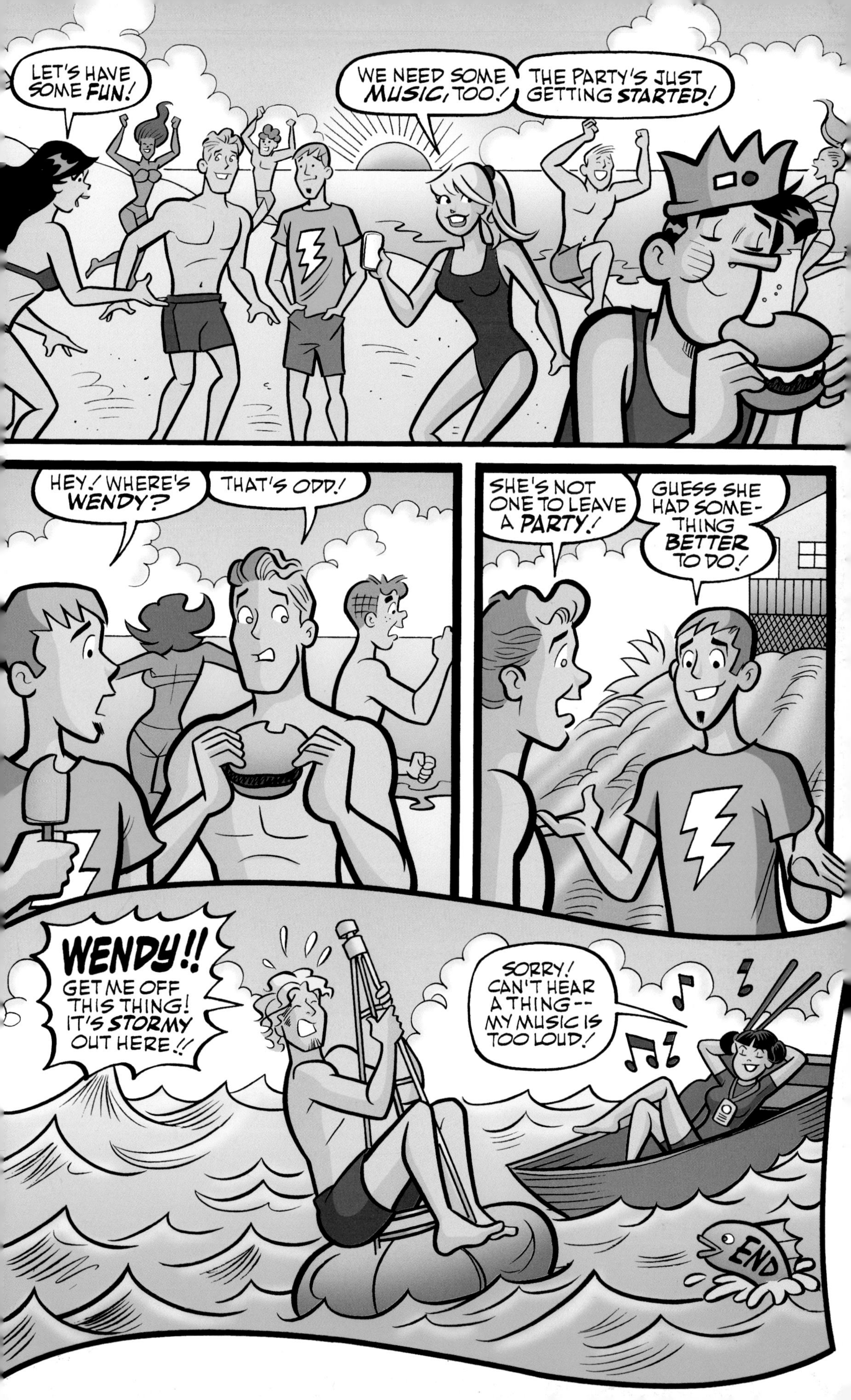
LET'S HAVE SOME FUN!
WE NEED SOME MUSIC, TOO!
THE PARTY'S JUST GETTING STARTED!
HEY! WHERE'S WENDY?
THAT'S ODD!
SHE'S NOT ONE TO LEAVE A PARTY!
GUESS SHE HAD SOME-THING BETTER TO DO!
WENDY!! GET ME OFF THIS THING! IT'S STORMY OUT HERE!!
SORRY! CAN'T HEAR A THING-- MY MUSIC IS TOO LOUD!
END

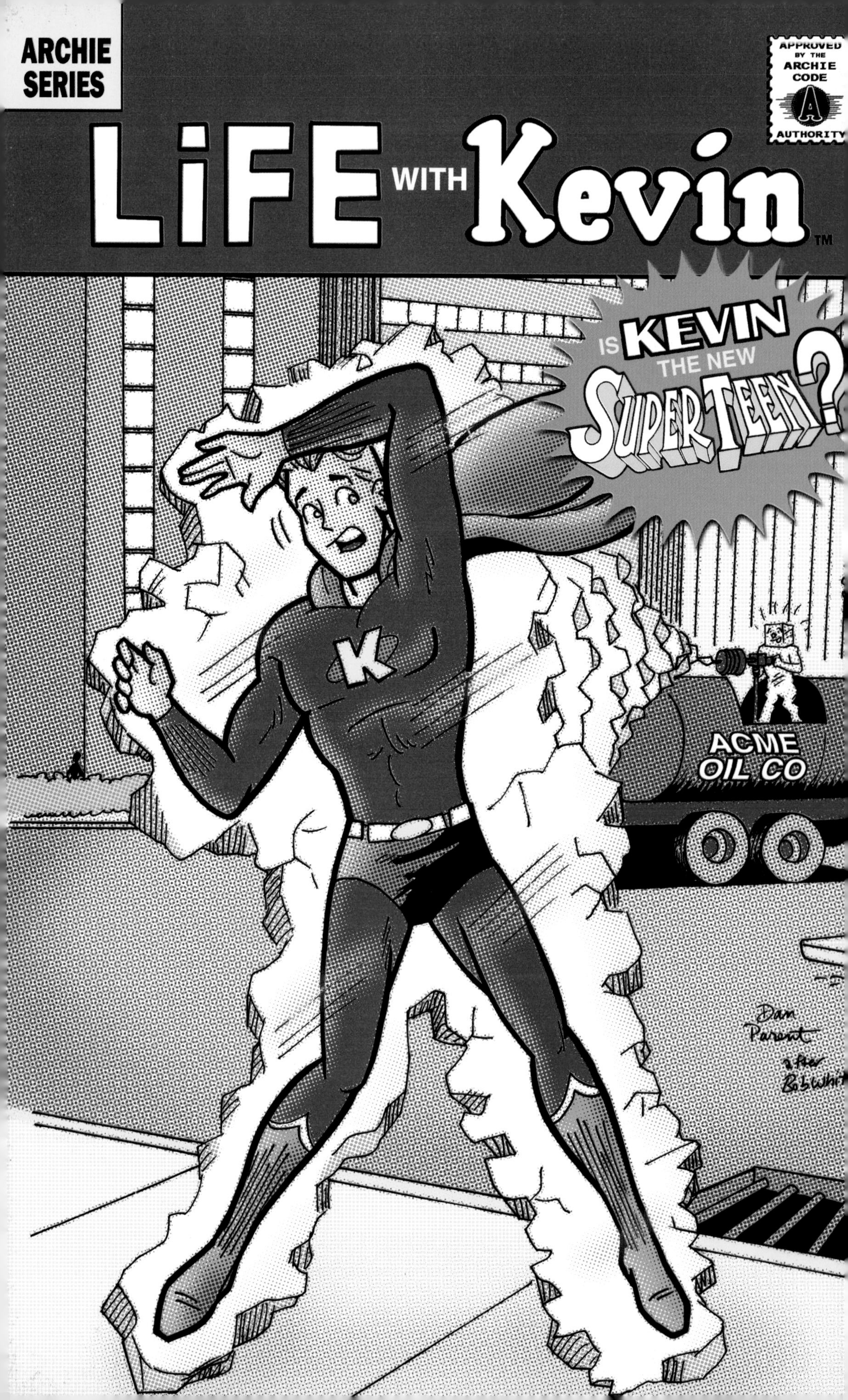
ARCHIE SERIES
APPROVED BY THE ARCHIE CODE AUTHORITY
LiFE WITH Kevin™
IS KEVIN THE NEW SUPERTEEN?
ACME OIL CO
Dan Parent

Chapter 4

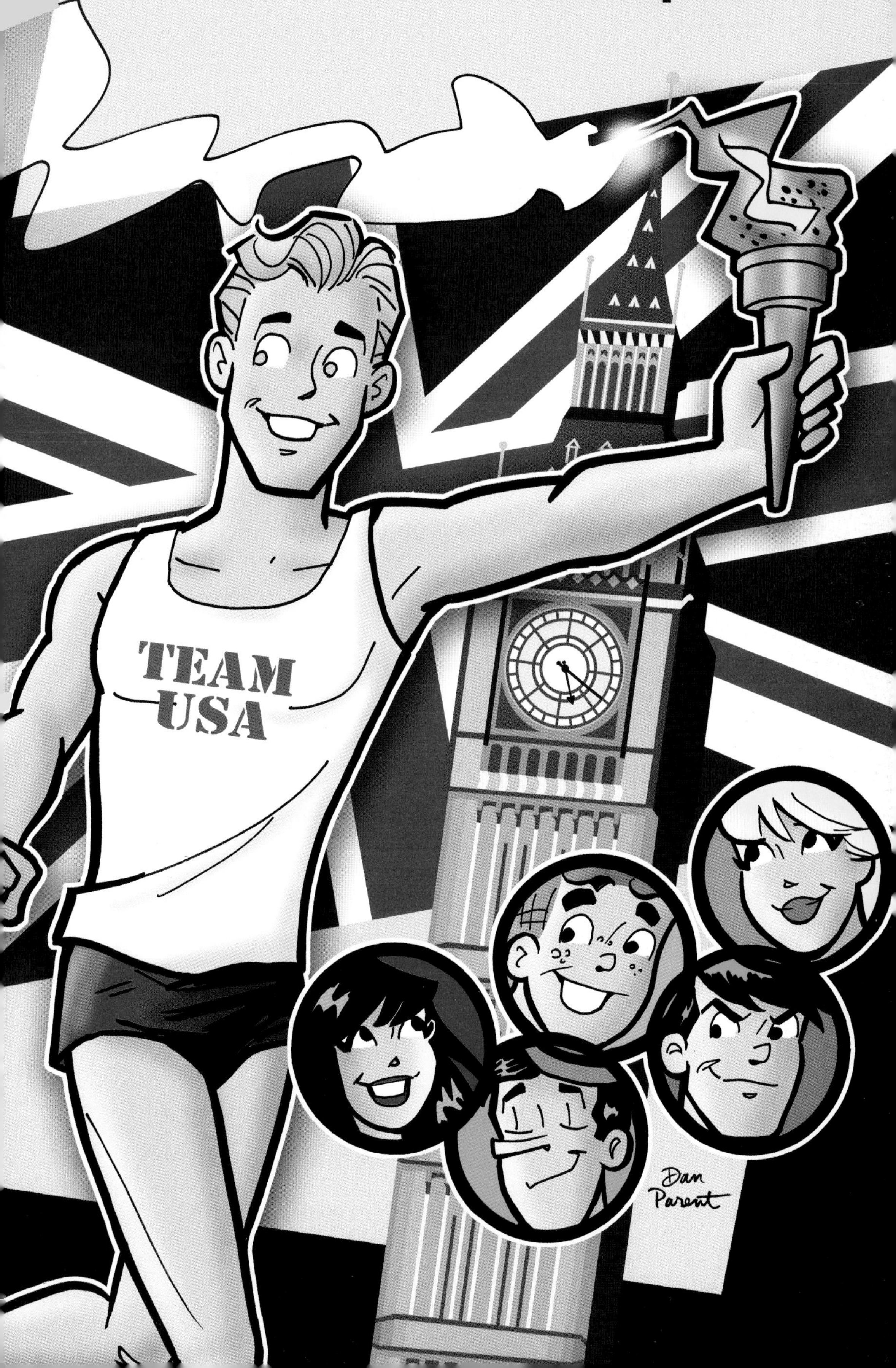

TEAM USA
Dan Parent

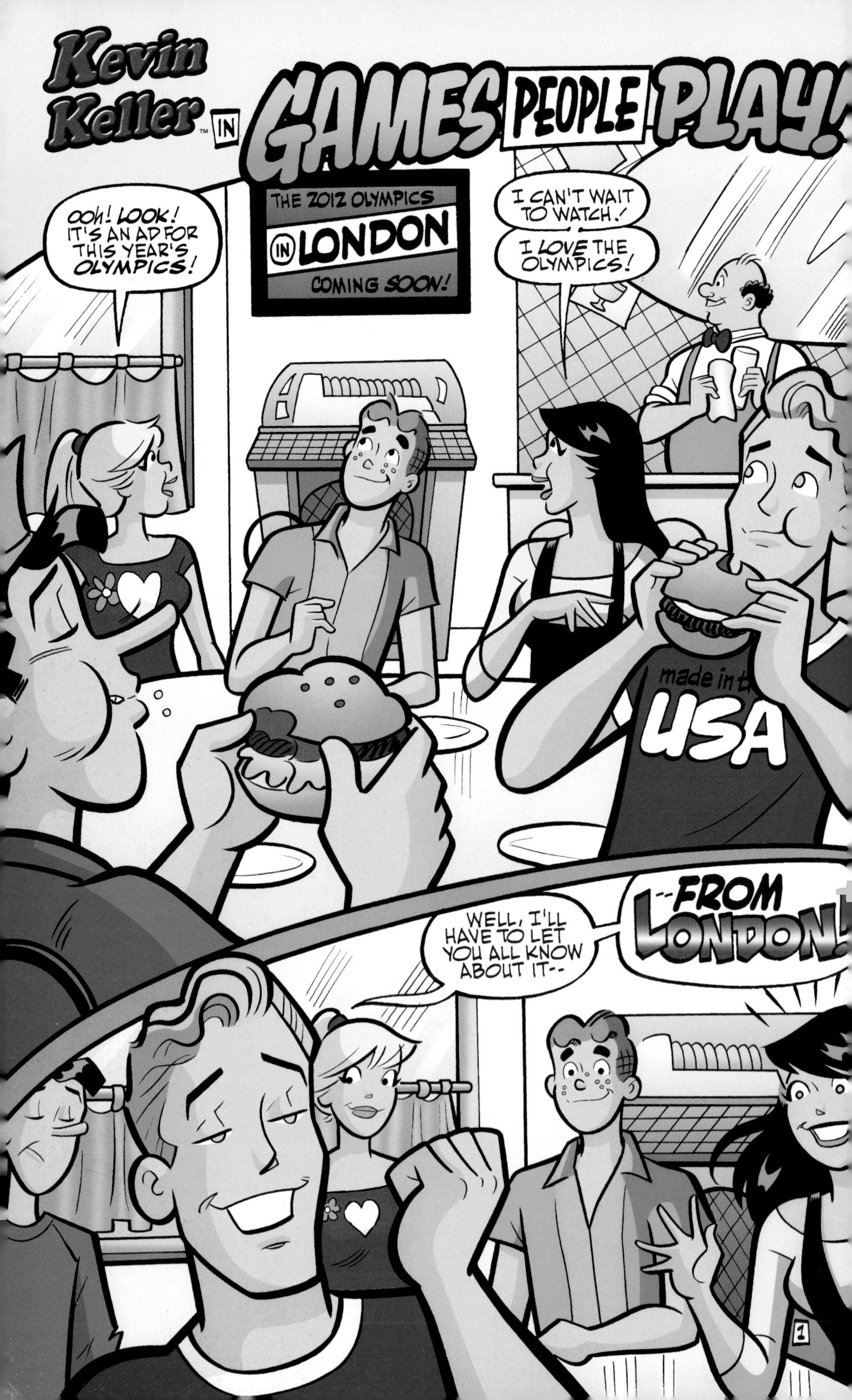
Kevin Keller™ IN GAMES PEOPLE PLAY!
THE 2012 OLYMPICS IN LONDON COMING SOON!
OOH! LOOK! IT'S AN AD FOR THIS YEAR'S OLYMPICS!
I CAN'T WAIT TO WATCH!
I LOVE THE OLYMPICS!
made in the USA
WELL, I'LL HAVE TO LET YOU ALL KNOW ABOUT IT--
--FROM LONDON!
1

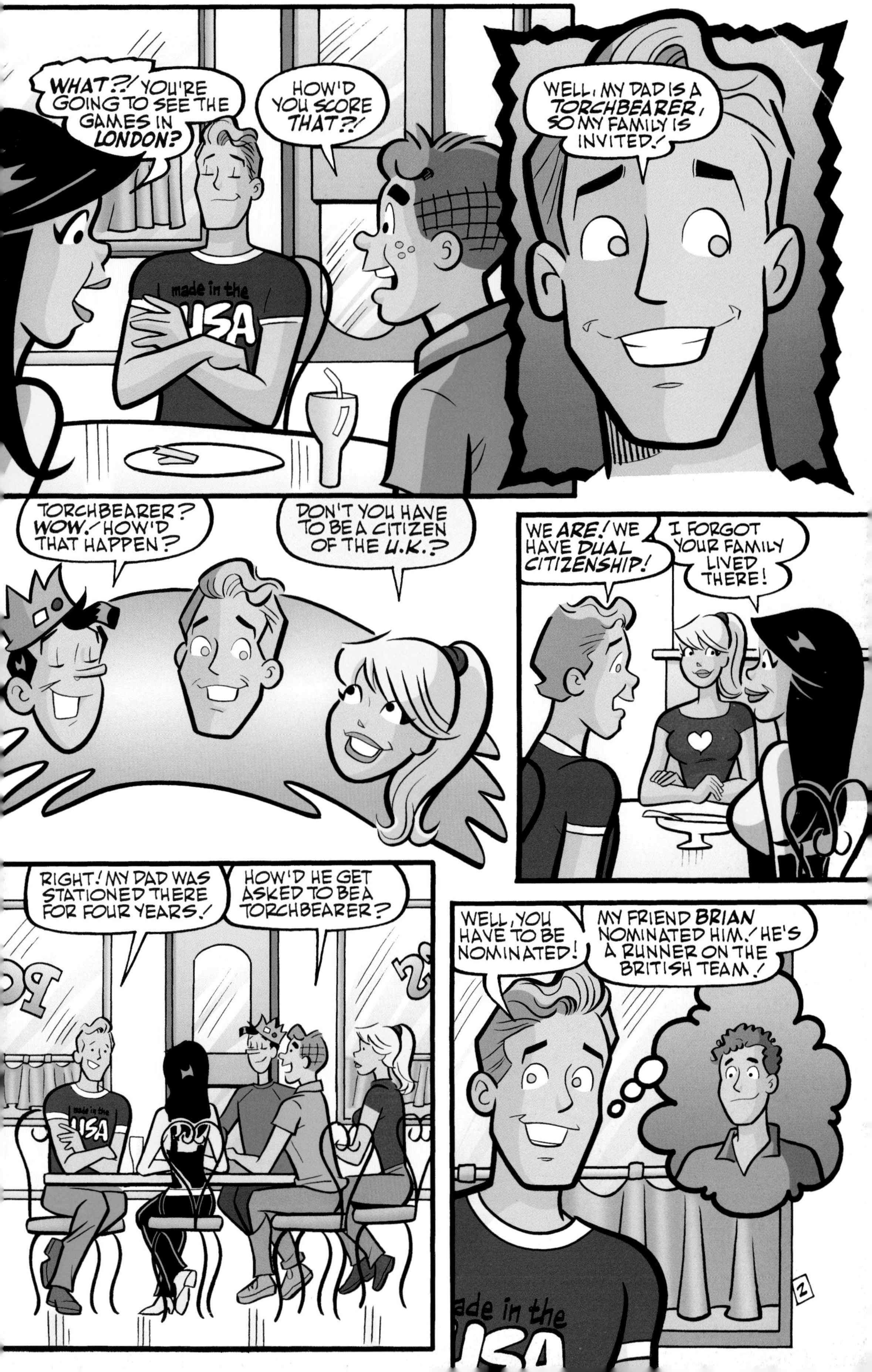
WHAT?! YOU'RE GOING TO SEE THE GAMES IN LONDON?
HOW'D YOU SCORE THAT?!
WELL, MY DAD IS A TORCHBEARER, SO MY FAMILY IS INVITED!
TORCHBEARER? WOW! HOW'D THAT HAPPEN?
DON'T YOU HAVE TO BE A CITIZEN OF THE U.K.?
WE ARE! WE HAVE DUAL CITIZENSHIP!
I FORGOT YOUR FAMILY LIVED THERE!
RIGHT! MY DAD WAS STATIONED THERE FOR FOUR YEARS!
HOW'D HE GET ASKED TO BE A TORCHBEARER?
WELL, YOU HAVE TO BE NOMINATED!
MY FRIEND BRIAN NOMINATED HIM! HE'S A RUNNER ON THE BRITISH TEAM!

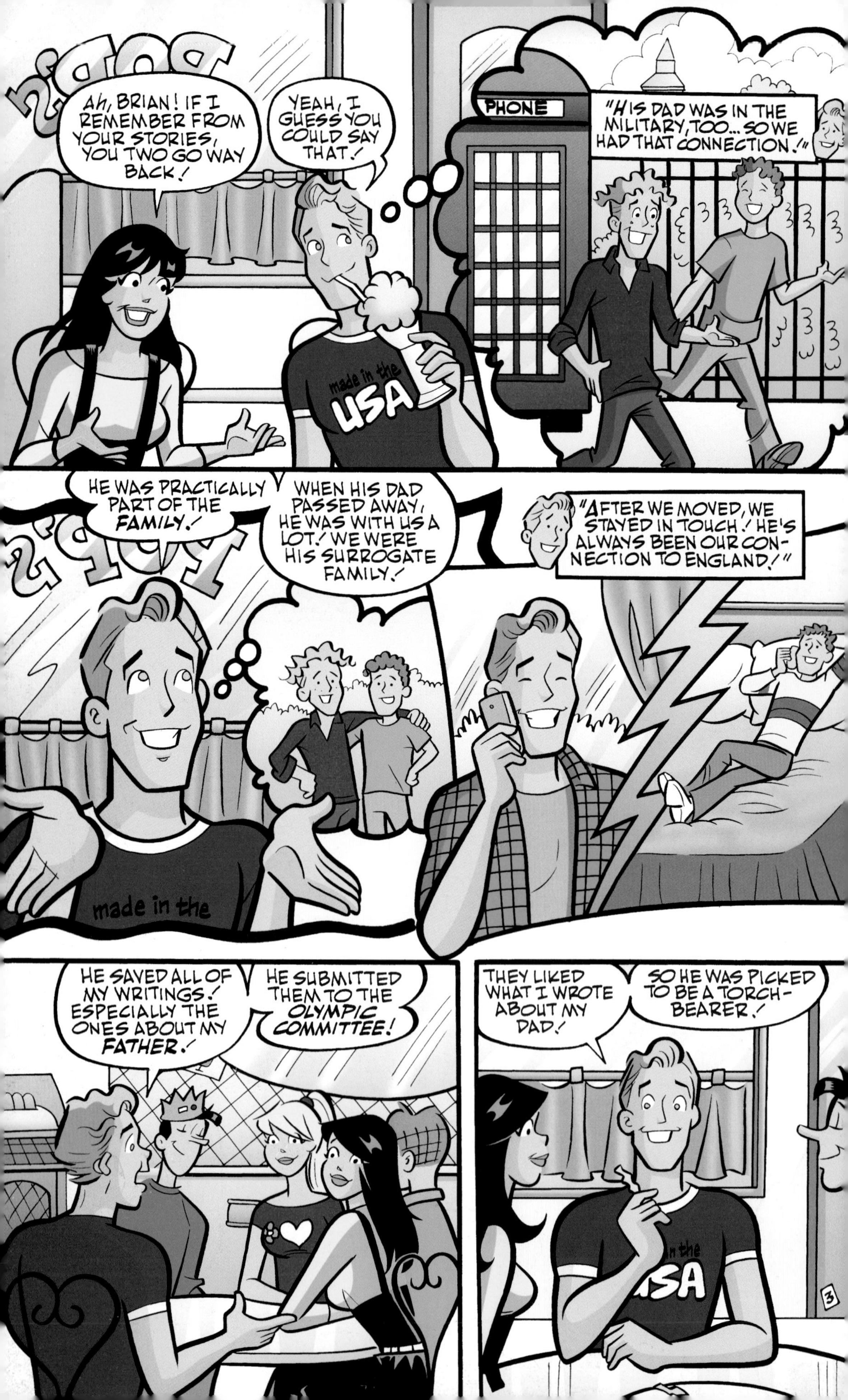
POP'S
AH, BRIAN! IF I REMEMBER FROM YOUR STORIES, YOU TWO GO WAY BACK!
YEAH, I GUESS YOU COULD SAY THAT!
PHONE
"HIS DAD WAS IN THE MILITARY, TOO... SO WE HAD THAT CONNECTION!"
made in the USA
HE WAS PRACTICALLY PART OF THE FAMILY!
WHEN HIS DAD PASSED AWAY, HE WAS WITH US A LOT! WE WERE HIS SURROGATE FAMILY!
"AFTER WE MOVED, WE STAYED IN TOUCH! HE'S ALWAYS BEEN OUR CONNECTION TO ENGLAND!"
made in the
HE SAVED ALL OF MY WRITINGS! ESPECIALLY THE ONES ABOUT MY FATHER!
HE SUBMITTED THEM TO THE OLYMPIC COMMITTEE!
THEY LIKED WHAT I WROTE ABOUT MY DAD!
SO HE WAS PICKED TO BE A TORCH-BEARER!
3

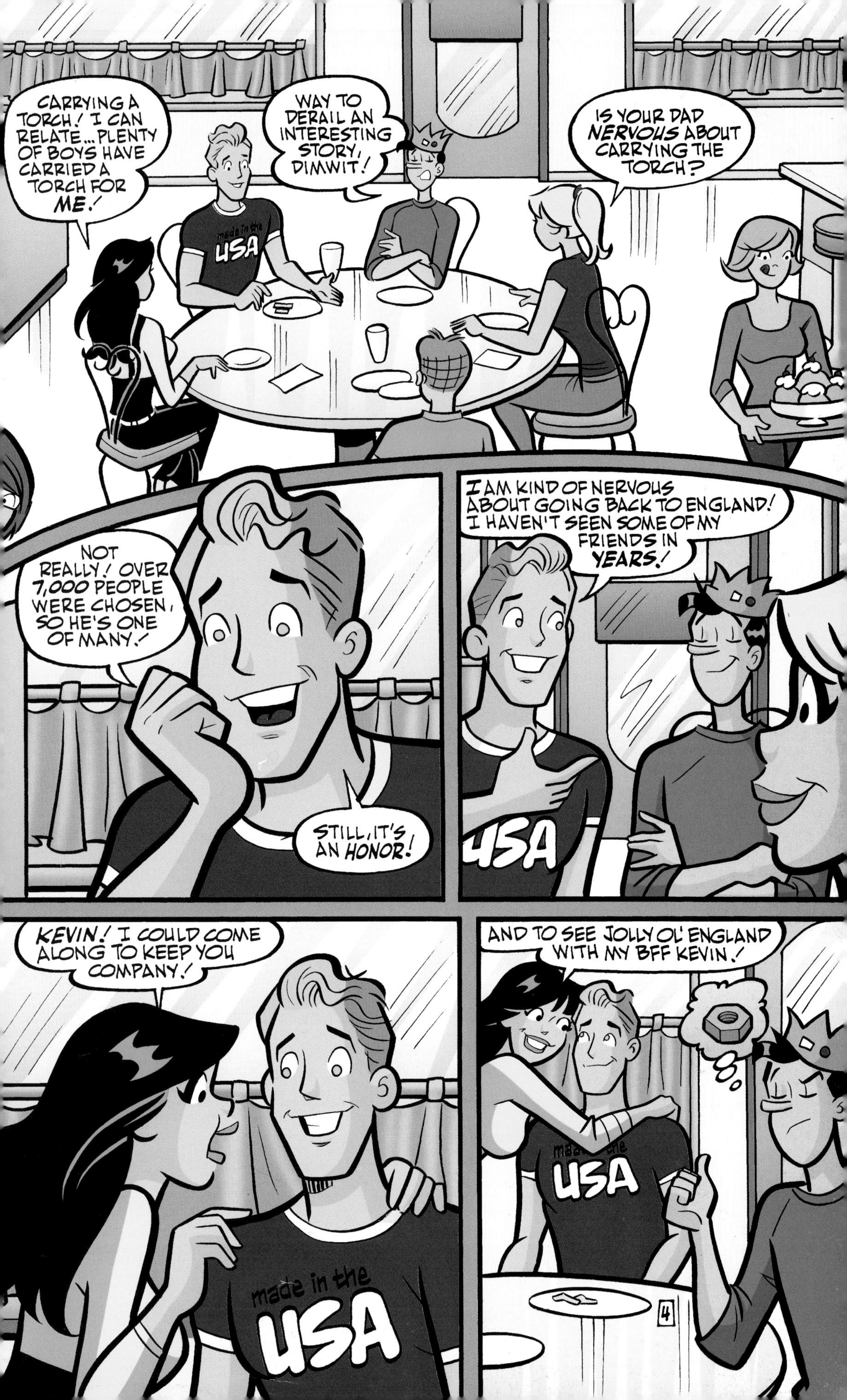
CARRYING A TORCH! I CAN RELATE... PLENTY OF BOYS HAVE CARRIED A TORCH FOR ME!
WAY TO DERAIL AN INTERESTING STORY, DIMWIT!
IS YOUR DAD NERVOUS ABOUT CARRYING THE TORCH?
made in the USA
NOT REALLY! OVER 7,000 PEOPLE WERE CHOSEN, SO HE'S ONE OF MANY!
STILL, IT'S AN HONOR!
I AM KIND OF NERVOUS ABOUT GOING BACK TO ENGLAND! I HAVEN'T SEEN SOME OF MY FRIENDS IN YEARS!
USA
KEVIN! I COULD COME ALONG TO KEEP YOU COMPANY!
made in the USA
AND TO SEE JOLLY OL' ENGLAND WITH MY BFF KEVIN!
USA
4

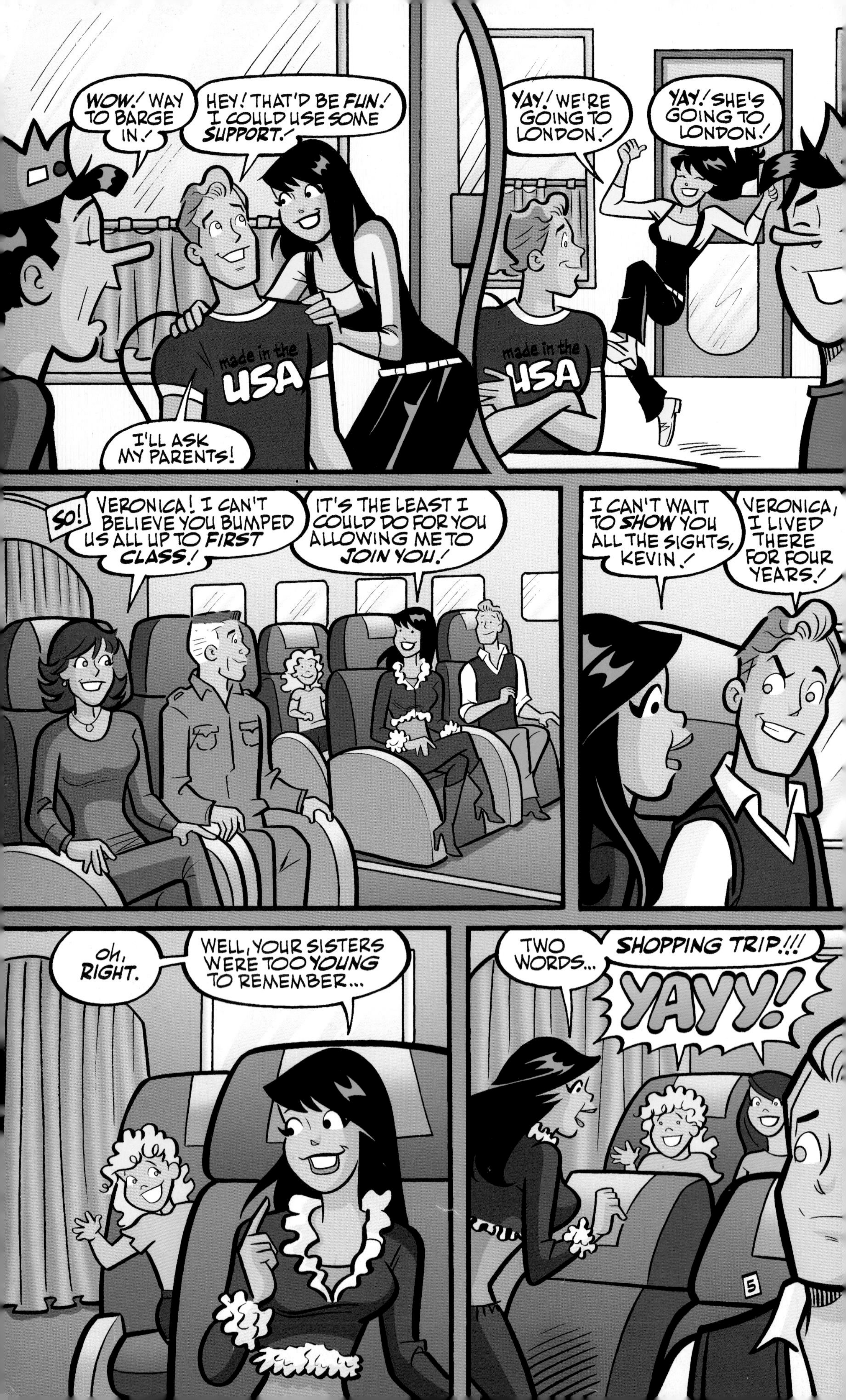
WOW! WAY TO BARGE IN!
HEY! THAT'D BE FUN! I COULD USE SOME SUPPORT!
I'LL ASK MY PARENTS!
made in the USA
YAY! WE'RE GOING TO LONDON!
YAY! SHE'S GOING TO LONDON!
made in the USA
SO! VERONICA! I CAN'T BELIEVE YOU BUMPED US ALL UP TO FIRST CLASS!
IT'S THE LEAST I COULD DO FOR YOU ALLOWING ME TO JOIN YOU!
I CAN'T WAIT TO SHOW YOU ALL THE SIGHTS, KEVIN!
VERONICA, I LIVED THERE FOR FOUR YEARS!
oh, RIGHT.
WELL, YOUR SISTERS WERE TOO YOUNG TO REMEMBER...
TWO WORDS...
SHOPPING TRIP!!!
YAYY!
5

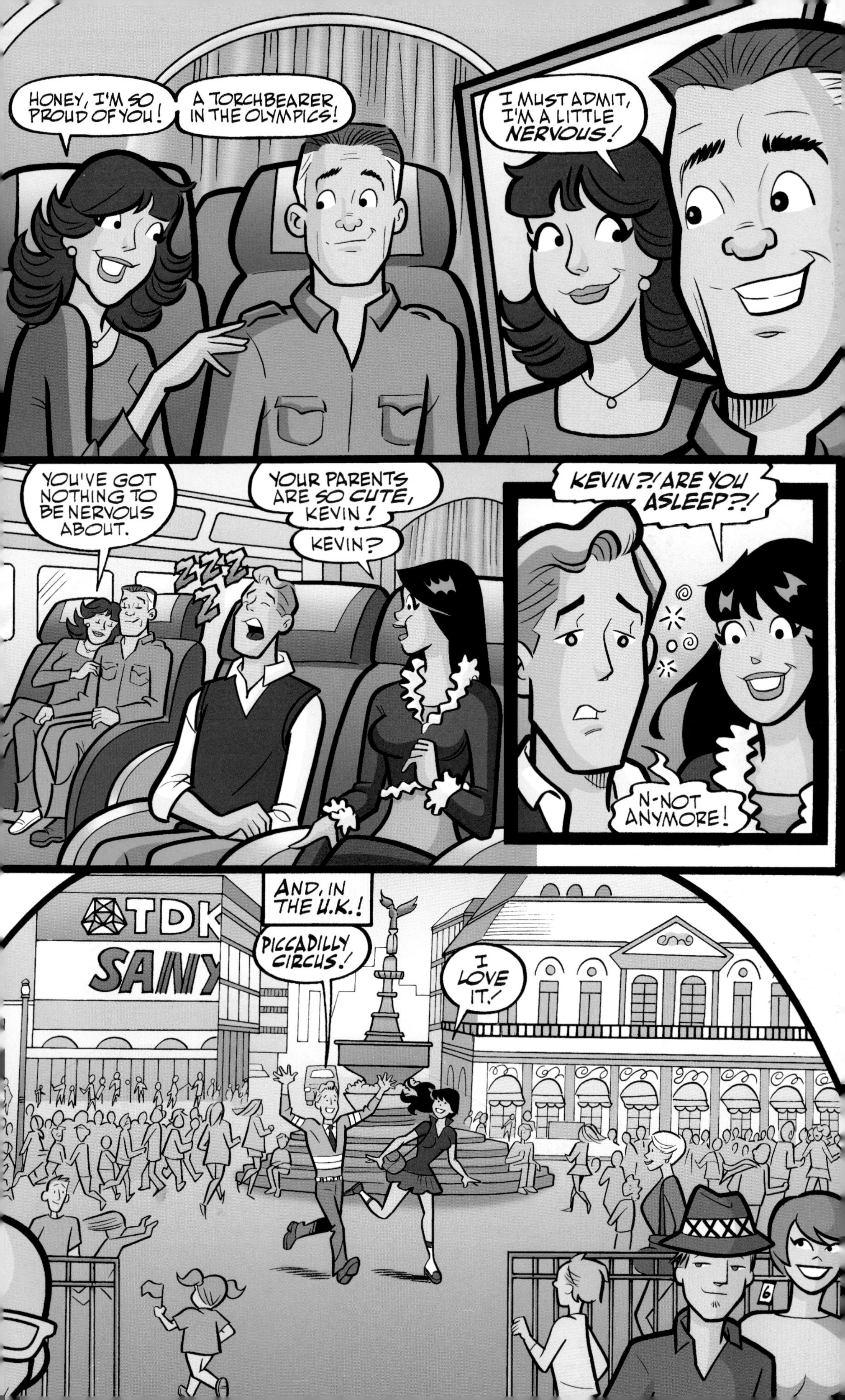
HONEY, I'M SO PROUD OF YOU!
A TORCHBEARER IN THE OLYMPICS!
I MUST ADMIT, I'M A LITTLE NERVOUS!
YOU'VE GOT NOTHING TO BE NERVOUS ABOUT.
YOUR PARENTS ARE SO CUTE, KEVIN!
KEVIN?
ZZZZ
KEVIN?! ARE YOU ASLEEP?!
N-NOT ANYMORE!
AND, IN THE U.K.!
TDK
SANY
PICCADILLY CIRCUS!
I LOVE IT!
6

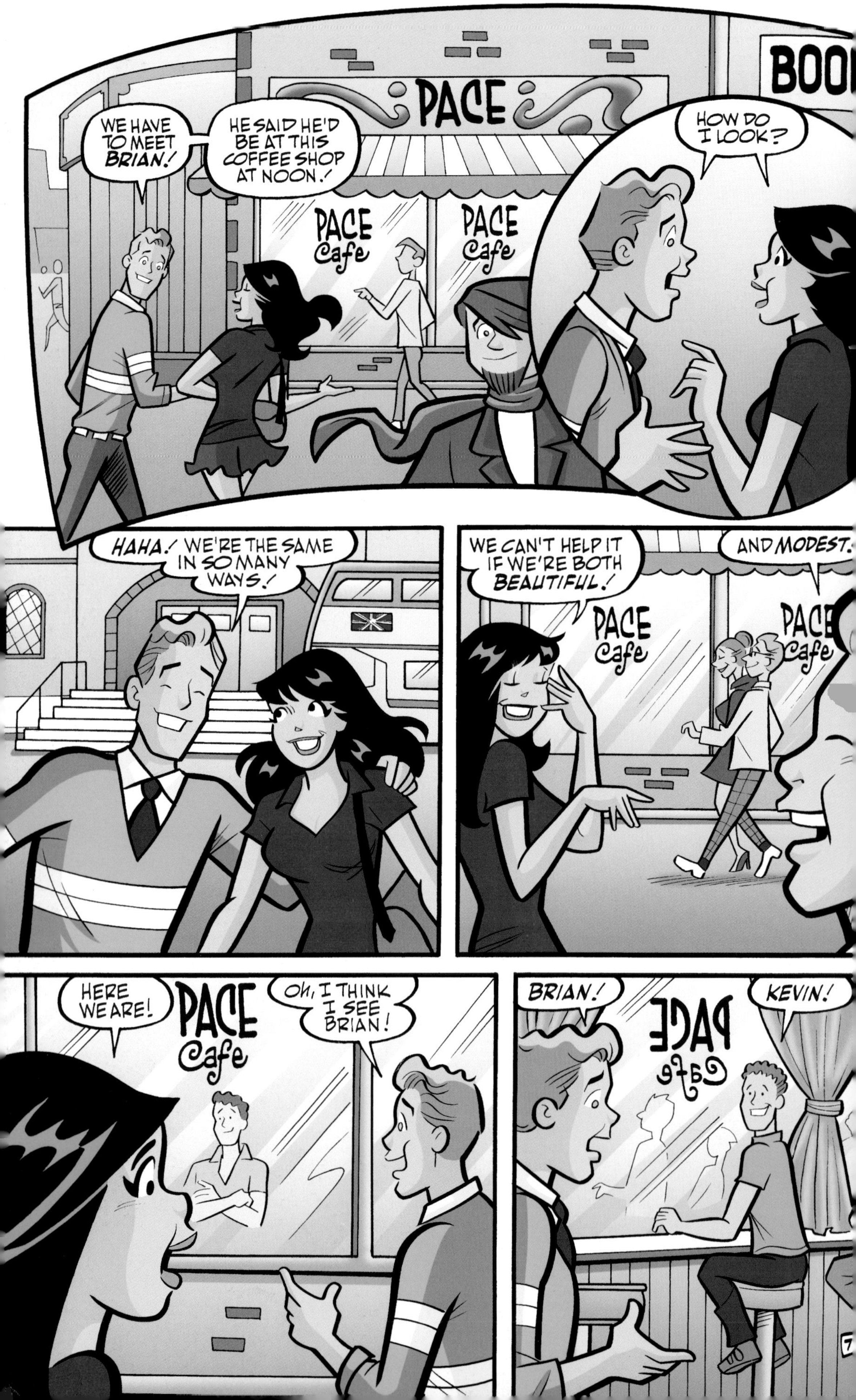
PACE
BOO
WE HAVE TO MEET BRIAN!
HE SAID HE'D BE AT THIS COFFEE SHOP AT NOON!
PACE Cafe
PACE Cafe
HOW DO I LOOK?
HAHA! WE'RE THE SAME IN SO MANY WAYS!
WE CAN'T HELP IT IF WE'RE BOTH BEAUTIFUL!
AND MODEST.
PACE Cafe
PACE Cafe
HERE WE ARE!
PACE Cafe
Oh, I THINK I SEE BRIAN!
BRIAN!
KEVIN!

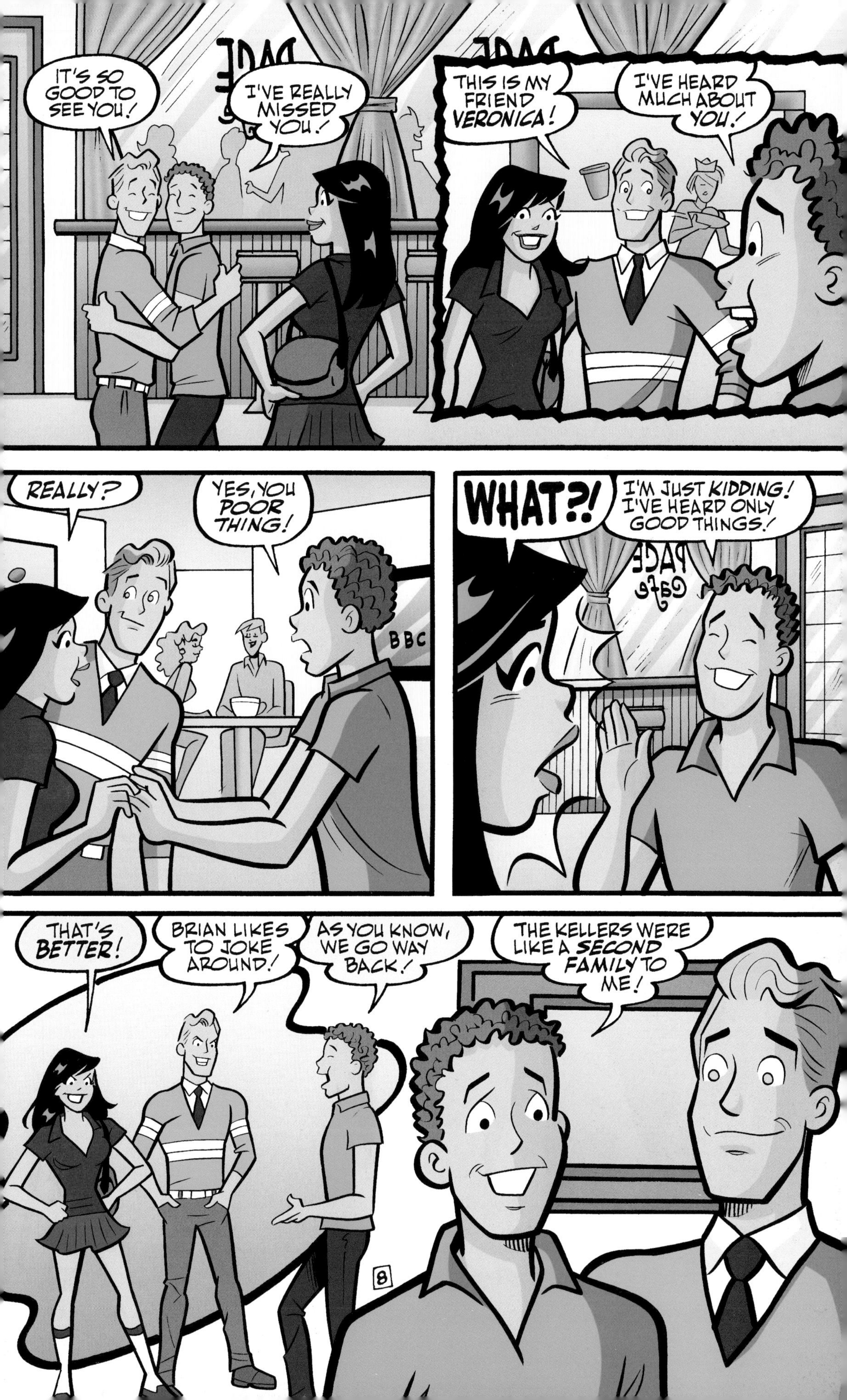
IT'S SO GOOD TO SEE YOU!
I'VE REALLY MISSED YOU!
THIS IS MY FRIEND VERONICA!
I'VE HEARD MUCH ABOUT YOU!
REALLY?
YES, YOU POOR THING!
BBC
WHAT?!
I'M JUST KIDDING! I'VE HEARD ONLY GOOD THINGS!
THAT'S BETTER!
BRIAN LIKES TO JOKE AROUND!
AS YOU KNOW, WE GO WAY BACK!
THE KELLERS WERE LIKE A SECOND FAMILY TO ME!
8

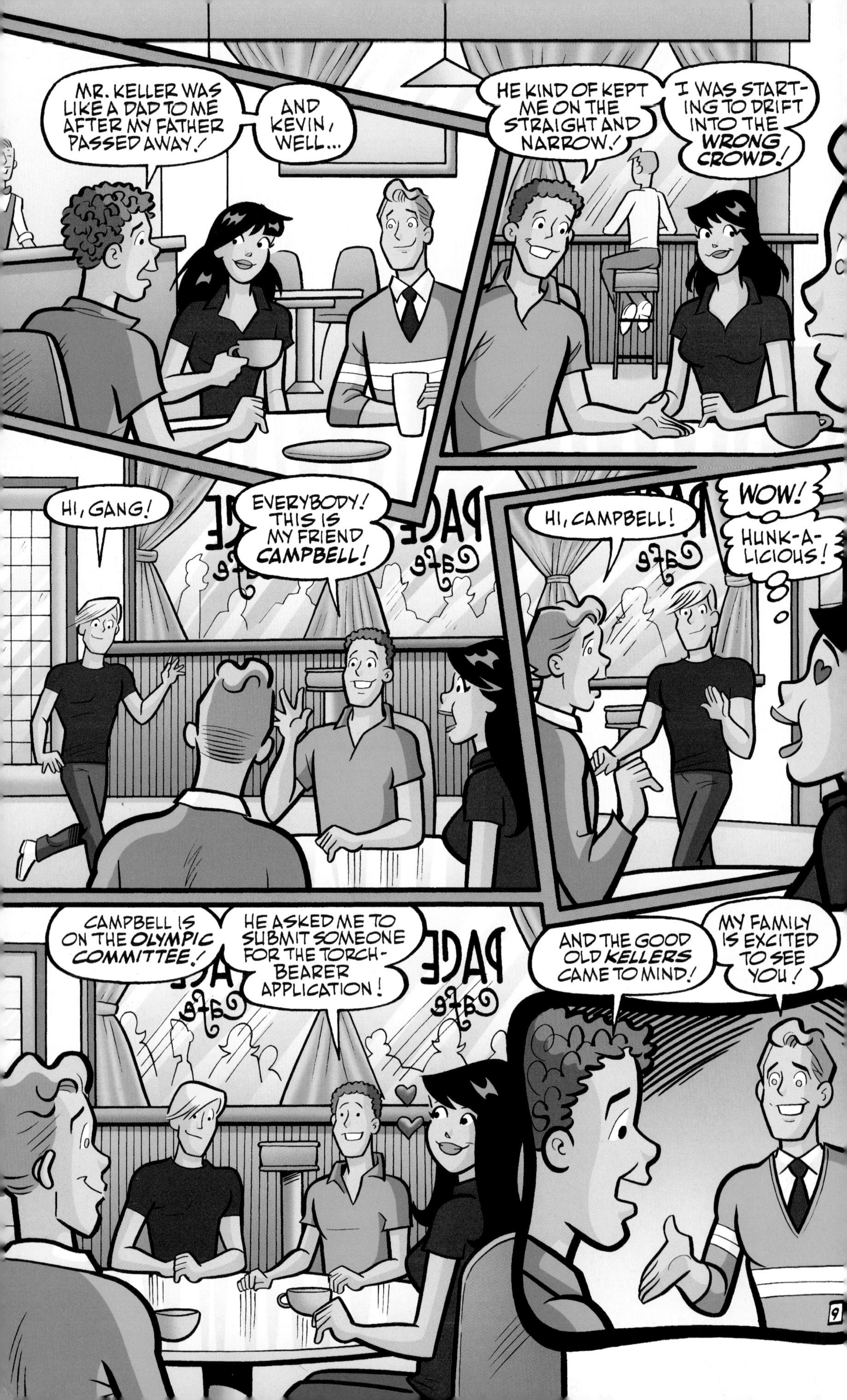
MR. KELLER WAS LIKE A DAD TO ME AFTER MY FATHER PASSED AWAY!
AND KEVIN, WELL...
HE KIND OF KEPT ME ON THE STRAIGHT AND NARROW!
I WAS STARTING TO DRIFT INTO THE WRONG CROWD!
HI, GANG!
EVERYBODY! THIS IS MY FRIEND CAMPBELL!
PAGE
Cafe
HI, CAMPBELL!
WOW!
HUNK-A-LICIOUS!
CAMPBELL IS ON THE OLYMPIC COMMITTEE!
HE ASKED ME TO SUBMIT SOMEONE FOR THE TORCH-BEARER APPLICATION!
AND THE GOOD OLD KELLERS CAME TO MIND!
MY FAMILY IS EXCITED TO SEE YOU!
9

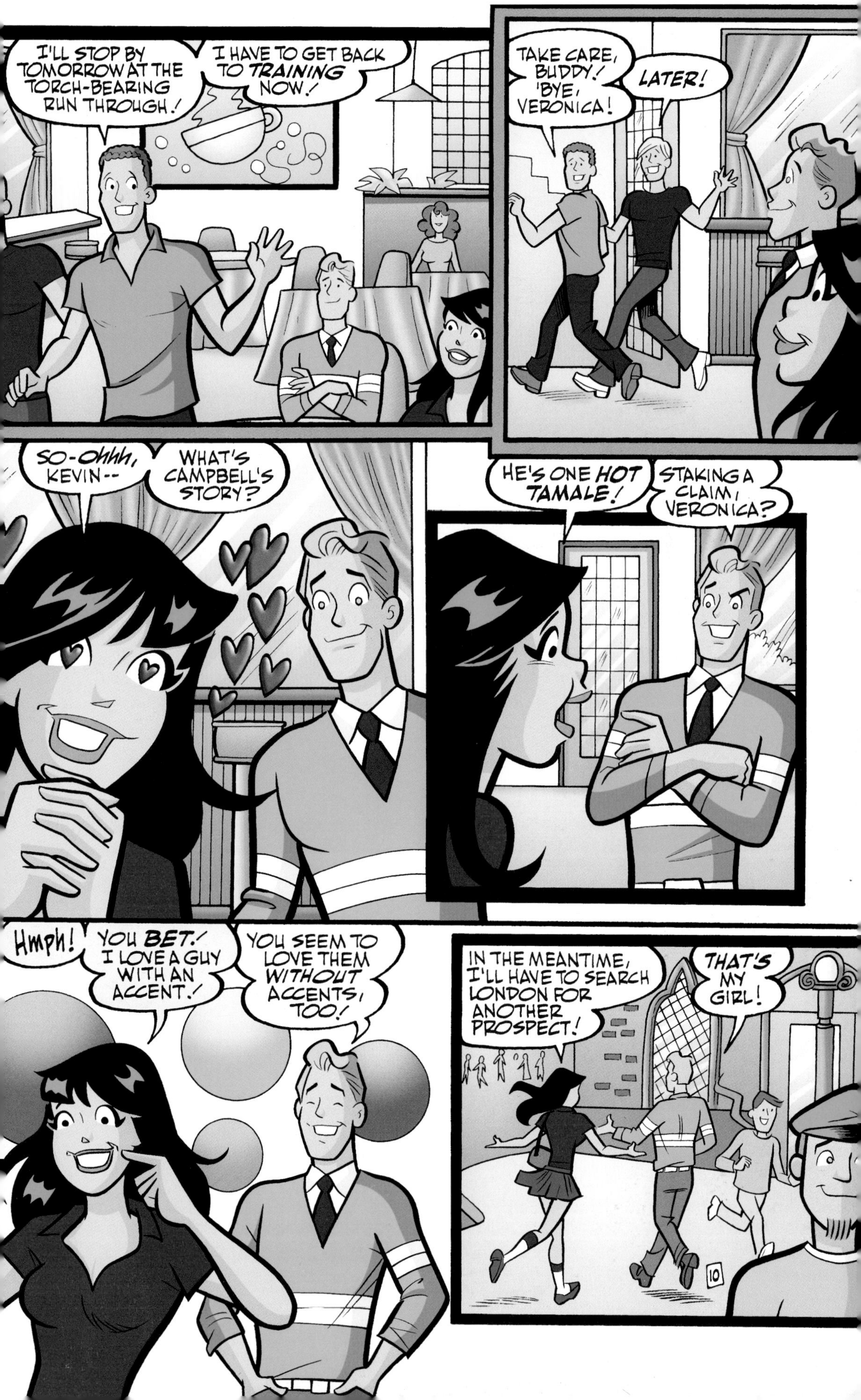
I'LL STOP BY TOMORROW AT THE TORCH-BEARING RUN THROUGH!
I HAVE TO GET BACK TO TRAINING NOW!
TAKE CARE, BUDDY! 'BYE, VERONICA!
LATER!
SO-Ohhh, KEVIN--
WHAT'S CAMPBELL'S STORY?
HE'S ONE HOT TAMALE!
STAKING A CLAIM, VERONICA?
Hmph!
YOU BET! I LOVE A GUY WITH AN ACCENT!
YOU SEEM TO LOVE THEM WITHOUT ACCENTS, TOO!
IN THE MEANTIME, I'LL HAVE TO SEARCH LONDON FOR ANOTHER PROSPECT!
THAT'S MY GIRL!
10

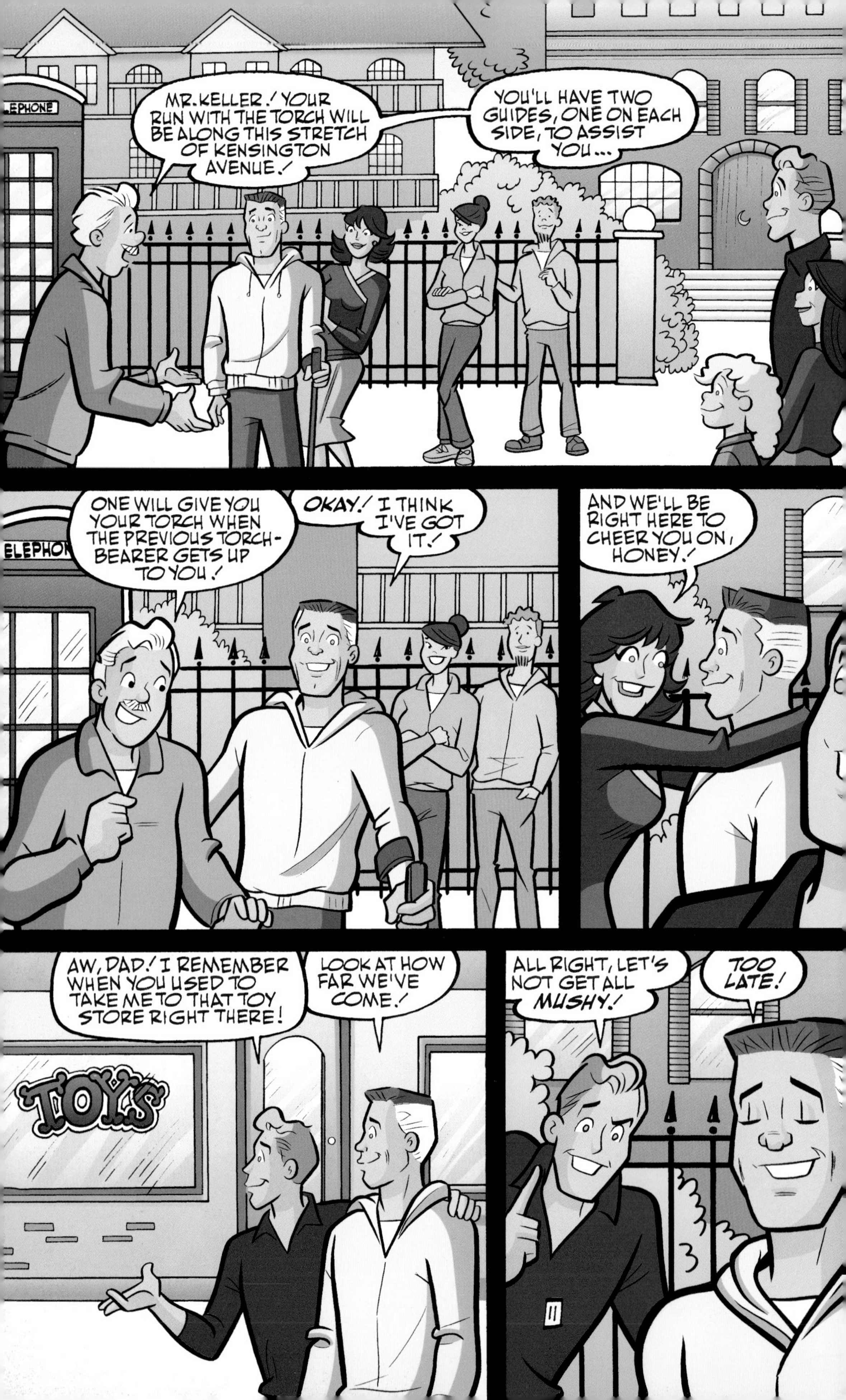
ELEPHONE
MR. KELLER! YOUR RUN WITH THE TORCH WILL BE ALONG THIS STRETCH OF KENSINGTON AVENUE!
YOU'LL HAVE TWO GUIDES, ONE ON EACH SIDE, TO ASSIST YOU...
ELEPHON
ONE WILL GIVE YOU YOUR TORCH WHEN THE PREVIOUS TORCH-BEARER GETS UP TO YOU!
OKAY! I THINK I'VE GOT IT!
AND WE'LL BE RIGHT HERE TO CHEER YOU ON, HONEY!
TOYS
AW, DAD! I REMEMBER WHEN YOU USED TO TAKE ME TO THAT TOY STORE RIGHT THERE!
LOOK AT HOW FAR WE'VE COME!
ALL RIGHT, LET'S NOT GET ALL MUSHY!
TOO LATE!

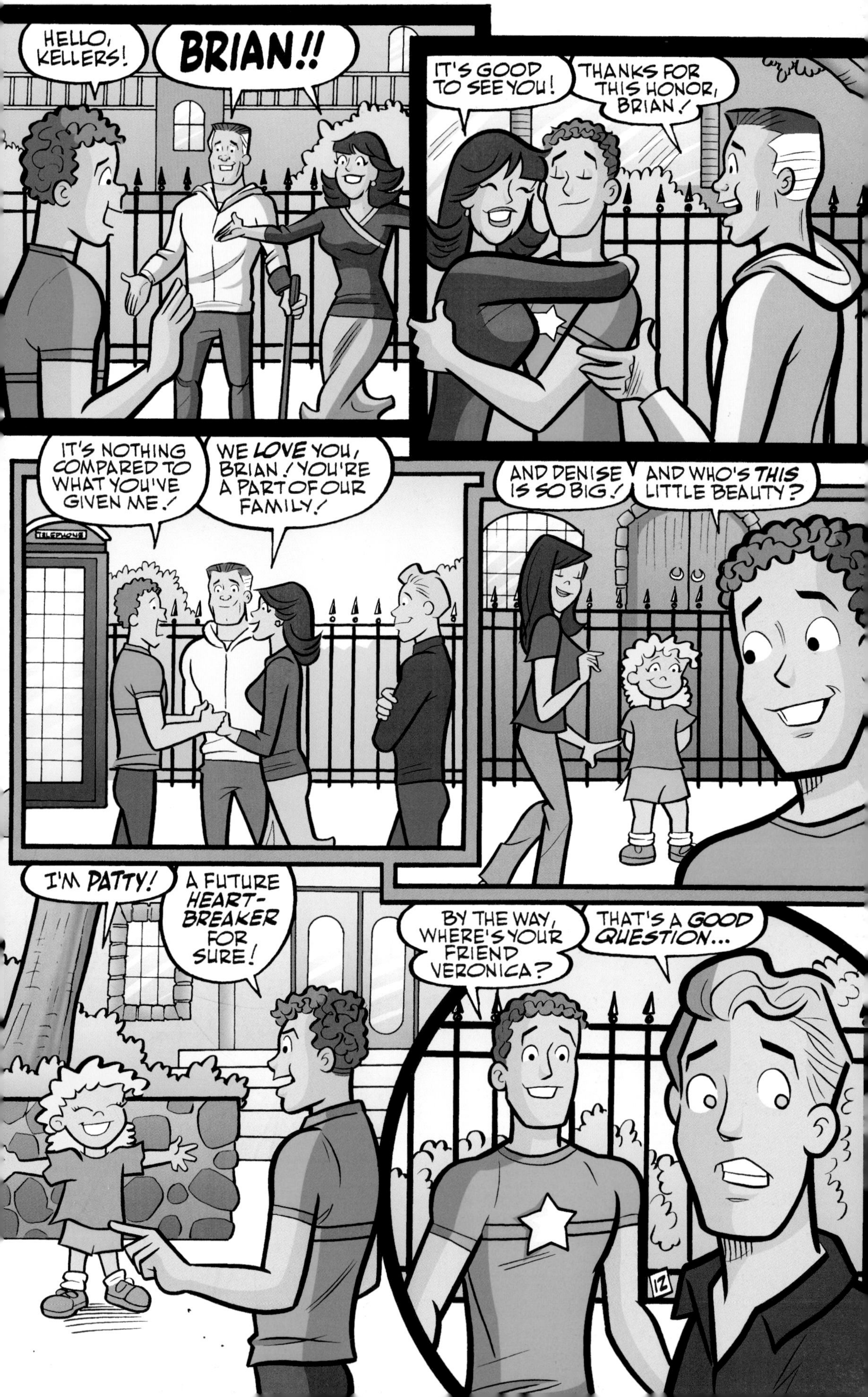
HELLO, KELLERS!
BRIAN!!
IT'S GOOD TO SEE YOU!
THANKS FOR THIS HONOR, BRIAN!
IT'S NOTHING COMPARED TO WHAT YOU'VE GIVEN ME!
WE LOVE YOU, BRIAN! YOU'RE A PART OF OUR FAMILY!
TELEPHONE
AND DENISE IS SO BIG!
AND WHO'S THIS LITTLE BEAUTY?
I'M PATTY!
A FUTURE HEART-BREAKER FOR SURE!
BY THE WAY, WHERE'S YOUR FRIEND VERONICA?
THAT'S A GOOD QUESTION...
12

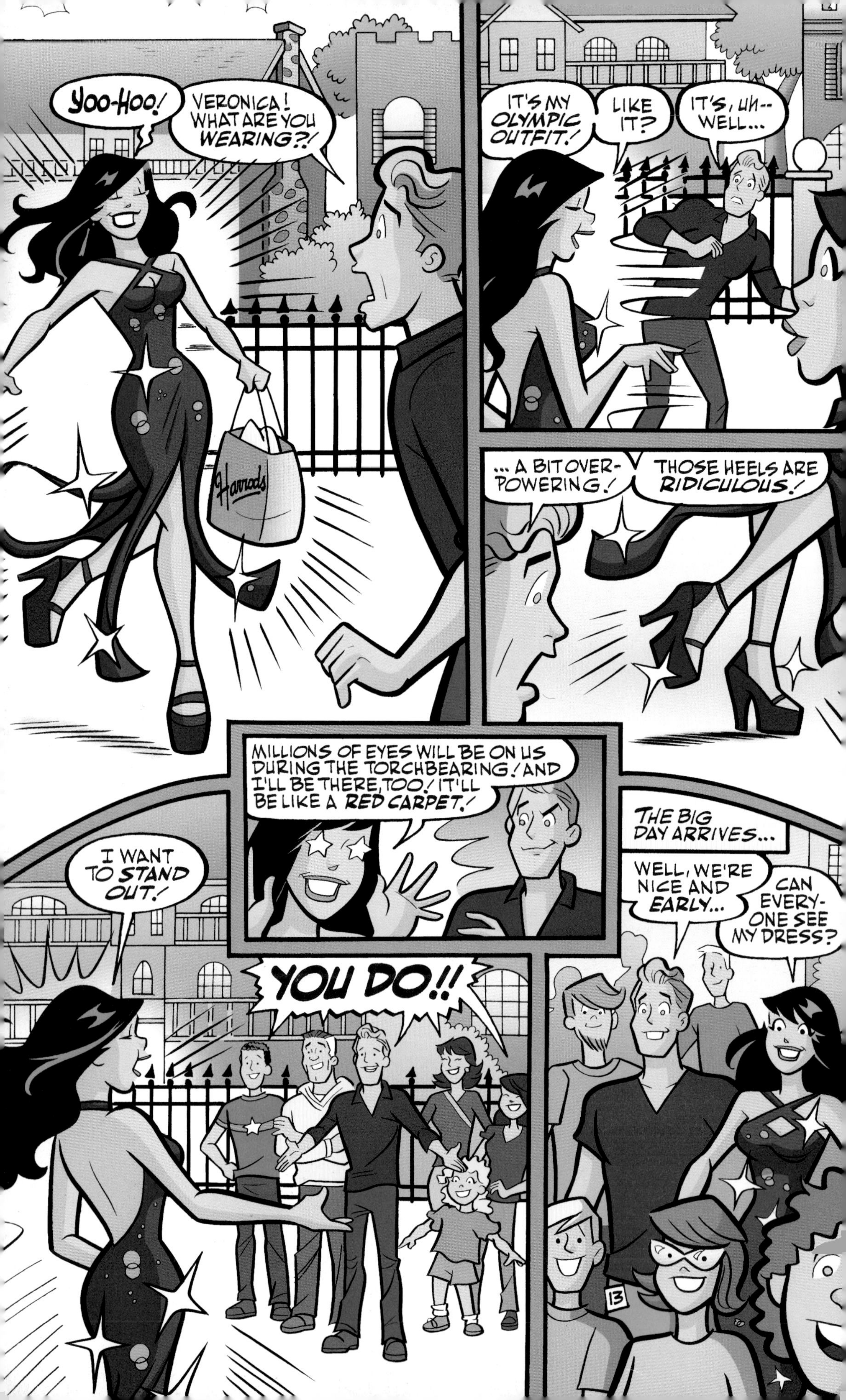
YOO-HOO!
VERONICA! WHAT ARE YOU WEARING?!
Harrods
IT'S MY OLYMPIC OUTFIT!
LIKE IT?
IT'S, UH-- WELL...
... A BIT OVER-POWERING!
THOSE HEELS ARE RIDICULOUS!
MILLIONS OF EYES WILL BE ON US DURING THE TORCHBEARING! AND I'LL BE THERE, TOO! IT'LL BE LIKE A RED CARPET!
I WANT TO STAND OUT!
YOU DO!!
THE BIG DAY ARRIVES...
WELL, WE'RE NICE AND EARLY...
CAN EVERY-ONE SEE MY DRESS?
13

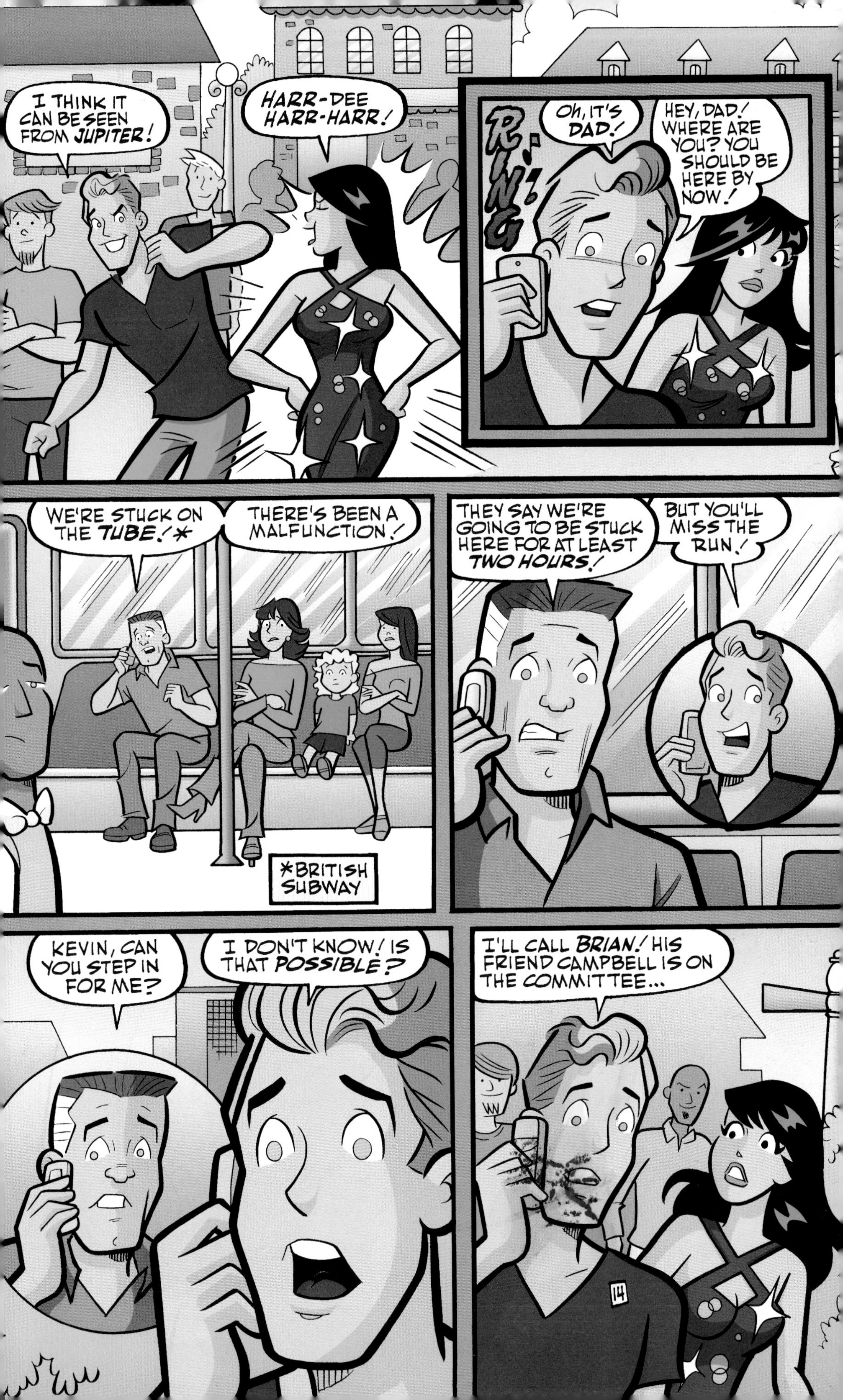
I THINK IT CAN BE SEEN FROM JUPITER!
HARR-DEE HARR-HARR!
RING
OH, IT'S DAD!
HEY, DAD! WHERE ARE YOU? YOU SHOULD BE HERE BY NOW!
WE'RE STUCK ON THE TUBE!*
THERE'S BEEN A MALFUNCTION!
*BRITISH SUBWAY
THEY SAY WE'RE GOING TO BE STUCK HERE FOR AT LEAST TWO HOURS!
BUT YOU'LL MISS THE RUN!
KEVIN, CAN YOU STEP IN FOR ME?
I DON'T KNOW! IS THAT POSSIBLE?
I'LL CALL BRIAN! HIS FRIEND CAMPBELL IS ON THE COMMITTEE...
14

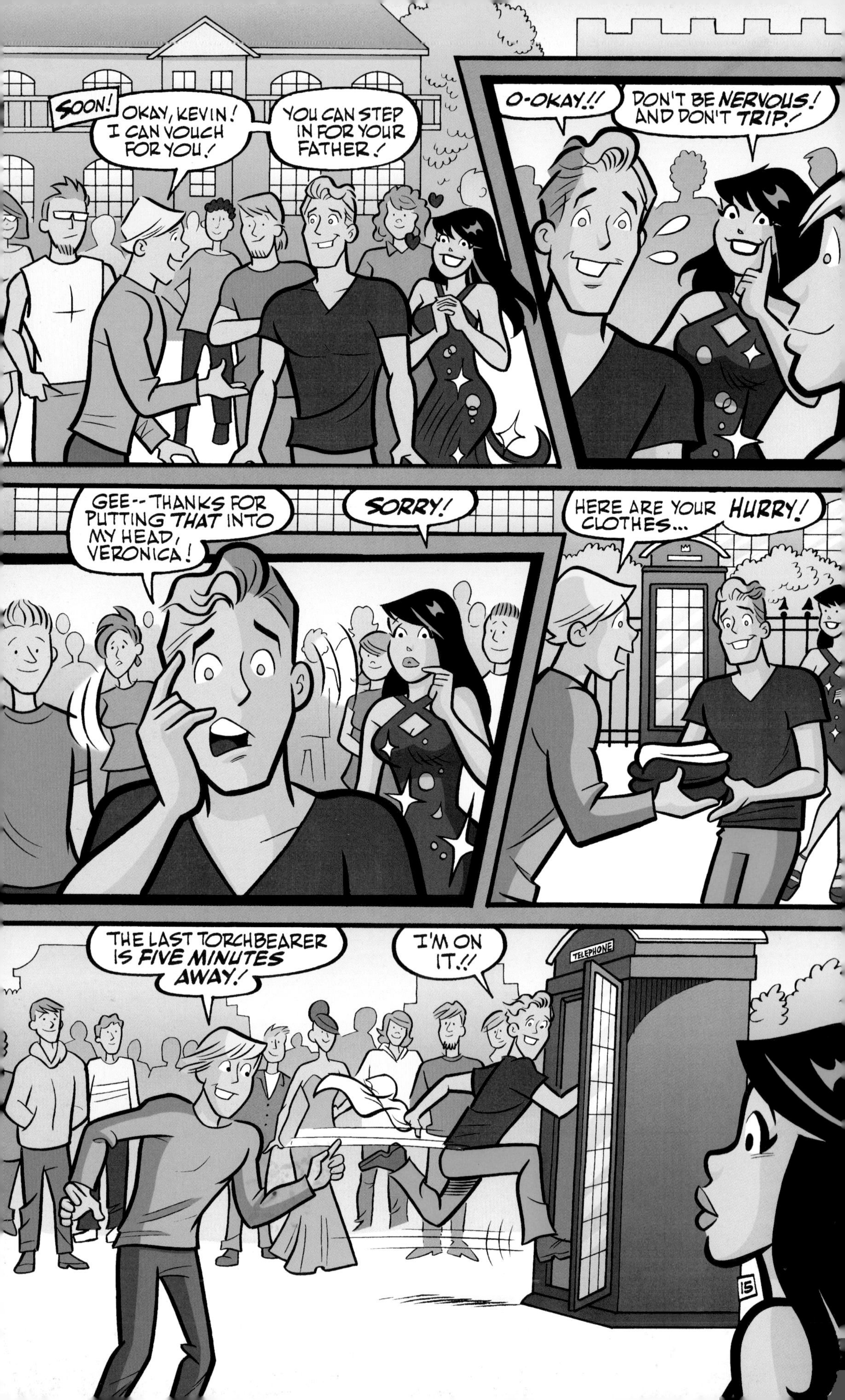
SOON!
OKAY, KEVIN! I CAN VOUCH FOR YOU!
YOU CAN STEP IN FOR YOUR FATHER!
O-OKAY!!
DON'T BE NERVOUS! AND DON'T TRIP!
GEE--THANKS FOR PUTTING THAT INTO MY HEAD, VERONICA!
SORRY!
HERE ARE YOUR CLOTHES...
HURRY!
THE LAST TORCHBEARER IS FIVE MINUTES AWAY!
I'M ON IT!!
TELEPHONE
15

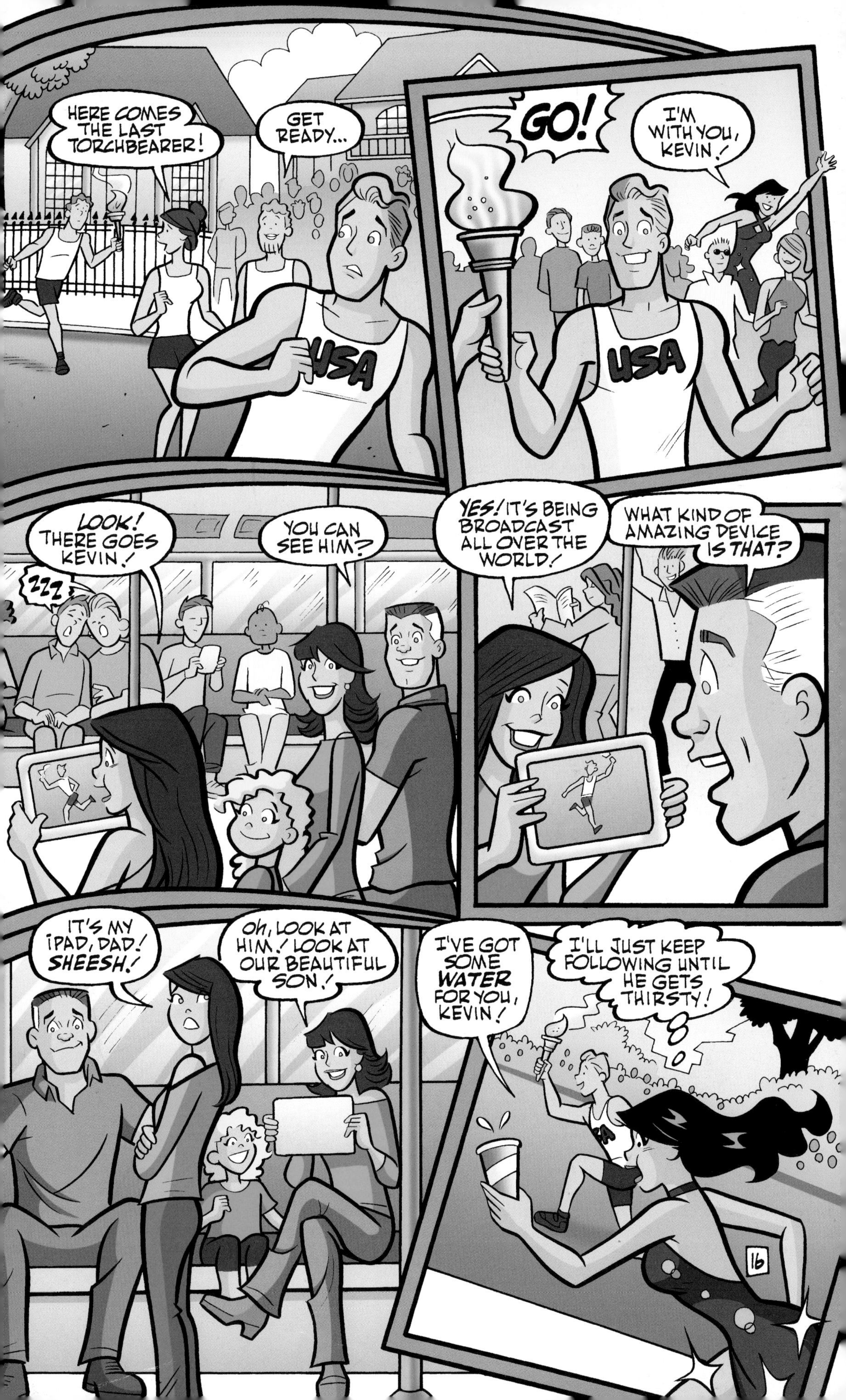
HERE COMES THE LAST TORCHBEARER!
GET READY...
GO!
I'M WITH YOU, KEVIN!
LOOK! THERE GOES KEVIN!
ZZZ
YOU CAN SEE HIM?
YES! IT'S BEING BROADCAST ALL OVER THE WORLD!
WHAT KIND OF AMAZING DEVICE IS THAT?
IT'S MY iPAD, DAD! SHEESH!
Oh, LOOK AT HIM! LOOK AT OUR BEAUTIFUL SON!
I'VE GOT SOME WATER FOR YOU, KEVIN!
I'LL JUST KEEP FOLLOWING UNTIL HE GETS THIRSTY!
USA
16

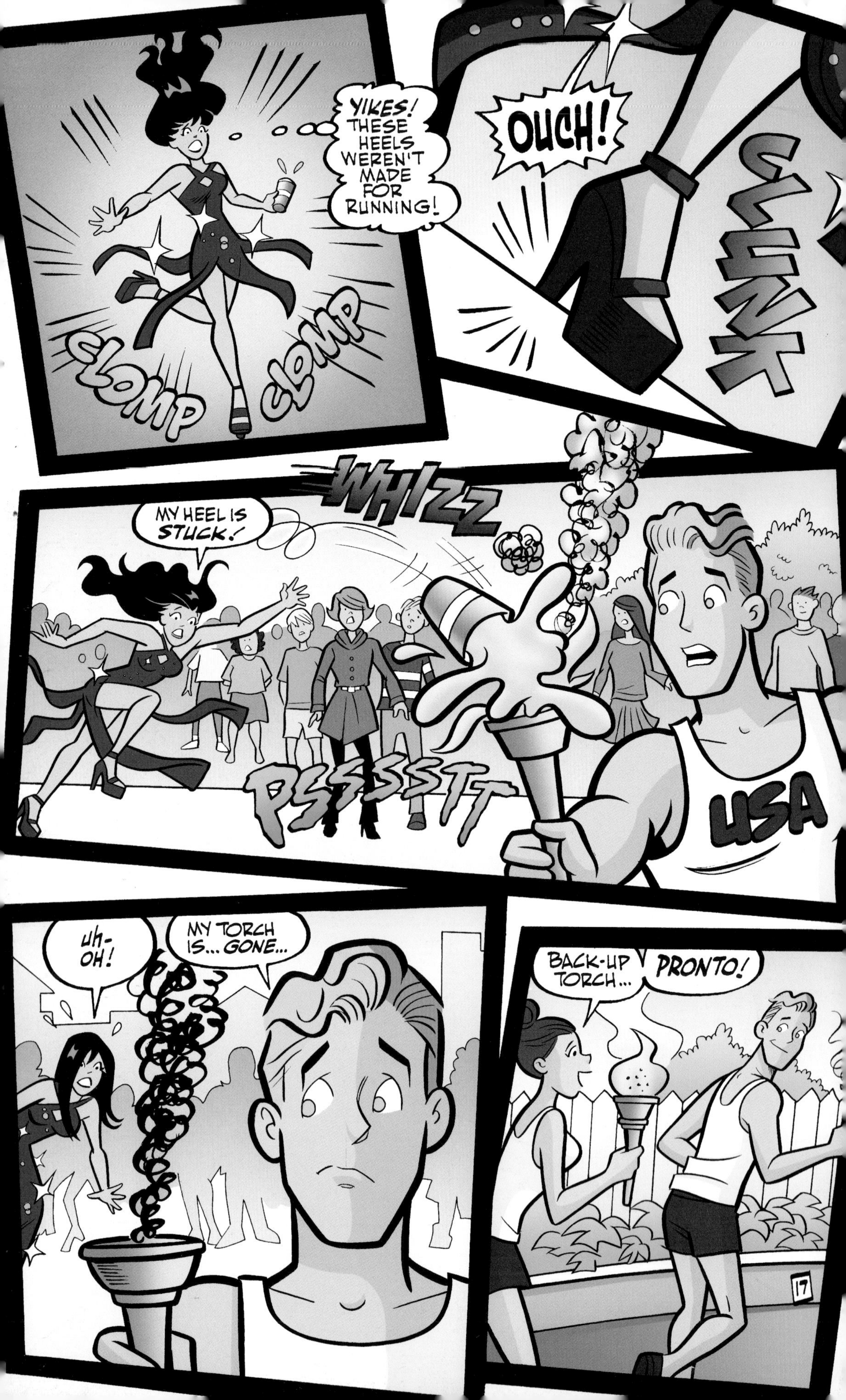
YIKES! THESE HEELS WEREN'T MADE FOR RUNNING!
CLOMP
CLOMP
OUCH!
CLUNK
WHIZZ
MY HEEL IS STUCK!
PSSSSTT
USA
UH-OH!
MY TORCH IS... GONE...
BACK-UP TORCH...
PRONTO!
17

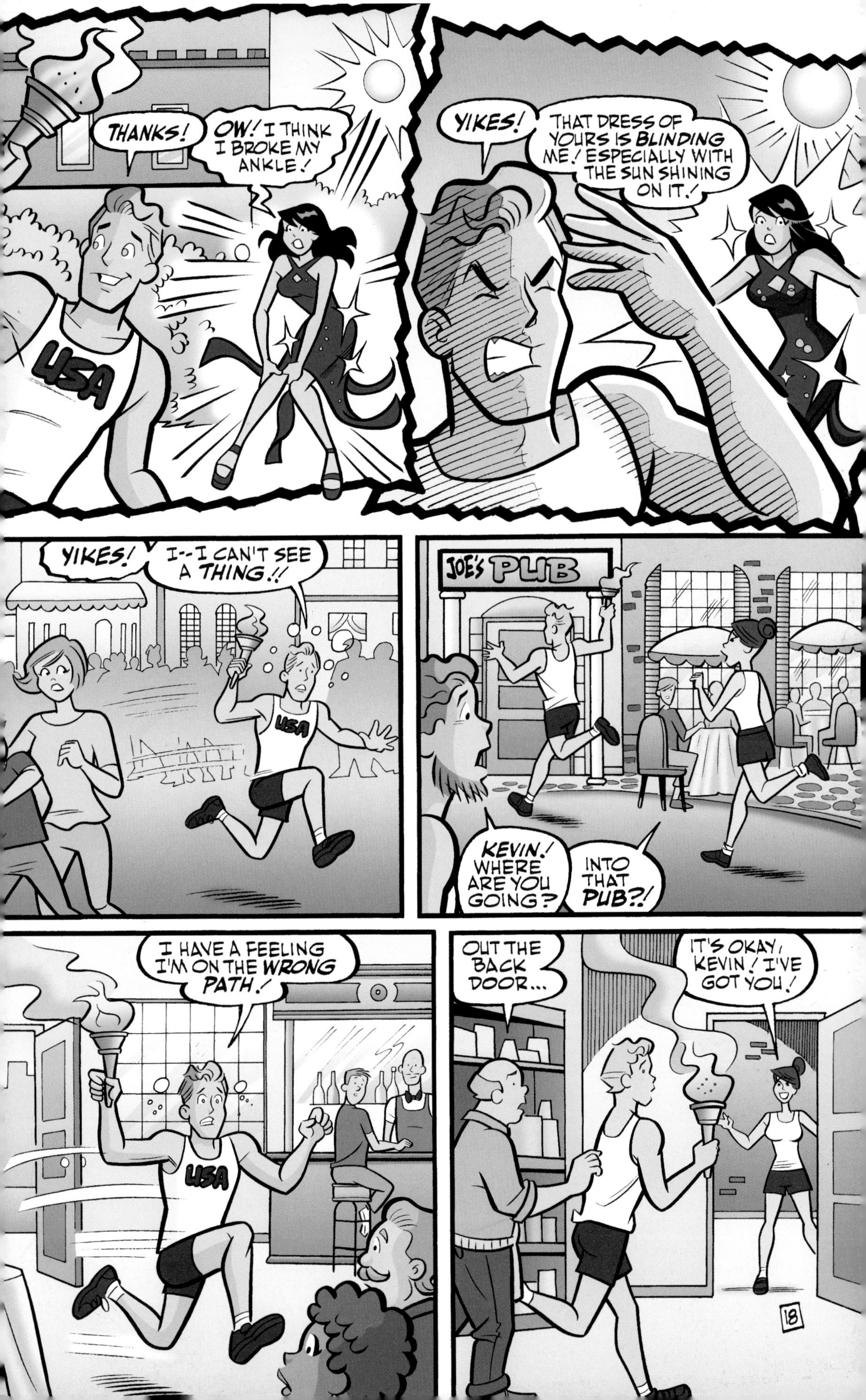
THANKS!
OW! I THINK I BROKE MY ANKLE!
YIKES!
THAT DRESS OF YOURS IS BLINDING ME! ESPECIALLY WITH THE SUN SHINING ON IT!
USA
YIKES!
I-- I CAN'T SEE A THING!!
USA
JOE'S PUB
KEVIN! WHERE ARE YOU GOING?
INTO THAT PUB?!
I HAVE A FEELING I'M ON THE WRONG PATH!
USA
OUT THE BACK DOOR...
IT'S OKAY, KEVIN! I'VE GOT YOU!
18

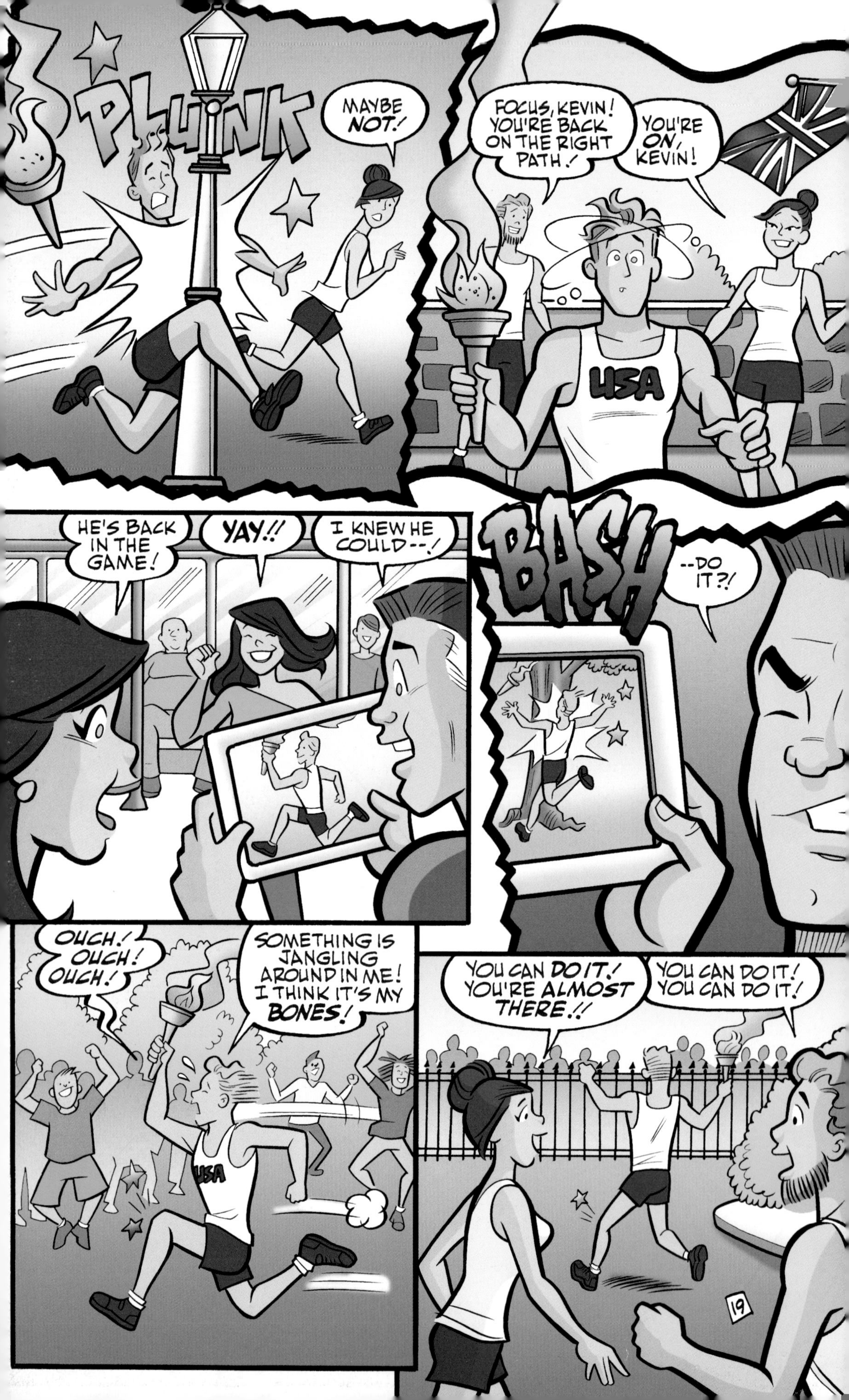
PLUNK
MAYBE NOT!
FOCUS, KEVIN! YOU'RE BACK ON THE RIGHT PATH!
YOU'RE ON, KEVIN!
USA
HE'S BACK IN THE GAME!
YAY!!
I KNEW HE COULD--!
BASH
--DO IT?!
OUCH! OUCH! OUCH!
SOMETHING IS JANGLING AROUND IN ME! I THINK IT'S MY BONES!
USA
YOU CAN DO IT! YOU'RE ALMOST THERE!!
YOU CAN DO IT! YOU CAN DO IT!

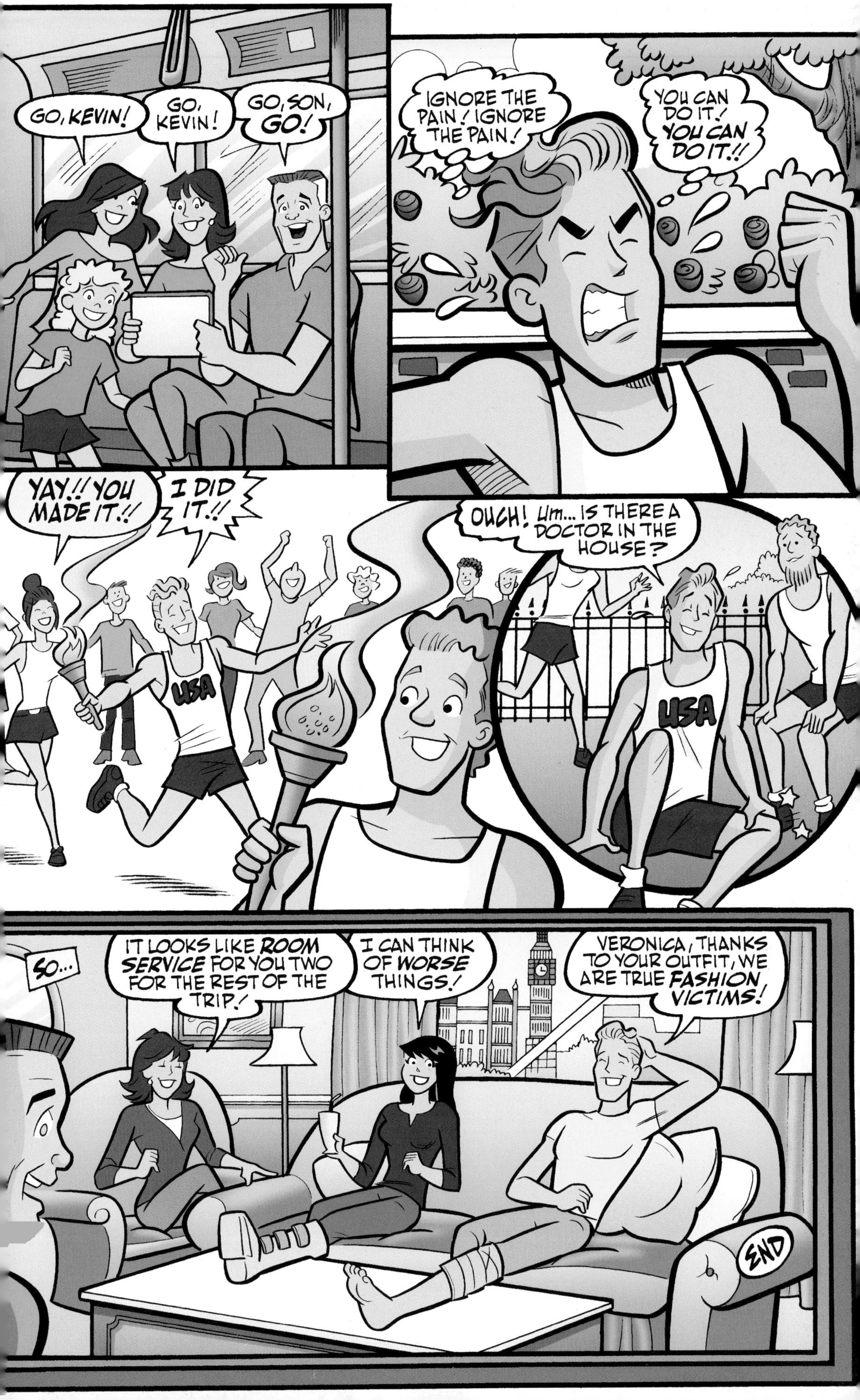
GO, KEVIN!
GO, KEVIN!
GO, SON, GO!
IGNORE THE PAIN! IGNORE THE PAIN!
YOU CAN DO IT! YOU CAN DO IT!!
YAY!! YOU MADE IT!!
I DID IT!!
OUCH! Um... IS THERE A DOCTOR IN THE HOUSE?
SO...
IT LOOKS LIKE ROOM SERVICE FOR YOU TWO FOR THE REST OF THE TRIP!
I CAN THINK OF WORSE THINGS!
VERONICA, THANKS TO YOUR OUTFIT, WE ARE TRUE FASHION VICTIMS!
END

Afterword
by Dan Parent

It's exciting to be writing the afterword to the second collected edition of Kevin Keller stories. The world has embraced Kevin and I sort of feel like a proud father at this point! I'm so proud to have been able to bring Kevin into the world of Archie Comics (let's have a hand for Jon Goldwater here, who green-lighted introducing Kevin to the masses). And as Kevin's role in the Archie universe expands, the world of Riverdale becomes a brighter and better place.

This set of stories begins as Kevin settles into everyday life in Riverdale, dealing with being the new class president, his new friends in school, and of course, the world of dating. Dating is usually a mixed bag of emotions for most teenagers, even Kevin. Sure, he's good looking and popular, but that's not always a free pass to the world of perfect relationships.

Of course, being a gay teenager just adds to the complications. First off, there's still discrimination to deal with. And there's dealing with the issues that your date may be going through. Then there's the general awkwardness of dating that EVERYBODY goes through, gay OR straight. We've seen Kevin enter this world of dating with mixed results. Sort of like, well, you know, most teenagers!

And that's Kevin Keller for you. He's your typical teenager. He wants to excel in school. And hang out with his friends. And date. And fall in love someday. He's the all-American boy next door. And he's gay. And he gets to live in a cool town like Riverdale.

Maybe not every gay teen has an ideal experience like Kevin has in Riverdale. There are many who are struggling out there, so maybe we're not showing the way things are with all gay teens. But we're showing the way things SHOULD be! Everybody deserves their own Riverdale! That's a great goal for everyone!

Dan Parent

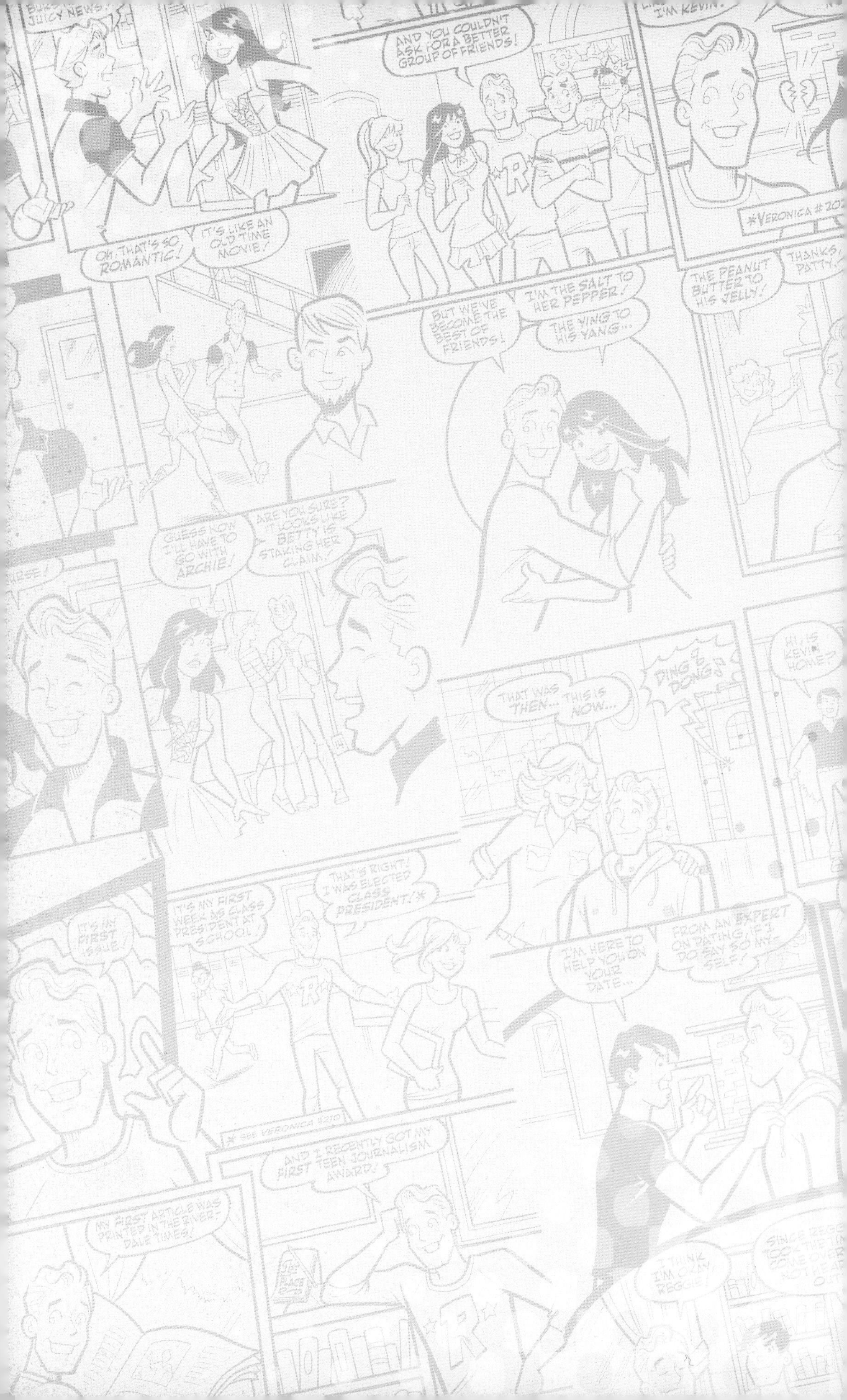
JUICY NEWS!
I'M KEVIN!
AND YOU COULDN'T ASK FOR A BETTER GROUP OF FRIENDS!
OH, THAT'S SO ROMANTIC!
IT'S LIKE AN OLD TIME MOVIE!
THE PEANUT BUTTER TO HIS JELLY!
THANKS, PATTY.
BUT WE'VE BECOME THE BEST OF FRIENDS!
I'M THE SALT TO HER PEPPER!
THE YING TO HIS YANG...
GUESS NOW I'LL HAVE TO GO WITH ARCHIE!
ARE YOU SURE? IT LOOKS LIKE BETTY IS STAKING HER CLAIM!
HI, IS KEVIN HOME?
THAT WAS THEN... THIS IS NOW...
DING DONG
IT'S MY FIRST ISSUE!
IT'S MY FIRST WEEK AS CLASS PRESIDENT AT SCHOOL!
THAT'S RIGHT! I WAS ELECTED CLASS PRESIDENT!*
I'M HERE TO HELP YOU ON YOUR DATE...
FROM AN EXPERT ON DATING, IF I DO SAY SO MY-SELF!
* SEE VERONICA #210
AND I RECENTLY GOT MY FIRST TEEN JOURNALISM AWARD!
MY FIRST ARTICLE WAS PRINTED IN THE RIVER-DALE TIMES!
1ST PLACE
I THINK I'M OKAY, REGGIE!

OFFICIAL

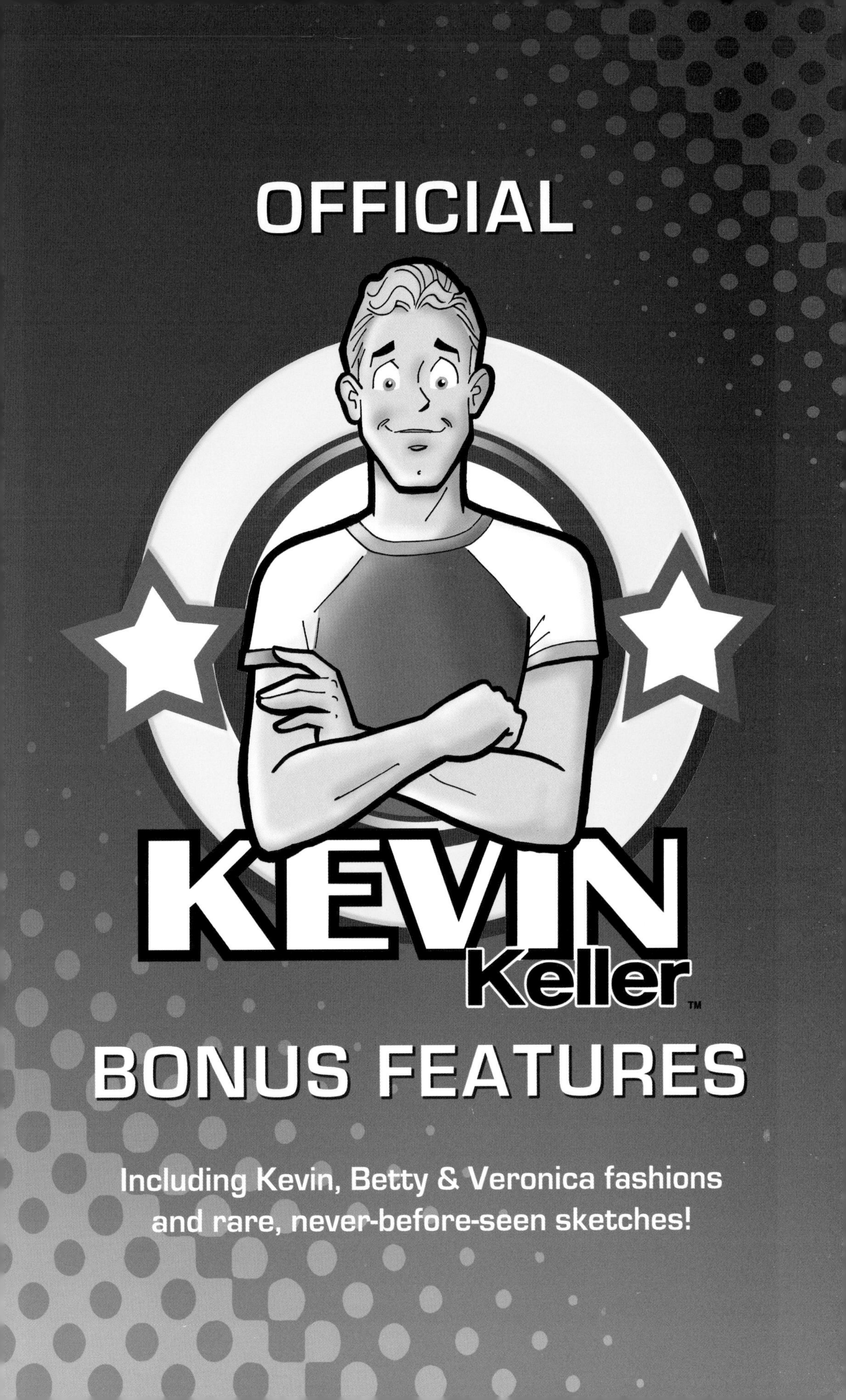

KEVIN Keller™

BONUS FEATURES

Including Kevin, Betty & Veronica fashions and rare, never-before-seen sketches!

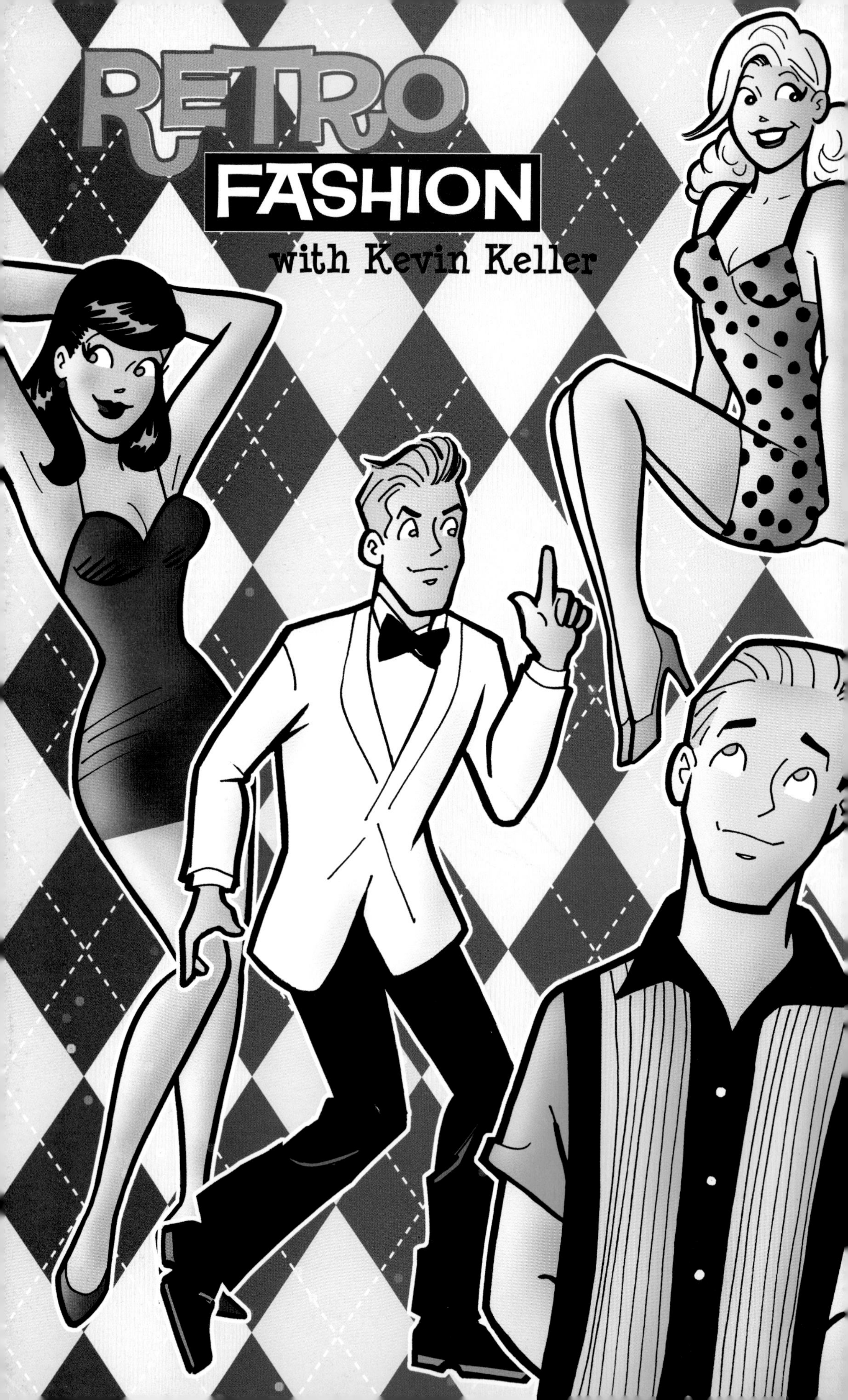
RETRO
FASHION
with Kevin Keller

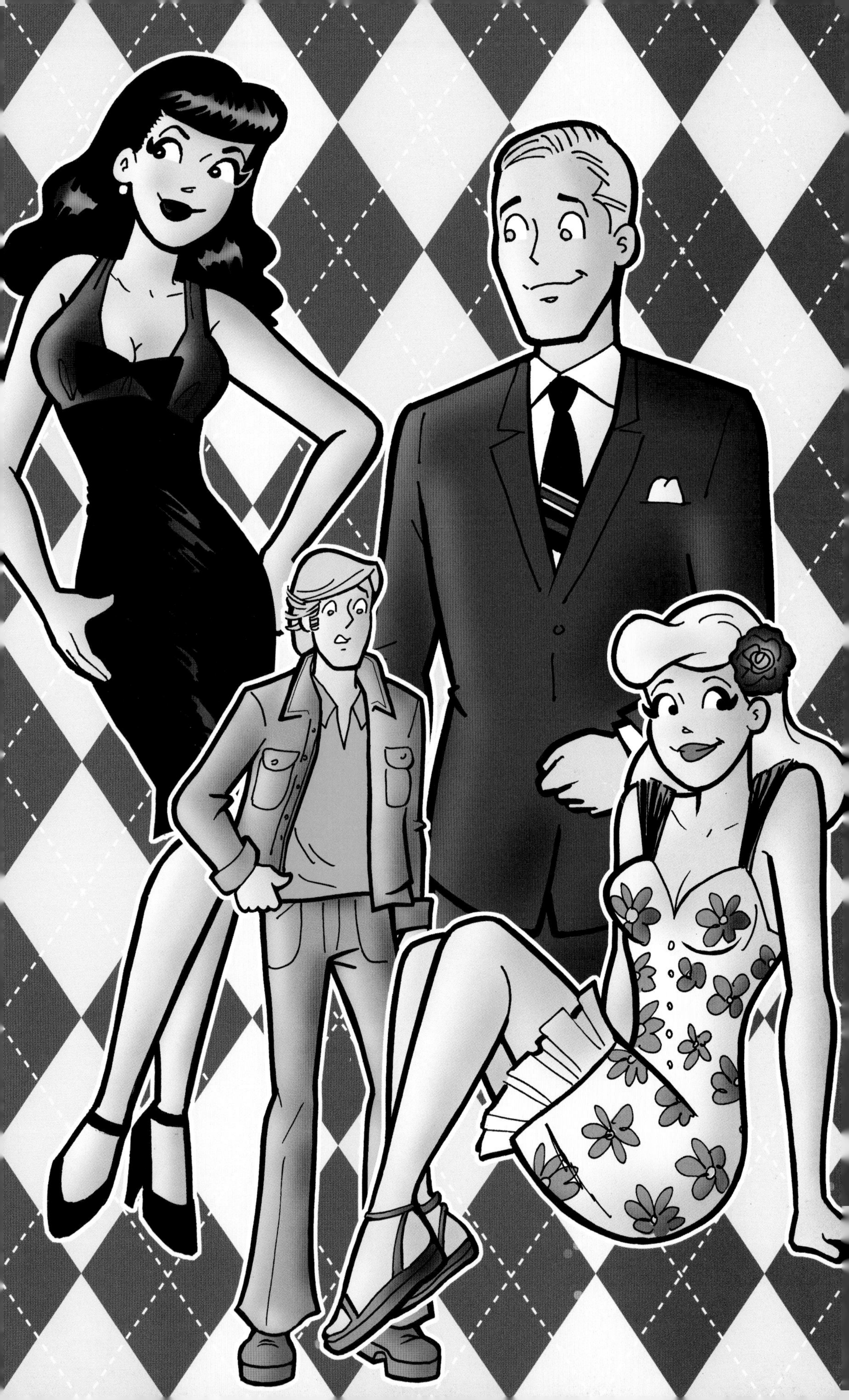

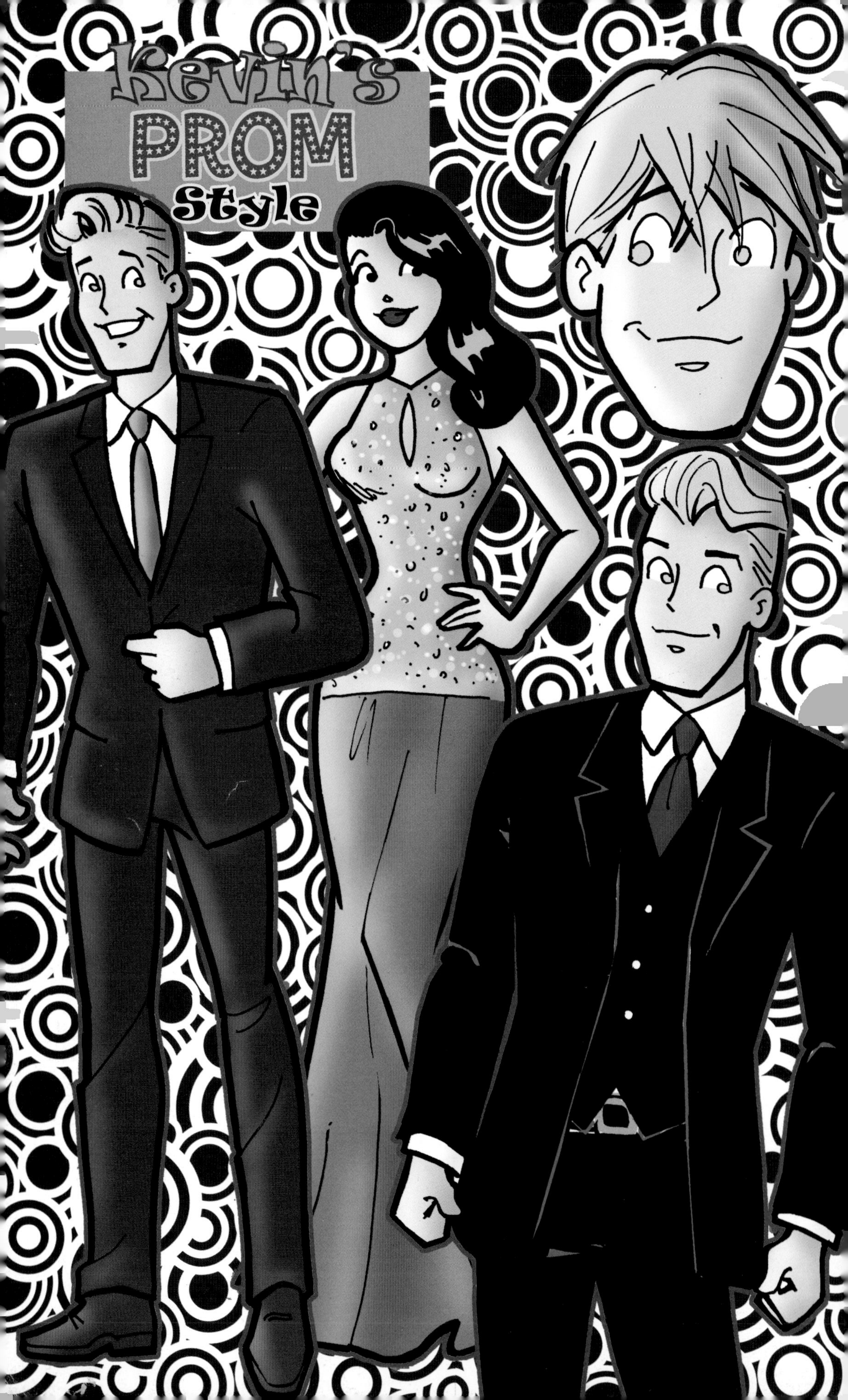
Kevin's
PROM
Style

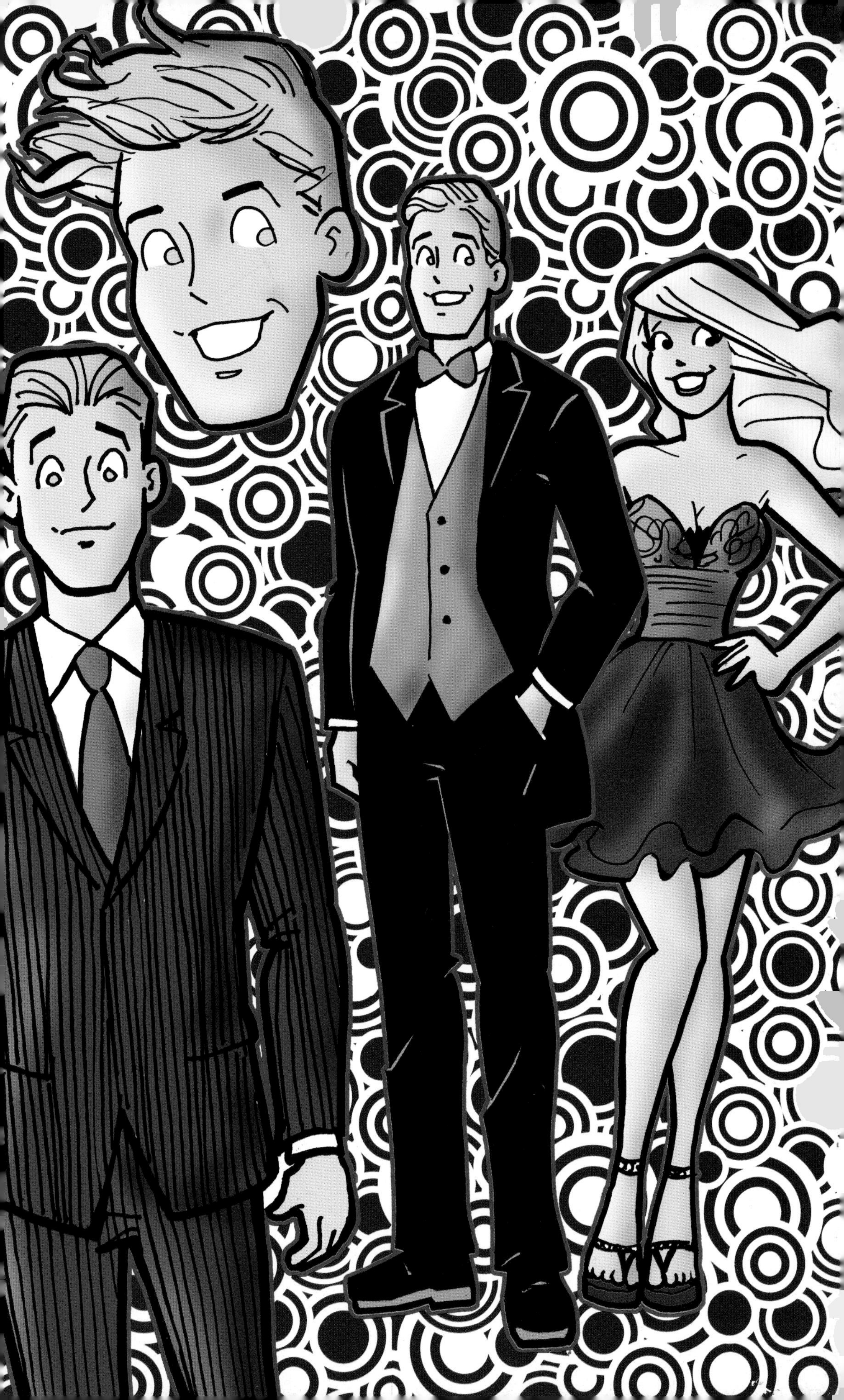

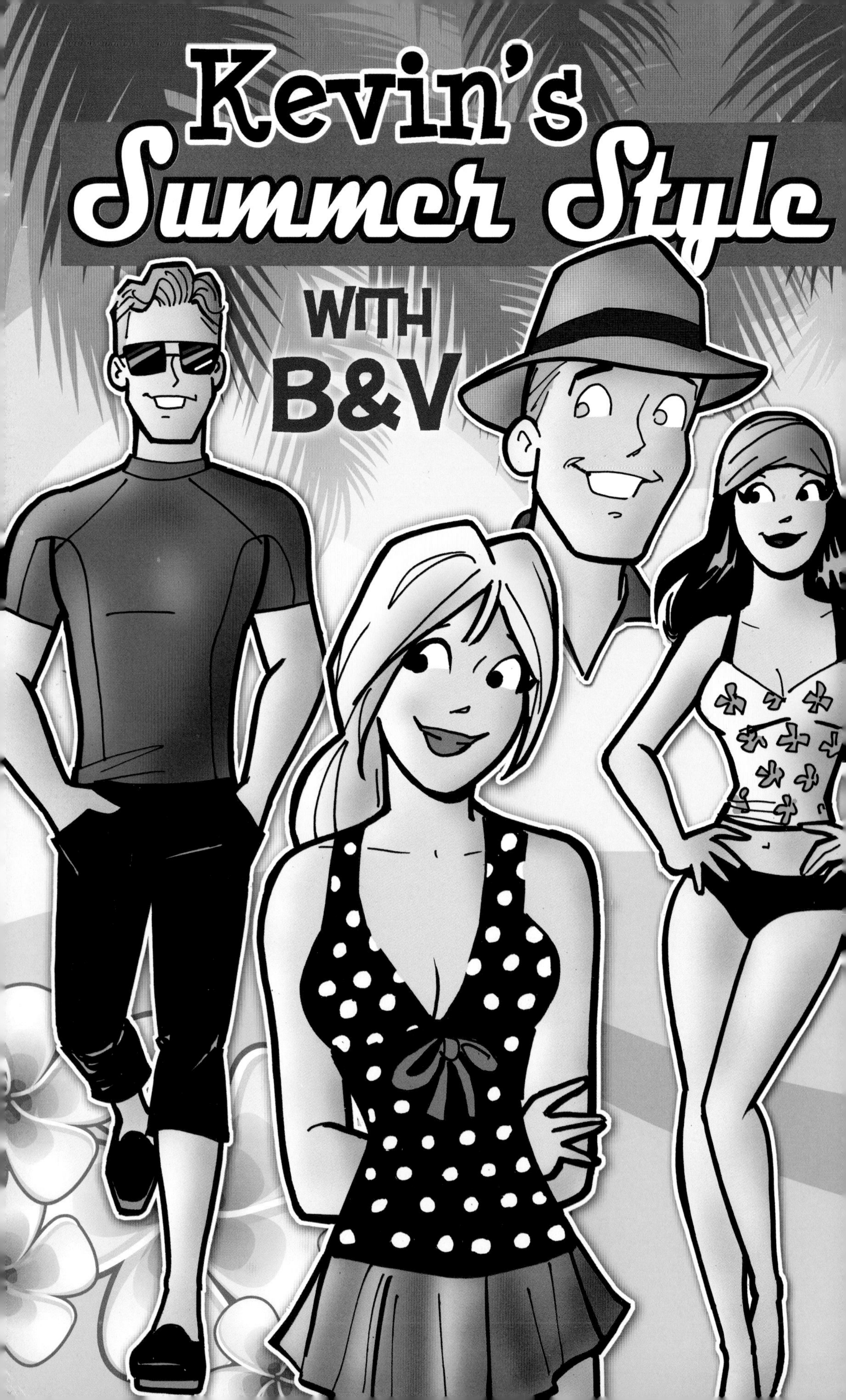
Kevin's
Summer Style
WITH
B&V

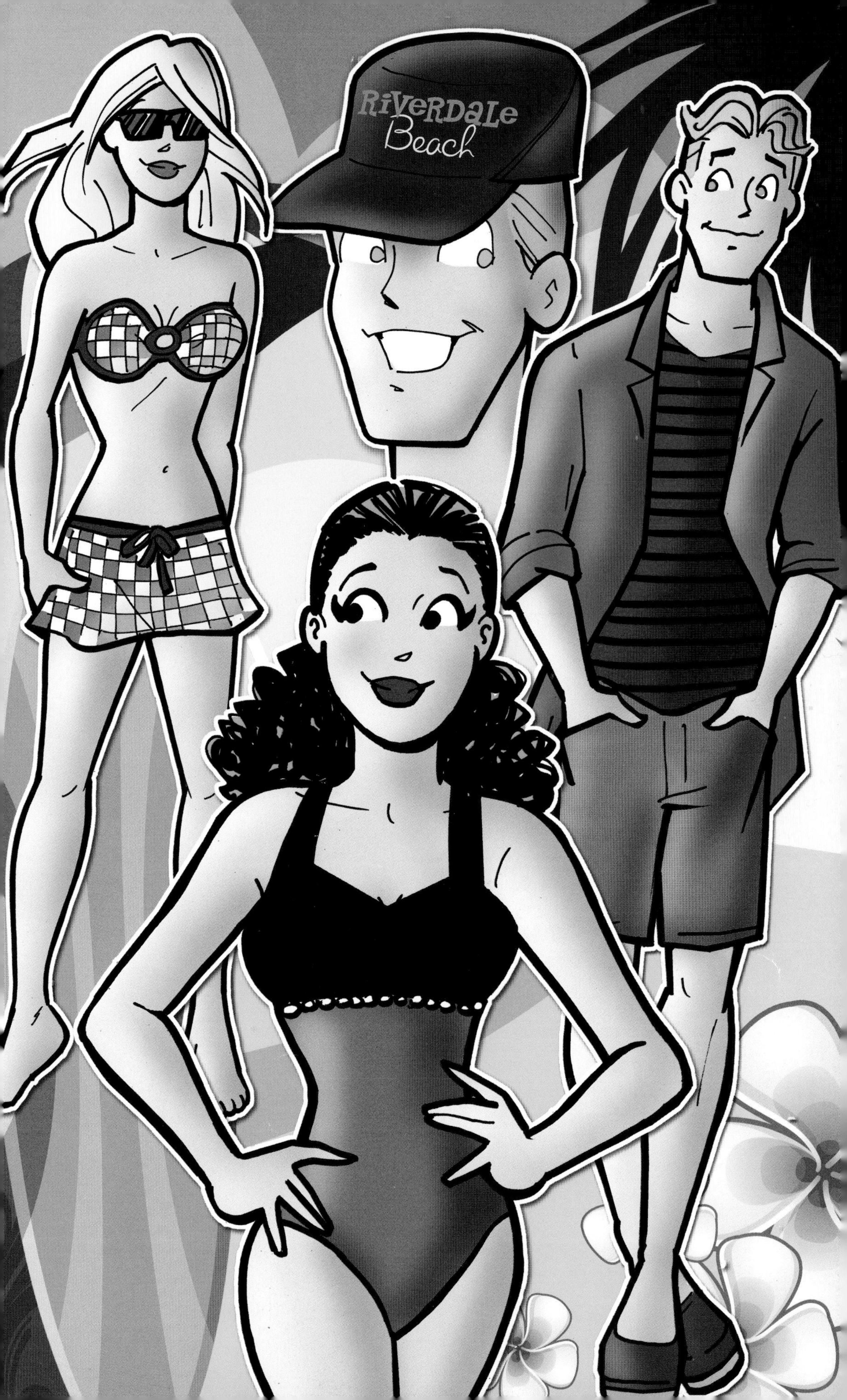

RiVERDALE
Beach

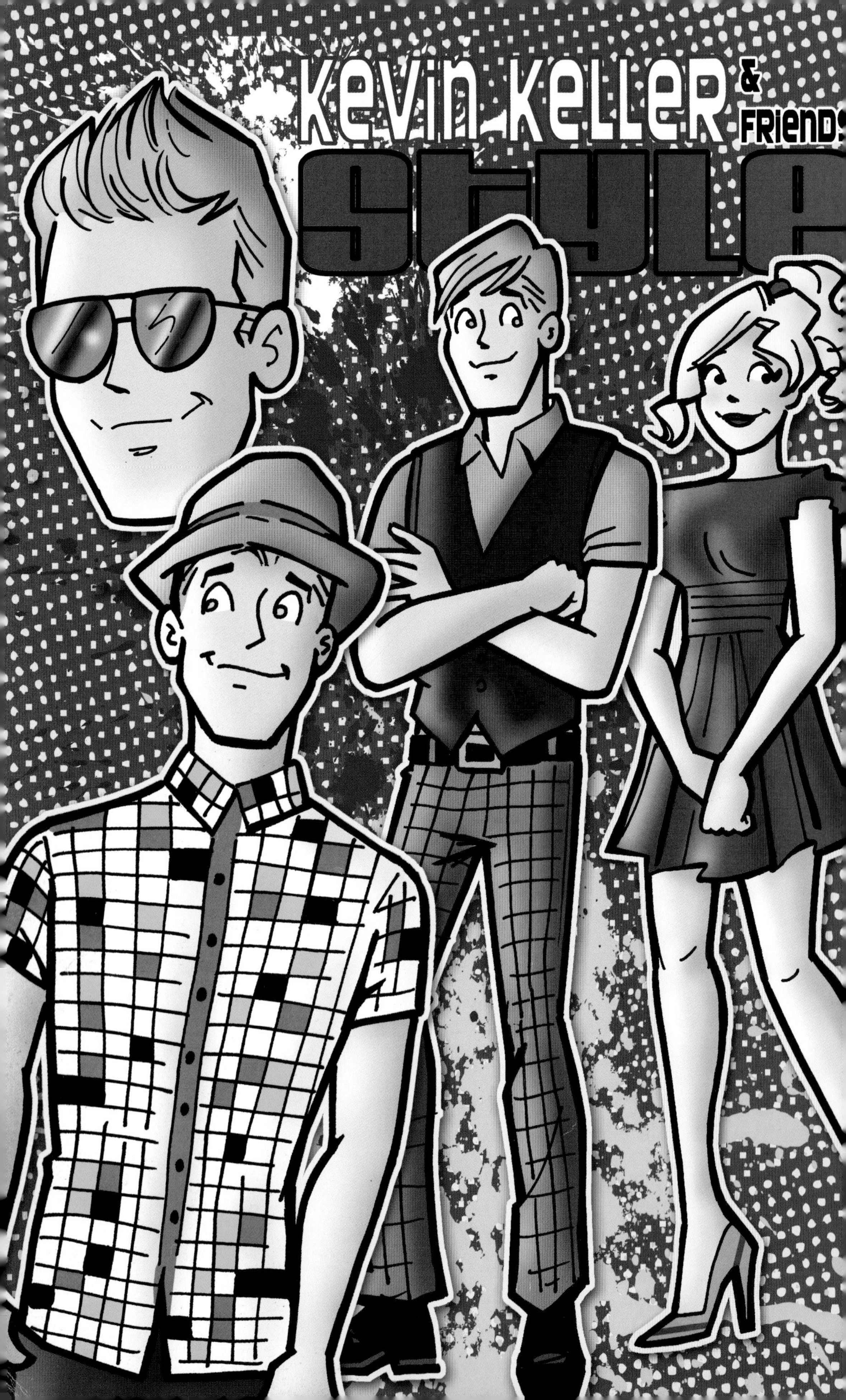
Kevin Keller & Friends
Style

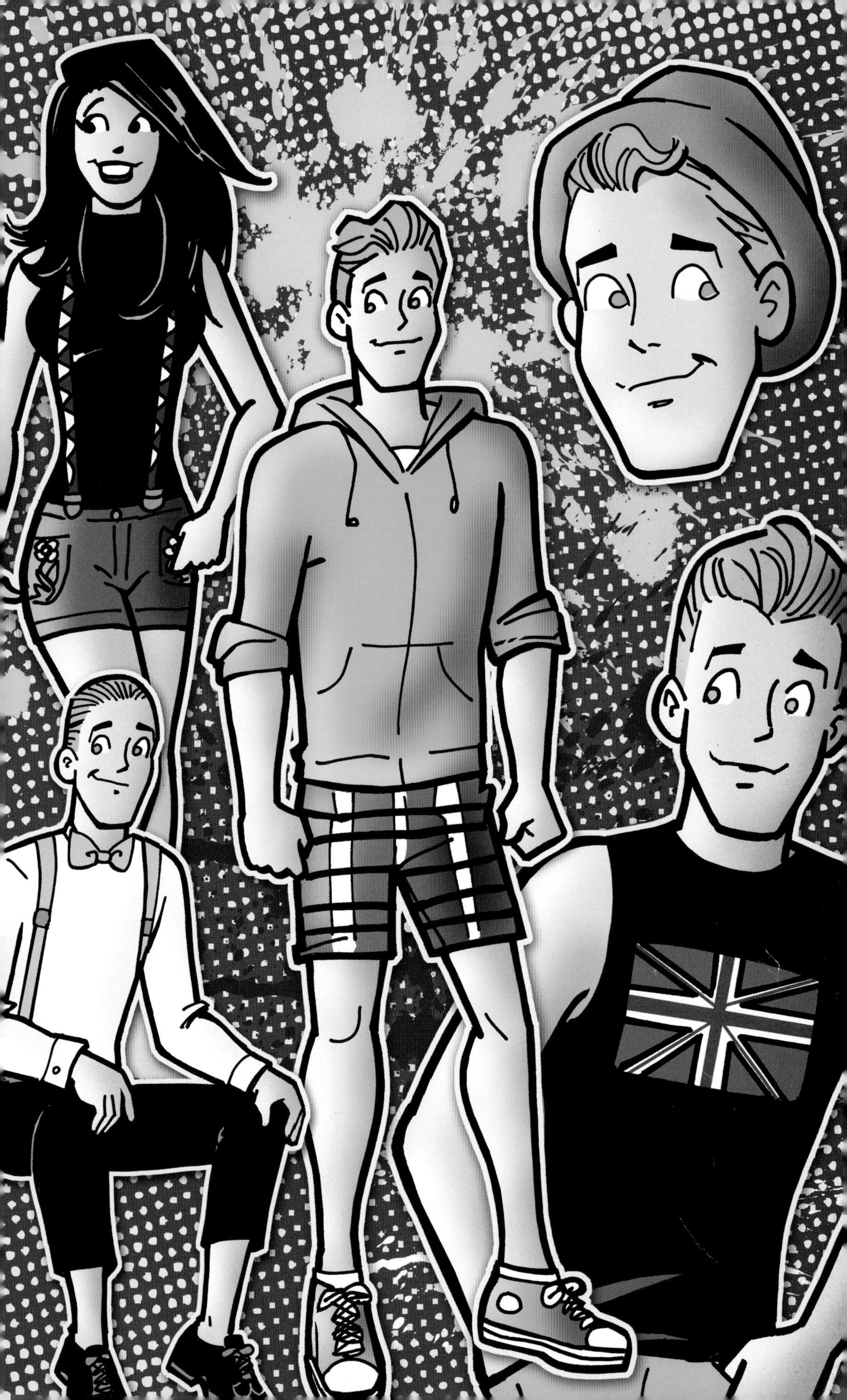

UNRELEASED PROMOTIONAL SKETCH 1

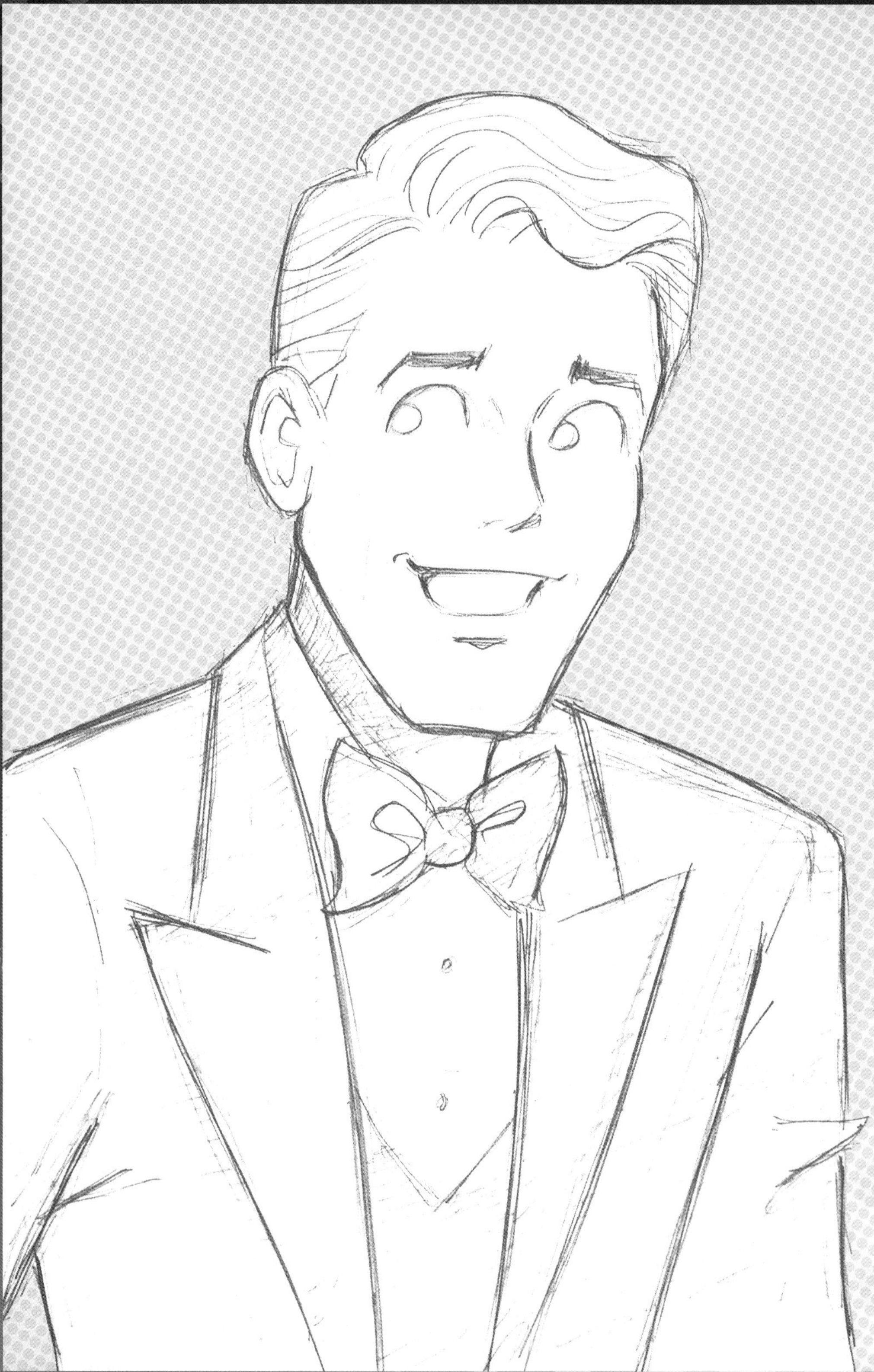

UNRELEASED PROMOTIONAL SKETCH 2

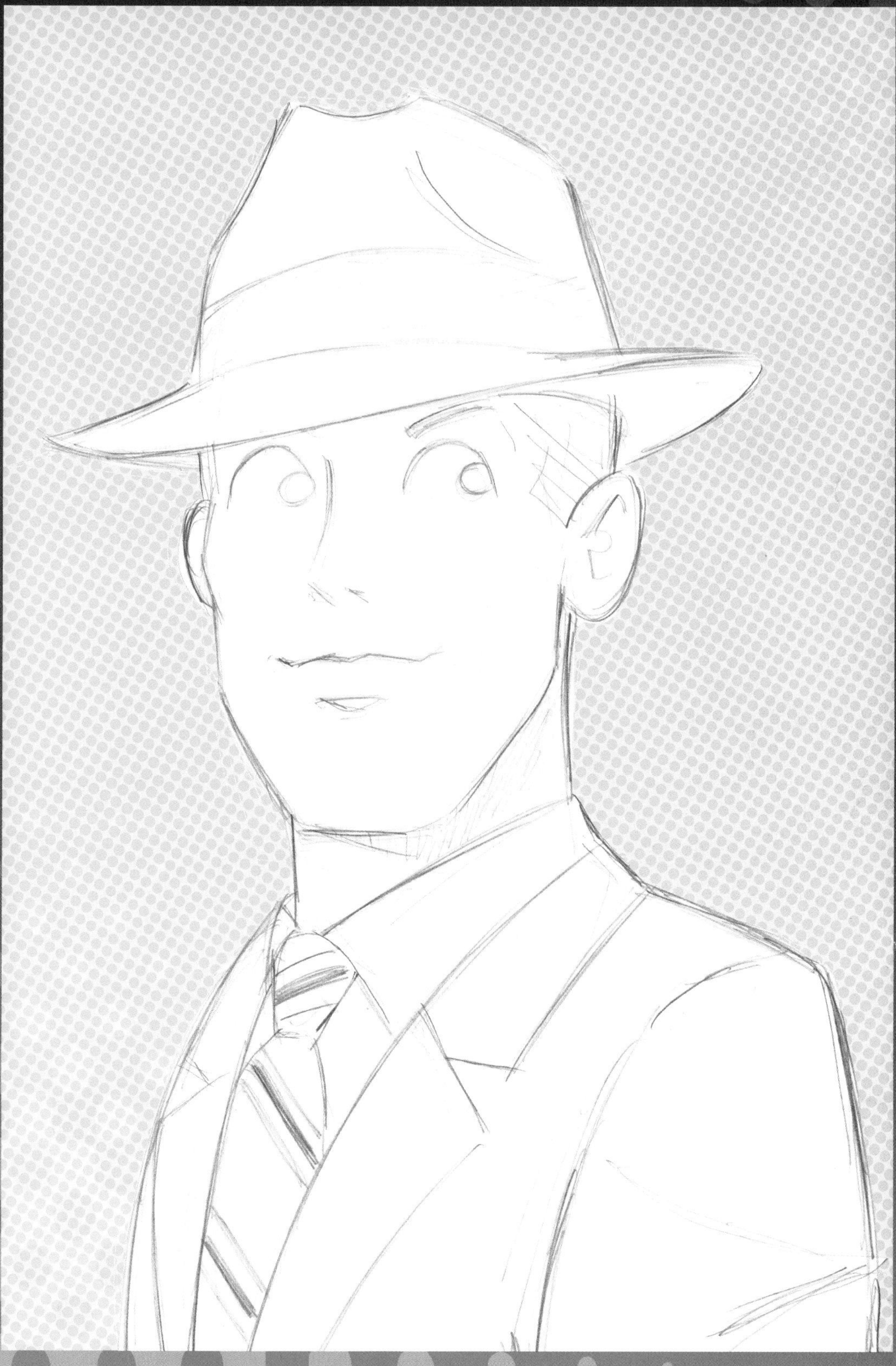

UNRELEASED PROMOTIONAL SKETCH 3

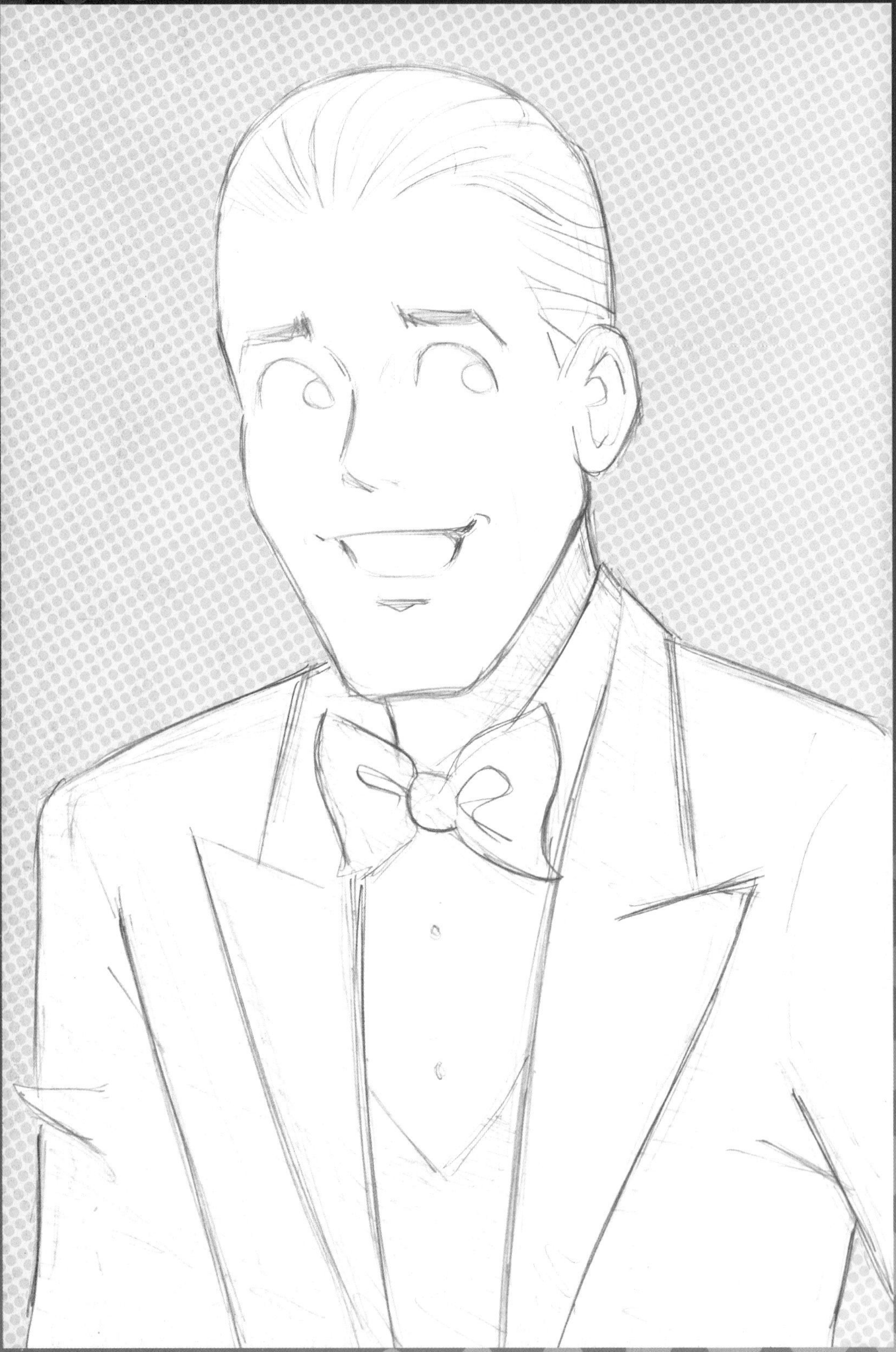

ISBN: 978-1-936975-58-7ISBN: 978-1-936975-35-8ISBN: 978-1-879794-93-1